"Do you want the abandon ship order given?"

One man, suddenly roused from a sound sleep and standing half-clad on the deck of a severely damaged ship, was confronted with a fateful decision. Charles Butler McVay III was truly a man alone. There was one of two choices to make. Either pass the word to abandon ship and watch over a thousand men drop into the uncertain peril of the open sea or harken back to those vast files of naval records that prove beyond a shadow of a doubt that many a good ship has been prematurely deserted at great cost of human life and the eventual and unnecessary loss of a fine ship. A captain must give the final word—right or wrong.

ORDEAL BY SEA

ALSO BY THOMAS HELM

MONSTERS OF THE DEEP
SHARK!
TREASURE HUNTING AROUND THE WORLD
THE SEA LARK

ORDEAL BY SEA

The Tragedy of the USS *Indianapolis*

THOMAS HELM

Foreword and Afterword
by Captain William J. Toti, USN

A SIGNET BOOK

SIGNET
Published by New American Library, a division of
Penguin Putnam Inc., 375 Hudson Street,
New York, New York 10014, U.S.A.
Penguin Books Ltd, 27 Wrights Lane,
London W8 5TZ, England
Penguin Books Australia Ltd, Ringwood,
Victoria, Australia
Penguin Books Canada Ltd, 10 Alcorn Avenue,
Toronto, Ontario, Canada M4V 3B2
Penguin Books (N.Z.) Ltd, 182–190 Wairau Road,
Auckland 10, New Zealand

Penguin Books Ltd, Registered Offices:
Harmondsworth, Middlesex, England

Published by Signet, an imprint of New American Library,
a division of Penguin Putnam Inc.

First Signet Printing, June 2001
10 9 8 7 6 5 4 3 2 1

 REGISTERED TRADEMARK—MARCA REGISTRADA

Printed in the United States of America

TO ALL THOSE WHO SERVED ABOARD THE
USS *INDIANAPOLIS* IN HER FINAL HOURS,
THIS BOOK IS RESPECTFULLY DEDICATED.

CONTENTS

FOREWORD
by Captain William J. Toti, USN

THE group of men that stood before me on a warm Hawaiian afternoon in February 1998 could have passed for those in any retirement community. As I looked at them, I searched for something in their faces that might reveal the incredible suffering they had endured, something that might identify them as the heroes they were. There did seem to be an intensity of spirit—a fire in their eyes—that belied their advancing years, but other than that, as hard as I looked, they just appeared to be a bunch of elderly men.

I was in awe of them just the same, for these were the survivors of the armored cruiser *Indianapolis* (CA-35), whose ship had been sunk in the final days of World War II.

They were assembled that day in Pearl Harbor to witness the inactivation of my submarine bearing the same name. As captain, I thought it appropriate to

ask these men to stand with my crew as we decommis-
sioned our boat, since the survivors never got to say
good-bye to their own vessel in this fashion.

I hoped their presence might drive home the realization that as bad as it is to decommission a perfectly
good submarine, a casualty caused by the end of the
Cold War, there are worse fates for a ship. I also
thought it would inspire my crew to have these men
stand in formation with us one last time as one crew—
the combined crew of the *Indianapolis*.

The ceremony went off beautifully. At the reception
following, however, one of the survivors—Paul Murphy, president of the survivors' association—approached me. He thanked me for inviting his crew to
the ceremony. He said that standing in formation as
the *Indy* crew once again, in Pearl Harbor, would be
something they would never forget. Then, when he
had me right where he wanted me, he threw in the
kicker.

"We were thinking," he said, "that there may never
be another USS *Indianapolis* to carry on the reputation of our ship. That means you're the last *Indy* captain. Another *Indy* captain needs you—and some of
us think you have a duty to respond to his call."

I was not surprised by this request. After three tours
in the submarine *Indianapolis*, I knew well the legend
of the cruiser for which we were named. I knew the
story of Captain Charles Butler McVay III. He was
the tenth and final captain of his *Indianapolis;* I was
the tenth and final captain of mine. I knew many of the
issues surrounding his court-martial. I even knew his
two sons.

I had spoken to many *Indy* survivors over the years
and knew that they were unanimous in their opinion
that their captain had been wrongly prosecuted. A
submarine sank the *Indy,* and I was a submarine commander. Hence, I could analyze the attack with a
trained eye to evaluate whether McVay's actions had
been appropriate. That was why these men were com-

ing to me. I was their logical choice to bring this issue to closure. It all made sense.

But I dreaded the request just the same.

Not because I feared controversy, for, with apologies to the late Senator Goldwater, passivity in response to injustice is no virtue, and controversy in defense of truth is no vice.

Not because it would be work—I already had done the research. Over the years I had become very familiar with the facts surrounding the sinking of the *Indianapolis*. I had twice laid wreaths at the site of her sinking. I even made an attempt to meet Commander Mochitsura Hashimoto, the captain of the submarine that sank her. I had read virtually every book, article, and document ever written on the event.

I dreaded the petition because I wasn't sure the survivors would want to hear what I had to say. Nevertheless, these men have inspired me greatly over the years, so I have attempted to honor their request. That is why I have agreed to amend *Ordeal by Sea*. I will address the issue of Captain McVay in the afterword to this book.

But first, it's important to set the stage. The 1945 sinking of the armored cruiser USS *Indianapolis* by the Imperial Japanese submarine *I-58* has been called the last great naval tragedy of World War II. Since I'm a career naval officer, you might expect that I've been aware of this story for all of my adult life. You'd be wrong. I first learned of the tale of the *Indianapolis* the same way many other Americans did—from a movie.

In 1975 I was an eighteen-year-old plebe at Annapolis. The town of Annapolis had only three or four theaters in those days, each playing a single feature. Popular movies ran for long periods of time, and during my plebe year, one of those theaters—the Circle—ran a single movie for most of plebe summer and well into plebe year.

That movie was *Jaws*.

We wondered how a movie could be so popular as

to run uninterrupted for so many months. We were
curious to see the movie, but as plebes, we weren't
allowed until well into the academic year.

If you were to go back to that first weekend in the
winter of 1975, you would have found a long queue
of cold midshipmen lined up in uniform outside the
Circle Theater to watch that movie. We were surprised
at the terror a few sharks could cause. But we were
even more surprised by the description, rendered so
well by Robert Shaw, of a great naval disaster that
few of us had ever heard—the sinking of the *Indianapolis*. I remember being asked by a civilian as we left
the theater whether the ship story was true. I was
embarrassed by the fact that I had no idea.

As it so happened, at that time I was taking the
required plebe course called the History of Seapower.
My professor was the man who quite literally wrote
the book—that is, he cowrote our textbook with Admiral Chester Nimitz—the great naval historian Edwin
B. Potter. I asked Professor Potter if the *Indianapolis*
story was true, and he said it was.

He described the *Indianapolis* sinking as among the
worst sea disasters to befall anyone since men began
going to sea in ships. He mentioned that the event
greatly disturbed his coauthor, Admiral Nimitz. We
talked about it for quite a while, realizing that at the
time this tragedy befell the crew of the *Indy*, most of
them were in their late teens—the same age we were.
We wondered if we would have had the strength of
character those sailors showed in 1945.

My next recollection of thinking about the *Indy* was
after graduating from the Academy. While I was in
submarine training, I had a friend and submarine
school classmate—Jim Rutherford—who was a great
fan of *Jaws*. He had the thing nearly memorized and
used to go about quoting Robert Shaw: "Twelve hundred men went into the water, three hundred seventeen came out. That was July the 29th, 1945. . . ."

When it came time to ask for our first ship assignment, it was Jim who conveyed to me the fact that

the Navy had just commissioned a submarine named *Indianapolis*. Even better—it was homeported in Pearl Harbor, Hawaii. The combination of a boat bearing that historic name, combined with the tropical climate we would be forced to endure, was too good to resist. We both asked for assignment to the *Indy*. Jim got his assignment, but I did not. Instead I was sent to the *Omaha*. The *Omaha*! Who ever heard of the *Omaha*?

But all was not lost. After serving nearly two years on that boat, I learned that the *Indy* had an opening for an officer and was about to deploy. Although this was none too pleasing to my wife of two weeks, I jumped at the chance to join Jim and other friends on the *Indy*. Thus began the first of my three tours on the submarine *Indianapolis*.

Five years later, I would return to *Indy* as the ship's Operations Officer and Navigator, and five years after that, I would report one last time—this time as her captain. My tours on *Indy* are what initiated my long acquaintance with the survivors of the cruiser, which in turn precipitated my desire to learn more about the ship and crew.

Over the years the cruiser *Indy* inspired me and my crew in ways you can't imagine. Nearly every event we went through over the past eighteen years, we did so with the cruiser *Indy* in mind. We had her hull number, CA-35, next to a small star on our submarine logo, to memorialize her service. We conducted wreath-laying ceremonies in her honor, beginning with our first deployment in 1982 and ending with our final deployment in July 1998.

This linkage caused me to gain a kind of kinship with the survivors. Occasionally, the subject of the various books describing their ordeal would come up, and I realized that as many times as their story had been told, nobody had ever gotten it quite right. On one issue most accounts agree. It is indeed the stuff of legend—a modern naval tragedy as compelling as that of Odysseus, one with no shortage of heroes. It would constitute a piece of fiction too outlandish to believe.

Recently, this incredible story has encountered a huge resurgence of interest.

It's ironic that this event—one that was front-page news in almost every newspaper fifty-six years ago—is again front and center on the national stage as the survivors enter the twilight of their lives. As of this writing, five books—including *Ordeal by Sea*—are in print or approaching publication, two movie projects are in various stages of development, Pioneer Productions of London has listed this incident as one of the ten greatest sea disasters in history and plans a television special on it, the Discovery Channel sent noted undersea explorer Curt Newport out on an aborted attempt to locate the wreck, and an A&E Channel and several TV news magazine specials have been or will be produced.

Why does this story continue to be so compelling?

Because these tragic heroes are America. The officer of the deck who was relieved just prior to the sinking, Lt. (jg) Charles McKissick, was from Midland, Texas, President George W. Bush's hometown. Other sailors were from Iowa, Oklahoma, Ohio, California, New Mexico, Vermont, and New York—almost every state in the union. These are heroes who are rapidly fading away. That's why I feel compelled to help tell the story at this time.

Why am I supporting this 1963 version of the events? Several reasons.

First, the Navy Department gave author Thomas Helm almost unlimited cooperation in the conduct of his research.

Second, of all the books I have read on the subject, this one seems to present the most accurate portrayal of people and events. It is not an official naval history, but a narrative, written just eighteen years after the event.

It also benefited from contemporary interviews of survivors while their memories were still fresh. For example, the author was able to conduct priceless interviews with Captain McVay himself, which yield, among other things, amazing revelations regarding Admiral Spruance's concerns about *Indy*'s declining survivability should a torpedo attack occur.

It was written by a former Navy man and a former crew member of USS *Indianapolis* who detached before the ship was torpedoed. He understood the ship in ways other authors could not. He got it right.

Most important, the author was driven for personal reasons to tell a story he felt needed to be told. He tells the story in a solid, introspective style that is clearer and purer than the more melodramatic renderings of recent accounts. *Ordeal by Sea* comes across as the most balanced of the several narratives.

The book was published in 1963, and reading it now is like opening a time capsule. So much has happened since then:

• Captain McVay committed suicide in 1968.
• The Japanese Ultra code material that shed light on what was known by the routing officials in Guam prior to *Indy*'s departure has been declassified.
• The Japanese submarine commander recently died.
• The survivors have stepped up their efforts to clear their captain's name.
• Legislative efforts have attempted to achieve the same result.
• Many of the survivors who so looked forward to future reconciliation of their status—reconciliation that many survivors believe is yet to come—have passed away.

I will attempt to update this story in the afterword. I can still picture the men who honored me by asking me to be the keynote speaker at their last reunion—old men, now in their seventies and eighties, some wheeling oxygen bottles behind them, some in wheelchairs. How could they, as young men, have endured so much? As the saying goes, some heroes train their whole lives to be such; others find heroism thrust upon them.

It was at that reunion where the survivors presented me with what has become one of my most prized possessions: a poster titled "Home at Last" with a photograph taken of the crew a few days after their rescue, signed by the hundred survivors present. And despite the disparity in our ages, their young sailor minds couldn't get past my rank, so instead of simply referring to me by my first name, they dedicated it to "Our friend, Skipper Bill."

This is their tale. It is not so much a naval story as a tale of survival. This is for them, with hope that they truly find home, at last.

CAPTAIN WILLIAM J. TOTI, USN
Springfield, Virginia
28 January 2001

PREFACE

FOR nearly a year and a half, just before the beginning of World War II, the *Indianapolis* was my home. I boarded her at Pearl Harbor on a rainy April afternoon in 1940 and remained as a member of her crew until August of 1941, when I was transferred to a patrol boat squadron at Kaneohe Naval Air Station on the island of Oahu. Because of this close association with the ship, it is only natural that I should have a deep personal interest in this story. For all of his cussing and grumbling about bad chow, poor living conditions, not enough liberty and certainly not enough pay, a sailor seldom fails to form a deep and lasting attachment for his ship. Of more importance were the friends I made while aboard the *Indianapolis*, some of whom were still with her in the final hour.

When writing a book such as this, with all of its attendant research, there is the wish that everyone who contributed help in both large and small measure could be personally acknowledged and thanked in these pages. But that list runs well into the hundreds, including former seamen and admirals, a number of marines and even people who were not aboard on the final voyage but who nevertheless played an important part in the overall account of this greatest of all United States naval sea disasters.

A special note of thanks must go to many offices in the Navy Department for almost unlimited co-operation in the search for facts and checking for accuracy on seemingly unimportant details. Last, but far from least, sincere thanks to my beloved wife, Dorothy, without whose excellent assistance and unstinting devotion to the more menial aspects of the task this book could not have been written.

It would be virtually impossible to say just when I began to do research on the sinking of the *Indianapolis*. I strongly suspect, however, that the seed was planted on that August day in 1945 when newspapers around the world carried banner headlines announcing the surrender of Japan. In these same papers there was the all too brief story stating simply that the heavy cruiser CA-35, known as the *Indianapolis,* had been sunk two weeks earlier and what remained of her crew had not been rescued for nearly five days.

Seven years later, in collaboration with one of the survivors, I wrote an account of the sinking, and it was published in a national magazine. Since that time my file of information has continued to grow until finally there was no other choice but to write the full story.

This is not intended to be a controversial book saying who was finally to blame for the disaster, nor is it propounded to be official naval history. Instead, it is simply the narrative of a warship that served her country well and came to a tragic end with ultimate Allied victory only a few short days away. More important, it is the story of men who survived an ordeal probably unparalleled in the history of seafaring.

Throughout the research and final writing I have talked and corresponded with most of the survivors. In every case the incidents related herewith are faithfully recounted just as they were told to me. Nothing has been fictionalized in the interest of making a story.

In the years I have been so closely associated with the *Indianapolis* story one pathetic but very real fact has forever been in focus. It concerns those few people who still cling to that thin frayed thread of hope, or perhaps fear, that their loved one who was listed among the missing might have somehow managed to swim to an uninhabited island and still be marooned and living there as a sort of modern Robinson Crusoe. With the belief that the truth, no matter how harsh, is always better than lingering doubt, it should be known that when the Navy finally gave up the search nearly a week after the survivors were found, the door was forever closed on even the remotest possibility that any man could have been missed.

The wonder of it all is that any of the 317 survivors lived through the ordeal and came back to tell the rest of the world what happened.

THOMAS HELM

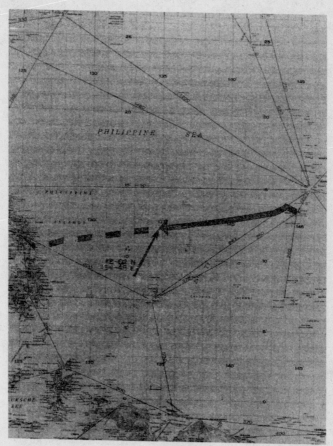

A map of both the USS *Indianapolis*'s proposed route following delivery of the atomic bomb and the site of its encounter with the *I-58*. The solid line indicates the course traveled by the *Indianapolis* prior to the attack. The broken line projects what would have been the remainder of the ship's journey. (*National Archives*)

ONE

≈≈≈

WAKE OF A WARSHIP

AT 2300 Navy time or eleven p.m. 29 July 1945, Commander Mochitsura Hashimoto mounted the conning tower of his submarine *I-58*. As his eyes were becoming accustomed to the darkness, he gave orders for the submarine to be raised to a depth of sixty feet and the speed to be increased from two to three knots. When the submarine leveled off, the periscope went up and Hashimoto took a quick look around the surface of the sea. There was a bright half of a moon well up in the eastern sky showing occasionally through patches of cloud covering, but for the most part the sea was dark. There was nothing in sight, and as they needed to exchange the air in the submarine and recharge the batteries, Commander Hashimoto directed the surface and aircraft radar crews to their stations.

"Blow main ballast!" he ordered.

The *I-58* rose quickly, and in seconds the yeoman of signals undogged the conning tower hatch and stepped out onto the bridge. He was followed immediately by the navigator and Hashimoto. It was good to breathe fresh air again, and the men indulged in a few deep-breathing exercises.

Suddenly the navigator turned to his commander. "Bearing red nine zero degrees—a possible enemy ship," he said excitedly.

Hashimoto jerked his binoculars from their case, put them to his eyes and trained the glasses in the direction indicated by the navigator. A large black object was clearly visible on the horizon! Right at the moment the rising moon in the eastern sky was shining brightly through an open patch in the clouds, making a silhouette of the approaching ship.

Staccato orders electrified the crew. "Dive!" "Open the vents!" "Flood main ballast!"

The bridge was cleared, and as the conning tower hatch slapped shut, Hashimoto was at his periscope. He felt the blood surging through his veins as he watched the approaching ship. This was not just another merchantman nor even a destroyer. It was something bigger—much bigger. Hashimoto hardly dared believe what his eyes were telling him. Through the periscope he thought he could make out two turrets forward and two aft, separated by a large tower mast. If he was right, this was an *Idaho*-class battleship! At last *I-58* could strike a major blow for Japan. Built in the spring and summer of 1944 and formally commissioned on 13 September at the naval yard in Sasebo on the northwestern end of the island of Kyushu, *I-58* had been expected to contribute immensely in turning the tide of battle in favor of Japan, but until now she had never been in a position to make a major kill.

With an overall length of 335 feet and an underwater displacement of 3,000 tons, the submarine had a cruising range of 15,000 miles and carried a complement of 105 officers and enlisted men. At this moment two thirds of the crew were asleep. Yielding to cramped quarters, they were scattered about in almost every available spot. Some were stretched out on top of torpedoes, others were tucked away in narrow bunks and many more sought the limited comfort of the bags of rice that were so much a part of the stores of any Japanese ship. When Hashimoto dropped down from the conning tower and gave the order for all hands to stand by their battle stations, submariners from the lowest to highest in rank jumped into action.

In the faltering moonlight Hashimoto could see his target for only brief intervals. He had no way of estimating the distance, so he could not be sure of its size. While he did not know it, the poor light had already caused him to make an error in deciding that the approaching ship was a battleship with four turrets. She was, in fact, the heavy cruiser USS *Indianapolis*, with three.

The USS *Indianapolis*, designated CA-35, was the first peacetime warship to be built in the United States after the London Treaty of 1929. The war to end all wars was now ten years in the background. Germany had been forever obliterated as a threat. Château-Thierry, the Argonne and the *Lusitania* were just names that people of the western hemisphere occasionally reflected on with mixed emotions.

The New York Shipbuilding Company of Camden, New Jersey, was awarded the contract and the *Indianapolis* slid down the ways on the morning of 15 May 1931. It was a gala occasion, with Miss Lucy Taggart, daughter of Senator Thomas Taggart from Indiana, acting as a sponsor. Senator Taggart had at one time in his political career been mayor of Indianapolis.

The heavy cruiser was put in full commission at the Philadelphia Navy Yard a year and a half later on 15 November 1932, with Captain John M. Smeallie on board as her first commanding officer. At the time she carried a complement of only forty-nine officers and 553 enlisted men.

Leaving the Navy yard early the following January, the *Indianapolis* nosed out into the Atlantic for her shakedown cruise and then turned south for gunnery practice off Guantánamo Bay, Cuba. There she was

joined in the latter part of February by the destroyer
Babbitt, and the two ships crossed the Caribbean, were
locked through the Panama Canal and then paid a visit
to Chile.

Returning to Atlantic waters in the spring of 1933,
the *Indianapolis* paused only long enough for some of
the crew to go on leave and then proceeded to Campo-
bello Island, New Brunswick, to receive President Franklin D. Roosevelt and his party on board for a summer
cruise. Many of that first crew still recall the late President fishing with enthusiasm from the fantail—the same
fantail that was to become a scene of horror exactly
twelve years later as hundreds of frightened and confused men waited for the order to abandon ship.

On 1 August 1933, the *Indianapolis* discharged the
presidential party at Annapolis, Maryland, quickly
took aboard Secretary of the Navy Claude A. Swanson
and departed on an inspection tour of naval bases in
the Canal Zone, California and Hawaii. President
Roosevelt came aboard again on 31 May 1934 to review the proud fleet from her bridge as it steamed in
parade off of New York.

After over two years of active command, Captain
Smeallie was relieved by Captain W. S. McClintic on
11 December 1934. The *Indianapolis* spent the following summer in dry dock and overhaul at Hampton
Roads Naval Base in Virginia, where she was fitted
out as a flagship and put to sea with Captain Henry
K. Hewitt in command.

For the third time President Roosevelt went aboard
the *Indianapolis*—this time in November of 1936 for
a cruise to South America.

Her next captain was the illustrious Thomas C. Kin-
kaid, followed by Captain J. F. Shafroth, Jr., who was
relieved in July 1940 by her first wartime commanding
officer, E. W. Hanson, a captain who was genuinely ad-
mired by every man aboard from the youngest seaman
to the most-seasoned line officer. On the morning of 7
December 1941, while Japanese planes were attacking
the fleet and shore installations at Pearl Harbor, the

Indianapolis was at sea carrying out simulated bombardment of Johnston Island some 500 miles to the southwest of Oahu. When word of the attack was received, she immediately joined a task force searching the sea around the Hawaiian Islands for Japanese ships. When a week had passed and there was no sign of the enemy, the *Indianapolis* was ordered back to Pearl Harbor.

Fueled and provisioned, the heavy cruiser steamed westward across the Pacific toward her first encounter with the enemy. It came on the afternoon of 20 February 1942 about 350 miles south of Rabaul, New Britain, well into Japanese-dominated waters. At the time the *Indianapolis* was part of a task force built around the carrier *Lexington*. The battle was engaged when a flight of eighteen twin-engine bombers attacked the group of ships. It was during this battle that Navy Lieutenant (j.g.) Edwin H. "Butch" O'Hare shot down six enemy planes in one flight and earned the Congressional Medal of Honor. The next few months were ones of frequent bombardment of enemy bases and numerous battles.

In July the *Indianapolis* returned for repairs to Mare Island, California, where Captain Hanson was relieved by Captain Morton L. Deyo. When the overhaul was complete she headed for the bleak cold waters of the North Pacific to help stem the tide of Japanese forces who were rapidly gaining a foothold in the Aleutians. The treacherous fog-shrouded waters around these Alaskan islands were to be the hunting ground of the *Indianapolis* for over a year, and she fought many battles at such places as Kiska, Adak and others.

War in the North Pacific was far from an easy tour of duty. Aside from the knowledge that the enemy was well entrenched on certain of the islands there was the problem of weather. There are few places on the face of the earth where the year-round weather is so inhospitable as in the Aleutians. A day may begin with a clear sky spread benignly over a calm sea and seabirds wheeling and turning in the sunlit air. Sailors pull off their watch caps and unbutton their peacoats. Islands that rise abruptly out of the sea are drenched in sunlight, and the more optimistic are inclined to believe that here, at last, is a nice day. Before the breakfast dishes are cleared from the mess table, however, a lookout will possibly announce the approach of a fogbank, and minutes later the wind will begin to blow. All at once the sky is obscured and swirling snow fills the air. The Aleut has a name for this sudden storm. He calls it a williwaw. He simply crawls into the nearest shelter and waits for the elements to spend their fury. Then he crawls out and continues about his daily business. Naval ships do not find their task so simple. High winds mean disturbed seas. Large ships must keep to deep water. Smaller ships, the destroyers and lesser patrol craft, tuck themselves away in sheltered coves and wait for the storm to pass.

But keeping to deep water was not always an easy task for the *Indianapolis*. Waters surrounding the Aleutians were virtually uncharted. Unless proceeding in open water in the Bering Sea to the north or the Pacific Ocean to the south, the skipper frequently had to con his ship along at the slowest possible speed, relying on sonic depth-finding devices and sometimes resorting to the primitive lead line.

It was a cold and dreary life probing through fogbanks and snowstorms, battling high winds and icy seas and never knowing just how near or how far away a powerful enemy bastion might be. Scout planes were launched from catapults to reconnoiter a suspected island, and it was always a nip-and-tuck game getting them back again before they were stranded in the air by foul weather.

Intelligence was practically nil, but by constantly probing at various points it was finally decided that the main Japanese stronghold in the Aleutians was concentrated on the tiny island of Kiska near the westernmost end of the chain. On 7 August 1943 the *Indianapolis* and other ships of the Task Force were lying offshore waiting for the fog to lift. As soon as they could see the dim outline of their target they began laying down a devastating barrage. So confident had the Japanese forces been that their position was unknown, they were caught by complete surprise. For fully a quarter of an hour after the bombardment started, the shore batteries on Kiska were silent. When they did become operational, many began firing into the cloud-shrouded sky, apparently in the belief that they were under attack by bombers. Gunnery crews aboard the *Indianapolis* and the other ships were confident they were "on target," but the fickle Aleutian weather would not let them claim a positive victory. When the shelling was nearly complete, a massive wave of fog again swelled up out of the sea and covered the entire area. In the final minutes scout planes made hasty sorties over the harbor and reported sinking ships and heavy destruction of shore batteries and other installations, but they could not be sure how effective the job had been.

During the time the *Indianapolis* was in Alaskan waters Captain Deyo was relieved in January 1943 by Captain Nicholas Vytlacil, and in August of that same year, under the latter's command, the ship returned to Mare Island for a brief overhaul and another change of command. This time Captain Einar Johnson relieved Captain Vytlacil, and once again the vessel went back to the Aleutians.

When it was felt that the Aleutians were secure, the *Indianapolis* was ordered to the Central Pacific and immediately participated in the operations leading to the occupation of the Gilbert Islands. She was in the heat of the battle, with invasion bombardments of Tarawa, Makin and the Marshall Islands. Admiral Raymond A. Spruance selected the *Indianapolis* as his flagship, and on 23 June 1944 the heavy cruiser moved in on Saipan to furnish fire support. Six days later the cruiser's eight-inch main battery smashed shore installations on the island of Tinian—the same island to which the *Indianapolis* was destined to deliver the first atomic bomb just a little over a year later.

Back at Mare Island for still another overhaul, the ship was to welcome aboard her tenth and last skipper.

On 18 November 1944 Captain Einar Johnson was
relieved by Captain Charles Butler McVay III.

Captain McVay was what might have been termed a
dyed-in-the-wool Navy man. His father, Charles Butler
McVay, Jr., had graduated from Annapolis with the class
of 1890 and commanded such ships as the *New Jersey,
Oklahoma* and *Saratoga* during World War I. He held
the important posts of Commandant of the Washington
Navy Yard, Chief of the Navy's Bureau of Ordnance
and at the time of his retirement as Admiral in 1932
was Commander-in-Chief of the U.S. Asiatic Fleet.

McVay's naval background extended even beyond
that. While not a true Navy man so far as rank was
concerned, the captain's grandfather had been closely
associated with naval activities and was made an hon-
orary member of the 1890 graduating class of Annapolis, an honor bestowed on the elder McVay for his
unswerving moral and financial support in the faltering
days that followed the Civil War.

When Captain McVay III took command of the *Indianapolis* in November of 1944, it was the realization
of a long-cherished dream. He had graduated from Annapolis with the class of 1920 and reached the rank of
captain on 18 June 1942. At the age of forty-six, as he
stepped aboard the *Indianapolis* and began to prowl her
decks in the manner of any new captain, he was com-
forted in the knowledge that the Axis in Europe were
beginning to bend and the Allied forces were making
impressive forward steps against Japan. At the same
time, he knew that war in the Pacific was still a deadly
reality. He watched the *Indianapolis* go through a brief
period of overhaul and then he took her to sea.

Once back in the Forward Zone and with Admiral
Spruance's Flag aboard again, the *Indianapolis* was
plunged into the thick of battle. She joined Admiral
Marc A. Mitscher's carrier task force to launch the
first attack on Tokyo since the famous Doolittle raid
in April of 1942. The action was designed to cover
United States landings on Iwo Jima. The task force
approached the island of Honshu in the midst of a

tropical storm and by the time the weather abated the ships were in range of Tokyo. The full-scale attack, which was an enormous success, began in earnest. The Navy lost forty-nine planes but more than made up for it by destroying 499 Japanese planes and sinking a carrier, nine coastal vessels, a destroyer, two destroyer escorts and a cargo ship. In addition to these Japanese air and sea losses, United States guns laid waste to aircraft installations, factories and other industrial targets. Through it all, the *Indianapolis* continued to play her role of fire-support ship. When the job was done, CA-35 turned south to back up the Iwo Jima landings.

Admiral Spruance had chosen the *Indianapolis* as his flagship because there was adequate berthing space aboard to accommodate his staff, and also the heavy cruiser had the speed to keep pace with the fast carriers. But he had still another reason for this selection, one that might have shocked some of the crew and civilians alike had they known—the *Indianapolis* was an old ship and not as valuable to the fleet as some of her younger sisters. The admiral never hesitated to have her used close inshore during amphibious landings and bombardments, and lack of a destroyer for an anti-submarine escort never prevented him from going where he thought necessary during an operation.

One day when Admiral Spruance and Captain McVay were on the bridge together the admiral noticed that the *Indianapolis* was slow in returning to even keel after a fast turn under full rudder. He discussed this with McVay, who told him that the ship had been inclined the last time she was at Mare Island for overhaul and it was discovered that due to the increasing weight of armament and equipment being added to her superstructure the metacentric height was now less than one foot. This meant that the cruiser was just about as heavy above water as she was below, decidedly not a healthy condition for a capital ship that should be able to recover from a knockdown in a typhoon or suffer heavy damage in battle and still remain on an even keel. Fully aware of her watertight integrity, Admiral Spruance knew that a ruptured seam in either bow or stern could be corrected for in short order, but he was worried about what a torpedo might do if it slammed into her vitals amidship. It was at this time that he uttered a statement which was to be little short of a prophetic warning: "Should the *Indianapolis* ever take a torpedo hit in the right place, she would capsize and sink in short order." Neither Admiral Spruance nor Captain McVay let this problem deter them in their assignment of the *Indianapolis*. She was kept in the heat of battle until crashed by a kamikaze in the Okinawa campaign.

On the day before the landing of 31 March 1945 in the hour just before dawn, a single-engine Japanese suicide plane was spotted as it bore in on the ship. Anti-aircraft guns opened up but made contact only seconds before the plane struck, barely missing the bridge and hitting on the port side of the fantail. By good fortune, only nine men were killed and hardly twice that number injured. Casualties could easily have been ten times as great had the plane hit almost any other part of the ship.

When order was restored, divers went over the side and made a temporary patch. Realizing that the *Indianapolis* would be out of commission for a while, Admiral Spruance quickly shifted his Flag to the battleship *New Mexico*, and the *Indianapolis* proceeded to Kerama Retto roadstead for further repairs. Kerama Retto is a ragged group of island mountains jutting up out of the sea fifteen miles west of Naha in the southern end of the Okinawa chain. It offered sheltered water for refueling, minor surface repairs and transfer of ammunition. The natural harbors between the islands provided deep water for as many as seventy-five large ships, with good holding bottom for anchors. What was even better, both ends of the roadstead could be closed with nets to prevent the sneak entry of enemy submarines. It was a comfortable, safe anchorage except for one fact. Fog often rolled in from the China Sea and left only the mast tops of the ships exposed. When the kamikaze planes found Kerama Retto in such a state, they could pick out their targets by the mast peaks and go down on them in a blaze of glory while the gunners of the close-range anti-aircraft guns were helplessly blinded.

The *Indianapolis* escaped further suicide plane attacks, but her stay in the harbor at Kerama Retto was not without incident. It was well known that the irregular mountains close by were populated with Japanese soldiers, and from time to time some of the more fanatical of these would swim out to the ships, climb up the anchor chain and kill a few sailors. Some even brought along crude bombs, which exploded with a loud bang, often causing more excitement than damage. In the predawn hours, shortly after the *Indianapolis* had anchored, a seaman on deck watch stumbled over the inert body of a marine with a bad gash on his head. Belief that he had been struck down by a suicidal Japanese soldier from the nearby islands quickly spread, and immediately the entire ship's company was roused. The intercom ordered all hands to remain in their own quarters and watch for signs of the enemy who might be aboard. When the night fog was swept away by a morning breeze and daylight returned, the excitement subsided. The ship had been searched from bow to stern and the enemy had not been found. How the marine guard had been injured was to remain a mystery.

As soon as the *Indianapolis* was seaworthy again, it was decided to send her back to the States for major overhaul. Once more she weighed anchor and pointed her bow eastward until she was steaming under the Golden Gate Bridge and up across San Pablo Bay to that long finger of land known as Mare Island. She had been here many times before, and it almost seemed like home. Men stormed the nearby town of Vallejo, and many had to be returned to their ship by understanding members of the Navy's Shore Patrol. The more introspective drank only a few beers and took in a movie, and one man got married by a local J.P. who kept his light on all night.

To all intents and purposes, the *Indianapolis* was snugged up in the Mare Island Navy Yards just like dozens of other combatant ships. During the next three months shipyard workers stayed on the job around the clock rebuilding the port quarter that had been so badly mauled by the suicide plane's bomb. Some officers and enlisted men who had been at sea much too long were turning over their duties to new-comers, ensigns replacing ensigns and seamen replacing seamen.

On Thursday, 12 July 1945, Captain McVay noted with satisfaction that the job was almost completed. A couple of weeks more and his ship would be in first-class condition and ready to take to sea for a two-week training cruise before being ordered back to the Forward Area. On that day, however, he received an unexpected order—the *Indianapolis* was to be ready for sea in four days! This would take a bit of doing. Nonessential shipyard workers were hurried ashore and those who remained were instructed to polish off the final touches on the double. Many of the ship's crew were scattered out over a variety of shore-based trade schools and a considerable number were on leave. All were recalled, with orders to return immediately, and shore liberty was suddenly a thing of the past. Deck and engine-room crews who had indulged in the relaxed routine of Navy yard life were jolted back to reality as preparation for sea became more furious. There was an air of secrecy surrounding the ship, and in true Navy fashion rumors flew thick and fast.

Captain McVay and his division officers, along with many of the leading petty officers, viewed the unex-pected orders with more than a little concern—and not without good reason, for nearly a quarter of the ship's company now consisted of completely green sailors.

Saturday morning the *Indianapolis* put to sea for a

brief trial run and twenty-four hours later she was
back at dockside. Now the lid of secrecy was slapped
shut with a bang. There was absolutely no liberty for
anyone, and all stations were on standby duty. As
soon as the cruiser was tied up, Captain McVay was
called to Naval Headquarters in San Francisco and
told only that he was to bring his ship to Hunter's
Point Navy Yard in San Francisco Bay that afternoon
to receive two Army officers and two top-secret pieces
of cargo, one large and one small. The larger one was
to be stowed on the quarterdeck and guarded around
the clock by the Marine detachment aboard. The
smaller package would be watched over by the two
Army officers and it would be kept in their quarters.

Even as McVay listened to his brief but obviously
vital sailing orders, the strange cargo was moving fast.
A convoy consisting of a closed black truck accompanied by seven large black cars filled with security
agents sped out of Santa Fe, New Mexico, bound for
an airport outside of Albuquerque. There the big crate
and the small package were immediately transferred
to an Air Force cargo plane, accompanied by Major
Robert R. Furman and Captain James F. Nolan. Furman and Nolan, top scientists in the Manhattan Project, were traveling in the guise of army officers in true
cloak-and-dagger style. The cargo plane touched down
at Hamilton Field outside San Francisco, where security agents were waiting with another truck and more
cars, and the cargo was whisked from the airport to
the dockside at Hunter's Point. Back aboard the *Indianapolis,* Captain McVay knew only that he was to
carry the two pieces of cargo to the island of Tinian
as quickly as possible. The parting admonishment to
him had been that every hour he could shave off the
trip would shorten the war by just that much.

There was plenty of activity aboard the cruiser all
during Sunday night, and long before sunrise the mysterious cargo was aboard. The day was 16 July 1945,
and at 0830 hours the *Indianapolis* was under way.
Three hours earlier a blinding fireball had risen over

the New Mexico desert near Alamogordo. The Trinity Shot had proved successful, and the Atomic Age had begun.

Lieutenant Richard Banks Redmayne had joined the *Indianapolis* at Saipan in February 1945 as junior engineering officer. His senior was Commander Glen F. DeGrave. On the way across the Pacific between Hunter's Point and Pearl Harbor, Lieutenant Redmayne had more or less taken charge of the engine room, and despite several fires caused by rubbish left by the shipyard workers, which were quickly extinguished, the *Indianapolis* maintained a speed of 29.5 knots. When the ship nosed into Pearl Harbor for refueling, Captain McVay was satisfied that the lanky six-foot Redmayne was fully qualified to be engineering officer, and Commander DeGrave was put on the beach for a well-deserved tour of shore duty.

Repeatedly, Redmayne plied the ship's intelligence officer as to the nature of the mysterious cargo. He could glean only that the crate being guarded by marines was something destined to shorten the war.

Down in the crew's quarters the same question was being asked.

"It's nothing more than a big box of soft mattresses for the admirals and generals," one sailor said.

"You're all wrong," another opined. "It's a new car for General MacArthur."

On and on the guessing game continued.

"If you'd use your head," a sailor sagely said, "you'd know it's just cases of whiskey for the officers."

"Then let's get into it," another suggested. "The Gyreens are guarding it from topside, but who's to say we can't tap it from the bottom?"

Watertender Second Class Harold Flaten looked on the plan with anticipation. The job would be relatively simple. All they needed to do was cut a hole through the deck under the box and extract the cases of spirits. Immediately, elaborate plans were made. A shipfitter was to bring the cutting torch and a yeoman was to "borrow" one of the blueprints showing the details of the structure of that section of the quarterdeck. Then there were those designated to stand guard duty to give timely warning should a deck-prowling officer or master-at-arms happen along at the wrong time.

Of course it was all just good clean fun and no attempt was ever made actually to cut through into the box, but the plotting and planning occupied many off-duty hours, and gallons of coffee were swallowed.

As the *Indianapolis* continued to drive westward across the Pacific, no one realized she was setting a speed record, but when the island of Tinian was sighted on Thursday morning 26 July some of those aboard interested in statistics did some quick arithmetic and came up with unbelievable figures. In just ten days the venerable cruiser had crossed five thousand miles of ocean, averaging about five hundred miles per day.

The sight of the tiny Pacific island of Tinian was most welcome to Captain McVay. The big job was done. While he still did not know the nature of his strange cargo, he was positive it was vital to the war effort and here it was, ready to be safely delivered on Thursday morning.

The sea was calm as the *Indianapolis* cautiously picked her way into the tiny harbor and anchored a short way offshore. Immediately a swarm of small boats containing admirals, generals and other top brass were beside the cruiser and when the officers climbed aboard, everybody was asking questions, but only a select handful had the answers, and they were not talking. The atomic bomb was the best-kept secret of the war—perhaps the best-kept really big secret in military history. Furman and Nolan, the masquerading scientists who had watched over the bomb components all the way from the New Mexico desert, had certain signals to look for on the faces of a few key people, and within minutes they knew for the first time that the Trinity Shot near Alamogordo had been highly successful.

The big crate and the little metal cylinder were hoisted over the side and deposited in an LCT. Interest in the *Indianapolis* suddenly evaporated as all of the high-ranking officers left and followed the landing craft ashore. The Marine detachment breathed a sigh of relief and settled down to a normal routine.

The *Indianapolis* hoisted anchor late that afternoon, and by morning was off Guam. Apra Harbor was a traffic jam with big ships and little ships and rapidly growing shore installations. When his vessel was securely moored, Captain McVay went ashore, as did several other officers and a few enlisted men. At CINCPAC headquarters, McVay was told that refueling and the bringing aboard of stores and ammunition would continue through the day and night and that he should be ready to sail Saturday morning. The cruiser's orders had already been cut. She was to proceed to Leyte for a two-week training period with Rear Admiral Lynde D. McCormick's unit, then join Vice Admiral J. B. Oldendorf's Task Force 95 off Okinawa. Captain McVay had lunch with Admiral Spruance, but no definite date was set for the return of the Flag. At the moment, Spruance was deeply involved in plans for the invasion of Kyushu.

While ashore Captain McVay happened upon an old Annapolis buddy, Captain Edwin M. Crouch, who graduated a year after McVay with the class of '21. Crouch, Director of Maintenance Division, Bureau of Ordnance, Washington, D.C., was scheduled to fly to Leyte in the next few days for a period of temporary duty. McVay invited him to make the trip on the *Indianapolis* as a passenger and Captain Crouch, accepting the invitation, went aboard several hours later.

Some of the other officers also met old friends, and a few aviation radiomen spent all day Friday scrounging spare parts from the overstocked warehouses. Doctor Melvin Modisher, foraging through the rosters, suddenly discovered that his friend Doctor Robert R. Berneike was now Lieutenant (j.g.) Berneike, medical officer for a group of mine sweepers based at Guam. Doctor Modisher insisted that Berneike come aboard the *Indianapolis* for the afternoon and stay for dinner.

When the evening meal was finished, he introduced his friend to Doctor Earl Henry, the ship's dentist, and the latter led the doctors to his stateroom, where he proudly displayed a detailed model of the *Indianapolis*, which he had devoted months of his spare hours to building. It was an exact replica, complete in every detail even down to the last chock and scupper.

The *Indianapolis* cleared Apra Harbor at 0910 hours on 28 July. Her voyage across to Leyte should have been simple and uneventful. Captain McVay was given a routine warning that three submarine contacts had been reported within two hundred miles of the ship's plotted course. He asked for an escort but was told that no destroyer or destroyer escort was available. It made little difference. The big cruiser had been traveling unescorted for most of her career, and one more such voyage would not matter.

Had she been a tanker or a destroyer on limited duty, there would have been fleet orders to cover her Guam departure and estimated time of arrival at Leyte in the Philippines. Combatant ships such as the *Indianapolis*, however, were generally assumed to be capable of making their own way. True, a radio message was sent from Guam giving the estimated time of arrival of the *Indianapolis*, and half a dozen responsible officers in the Forward Area should have made note of it, but with hundreds of arrival and departure signals being logged in a normal day, there just simply was not enough time to make a detailed study of each report. Most important, however, her top-secret mission had left her name deleted from most arrival and departure boards in the Philippine Sea Frontier. She had returned to active duty the day she dropped her atomic cargo at Tinian, but so well guarded had been her mission that only a limited few actually knew this.

Standing proudly out to sea, the *Indianapolis*, with 1,196 men on board, did not look like a warship that would soon be in dire need of help. She was lean and sleek and capable of turning up a speed that would enable her to outrun any enemy submarine.

TWO

![wavy divider]

INTO THE NIGHT

AT about 2345 on the evening of 29 July, Coxswain Edward Keyes climbed the ladders from the quarterdeck to the navigation bridge of the *Indianapolis* and took over the duty as boatswain's mate of the watch. The nineteen-year-old sailor from Deerbrook, Wisconsin, always preferred to relieve his watch a few minutes early because it left time for a cup of coffee, and besides, it was too hot belowdecks for comfortable sleep. Fitting the boatswain's pipe lanyard over his head, Keyes picked up his mug of hot coffee and walked across the bridge to the starboard wing. He looked up to the sky at the roiled mass of dark clouds with just an occasional flash of moonlight showing through. In the darkness below him there was nothing to see save the luminescent curl of foam thrown back by the bow of the heavy cruiser as she made her way westward across the Pacific Ocean midway between Guam, the southernmost island in the Mariana group, and Leyte in the Philippines.

18

Making turns for 17.5 knots, the *Indianapolis* was steaming along at an unhurried pace across a gently heaving sea with four of her eight boilers on the line—two in her two forward firerooms and two in the two after firerooms. With her propulsion plant thus split, better damage control was afforded.

World War II was rapidly drawing to a close. Nazi Germany and Fascist Italy were no more and in the Pacific, Guadalcanal, Coral Sea, Iwo Jima and Tarawa were already just place names where great battles had been fought and won by Allied forces. Everyone from admirals to boots knew that Japan was on her knees and it would be only a matter of months before a full-scale invasion of the home islands would begin, bringing about a rapid if bloody surrender. Almost a year earlier the joint chiefs of staff had approved a timetable that decreed Kyushu to be invaded on 1 October 1945, with a final assault on Tokyo to follow in December.

Sunday on the *Indianapolis* had been almost as quiet as in the peacetime Navy. The weather had been overcast and the waves choppy. Church services were held in the morning, and the cooks dished out a really first-class Sunday dinner of fried chicken with all of the trimmings for the noon meal. By 1300 the mess cooks had cleared the tables, and the ship continued on somewhat of a holiday routine. Poker and crap games, as well as a little acey-deucey and cribbage, developed in various parts of the ship. Watches went on duty and came off, and Cleatus A. Lebow, fire-controlman third class, under the supervision of his division officer, took the final exam for his second chevron. The port lookouts spotted a dark, squat shape of a ship on a northbound course and word was quickly passed to the bridge. Signal hoists were raised, blinker lamps began flashing and a moment later the excitement was passed. The ship was an LST, and she was talked to briefly by voice radio. Then this last contact with the outside world cut the wake of the *Indianapolis* and proceeded on its northward course.

Along about midafternoon the boatswain's mate of

the watch flipped the lever on the public-address control box and blew on his pipe to attract attention. "Now hear this!" In terse words he informed the ship's company that the medical force was giving cholera shots in the after mess hall. Lieutenant Commander Lewis Haynes and Lieutenant (j.g.) Melvin Modisher, senior and junior medical officers aboard, were in charge of the inoculations, assisted by the two chief pharmacist's mates Watts and Schmueck. Also helping were several hospital corpsmen who had been studying for a rating exam that was to come up in the next few days. Well, the interruption did not matter much. They could study as long as they wanted in the air-conditioned sick bay during the night and sleep late on Monday morning.

Sunday evening passed uneventfully. Nearly twelve hundred sailors nibbled at a supper of cold cuts because the cooks had worked so hard over the fried chicken dinner. Some topped off the rather uninspired meal with a visit to the ship's soda fountain down on the second deck on the port side for one of those large scoops of ice cream in a paper cup generously smothered with thick syrup and chopped nuts—a dish known to all Navy men as a gedunk.

Steaming westward across the Pacific the men of the *Indianapolis* were unaware that they were not alone. They did not know that below the surface was the dark and sinister shape of the Japanese submarine *I-58*. Her crew and skipper were veterans, and each man was honed to a fine edge. The *I-58* had put to sea from Kure on the main Japanese island of Honshu on 16 July 1945, the exact same date the *Indianapolis* had cleared Hunter's Point in San Francisco Bay. A fortnight had passed and neither ship had engaged in battle. The *I-58* was hungry for a kill!

No one aboard the *Indianapolis* was very much concerned about submarines in that section of the Pacific. To be sure, a message from Guam had been picked up by Radio Central and duly sent to the bridge. It was so routine that hardly anyone paid any attention to it. The message was a submarine alert that had come from the SS *Wild Hunter* on her way to Manila with army cargo. Captain Anton Wie of the *Wild Hunter* had seen a periscope at 10 degrees 25 minutes North and 131 degrees 45 minutes East. Captain Wie reported that the armed guard aboard his ship had fired a few rounds at the periscope and that it had vanished. His sighting was some seventy-five miles south of the position the *Indianapolis* would reach around midnight. It was not difficult to become callous to minor submarine alerts in wartime. If each had been taken seriously, every ship in enemy waters would have spent most of the war in a state of something close to general quarters, with the result that officers and sailors alike would have burned out quickly from the constant tension. Anyway, submarine alerts in the western Pacific were as common as barnacles on a ship's bottom. They came in over the regular radio schedules from planes, warships and merchant vessels. Frequently they were just plain errors. A chunk of driftwood bobbing along on the surface might resemble a periscope, and the warning would be sent.

Captain McVay had been following fleet orders—zigzag during periods of good visibility day or night. As a top-flight naval officer, he would not take issue with the Navy Department concerning the honest value of the practice of zigzagging. There were many junior officers and experienced sailors aboard who were strongly opposed to the practice because it put a burden on everyone aboard as the helmsman was forever swinging the ship first to starboard and then to port. With each turn the ship was forced to lean sharply away from the angle she had just assumed. Such maneuvers might have been applicable back when the Navy was younger and fire control was mostly a matter of human sight. But with radar and modern range-finding equipment, the enemy ship had only to study the zigzag pattern electronically for a few minutes and then get the range. Half a year later on a cold winter day in Washington, D.C., the Navy

and the press would pay a lot—perhaps an undue
amount—of attention to whether the USS *Indianapolis* was steering a true course or zigzagging across an
empty expanse of the Pacific Ocean.

After the supper of cold cuts many of the men assembled in the starboard hangar to watch a movie.
Most of the old salts had seen it when they were children, and some of the younger sailors thought it a
little on the corny side, but most important, it was
entertainment.

Just watching a movie for the sake of it was not to
First Sergeant Jacob Greenwald's liking, so he spent
most of Sunday evening visiting friends in the photo-
graphic lab, and on his way back to his bunk in chiefs'
quarters, he stopped by for a short visit with a friend
who ran the ship's soda fountain. Greenwald had been
born into a close-knit family on 19 December 1917
and with three older brothers and a sister he had
grown up the hard way. He and his brothers had kept
their pockets full of change by cutting lawns, delivering papers and pulling weeds at a nearby truck farm.
The job he liked most was caddying at the Lincoln
Country Club in Lincoln, Nebraska. At the age of
twenty-two he and his three best friends had seen an
"A" frame poster on the sidewalk in front of the post
office, and with an urge for adventure and a desire to
see the world, they enlisted.

The second dog watch went on duty at 1800 hours.
Twenty-eight-year-old Lieutenant (j.g.) Charles B.
McKissick from Midland, Texas, was the OOD on the
bridge. The solid cloud cover which had persisted all
afternoon was now becoming ragged, but visibility was
poor and it showed no signs of improving. Shortly
after he went on duty, McKissick talked with the captain and as the two looked at the sky McVay told the
OOD that he could secure from zigzagging and re-
sume the base course.

McKissick issued the orders, and the ship steadied
down on her base course of 262 degrees True, her
clipper-type bow pointed just a few degrees south of

west and straight toward Leyte. McKissick passed the order to the OOD who relieved him of duty shortly after eight p.m. and stopped off to watch a movie in the wardroom. Because the enlisted men had a movie tonight in the starboard hangar, the officers had one in the wardroom. This was the result of a standing order Captain McVay had issued shortly after assuming command on 18 November 1944. It was simple and explicit: Should conditions exist that make it impractical for the enlisted personnel to enjoy a movie, there would be no movie shown in officers' quarters.

With the whole world in the midst of a global struggle it is understandable that some might question the importance of a captain of a warship concerning himself with a subject seemingly so trivial as the showing of movies. But a ship at sea is a tiny kingdom within itself with the crew its population and the captain its ruler. Almost as in feudal times, if the king was a just king and showed no favoritisms or undue privileges to the upper classes the population was happy and content. When things were out of balance, however, there was unrest and there arose the problem of discipline.

Although he was a graduate of Annapolis and a regular line officer in the Navy with full understanding that it was unwise for officers and crew to mingle socially, Captain McVay was a fair man. Junior officers and enlisted men respected him for his attitude. Many a sailor from deck force to engine room had his day brightened from time to time when the skipper stopped by to ask how things were going. That the entire ship's complement felt a warm regard for their captain was a fact to be borne out later during an unprecedented court-martial trial.

The evening watch had come on duty around eight p.m. Young men, fresh out of boot camp, had taken up stations on five-inch guns and bridge wings and inside the ship; boys who hardly knew the difference between a carburetor and a voltage regulator had gone down into firerooms and begun watching dials and gauges. With the war in the Pacific rapidly drawing to a close, the

Navy was in a hurry to get the job done. Ships were being shoved to sea as fast as they could be outfitted and manned, and the veteran *Indianapolis* was no exception. After all, she had a good skipper, a dozen seasoned officers and many experienced petty officers.

Around nine p.m. shipboard life began to settle down. Movies were finished in the starboard hangar and in the wardroom. Belowdecks conditions were almost intolerable. A man could drop into his sack and toss and turn until he either fell asleep from exhaustion or give it up as a bad job and take a blanket and pillow to the weather decks where he would not be stewing in his own sweat. Because of poor ventilation belowdecks the *Indianapolis* was proceeding under what had come to be known as Condition Yoke Modified. No *Bluejackets' Manual* or any other official Navy book explained what Condition Yoke Modified might mean, but it was a real situation to men aboard the *Indianapolis* and in the closing years of the war.

All major warships were constantly under one of three "conditions" while at sea. These were either X-Ray, Yoke or Zebra. Condition X-Ray was the most favorable. It meant that the ship was cruising under normal conditions with no expectation of any damage. In this case little attention was paid to keeping watertight doors shut, and there was plenty of ventilation to berthing quarters belowdecks. Condition Zebra was the final extremity when the ship was buttoned up for battle with almost every single compartment and passageway shut off from another by watertight steel doors with hatches and scuttles dogged down hard and fast.

Condition Yoke, however, was quite another story. Halfway between the cruising condition of X-Ray and the general quarters condition of Zebra there were conditions Yoke and Yoke Modified. Yoke, itself, in the jargon of the Navy simply means that the ship is in waters where an attack or accident might and even probably will occur, but Condition Yoke Modified was a somewhat hypothetical situation that existed more in the mind than in the realm of hard cold facts. Offi-

cers and men alike knew they could not sleep in superheated compartments—spaces that were mechanically
heated by boilers and firerooms or from the blistering
tropical sun.

In the late days of the war, ships were beginning to
slide down the ways with elaborate blower systems
which brought fresh cool air from topside down into
the berthing and working quarters. Some craft, hospital vessels in particular, even had built-in air condi-
tioning systems to make life aboard more pleasant.

The *Indianapolis* had none of these modern conve-
niences. She had been built in a day when sailors were
supposed to be a hard-bitten lot who could put up
with any kind of deprivations as long as they were
fairly well fed while at sea and had a few dollars to
spend at the end of a cruise.

So, Condition Yoke Modified meant that on the night
of July 29 the *Indianapolis* was steaming westward
across the Pacific in about the same condition of watertight integrity as she would have fifteen or twenty years
earlier when the only potential hazard was a derelict
ship or an unexpected storm. While the hatches were
dogged, the scuttles were open to admit the slightest
breath of fresh air from topside. This was not an over-
sight on the part of officers or leading petty officers. It
was simply standard procedure for all overaged warships
still plodding about the Pacific in the final days of the
war. After all, there were nearly twelve hundred men
aboard, and Tuesday they would have to be alert and
on their toes when the ship joined Rear Admiral Lynde
D. McCormick's unit in Leyte Gulf for a two-week period of training before proceeding on to join Vice Admiral J. B. Oldendorf's Task Force 95 off Okinawa.

To the casual observer a warship may seem to go
to sleep shortly after taps has sounded, but closer examination will show that it is still very much awake
at scores of key points from bow to stern. High in
their perch known as Sky Aft behind number two
stack Ensign Harlan M. Twible and Lieutenant (j.g.)
L. J. Clinton had the evening watch. Twible was proud

of his uniform. Those gold ensign bars had not come without struggle. His father, an immigrant from Ireland, was a mill worker in Gilbertville, Massachusetts. During the Depression the sons of woolen mill hands seldom made a practice of going to college, but the Twible family was different. It was never doubted for one minute that any of the children would graduate from college. Just prior to Pearl Harbor, Twible had applied for appointment to Annapolis but was turned down. A year later he took the competitive examination and was accepted. Things had been happening fast for him in the past few months. First there had been graduation with the Spring Class at Annapolis, followed by his marriage to Alice Southworth of Ware, Massachusetts, and then a trip across the States to be the last officer to go aboard the *Indianapolis* before she steamed out into the Pacific on her final cruise. Lieutenant Clinton, fresh out of a PT boat squadron, had also been aboard the *Indianapolis* for only a short while, and the two men had many things to occupy their time on the evening watch.

There was one thing Ensign Twible did not talk about that night in Sky Aft. In fact he had not mentioned to anyone on board that a strange feeling had come over him when he first boarded the *Indianapolis* at Mare Island. He did not know quite how to explain it even to himself, but somehow he felt things were not quite right with this ship. He was not one prone to brood on disaster or take a pessimistic view of matters, but he simply could not shake a sense that the ship would never return. Before leaving San Francisco he had written his two brothers and mentioned these innermost thoughts to them, adding on a brighter note that there was no need for them to worry because he was confident that whatever happened to the ship he would return safely.

Another new naval officer, Ensign John Woolston, was on duty tonight down in Damage Control. Born in Seattle, Washington, Woolston decided he wanted to be a naval architect when he was in the fifth grade, and the following year he was the proud possessor of an MIT

catalogue. Naval architecture had not been just a passing
fancy with John Woolston. When he was sixteen, he
graduated from Broadway High School in Seattle, Washington, with a scholarship to MIT in his pocket and
entered there in the fall of 1941 when he was seventeen.
Upon graduation three years later, he joined the Navy's
V-12 plan and was commissioned an ensign in March of
1945. After a hurry-up course in Damage Control School
at Philadelphia, during which time he was married, he
was routed west and boarded the *Indianapolis* on 2 May.
The day Ensign Woolston stepped aboard his first ship
he began to study her from the inner bottoms to the
tip-top of the foremast. He had learned how to absorb
facts early in life, and it was not long before he could
have walked blindfolded through the ship from the chain
lockers in the bow to the emergency steering room aft
just above the rudder.

There were many other men on duty at various
parts about the *Indianapolis* during the evening watch.
On the weather decks little knots of men clustered
about battle stations—gunnery crews on five-inch and
40-mm guns and inside the three turrets that operated
the eight-inch main battery. Men like Grover Carver,
a farm boy from Simpson, Louisiana, who would reach
his twenty-first birthday in a little over a month. When
he went aboard the *Indianapolis,* he was placed in the
Fourth Division and tonight he was on duty beside a
five-inch gun.

Down in the belly of the ship Richard E. Houck,
Frank Burkholtz and William Mills were standing the
evening watch in Central Station. All three sailors
were from Ohio. Houck, an ex–farm boy from the
southern part of the state, was the youngest of seven
children, and while he found plenty of companionship
in a big family, he was never able to develop a love for
the agrarian life. Plenty of whole milk, fresh churned
butter and vegetables straight from the garden made
for good eating. Even during the Depression years it
was pretty certain that no member of a well-organized
farm family would go hungry, but young Dick Houck

studied the bountiful pastoral scene with a jaundiced
eye. A man could follow a mule or drive a tractor
down ten thousand miles of corn rows and grow old
without seeing anything of interest beyond an occasional flock of crows. But the whole world was waiting
and it was a world filled with adventure in far-off
places for one who had courage to go and seek it. He
unceremoniously pulled up stakes and found adventure right away when he got a job with the telephone
company and was sent straight to South America.

He returned to the States for a short leave and then
was in Alaska stringing countless miles of copper wire
and climbing endless poles in the land of Robert Service
and sourdoughs. When he finally came home again he
found all of his brothers had enlisted in various branches
of the service. Young Dick Houck knew his profession
offered him unlimited deferment so far as military service was concerned, but it just did not seem right to
take advantage of it. He paid a visit to the local draft
board and told them of his qualifications and suggested
that he be inducted and assigned to the Army Signal
Corps—a logical suggestion, since he knew telephones
inside and out. But some draft boards in 1943 were noto-
riously unconcerned with a man's qualifications. The
main problem was to meet a quota and just after the
New Year had been rung in Richard Houck found himself inducted into the Navy. He was shipped off to Great
Lakes Naval Training Station, then to Pearl Harbor on
a transport and aboard the *Indianapolis* in time for the
Marianas campaign.

A veteran in telephone work, at the age of twenty-
seven, Houck was placed in the ship's intercom service. Young Seaman First Class Burkholtz and Electrician's Mate Third Class Mills from the Buckeye State
began to look on world-traveler Houck as a sort of
second father away from home.

It takes some people longer than others to get to
sleep, and sailors on a warship are no exception. When
the bugler sounds tattoo most of the men have already
completed their nightly toilet and are about ready to

dab out the final cigarette or make a thumbnail mark on a magazine or book page they are reading. Some will make a fast trip back to the head as assurance that they will not have their sleep interrupted a few hours later and find themselves stumbling through darkened passageways to answer a call of nature.

But then there were always the "night crawlers," and no warship has ever been without them. These are the sailors who leave everything to the last minute. Tattoo is sounded, followed shortly by the peaceful notes of taps. The lights go off and it is only then that the night crawlers become active. Bull sessions are brought to inconclusive halts, flashlights snap on, locker doors open and click shut and there are the muffled sounds of bare feet padding about the hushed deck. Here and there a variety of objects are dropped ranging from the top of a fountain pen to a carton of sea stores. Others have failed to put up their laundry or turn down their bunks. Then there is always the man who tosses a glowing cigarette into the butt kit and sets the whole pot to smoldering and the objectionist who climbs out of his sack and carries the offending receptacle to the head for disposal, muttering a few carefully selected profanities indelicately directed at careless smokers in general.

On an aging warship in the tropic latitudes during World War II there were always the displaced sleepers who could be found moving about from every division on the ship—engineers, radiomen, quartermasters and watertenders. During the afternoon they may have vowed they would last out another night in the berthing space assigned to them in the superheated quarters below deck, but when put to the test many found that sleep was simply out of the question. The only way to avoid a sleepless night of sweating was to lug a blanket to a sheltered place on the weather deck and bed down.

Such a decision was made with the full realization that deck crews would be out in force with saltwater hoses and swabs just about sunrise and those who had

sweltered through the torrid night below would have
a full hour's more sleep.

Some of the luckier ones, such as Quartermaster First
Class Robert Gause and Yeoman Second Class Victor
Buckett, had been aboard the *Indianapolis* long enough
to find safe and cool sleeping quarters above deck in
the port catapult tower. But soon there were others who
also discovered that a good place to sleep in cool comfort was the big empty cylinder that supported the port
catapult from which the OS2Us were launched.

Born on 10 April 1922, on Jefferson Avenue in Ma-
maroneck, New York, Yeoman Victor Buckett grew
up as an only child and was well on his way toward a
life in the entertainment field or the world of sports.
He could not tell which. By the time he graduated
from high school he had earned no less than eight
letters in sports, was class president and voted the
wittiest man in his class for his ability to impersonate
famous show people. After the bombing of Pearl Harbor, he resigned his job with the Muzak corporation
in New York City and walked down to the recruiting
station. Ten months later he was sworn into the Navy
and sent to training at Great Lakes. When he went
aboard the *Indianapolis* he wanted to be a quartermaster and was in NAN division for a short while
until one day while he was on the bridge an officer
asked if there was anyone on duty who could use a
typewriter and young Buckett spoke up. From this
moment on his duties were clear—and not a bad
change from a simple striker in the quartermaster division. Now he was a yeoman with the primary job of
typing up the ship's log. What was more, he had ar-
ranged an "office" in the cool port catapult tower
which he shared during the daylight working hours
with Aerographer's Mate Second Class Edward S.
Alvey. Alvey was no stranger to him, however. In fact
Buckett had stood up as best man for the younger
aerographer a few days before the ship had left Frisco.

Men like little Seaman First Class Ernest McKenzie
and his buddy, Seaman Second Class Thomas Lock-

wood, were on the move after taps that night. McKenzie had grown up to all of his five feet four inches on a small farm outside Columbia, Missouri. The day he turned seventeen he resolved to join the Navy. He quickly persuaded his parents and convinced them they should sign the necessary papers. In short order he was on his way to the naval training center at Farragut, Idaho, and from there he was sent to the escort carrier *Bismarck Sea* at Astoria, Oregon. He was aboard when the *Bismarck Sea* received a mortal wound from a kamikaze plane just about sundown on the evening of 21 February 1945 about forty-five miles east of Iwo Jima. A suicide plane boring in toward the port bow was taken under fire and splashed, but a second kamikaze escaped detection until it was only a thousand yards away on the starboard side. It crashed the *Bismarck Sea* abreast the after elevators, causing a heavy internal explosion. Orders were given to abandon ship and little Ernest McKenzie hit the water without a life jacket and was almost run over by the sinking ship. A destroyer picked him up several hours later along with 725 other survivors.

McKenzie was shipped back to the States for a thirty-day survivor's leave and then reported to Alameda, California. It was here that he ran into his school friend from Columbia, Missouri, Tommy Lockwood, who had recently been assigned to the *Indianapolis*. The two young sailors were overjoyed that they had found each other, and McKenzie requested that he be assigned to the same ship and got his wish. He reported aboard on 6 July 1945.

On this Sunday night he had finished the day by standing the four to eight watch on one of the 40-mm guns. He had a berth in the port hangar, but when he had first gone aboard a few weeks earlier he had been assigned a bunk in the crew's quarters belowdecks. After a couple of nights at sea he cornered his division officer and explained that he had just survived the sinking of the *Bismarck Sea* and he simply could not rest easily in such close confines. The understanding

officer took pity on him and gave him a pass to sleep
in the hangar. Tommy Lockwood was not so lucky.
His bunk was down in the hot inside. On this fateful
Sunday night McKenzie bumped into his friend as
they came off duty.

"I think I'd rather stay awake all night than go
down in that sweatbox," Lockwood complained.

McKenzie thought over the problem for a minute and
remembered a pile of folding canvas cots stored near
the port hangar. They belonged to the Marine Guard,
but no one was using them. He told Lockwood to get
his pillow and blanket and be his guest in the big
airy hangar. (A chance meeting on a darkened deck,
a scrounged folding cot—a passport to deliverance?)

Down in the electrician's station in number one fireroom, twenty-year-old David Thompson from Adams-
ville, Ohio, kept a sharp watch on the various meters
and switches that make up the electrical panel. He
was an electrician's mate third class and had been
aboard the *Indianapolis* for a little over a year. Despite his youth he was already leading petty officer of
the watch. When his relief showed up early, Thompson picked up his tool kit and his life jacket and
headed for his bunk in the crew's quarters. Why had
he decided on this night alone to take his life jacket
with him? He had never done it before. It was not
premonition, because Thompson did not think about
such things.

All about the ship life and activity continued long
after taps had sounded: men coming off watch and going
on watch, men dragging their bunks topside. The master-
at-arms rapped on a few officers' doors and told them
they had left a porthole open, reminding them that it
should be closed after sundown. In more remote parts
of the ship clusters of enlisted men were gathered
around dim lights, putting the finishing touches to card
and crap games. Firecontrolman Third Class Rudolph
Gemza, just turned twenty-eight, spent Sunday evening in a hard-and-fast crap game and really lost his
shirt. In fact, in a futile effort to recoup his losses, he

had tossed in a handmade sheath knife he had been working on for more than a month, and the fickle whim of the galloping dominoes decreed that he should lose even this.

From Sky Control to firerooms and from bow to stern, the *Indianapolis* was very much alive. It did not matter whether the crew was just trying to find a place to sleep, win a crap game or relieve a watch, there were life and movement all about the ship as she steamed steadily toward her point of no return.

THREE

≋

THE LAST WATCH

NIGHT or day the most important part of any ship is the navigation bridge, for here is the brain that must remain sharply alert from the moment the ship gets under way until she is once more at anchor.

The evening watch was slowly wearing on. At just about 2230 the moon officially rose, but no one aboard the *Indianapolis* saw it because of the thick cloud cover in the eastern sky. During that watch there were somewhere between ten and fifteen officers and enlisted men on duty. High above number two turret the bridge was far removed from the rumble and hum of engines and motors and the swish and splash of waves racing along the side of the hull. It was a quiet part of the ship, as the bridge usually is except in time of storm or battle. It was a place of charts and dials and instruments. Simple instruments like the magnetic compass, almost as old as the science of navigation itself, stood beside the more modern gyro compass. There was the radarscope with its thin finger of yellow light sweeping endlessly in a clockwise rotation, feeling the surface of the sea for miles in all directions, forever searching for some solid object that would leave a pip or tiny smear of light in the wake of the moving finger. Then there was the fathometer, an instrument that constantly reminded the navigator of the depth of the water over which he was sailing. Tonight the water was deep. In fact the *Indianapolis* had just passed a few miles north of the Challenger Deep— the deepest spot in any ocean of the world. Seven miles of nothing but water. If Mount Everest were sheared off at sea level and dropped into Challenger Deep it would sink and still be covered by a mile of water. But as the ship continued on her westward course the ocean bottom began slowly to rise. By the middle of the midwatch the fathometer was recording fifteen hundred fathoms separating the ship's keel from the bottom—about two miles down.

There was not much to do on a night like this. The helmsman kept the ship on course. Talkers—sound-power men with headphones and a microphone—were in frequent contact with the engine rooms, Radio Central, the various radar control centers and other important points about the ship.

Lieutenant Richard Banks Redmayne, the ship's new engineering officer, was on the bridge during the evening watch as supervisor of the watch under instructions. He had stood no bridge watches until the *Indianapolis* departed from Guam. The tall, angular twenty-six-year-old naval officer from Westwood, Massachusetts, would celebrate his twenty-seventh birthday in just ten days. He had been at sea almost constantly since he had reached voting age. He had graduated from the Massachusetts Maritime Academy in 1941 as an officer, and when war clouds began to gather over the United States he transferred to the U.S. Navy as an ensign. On another fateful Sunday, 7 December 1941, he had found himself as chief engineer on a converted four-piper, the USS *Hulburt,* at Pearl Harbor. There was not much for an overaged destroyer to do while the sky was full of enemy planes except shoot back and hope for the best.

After 7 December, Redmayne moved out to other areas of the Pacific. He participated in the Aleutian Campaign before joining the *Indianapolis* in February 1945. He was shortly made senior assistant engineering officer and was aboard during the Iwo Jima campaign, carrier raids off Japan and the preinvasion bombardment of Okinawa, where the *Indianapolis* was damaged by a kamikaze and forced to return to the States for repairs. It was when the ship reached Pearl Harbor on what was to be her final westward crossing in July that Lieutenant Redmayne had taken over the duties of Chief Engineer from Commander Glen F. DeGrave.

Lieutenant Redmayne enjoyed the evening watch. He was confident he had done a good job in bringing the *Indianapolis* safely and quickly to Tinian and then on to Guam and he knew that the other officers respected him for it. Tonight he had spoken briefly with Captain McVay during one of the skipper's frequent trips to the bridge before retiring to his emergency cabin shortly after eleven o'clock. The ship's gunnery officer, Commander Stanley W. Lipski, was in charge of the bridge as supervisor of the watch, and Redmayne found this Annapolis graduate with two years' duty on the *Indianapolis* pleasant company.

Commander Lipski was what might have been termed a sailor's sailor. He could have easily stayed safely ashore during the war. In fact the Navy Department urgently requested that he stick glued to the chair behind a desk in the confines of Washington because he was an expert in the Russian language and had so many other qualifications that would make him valuable ashore. Stanley Lipski took a dim view of desks. He was a qualified gunnery officer and felt his talents could best be utilized on the open sea aboard a man o' war. He had put up a paper and red tape battle to abandon his desk and he voluntarily shoved up into the Forward Area.

The zero hour was rapidly approaching.

*   *   *

Through the wave-dashed orifice of the *I-58* a squat man was hungrily sizing up his approaching target. There was excitement aboard the submarine, and clustered about the captain were the Kaiten pilots begging for permission to be launched against his enemy ship. These fanatical young submariners—like their airborne brother, the kamikaze pilot—had sprung into existence during the war. The Kaiten was, in effect, a midget submarine weighing about eight tons. The entire forward section was the explosive warhead of a huge torpedo with the pilot and the power plant occupying the after section. The Kaiten could travel a maximum distance of about thirty miles and had a top speed of twenty knots. Once launched from the mother sub, there was no turning back. The suicide submarine was equipped with a small periscope that allowed the pilot to keep his target in sight until the final moment when torpedo and ship exploded. Should he miss his target, the pilot was doomed anyway. But his end would not be the glorious death so appealing to the Japanese warrior. He would simply continue running until the fuel supply was exhausted; then slowly the human torpedo would sink, and as it went deeper and deeper, the mounting pressure would cave in the bulkheads and the pilot would suffocate.

Even before Pearl Harbor, Commander Hashimoto had known war and death while he served on the Yangtze River in gunboats and mine sweepers. There was something about him that resisted the urge to send his countrymen on a certain suicide mission if the job could be successfully accomplished by mechanical means. He told the Kaiten pilots to stand by and instructed his torpedo officer to prepare for a run of fifteen hundred yards and to make ready to fire six torpedoes fan-wise when he gave the order.

Lieutenant Redmayne left the bridge a few minutes before midnight. Making his way down to the wardroom, he found it quiet. He looked into the pantry where the steward's mate of the watch was leaning

across a table reading an out-of-date magazine. There
was the smell of coffee from a pot gently fuming on
a hot plate in the corner. Looking up from his magazine, the steward's mate asked the engineering officer
if there was anything he wanted. Redmayne had not
had enough supper, so the on-duty steward's mate
made him a ham sandwich. Not anything to brag
about—just a slice of boiled ham between two slices
of bread with a little mustard on one side. While Lieutenant Redmayne was sipping his coffee, Ensign John
Woolston also dropped by the wardroom pantry for a
midnight repast, and the two talked briefly.

By five minutes before midnight, more than two
hundred men and officers had gone off watch and an
equal number had taken their places. They came and
went from all parts of the ship and carried with them
a wide variety of rates and ranks.

There were thirty-nine seagoing marines aboard and
while they had been hard pressed to guard that mysterious box that housed the first atomic bomb from
Frisco to Tinian, the pressure was off of them now,
but they still had a few watches to stand.

Marine Private First Class Giles McCoy walked aft
to the ship's brig under the fantail, relieved the marine
who had been on duty, and then checked on his two
prisoners who were quietly serving out their time behind bars. Both were sleeping, so McCoy pulled a
magazine out of his hip pocket and made himself as
comfortable as he could on an empty bunk. All
around him in the darkened compartment sailors were
sleeping, but there was the dim glow of a battle light
on the bulkhead over his head and he settled down
to while away the next four hours. It was just as well
that he had not selected this night to make any deep
inroads into *Anthony Adverse* or *Gone with the Wind*,
because he had only a precious few minutes to read.

Back behind number two stack in Sky Aft, Ensign
Harlan Twible and Lieutenant (j.g.) Leland Jack Clinton
began to wonder, as the midnight hour approached, why
they had not been relieved. It was not anything unusual,

however, even for officers. The same thing went on in every department, and gunner's mates, chief petty officers and boot seamen had the same problem. Lieutenant Clinton told Ensign Twible to hold the fort while he went below to be sure their reliefs had been aroused. It could have been Twible who elected to go, for there was certainly no protocol connected with such a chore. But Clinton went and Twible stayed.

Gunner's Mate First Class Johnny Fitting of the Fifth Division was relieved some fifteen minutes before the hour of midnight and hurried down to his bunk in the crew's berthing quarters. Fitting had enlisted with his boyhood friend Joseph L. Nichols the day after the Japanese struck Pearl Harbor in 1941. Five days later they were on their way to the San Diego Naval Training Station and they would not see their home state of Idaho for nearly four years. Fitting was to be a gunner's mate, while Nichols would stick to the deck division and earn the rate of boatswain's mate second class.

The two had been on the *Indianapolis* since they left boot camp in San Diego. When she had returned to the States for repairs, they were both granted leave and returned to the north central village of Kooskia, Idaho, on the Clearwater River. For Nichols and Fitting it was not just an average wartime leave with plenty of fried chicken and lemon meringue pies. These two sailors were going to marry sisters. This they did and after much too limited honeymoons they hurried back to California and checked in aboard the ship that had been "home" to them from almost the beginning of World War II.

As gunner's mate first class, Johnny Fitting was earning enough pay to invest in an electric fan. There was a 110 outlet just above his bunk, and as a first-class petty officer he indulged in this modicum of comfort. Sunday night, however, he found that someone had "borrowed" the outlet adapter needed to supply the necessary current for his small fan.

"Damn it!" he fumed. "Hey, Joe, did you see who got my plug?"

But Nichols, in the bunk below his, was already asleep. Since there was no way to make the fan work, Fitting rolled up his bedding and carried it topside. Boatswain's Mate Nichols and Gunner's Mate Fitting had been at one another's side throughout the entire war in the Pacific. Strange the workings of fate.

2400 hours. The beginning of a new day on the Navy's big twenty-four-hour clock—30 July 1945! Coxswain Edward Keyes, as boatswain's mate of the midwatch, made a quick count. There were thirteen officers and enlisted men on the bridge.

The ship's damage control officer, Lieutenant Commander Kyle C. Moore, was supervisor of the midwatch. He had been aboard the *Indianapolis* for three years and had qualified as supervisor of the watch only a year earlier. With the initials K. C., Moore could not escape the nickname of "Casey" the moment he entered the service. The Navy has a wonderful ability for changing names. Once aboard ship, one ceases to go up and down stairs because the stairs have become ladders. No longer is there a floor beneath the feet because all level surfaces on which one walks are decks. Walls suddenly become bulkheads, dining room tables are mess tables and bathrooms become heads. Consequently, the Navy does not let a man escape a nickname if there is anything about his name or physical makeup that might possibly suggest one. Big two-hundred-and-fifty-pound men are always known as Tiny. A man who makes a practice of reading books immediately becomes known as Professor. The sailor who is overly addicted to beer while ashore on liberty just naturally acquires the handle of Suds. Of course all radiomen are generically known as Sparks, and young ensigns fresh out of Annapolis are referred to as Shavetails.

Casey Moore had no objection to his nickname. In fact, he was proud of it because he knew that men of the Navy seldom bother to give a nickname unless they liked the man in question. He loved the Navy and was glad the men and his fellow officers liked him. An ex-newspaperman and photographer from Knoxville, Tennessee, he was skilled with a camera and on many occasions, Admiral Raymond A. Spruance had called on him to record permanently on celluloid scenes at Tarawa, Kwajalein, Saipan and a dozen other places where the admiral's flagship took part in action.

The war wore on and Casey Moore rose in rank. He was forced to set aside his camera as his duties as damage control officer became more complex and time-consuming. Tonight he looked at the crew on the bridge with him. He had not drawn a bad lot. His OOD was Lieutenant John I. Orr, a competent officer with three years of sea duty behind him. Lieutenant Orr knew what war was about. Just before boarding the *Indianapolis,* he had been aboard the USS *Cooper* (DD 695) when she was torpedoed and sunk in Ormoc Bay. Orr's junior OOD, Lieutenant (j.g.) Paul L. Candalino, and Ensign Paul T. Marple had been aboard for only a few weeks, but he did have some seasoned enlisted men on the bridge with him. There was Donald F. Mack, the bugler; Edward Keyes, boatswain's mate; and Jimmy French, quartermaster.

Moore made a quick tour of the bridge and satisfied himself that the lookouts were qualified and alert. He noted that the helmsman was keeping the ship on her true heading of 262 degrees. Orders to cease zigzagging had gone into effect during the evening watch, and now the clean clipper bow of the *Indianapolis* was pointed straight toward the island of Leyte in the Philippines. True, the moon would appear briefly at intervals as scudding clouds left an opening here and there, but certainly not long enough for an enemy submarine to line up her torpedo tubes.

Shortly after 2300 hours, Captain McVay had made his final tour of the bridge and was now retired in his emergency cabin on the port side of the bridge aft. Commander Johns Hopkins Janney, the ship's gunnery officer, was also asleep in a similar compartment on the opposite bridge wing.

With qualified officers and enlisted men on the

bridge there was not much to worry about. After all
the war was almost over. Hitler and Mussolini had
fallen flat on their ugly faces in Europe, and Tojo
was the next to go. A few months earlier Japanese
submarines and kamikaze planes had been a real
threat to any shipping in the forward area. Now, with
B-29 bombing raids on Japan occurring almost daily
and naval bombardment biting into the very heart of
the home islands, the bulk of the Imperial Submarine
Navy was ranging less far afield with each passing day.

Midnight—a moderately heaving sea and clouds
covering a half moon now nearly three hours old. The
Indianapolis, with her 9,950 ton displacement spread
over 610 feet, sliced her way westward into what must
forever be referred to as an approximate position of
134 degrees 48 minutes East and 12 degrees 2 minutes
North. The exact latitude and longitude will never be
known because at 0001, or just one minute after midnight, death in the form of a monstrous blast occurred
near the bow on the starboard side of the ship. The
Indianapolis shook and seemed to stagger under the
blow. All thirteen men on the bridge suddenly found
themselves on the deck. Even as they tried to regain
their footing, they were knocked down again by a second explosion of the same magnitude just aft of number two turret almost directly below the navigation
bridge in the vicinity of the fortieth frame of the ship.
A wall of dull orange fire fringed with a seething hellish halo of inky-black smoke belched up from the guts
of the cruiser and with it a geyser of exploded water
leaping higher than the ship itself.

In his emergency cabin behind the bridge, Captain
McVay was hurled to the deck. As he struggled to a
standing position, his mind was rapidly trying to put
things together. He had been aboard when the *Indianapolis* was struck by a kamikaze plane months earlier—
but this was not kamikaze area and besides, it was the
middle of a dark night hundreds of miles from the nearest land. Quickly assimilating the sensations and compar-
ing them with existing facts, he knew there were still

several other very real and equally serious possibilities. The ship could have struck a pair of floating mines or a boiler, maybe two, might have exploded. After all, the tired old cruiser had been put through quite an ordeal of speed in the previous two weeks, and all four fire-rooms had been pushed to the limit. However, as Captain McVay scurried about the bridge looking for Lieutenant Orr, the OOD, he did not discount the possibility that a Japanese submarine had sent a couple of torpedoes into his ship—unlikely, but possible.

Soundpower talkers—those seamen spotted about the bridge with telephone communication to various parts of the ship—hurriedly regained their footing and attempted to make contact. Edward Keyes, boatswain's mate of the watch, scrambled to the public address system control box. Training dictated that he should alert the ship with a sharp blast from his silver pipe that hung from his neck. The instant Keyes touched the control box lever he knew it was useless— the *Indianapolis* no longer had electrical power. The silver pipe was never blown.

The supervisor of the watch, Lieutenant Commander Casey Moore, recovered his footing and left the bridge in a rush. As damage control officer, he had to know what had happened.

Coxswain Keyes approached Lieutenant Orr and explained that his public address box was dead. "Get below and alert all hands to come topside and prepare to abandon ship!" Orr shouted, remembering the sinking in Ormoc Bay.

Following Moore down the ladder to the quarterdeck and ducking into the passageway on the port side, Keyes ran forward to the hatch leading down to the second deck. In Stygian darkness the hatch was choked with men fighting their way up the ladder to the main deck through volumes of smoke and acrid fumes. Frightened men, coughing, shouting and stumbling onto decks made slick with oil from ruptured pipes. All around him he could hear the cries of the wounded.

Spinning about, Keyes ran back out onto the quar-

terdeck and down in crew's mess. Already there was
a decided starboard list and the job with which he was
faced was not an easy one. He must burrow deeper
and deeper down into the very belly of the ship shouting over and over again: "All hands topside; prepare
to abandon ship!" Coxswain Keyes did his job well,
for men from remote compartments and out-of-the-
way sections of the ship were later to recall someone
running along darkened passageways shouting the
fearful warning that every sailor dreads. When he felt
he had covered the area as well as he could, Keyes
made his way back topside and to the bridge.

On the signal bridge, just below the navigation bridge,
Kenley M. Lanter, signalman third class, had skidded
across the deck with the first blast and scrambled to his
feet in a daze only to be knocked down by the second
torpedo. Lanter had stood the four-to-eight watch on
the signal bridge and after the movie he had gone down
to his regular bunk in the crew's quarters. When he
could not get to sleep because of the heat, he resignedly
picked up his pillow and blanket and made his way back
to the signal bridge. He flaked out close to the splinter
shield and was about to doze off, when several sailors
still on the evening watch moved up close to him. They
were rattling on in a typical Navy bull session; a good
way to pass the time if you had nothing to do, but not
exactly a lullaby for a man trying to go to sleep. "Come
on, you guys," Lanter had mumbled sleepily. "Knock
off the chatter and let a workingman get to sleep." Much
to his surprise, they had moved away and he balled his
pillow and stuffed it under his head. The topside air was
cool and soon he began to drift off to sleep. After the
rude awakening and when he managed to get on his
feet, he found his dungarees, shirt and shoes and pulled
them on in a hurry. He had his life jacket with him, and
before he tried to find out what had happened, he tied
it on. What had happened?

Nobody on the signal bridge knew for sure. Signalman
First Class Robert P. Bunai was senior petty officer on
duty and he immediately began gathering papers. "Hey,

you guys, help me with this stuff." Lanter and Signalman Third Class Frank J. Centazzo scurried about gathering up the classified material that was now scattered like dry leaves all over the signal bridge: restricted papers, code books, and any other information which must never fall into enemy hands were hurriedly collected and jammed into a weighted canvas bag that had been provided for just such an emergency. If the ship were going to sink, these important documents would also sink and not be left floating about the surface to be picked up by the enemy.

When Captain McVay found Lieutenant Orr he was ringing up the engine room on the annunciator and giving the order to stop all engines. There was no response—not even the slightest suggestion that the message had even left the bridge or been received. Only three or four minutes had passed, but already the *Indianapolis* had assumed a decided list.

Resignedly Orr turned to the captain. "I'm afraid the entire ship's electrical system is out, sir," he said.

There was very little that existed in this situation that could be covered in the rule books. The ship had been hit and obviously hit hard. Lieutenant Commander K. C. "Casey" Moore, the ex-photographer from Knoxville, Tennessee, rushed back to the bridge with findings from his brief exploration below. Moore was a practical man and he did not waste words when he told the skipper that he thought the ship was going to sink.

"Do you want the abandon ship order given?" he asked.

One man, suddenly roused from a sound sleep and standing half-clad on the deck of a severely damaged ship, was confronted with a fateful decision. Charles Butler McVay III was truly a man alone. There was one of two choices to make. Either pass the word to abandon ship and watch over a thousand men drop into the uncertain peril of the open sea or harken back to those vast files of naval records that prove beyond a shadow of a doubt that many a good ship has been prematurely deserted at great cost of human life and the eventual and unnecessary loss of a fine ship. A captain must give the final word—right or wrong.

"Maybe we can hold her," he said. "Go below and have a second look and report back as quickly as possible."

Moore nodded and once again hurried down the steel ladders that separated the navigation bridge from the quarterdeck.

Seaman First Class Marvin Kirkland from the Florida town with the tongue-twisting name of Thonotosassa had spread a blanket in an out-of-the-way spot on the communication platform between number one stack and the port catapult. He had forgotten his pillow, so he improvised by stuffing his shoes in his white hat. Thus provided with somewhat spartan bedding, he settled down for the night. When the first torpedo landed, he jackknifed into a sitting position and instantly pulled on his shoes. He was lacing them when the second and more violent explosion occurred, and with it a great mass of ugly red fire snorted down from the air exhaust shield around the stack and he heard men scream.

There were two thoughts in his mind as he clambered to his feet. First there was his life belt. He had left that way back in the shipfitter's shop on the starboard side just forward of number three turret. He had to get that and then he must go to his battle station, which was at the other end of the ship up near the bow but down on the second platform in the freshwater compartment. He was the "freshwater king," and his battle station was beside the tanks, wearing phones and standing by to twist valves that would either flood or drain the various tanks if it was deemed necessary by Damage Control.

As he was leaving the communication platform, two men stumbled toward him holding hands and screaming for someone to lead them to the sick bay. Kirkland took one look and shuddered. They were burned black. He wanted to turn and run—to run as far away from the sight of them as he could, but there was something about their voices that made him fight back his sense of revulsion. Someone had to help them because it was obvious they could not help themselves.

"Take hold of my shirt and follow along behind me," he said. "I'll tell you when we come to the ladder."

All about the weather decks men were running and shouting to one another. The ship was hardly moving through the water. Here and there a flashlight winked on and off now and then. This was practically a court-martial offense while traveling under blackout conditions in enemy water, but what difference did it make now? Kirkland saw a growing red glow from the forward section and realized that he could not get to the sick bay on the second deck. But how was he going to explain it to the two burned men who clung onto him?

Step by cautious step he helped them down to the quarterdeck and he was relieved when he saw a couple of hospital corpsmen trying to organize an emergency first-aid station near the opening of the port hangar.

"Bring them over here, Mac," one of the corpsmen shouted. "We'll do what we can for them until the doctor gets here."

Relieved of his responsibility, young Marvin Kirkland remembered his life belt. He ran across the quarterdeck to the starboard side and then back aft to the shipfitter's shop. He knew exactly where he had left the life belt, but when he began fumbling for it in the darkness, he found it missing. Someone had beat him to it. The ship was not going to sink, of course, but regulations did require that a man wear a life belt or jacket to his general quarters station. Trying to think where he could find one, he suddenly saw a bunch of men digging kapok jackets out of a big canvas bag. Running by, he stopped long enough to grab one for himself, and then he ducked down into number one mess hall. The compartment was rapidly filling with water and, in the gloom that was lighted with a dull red glow from a fire he could not see, there was a great mass of mess tables and broken benches floating about, and men were stumbling around through the confusion. Close by he heard someone calling. He turned and saw that it was his division officer, Commander Casey Moore, standing waist-deep in the water.

"Yes, you, sailor," Commander Moore shouted as he unlaced a fire hose from the rack on the bulkhead. "Get topside and see how much hose you can find. We've got plenty of fire forward and we're going to need all the hose we can find. Get some men to help you and get back here on the double!"

Waving an acknowledgment, Kirkland climbed back up to the quarterdeck. It was not until he was topside that he realized just how far the *Indianapolis* had rolled over to the starboard side. There might have been a spare fire hose in the starboard hangar, but now there was too much water in there to get it out, and besides, everybody was fighting their way up to the port side. Maybe he could find a length of hose in the port hangar. The deck was now sharply inclined, and twice Kirkland lost his footing as he climbed up the deck. The ship was still plowing forward very slowly, but the bow was almost under and waves were lacing across the quarterdeck. Conscientiously he stumbled about in the port hangar looking for a fire hose, but there was none to be seen. He could hear men shouting the order to abandon ship.

Reluctantly, Kirkland gave up his hopeless search and fought his way aft to his abandoned ship station on the fantail. There were two stacks of life rafts, four in each on the port and starboard sides. All around the stack on the starboard side men were swarming like bees trying to get into a hive. Kirkland joined them, wondering why the rafts were not being cut loose and tossed over the side. All at once he saw the reason. Someone with a .45 automatic in his hand was preventing this from being done. There was no way of telling whether he was an officer, a chief petty officer or one of the marine guards on board. But the man was demanding that everyone leave the raft stack alone until the word was passed to abandon ship.

Well, young Kirkland had already heard the *word* while he was searching for a fire hose in the port han-

gar. He had no desire to play hero or be a mutineer,
but his own instinct told him that the ship was sinking
fast. He fished a knife out of his pocket and started
cutting the straps that held the rafts. All at once the
whole pod began to break loose and slip down across
the sharply angled fantail deck.

The ship's navigator, Commander Johns Hopkins
Janney, who occupied the emergency cabin on the
starboard side of the bridge wing, dressed hurriedly
and stepped out onto the bridge. Even as he did so,
he recalled that he had mentioned to his brother officers that evening at dinner that the *Indianapolis* was
scheduled to pass a Japanese submarine sometime
around midnight. Of course the report was common
knowledge from the on-duty radiomen in Radio Central to the entire complement of the ship's wardroom,
but nobody gave it much serious consideration. It was
treated so lightly, in fact, that one of the line officers
jokingly replied that they had no reason to worry because the destroyer escort would clear a path for the
Indianapolis. The *destroyer escort* was a standing and
somewhat stale joke aboard the flagship of the Fifth
Fleet. She had made so many unescorted crossings of
the Pacific that her *destroyer escort*, which all capital
ships were entitled to, was a mythical company existing
only in the imagination. Now, to Commander Janney
the reference had taken on the importance of a prophetic warning, but neither he nor Captain McVay had
time to dwell on the supernatural. At the moment the
problem was real and urgent. Seconds ticked into minutes and the *Indianapolis* wallowed deeper and deeper
into the sea on her starboard side. There was little doubt
that two torpedoes had blasted into her.

"Go down to Radio Central and be sure they get
out the message that we've been hit and are sinking
fast," Captain McVay said. The Captain was certain
that if the generators supplying power to the transmitters
in Radio Central were out of commission the distress
call could be aired from Radio II with the use of standby generators. He did not have to concern himself with

the latitude and longitude because the navigator paused
for a fleeting moment at the plotting table to scribble
down the figures on a scrap of paper. Commander Janney was gone a moment later, bound for the radio
shack. That was the last anyone saw of him.

With the first blast, all lights in Radio Central had
winked out. When the second torpedo hit moments
later receivers, headphones, typewriters and radiomen
were suddenly thrown to the deck in a tangled mass.
A communications officer, Lieutenant Nelson Page
Hill, rushed into Radio Central a minute or two after
the torpedoes landed. In the uncertain glow of fire
and flashlight beams he saw an ugly picture. Even a
woodchopper could have taken a quick glance around
and guessed correctly that no distress message would
leave that compartment tonight. The deck was littered
with broken electrical equipment, paper and wounded
men. The phones were dead and there was no power
on the transmitter keys. Many of the radiomen were
rushing headlong through the after doorway that led
into the communications office where the decoding
machines were housed. Lieutenant (j.g.) David L.
Driscoll, communications officer of the midwatch, and
Lieutenant Hill made their way forward through the
same hatch. Everything behind them was on fire.

Messengers from the bridge began arriving with orders to send out a distress signal. Lieutenant Hill knew
that if there was any radio power left on the ship it
would be in Radio II behind the uptakes for number
two stack. He sent Radioman Third Class Elwyn L.
Sturtevant with the message. The chief warrant officer
in charge of Radio II, Leonard T. Woods, had somehow escaped the inferno in the forward part of the
ship and arrived at Radio II simultaneously with Sturtevant. He glanced briefly at the scribbled words, and
the key began clicking.

Did the distress message go out from the rapidly sinking cruiser, or was Radio II's transmitter also dead? This
was a vital question that would be asked repeatedly for
the next five days and for years to come. There was

never any doubt in the minds of those aboard that Captain McVay, Commander Janney, the messengers and radiomen had done their level best. Years later various people would come forward and claim they had received the message loud and clear. But on that fateful night in the middle of the summer of 1945, if anyone did copy the terse string of dots and dashes that were the *Indianapolis*'s dying call for help, they were not taken seriously. Ships, shore stations and ham operators around the world climbed out of bed on Monday morning without a backward glance at the radio log of the preceding night.

In the port catapult tower, Quartermaster First Class Robert Gause recovered his footing and hurried out into the darkness. Bounding like a kangaroo, he made his way to the port ladder and climbed up to the bridge. Passing the exhaust hood on the forward stack, he felt a severe burn on his right leg as he came in contact with a jet of live steam, but at the moment it did not seem to matter.

Captain McVay was fully dressed now and shouting for somebody to bring life jackets. Gause pondered for a moment then quickly untied his own kapok and shoved it into the skipper's hands. Seaman Second Class Loel Dene Cox had just been bounced around like a man on a trampoline. He was a striker in the NAN division and had drawn bridge lookout duty minutes before the torpedoes struck. He saw Quartermaster Gause give his kapok to the skipper and watched the "old man" struggling to tie it on. The jackets were new and just the day before Cox had tied his own and been ribbed by a few who saw him. "Going someplace, Cox?"

"I hope not in this thing, but if I do, I sure want to know how to get in it," he had replied.

Now, realizing the captain was having difficulty, Cox rushed to his side.

"Let me help you, sir." In a moment, the jacket was properly in place and fastened securely.

Vincent J. Allard, quartermaster third class, had been quartermaster of the evening watch but he had not left the bridge before the torpedoes hit. Allard knew the

Indianapolis inside and out and well he should, for he had been aboard since 1942. Seeing his leading petty officer turn over his jacket to the skipper, he rushed down the ladders to a spot where he knew there was a big supply. Minutes later he was back with a fresh jacket in his hand and Gause put it on.

Lieutenant Redmayne, having finished his sandwich, left the pantry and went to the officers' head to make his toilet before retiring. The first torpedo hit just as he was stepping back out into the passageway. Before he could recover his balance, the second one crashed aboard. He felt the bow section rise with a shudder and around him there was a snapping, popping, hissing noise. As he landed on the deck on all fours, it felt as if the palms of his hands had been pressed down upon a hot stove.

Regaining his footing, Redmayne became increasingly aware of the intense heat and the unmistakable sounds of fire around him. As the ship's engineering officer, his first thought was of the firerooms. He turned and ran aft. Breaking out onto the quarterdeck, he took a few delicious gulps of fresh cool air and then dashed into the starboard hangar. Everything was in shambles—cots, bedding, life jackets, wires and assorted aviation gear were strewn across the deck forming an impenetrable barrier. Cursing his luck, he ran back out onto the quarterdeck and across to the port hangar. There was confusion there too, but not so bad as on the starboard side. He shoved his way through and down to his battle station in the after engine room. Much to his surprise, things seemed almost normal. The lights were burning and the steady hum of turbines proved that the two inboard screws, numbers two and three, were still spinning. Gauges and dials were right on the button and about the only condition that radically departed from normality were the expressions of concern on every man's face from the duty officer to the youngest striker. What had happened? That was the question on everybody's lips.

It takes a special breed of man to consign himself willingly to the engine room of any ship and this is especially so in wartime. Isolated in the very bowels of the hull, he must be willing to wait for those on the weather decks to relay what is happening. Every engineer is constantly aware, at least subconsciously, that he is already far beneath the surface of the sea. He knows, too, that if conditions warrant he will be considered expendable and sealed off from escape in order to protect the ship's watertight integrity.

Communicating with the watch officer, Lieutenant Redmayne asked for a report. There really was not much to say—not at first—but it was noted a moment later that the inclinometer was registering a twelve- to fifteen-degree starboard list—nothing to attract more than a passing glance if the ship had been following a zigzag course. But the *Indianapolis* was on a true course. Added to this, it was suddenly discovered that the after fireroom was unable to make contact with the forward fireroom. Then pressure began to fall off on number two.

"Shut it down and make as many turns as possible on number three," Lieutenant Redmayne ordered.

The engineering officer's job was not to size up situations and make tactical decisions. The engine rooms received instructions from the bridge and his primary consideration was to keep the ship under way until he was ordered to stop or back down.

Number three screw, still turning, continued driving the ruptured bow of the *Indianapolis* forward. Through the rents caused by the two torpedoes, endless tons of seawater were flooding into the forward section.

On the dead annunciator a seaman on the bridge was frantically trying to arouse the engine room. *Stop all engines!* That was the order. He would have done far better to leave the brass handle of the engine order telegraph alone and run down to the after engine room to deliver the order in person.

Lieutenant Redmayne cringed at the waves of pain sweeping up his arms from his two burned hands. There were so many things he wanted to do—so much that should be done, but his fingers seemed like curled sticks. If this had been a normal emergency, he would be in sick bay now and Doctor Haynes or Doctor Modisher, the ship's medical officers, would already have given him a sedative to dull the pain and coated his hands with a soothing ointment. But this was not a normal emergency.

When a machinist's mate from the forward engine room found his way aft, Redmayne forgot his burned hands. In a fear-tinged voice the man told a succinct tale of hell in the forward fireroom. That he had managed to escape was a near miracle. Now Redmayne knew that the *Indianapolis* was in a very serious condition.

There was one faltering hope suggested by the "oil king." "If I pump all of the oil from starboard to port tanks, it may help correct the list."

Redmayne considered the idea and then told the "oil king" to give it a try. It certainly could do no harm.

Why was there no word from the bridge? Lieutenant Redmayne left the after fireroom and headed for the bridge to find out. He never made it. He had just passed through number two mess hall and was out on the weather deck when the vessel fell over on her starboard side. He began to make his way aft but when he reached number three turret he had to walk along the horizontal surface on the port side. The ship was settling lower and lower and the water was rapidly catching up with him. Finally there was nothing to do but step off into the sea and start swimming.

There is no ideal place to be on a ship when it is torpedoed in the middle of the ocean at midnight, but some places are worse than others. If Richard Houck, electrician's mate third class, had been offered a choice, it is hardly likely that he would have elected to be taking a shower. After being relieved from their evening watch in Central Station, he and his two friends, Frank Burkholtz and Bill Mills, had made their way along darkened decks to the shower room. Houck undressed and turned on the water and in a couple of minutes he had worked up a good lather. The first torpedo blast sent him skittering across the shower room floor. Before he could get up he was knocked down again and simultaneously there was no water, no lights and the ship was beginning to take on a starboard list.

"Hey, Houck!" he heard a voice call from the darkness. "What happened?"

Houck did not know. That he could not find his clothes seemed more important at the moment. As he groped about in the black room, he finally located his shoes and a towel. He worked his wet feet into the shoes, wrapped the towel around his waist and hurried out to the weather decks. The trouble would be fixed in a few minutes, and when the lights were on again and the water was running, he would go back and complete his nocturnal ablution. Nobody was going to swipe a pair of dungarees and a blue denim shirt. How he was going to long for that humble garb in the days to come.

Lieutenant Charles B. McKissick, who had relayed Captain McVay's order to cease zigzagging, had gone to bed in his stateroom on the starboard side after watching the movie in the wardroom. In the Navy, berths are usually assigned according to the occupant's rate, rank and time aboard. Naturally, and justifiably so, the officers are accorded better sleeping arrangements, more comfortable beds and a little more privacy than the enlisted men. On a large warship such as the *Indianapolis,* the ensigns generally find themselves in a cabin with two or three others of their rank. Full lieutenants and lieutenant commanders have slightly more spacious quarters, while commanders and the skipper usually have private rooms with most of the comforts of home.

Lieutenant (j.g.) McKissick was on the lower side of the middle group. His stateroom, designated as "JJ," was semiprivate. While he shared the compartment with five other officers, his bunk was comfortable, and they had steward service and their own washbasins and mirrors for shaving.

The "JJ" compartment was just forward of the op-

erating room on the second deck between the thirtieth
and fortieth frame. Straight across the ship on the port
side of the same deck was the Warrant Officer's mess.
The first torpedo hit just a few frames forward of
Lieutenant McKissick's room and the second straddled it a short way aft. The twenty-seven-year-old
naval officer from Midland, Texas, sat bolt upright in
his bunk. There was the clink and clatter of water
tumblers and mirrors as they fell and shattered on the
steel deck. The ship was plunged into darkness and
almost immediately the compartment was filled with
hot acrid fumes.

Fumbling in the darkness, clad only in his shorts and
undershirt, McKissick grabbed a towel from a rack close
to his bunk and jammed it down into the washbasin on
the bulkhead. He opened both taps wide but only a
trickle of water came through. Although there was no
pressure, enough water was in the pipes to soak the
towel. He wrapped it around his face as protection
against the choking fumes and felt his way across the
deck to the door that led into the passageway. Almost
as soon as he was out of his compartment he was wading
through ankle-deep water. Not knowing what had happened, McKissick could not have even guessed that he
was wading through seawater that was already flooding
the second deck near the bow although it had been
only two or three minutes since the torpedoes had found
their mark.

Stumbling about in the darkness, he found it increasingly more difficult to breathe even through the
wet towel he had wrapped around his face. Finally he
found a ladder that led to the main deck. It was so
hot that the rungs burned the skin on the palms of
his hands. When he reached the main deck, his lungs
began to buck and heave for a breath of fresh air. If
he could only get to a stateroom he could crawl
through a porthole. Every few seconds he could see
big bubbles of dull red flames boiling up in the direction of the quarterdeck. Never in his life had he felt
so alone. While he had no idea what had happened,

he was sure his ship had met with a terrible disaster and for a terrifying moment the thought crossed his mind that he might be the only survivor—if he could call himself a survivor.

By luck he found a port side compartment and felt along the bulkhead until he touched a port. The battle shield was in place and dogged down tight. Frantically his fingers searched around for a dog wrench. There should have been one in brackets just below or above, but the wrench was gone. Without the tool the nuts could not be turned. The towel over his face was rapidly drying out, and the smoke and fumes were growing more intense. He felt his strength waning and he did not know exactly where he was or how to get out. He reeled back to the passageway and just at that moment he heard a voice shout, "Does anybody want to get out?" The voice was the unexpected answer to a prayer. McKissick called back and within seconds he was following Seaman First Class James F. Newhall from Phoenix, Arizona, to the port side of the forecastle on a somewhat devious route that eventually led through a shell hoist.

Nearly asphyxiated, McKissick threw away his protective towel once he was topside and for a few seconds he was afraid he was going to be sick, but as he breathed deeply he soon overcame the nausea. Suddenly he became aware that he must be the only officer on the forecastle. He shouted to the collection of frightened men to break out life jackets and to bring up a fire hose to fight the fire that was getting increasingly worse belowdecks. By some miracle a dozen men were suddenly back with plenty of kapok life jackets. Someone dragged up a length of canvas fire hose and it was attached to a saltwater main, but when the valve was turned the flat hose lay as limp as a dead snake. There was no pressure in the main.

Lieutenant (j.g.) Melvin Modisher, junior medical officer aboard, had been hard at work all afternoon administering cholera shots to the crew and he had been glad to get to bed. Hardly a year older than

Lieutenant McKissick, Modisher had been born in
Sharpsville, Pennsylvania. He was in Temple University Medical School when he was inducted into the
Navy's V-12 program, and he graduated in December
1943. By then the war was just two years old. Already
married in 1942, he interned at Abington Memorial
Hospital in Abington, Pennsylvania. The Navy had its
sights on him and stayed on target until he was actually inducted and ordered to report aboard the *Indianapolis* in the late fall of 1944.

Doctor Modisher was a sensitive man. He hated war
with all of the injury and suffering it produced but he
was glad that he could play his small role as doctor
on a warship. He had been on board for little less
than a year, but he had seen much of war in that time.
On 19 February 1945, which was D day for Iwo Jima,
he remembered the *Indianapolis* in company with Task
Force 54 going about the business of shelling the coast
from predawn hours until just before H hour at 0900
and then falling back to the safety of the sea. When he
had sat down for the noon meal at a table with a clean
white cloth and plenty of well-cooked food, he simply
had no stomach for it. All he had been able to think of
were those endless waves of marines rolling ashore to
be cut down by Japanese gunfire.

Tonight, however, young Doctor Melvin Modisher
found himself very much in the thick of things. His
compartment was the last one forward on the port
side just across from the room occupied by the Catho-
lic chaplain, Father Thomas Michael Conway. There
were two other officers assigned to his room, but both
were on duty at the time the torpedoes struck.

At the first blast, Modisher was wide awake and lying
on his back in the middle of his compartment. In those
fleeting seconds before the lights went out he saw all
three bunks bounce into the air and then come to pieces.
Picking himself up, he stumbled across to a porthole that
was now open for some reason. He wondered what time
it was. Sticking his head out into the night air, he looked

up at the sky and caught a glimpse of the moon as it winked on and off behind scudding clouds.

Wearing only a T-shirt and a pair of shorts, Modisher searched around in the darkness until he found his kapok life jacket and quickly tied it on. Opening the door to his room he hurried out into the passageway and made his way forward to the hatch that led to the forecastle just forward of number one turret. When he gained the ladder, there were lots of other men going topside. Everyone had the same question on his lips—what had happened? No one had the answer but there was not much confusion—at least not in those first few minutes.

When he left his compartment, Doctor Modisher had intended to make his way aft to his battle station in the chiefs' quarters located near the fantail on the second deck. Before he had even started to leave the forecastle, however, he realized that he could do the most good by staying just where he was. There were those who had been badly burned and those with broken bones and somewhere in the darkness there was a man screaming in pain, crying out for someone to help him.

Lieutenant McKissick, Doctor Modisher and some hundred or more other men and officers on the bow section of the *Indianapolis* were perhaps the first ones to know for sure that the vessel was going to sink, and it did not take a lot of imagination to realize that she would remain afloat for only a few more minutes. With two gaping holes in the starboard side gulping countless tons of seawater, the entire forward end of the ship was digging deeper and deeper into the water. Far aft, number three screw still turned, and as the starboard side continued to fill, the ship began to roll and angle downward like a great fish dropping over into a graceful dive.

On the bow section the wounded and badly frightened slipped across the sinking forecastle into the water. The more agile climbed through the lifelines and found footing on the port side of the hull. As it dipped lower, they just walked out into the water as they would have done at a popular swimming beach. It was as easy as that—no jumping, no scrambling down a line, no big hurry.

Since the early days of sail, all seafarers have known that a sinking ship creates a suction that will carry all nearby flotsam, including swimming men, down to the ocean depths when it takes its final plunge. Basically, the peril of the suction of a sinking ship must always remain a mystery of the sea. Laboratory experiments can prove that a suddenly sinking mass may draw light floating objects beneath the waves with it, but laboratory conditions are far different from real life. Sometimes the phenomenon may depend on such vagaries of chance as whether a person was riding the crest of a wave or padding about in a trough, whether he was wearing a life jacket or swimming free and even whether he was inhaling or exhaling at the moment of the final plunge.

From captain to youngest seamen, men of the *Indianapolis* were beginning to go into the water within seven minutes after the two torpedoes struck. Young Seaman Second Class Glen Milbrodt, who had been born on a farm near Brunsville, Iowa, on 1 February 1927, had gone aboard the *Indianapolis* in May 1945. He was assigned to a 40-mm gun and was standing the midwatch when hell broke loose on the starboard bow. He asked his gun captain what they should do.

"Tie your life jacket on tight and go over the side!"

Fully clothed and wearing a new kapok jacket, the farm boy from Iowa who had spent only two weeks at sea went aft and dropped over the port side into the dark empty expanse of the Pacific Ocean.

Ensign Harlan Twible on duty in Sky Aft had waited for Lieutenant (j.g.) L. J. Clinton to report back saying that the midwatch officers Ensigns Donald J. Blum and Ross Rogers would be topside shortly. Lieutenant Clinton never returned, but Ensigns Rogers and Blum came up to relieve him about two minutes before midnight.

Twible may possibly be one of the very few who knew exactly when the first torpedo struck the *India-*

napolis. The impact slammed him against the splinter shield with a terrific jolt. When he looked at his watch a moment later, it had stopped at exactly 0001 hours, or one minute past midnight. It was a good timepiece, and Twible was certain that it was accurate. He was to wear the watch for the next four days in the water and even carry it home with him. Still fully wound, the hands never moved a tick past 0001.

The three ensigns—Twible, Rogers and Blum—watched in dismay as their ship began to sink. Great clouds of smoke and steam were rising from the forward stack and other points along the starboard side of the bow section.

Leaving Sky Aft, Harlan Twible made his way down toward the quarterdeck. He could hear clusters of excited men shouting to one another, interspersed with the cries of the wounded. When he reached the quarterdeck he saw the executive officer, Commander Joe Flynn, and ran over to him and asked what he should do.

"Get back to the fantail and be sure the men go off the high side of the ship," Flynn said.

On his way aft Twible chanced upon the type of real-life drama that has been so much a part of war from the dawn of civilization. As soon as he had gone aboard the *Indianapolis,* he had been assigned to court-martial duty. In the role of prosecutor, Twible was glad there were no serious offenses. For the most part all of the trials were just simple cases of AWOL or AOL. One he remembered rather vividly was that of a young sailor to whom the courts had meted out a sentence of seven days on bread and water for being AWOL. The sailor had served out his term during the *Indianapolis*'s fast run from Frisco. A court-martial officer cannot afford to take his petty cases too seriously, but at the time Twible had wondered if the offender had not been dealt with too harshly. Now, as he made his way aft, he saw the same sailor who had stood before him at mast, busily engaged passing out kapok life jackets from one of the large bags. Twible observed the young man with intense interest. It was

obvious that he could have simply grabbed a jacket
and let the other men fend for themselves. Instead the
ex-prisoner was so busy he had not bothered to get a
jacket for himself. In the weeks that followed, Ensign
Twible was to recommend the sailor for the Navy
Cross for meritorious action in the time of battle.

When he reached the fantail, Twible found several
hundred men milling about, slipping and sliding on a
deck that was rapidly lifting out of the sea and tilting
over to the starboard side.

Seaman Second Class Marvin Kirkland watched the
pod of life rafts he had helped cut loose skitter across
the deck and tumble into the water. Instinct told him
that he should follow them in a hurry, but it is not
easy to leave the deck of a ship and plunge unceremoniously into an inky sea. Besides, there were those in
authority who kept insisting that all hands should wait
for official orders to abandon ship.

In the fleeting moments of moonlight, Kirkland saw a
sailor suddenly break ranks. "I'm not going to stay here
and be dragged down with the ship," he shouted. In a
headlong rush he threw himself over the stern and
landed in the spinning blades of number three screw.
Kirkland squinted his eyes tightly to shut out the sight.

Determined that he would not meet the same fate, he
crawled through the lifelines on the port side and began
inching his way along the hull toward the middle section
of the ship. Struggling to keep his footing on the sharply
angled stern, he felt someone suddenly lunge against his
back. His first thought was that he had been pushed but
even in the fractional part of a second that it took him
to fall he realized that the shove was not deliberate.
Someone had simply stumbled into him. But it made
little difference now. He was falling down toward the
sea and the spinning shaft of number three screw. A
split second later a blast of multicolored lights was flashing through his brain, then total darkness.

Kirkland sank slowly for what seemed an interminable
length of time, but when he awoke he was swimming
with steady strokes away from the ship. At first he felt

nothing and then as complete consciousness returned he was aware of a great area of pain enveloping his face. Rolling over on his back and paddling with his left arm, the fingers of his right hand explored his aching face. What his fingers discovered was frightening. Where his front teeth had been there was nothing but the ragged edge of bleeding gums and lacerated lips. Then he remembered. He had fallen almost face first onto the shaft of number three screw, hitting his chin on the spinning bar. The impact had torn his lips and driven his upper front teeth up into his cheekbones. But now there was not time to dwell on what the results would be or the almost overpowering pain. The important thing was to swim far enough away so as not to be sucked down by the ship when she began to sink.

Up in the wardroom pantry, Ensign Woolston and the pantry steward were knocked to the deck with the first blast, and seconds later, when the next torpedo landed, the room burst into fire. The flames were short-lived, the red glow sweeping through the compartment long enough only to devour all of the oxygen and leave the space shrouded in oily smoke.

Woolston stumbled to his feet and weaved about in a daze on unsteady legs. Almost subconsciously he knew the only way out was through a porthole in the wardroom. He fumbled about in the darkness until he found a dog wrench and in a matter of seconds had two battle ports open. Just as his laboring lungs were gasping for that last breath of coveted oxygen he and the steward's mate thrust their heads out into the clean night air.

"Let's get out of here," Woolston shouted as he squirmed his way through the open port.

"O.K., sir. Just let me get a breath of clean air," the steward replied.

Woolston did not look back. Once out of the porthole, he made his way forward on the port side. Staring at the chaos about him, he realized he was an officer without a station. Damage Control Central was long gone. In that moment he knew the *Indianapolis* was sinking.

The young MIT graduate rushed out onto the fore-

castle, but two officers were already guiding the men
in trying to get the rafts ready. The same operation
was taking place on the communication deck on the
level above, and there was nothing he could do here.
He raced back down to the forecastle and then to the
main deck. The list was increasing, and he saw many
men at the port deck edge waiting for the word. No
one seemed to need help, so he hurriedly made his
way to the gun deck over the hangars. There was a
battery officer in charge here, but he saw that many
men were still without life jackets. He rushed over
and quickly began helping the crew until each had
a jacket.

In the time of catastrophe men sometimes react in
strange ways. When the torpedoes struck, the reaction
of those down in engineering spaces and berthing
compartments was normal as they struggled to get topside to see what had happened. But scattered about
other parts of the ship some behavior was less ortho-
dox. One man climbed out of his bunk, took a freshly
pressed suit of dungarees from his locker and dressed
almost as if he were getting ready to stand inspection.
He snapped on a flashlight and laid it on his bunk,
angling the beam so that he could see to comb his
hair. As a final touch, he picked up a brush and
knocked the dust off his shoes. Thus fully dressed, he
joined the milling throng and headed for the weather
deck. Another, who had earned quite a reputation as
a moneylender on board, heard the word to abandon
ship and suddenly remembered that the list of those
who owed him money was in his locker down on the
second deck. He called to one of his shipmates to get
an extra life jacket for him, then raced back down to
get the list of debtors. A sailor began to load a ditty
bag with articles he fancied he would need at a later
date. Some of the things he decided to take with him
were a box of pencils, a steel tape measure, a meer-
schaum pipe, a paperback edition of Thomas Hardy's
Return of the Native and a large magnifying glass.

One replenished the fuel supply of his cigarette

lighter while another sat on the side of his bunk calmly clipping his toenails. Here and there some paused long enough to tear treasured photographs out of scrapbooks and place them in their billfolds. Another sailor, determined to finish a letter he had started writing earlier, scrambled around in his locker, found his flashlight and brought the letter to a quick close. He folded the pages, addressed an envelope, and then carefully tucked the missive into his shirt pocket.

The majority, of course, assumed a realistic view of the situation and acted in a more normal manner. Boatswain's Mate Second Class Raymond B. McClain, on duty Sunday night as master-at-arms, was sleeping in the master-at-arms' shop. The torpedo blasts threw him out of his bunk and he hit the deck running aft through the mess hall and out onto the quarterdeck. Behind him he could hear men screaming for help. At one point he crossed a section of deck so hot that he felt the soles of his feet blister. But Mack, as most of the crew called him, was as tough as a hickory log and he kept on going.

Upon reaching the quarterdeck, he paused only long enough to rid his lungs of the fumes and smoke from below and then he raced on to his battle station, which was one of the 40-mm gun mounts on the hangar deck. Immediately he became a leaning post for the younger sailors manning the battle station. "What's the scoop, Mack?" "Are we going to sink?" "What do you reckon we oughta do, Mack?" "Did a boiler blow up, or is there a submarine out there shooting at us?"

"Nothing to worry about," McClain said. "But just so that we follow regulations, all you guys be sure you're wearing your life jackets."

He suddenly realized that while he was being certain all of his crew had life jackets he did not have one for himself. He asked if anyone had an extra. Of course, like most of the true sailors aboard the *Indianapolis* McClain was pretty sure she was not going to sink. After all, he had been aboard through many an engagement and he had seen the vessel hit hard time after time and remain afloat. Maybe this was a little worse than before, but you get to trust a ship after nearly four years aboard.

"Here, Mack, I went down to the hangar and got this for you."

It was a pale-faced kid who had been in the Navy for only a few months. He was bundled up in a kapok jacket of his own, but he had thought enough of the safety of the big boatswain's mate that he had left his station and raced down to one of the life jacket stations and picked up one for his friend. Never a sentimental man, McClain could not suppress a momentary tightening of his throat as he took the jacket from the young fellow who only a few years ago had been playing cowboys and Indians with cap pistols.

It was becoming more and more obvious that the gun crew would not be training on a target. The ship suddenly leaned sharply on her starboard side and McClain shouted, "Let's get ready to abandon ship!" The crew followed their boatswain's mate to the high side of the hangar deck. "O.K., guys, let's dive in," he said. Most of the men were young, but old and young alike dreaded the thought of deliberately jumping into the sea. McClain did not want to go either, but this big boy from Athens, Texas, had worked his way all through the war in the Pacific and he had seen ships sink. He did not need to be told now that the *Indianapolis* was on her way down.

He looked at the men's frightened faces and knew they needed a leader now more than at any time before—someone they could follow.

"If you won't do as I say, then do as I do!" With that he threw himself over the side and hit the water hard. The impact snatched the kapok jacket from him but he came up sputtering and managed to find it. Swimming away a few strokes, he rolled over and looked up toward the hangar deck. His trick had worked. The crew was following his lead and throwing themselves into the sea behind him.

Down on the second deck, Seaman Second Class

Avery C. Peterson found himself in quite a different predicament. Having joined the Navy on the fourth day of the fourth month in 1944 at the age of thirty-four, he had gone through training at Farragut, Idaho. As a firecontrolman striker he was assigned as telephone talker, and when the ship was not in battle condition his duties were in the soda fountain.

Tonight the top sergeant of the Marine detachment, Jacob Greenwald, had stopped by the soda fountain on his way back to his bunk in the chiefs' quarters. Peterson and the marine had each eaten a gedunk before taps. When Greenwald had taken his leave and headed aft, Peterson began closing up the soda fountain. In doing so he pulled the big wire screen down over the counter, tightened it with wing nuts and dogged the door. The ice cream maker had just settled down for a good night's sleep when he was suddenly thrown to the deck by the torpedo blasts.

As he regained his footing, he asked aloud, "What the hell happened?" Since there was no one around to give him an answer, he decided he had better get topside and find out. His route of escape was not going to be easy.

Shoving his way through a litter of paper cups, broken bottles and cans along the back side of the counter, he reached the door. It was jammed! Surely, he thought, with a little effort it will open. He worked in earnest but no amount of pushing or kicking cracked the door a single inch. Well, there was another way. He would open the screen mesh above the serving counter and get out that way. But the forces of evil were working against him. The screen was jammed shut!

As the ship began to roll starboard Peterson, on the port side, became more acutely aware of the unnatural slope of the deck beneath his feet. Then he heard men rushing about in the darkness shouting and trying to find their way topside.

"Hey, somebody, I can't get out of this place; the

door is jammed. Will you give me a hand and help me get it opened?" he yelled into the blackness.

With relief he heard a voice on the other side of the door. "You pull while I push," he called. Putting his shoulder against the door, he shoved and could feel the jerking from the other side—but the door would not budge.

"Maybe we can lift the screen mesh," he called to his unknown helper, and together they tugged. When it was obvious the screen could not be opened, the stranger in the darkness muttered, "Sorry, I can't stay any longer." Then he was gone.

"Don't leave me trapped in here like an animal!" Peterson screamed. He beat against the screen with his fists. Was it going to be his lot to sink into the sea surrounded by a few hundred gallons of ice cream, concentrates of soda pop and chocolate syrup and chopped nuts? No, it was not! He grabbed a small metal stool and attacked the screen mesh like a man possessed. When he had caused a rent, he threw the stool aside and ripped it open with his hands. Out he went into the passageway, through the greasy smoke up to the weather deck and the hangar where he had seen a bag of life jackets.

In Radar Aft behind number two stack Radarman Third Class Francis Rider, petty officer of the watch, and his buddy Seaman Second Class Allan Altschuler had the midwatch under way about ten minutes before midnight. There were ten other men on duty with them and tonight Altschuler had drawn telephone talker duty on the soundpower phones connected with the bridge. Overhead, at the top of the after mast, the big bedspring radar antenna revolved, searching the sea, which seemed devoid of any objects for forty miles in all directions. Those who watched the black dials would have gladly welcomed a slight pip on the screen. Even had it turned out to be nothing more than a floating fuel drum it would have afforded a little excitement—something to call the bridge about, something to enter on the log. But tonight there was nothing. Nothing the radar could "see" even though right at that moment there was a small spire of metal breaking the surface of the water only a few thousand yards away—the periscope of the *I-58* observing the *Indianapolis* as she steamed westward. Had that Japanese periscope been only a few feet higher out of the water, the fate of the 1,196 American sailors might have been entirely different. But the *Indianapolis* steamed complacently on while the crew of *I-58* lined up its torpedo tubes.

At the moment of impact, Altschuler was shoved across the deck, but he was able to steady himself on a nearby desk. He was sure that something serious had happened, although he did not know what. Radarman Third Class Francis Rider was not sure either, but he thought it wise to get his eleven-man crew out onto the weather deck in a hurry. Last to leave the shack, Altschuler hung up his phones and hurriedly followed the others. Just outside of Radar Aft, a seaman had ripped open a bag of kapok jackets, part of a double order that had been accidentally or providentially assigned to the ship just before leaving San Francisco. Almost as a team the men of Radar Aft put on their jackets and moved across to the port side. No one had planned it. Not one of the dozen men had even considered the prospects of abandoning ship, but now the trip to the high side seemed the natural thing to do. Even more natural was the business of walking down the port side of the hull and into the sea.

Seaman First Class Grover Carver was relieved from his battle station on the Fourth Division five-inch gun and ambled down to the after head with his friend Gunner's Mate Third Class Peter Mittler. True to Navy habits, Mittler, with the first name of Peter, had quickly become known to his close friends as "Peter Rabbit."

Carver and Mittler were making their final toilet when the torpedoes struck, and although the blasts had only caused them to stumble, they had looked at each other in dismay. Certainly no Japanese ships

were in this area of the Pacific at this stage of the war.
It must certainly have been an explosion in one of
the firerooms. Or maybe the ship had struck a mine.
Whatever the case, they would be sounding general
quarters in the next few seconds.

"Let's get back to the gun," Carver said.

Mittler agreed and, leaving behind their razors and
toothbrushes, the two sailors hurried up to number
one gun on the hangar deck.

No one in the gun tub knew what had happened,
and everybody was waiting for some word to come
over the speaker system. Carver picked up a sound
power headset and tried to make contact with other
parts of the ship, but the phones were as dead as if
they had been unplugged. Suddenly, the men on number one five-inch gun heard their gun captain calling
to them.

"We've taken two fish, lads," he announced in a
calm voice. "There's not much danger of sinking, but
just to be on the safe side let's get ready to abandon
ship just like it was a regular drill."

There was a big bag of kapok jackets just outside
the gun tub and Mittler, Carver and the rest of the
crew hurried to the station and started putting them
on. Carver was the self-appointed man to pass out the
jackets, and the procedure was calm and orderly for
the first few minutes, but then conditions changed
quickly. The ship began to make her first roll, and as
she did, scores of men converged on the pod of jackets. It was not a genuine panic, but Carver began to
realize that they were crowding in on him faster and
faster. To stem the tide, he began throwing the jackets
out to the crowd. There were plenty to be had, but
Carver was glad he was now able to disburse them
without getting trampled in the attempt. When the
sudden rush for jackets began to subside, he slipped
his own arms into one and just at that moment he lost
his footing as the *Indianapolis* took a sudden roll to
starboard. At the same instant he heard someone
shouting the word to abandon ship.

After finishing his written examination for firecontrolman second class in the afternoon, Cleatus Lebow
had eaten early chow and gone up to Sky Forward,
where he had stood the four-to-eight, or second dog,
watch—at last a chance to get a full night's sleep. He
did not have to go on duty until eight o'clock the
next morning.

On the way back from the bridge, he stopped off
in the firecontrol workshop up one deck level and just
behind number three turret on the port side. It was a
friendly place to while away an hour or two just bat-
ting the breeze with good companions. Tonight there
had been the usual gang: Rudolph Gemza, Lyle Rea-
ling, Donald "Polar Bear" Shown, Clarence Benton,
Guy Smith and Forest Gaither. Shown was not called
"Polar Bear" because of his proclivity for icy water
but just because he was a big man with a shock of
white hair on his head.

Lebow liked these occasional bull sessions. He had
grown up in a big family with four brothers and six
sisters, and there had always been plenty of talk to
listen to and join in with back home in Abernathy,
Texas. He had been born in the little town of Happy,
Texas, on 8 February 1924 and he had always thought
that the name of his birthplace was somewhat sym-
bolic of his childhood. He had become engaged in
April 1941 and was married nine months later, just
five days after the Japanese attack on Pearl Harbor.

Still mindful that he had a full night's sleep coming,
he left the firecontrol workshop a little after 2100
hours, went below and took a shower. On his way to
his bunk he passed the armory in the starboard aft
corner of number one mess hall.

"Hey, Lebow," a voice in the semidarkness called.
"Come on in and get a cup of lemonade."

Beginning to wonder if he was actually going to get
that full night in after all, Lebow stopped for another
bull session. The gang that hung out in the armory
was much like those up in the workshop: just good
companions with enough horseplay and ribald humor

to keep a guy laughing. The offer of lemonade was no
joke. Someone had scrounged a full gallon of lemon
concentrate. With a splash of this in the bottom of a
big china mug and diluted with six or seven ounces of
cold water, it made a fairly palatable drink, although
not as good as those big tubs of picnic lemonade back
in Abernathy, where tall glasses were half full of
cracked ice and the lemons had just been freshly
squeezed. To add to the pleasure there was always a
pretty girl to drink it with. But the concentrate made
a tasty substitute. In fact, he sat around in the armory
long enough to enjoy three mugs of the liquid before
taking his leave. That full night's sleep was something
that was destined to be long delayed. He had hardly
found his bunk and dozed off to sleep when he was
awakened by a frightening blast that almost tossed
him out of his bunk. He sat up quickly, pulled on his
shoes and scrambled in his locker for a shirt and a
pair of dungarees.

Under number three turret George Horvath, fire-
man first class from Cuyahoga Falls, Ohio, was sleeping in his shorts and T-shirt on single wool blanket.
Not much for a bed, but he had joined the ship after
a cruise across the Pacific on the USS *Chester*. In the
bombardment of Iwo Jima, the *Chester* was struck a
glancing blow by the *Estes* when the ships came too
close together during the heat of the battle. The damage was not sufficient to keep the cruiser from com-
pleting her mission but serious enough to send her
limping back to Mare Island for repairs. Entering port,
Horvath had garnered a short leave to scurry back to
Ohio to spend a few days with his wife Alice and their
two sons. The youngest was just about to celebrate his
first birthday, but Horvath could not stay. He hurried
back to California and was promptly transferred from
the disabled *Chester* to the nearly ready-for-sea *Indianapolis*. He was assigned to the evaporators helping
to make freshwater for the ship but no one told him
where to sleep. So George Horvath had become something of a gypsy. When he was hungry, he fell into the

nearest chow line and stowed his seabag in any corner he could find, and when night came on, he slept wherever he could. When the torpedoes struck, he was up and dressed almost before the ship stopped shuddering. Then he remembered he had been issued a kapok jacket, which he had left down in the evaporators two decks below. Although someone said they were passing out jackets forward, Horvath wanted to be sure he had one, so he dropped down the nearest hatch and worked his way to the evaporator station and retrieved his own. Back on deck he did not have to be told that the ship was sinking.

Up on the bridge Kenley M. Lanter finished helping Robert Bunai and Frank Centazzo stuff all of the scattered classified material in the weighted bag so it would go safely down with the ship. It made him sad to think about the *Indianapolis* sinking. He had come to love her and remembered the first time he had seen her. He had been transferred from the receiving station to the *Indianapolis* and as he walked solemnly down the Mare Island pier he had decided that his future home must surely be the biggest ship in the world. Because the tide was in, she seemed as tall as a skyscraper, and to a Georgia boy who had never before seen a really big ship, she seemed to reach from here to eternity as he came up on her stern. Everywhere there were men, dozens of them, scores of them milling about in clusters like ants working over a great aquatic anthill. Wide-eyed with awe, he had found his way up the gangplank, saluted the colors and made a quarter turn to repeat the salute to the OOD—they had taught him that in boot training at Great Lakes and in signal school at the University of Illinois. He had hardly had time to stow his seabag when a big boatswain's mate approached him and told him to lay to and help bring provisions aboard. Lanter had read *Twenty Thousand Leagues Under the Sea* when he was a boy and he remembered the *Nautilus* and Captain Nemo. This had been only a fanciful submarine off on a fictional voyage, but as he joined a work party bringing stores aboard the *Indianapolis* he began to wonder if he was not really a part of Jules Verne's crew. As he labored for what seemed to be endless hours under the July sun, he was firmly convinced that the *Indianapolis* was getting under way for a voyage that would last for at least a decade; otherwise no one would have considered taking such a vast quantity of provisions.

There was a decided angle to the bridge now. Footing was becoming more and more impossible. Lanter could hear the Captain talking with the exec.

"Skipper, this ship is doomed," Commander Joseph Ambrose Flynn said in a hushed voice. "The bow is already down and I think we'd better get off."

Standing there in the hazy darkness, Lanter strained to see McVay's countentance. Even a young sailor from Georgia knew that the "old man" had a tough decision to make. But it was not long in coming. McVay simply nodded and told the exec to see that the word was passed immediately to abandon ship.

Lanter remembered a pocket-sized copy of the New Testament his uncle had given him the last time he was home on leave. He had left it in the communication room behind the radio shack. Suddenly he wanted it very much. Slipping and stumbling down the ladder to the communication deck, he tried to get into the first doorway he found, but the dogs were jammed. He knew there was not much time left and he would have to forget about the Testament. Hanging on to one of the twisted dogs, he bowed his head and prayed: "Oh, God, please help me."

The ship was now lying over on her starboard side. Lanter crawled up the deck until he reached the port side and then he stood upright on the hull.

How does a man leave his ship? Not an easy question to answer. In the *Bluejackets' Manual* and other rule books pertaining to the sea, the business of abandoning ship is clear-cut and almost sterile. Under hypothetical conditions the ship is simply sinking into the water. Boats and rafts are lowered over the side, and men get into them in orderly groups and row away. But now there were no boats, no order and for Lanter nothing in the way of lifesaving equipment except the kapok jacket he was wearing. He walked slowly along the hull, reluctant to take the final plunge. A few feet in front of him he saw a young sailor he liked, with whom he had often talked. Just a few weeks earlier the man had been promoted to chief radioman. He had blond hair and freckles scattered about his face. Standing knee-deep in the water, he hesitated, afraid to go any deeper.

Closer still was another frightened and bewildered sailor, John Nelson Dimond. Although Dimond was only a seaman second class, he and Lanter had become friends shortly after the younger man had come aboard.

"We can't wait any longer, Johnny," Lanter admonished after making certain the seaman had his life jacket tied on properly. A moment later both men went into the water, and Lanter began to swim as hard as he could.

The ship's senior medical officer, Commander Lewis L. Haynes, was hurled from the bunk in his stateroom under the forecastle on the starboard side as the first torpedo struck its target. He got to his feet only to be knocked down again by a second torpedo blast. This time Doctor Haynes felt his hands sizzle as they touched the steel deck. In agony he regained his footing and in the gloomy darkness stared down at his fingers. Two deft hands that had been so steady and sure when removing a ruptured appendix or setting a bone now felt as though they were twisting and curling like a bird's feet gripping a branch. What was happening? As he stood upright he stumbled again as a third explosion rocked the ship.

When all of the tumult and shouting was quieted and the passing of the *Indianapolis* with the death of 879 sailors was over and done with, there would always remain the question of whether a third explosion did occur. To Doctor Haynes, as well as to a score of other survivors, and from the personal records of the

Japanese submarine commander who took credit for sinking the heavy cruiser CA-35, there *was* a third explosion. While the majority remember two, some officers and a goodly number of enlisted men remember only a single blast.

Shoving with his elbows to protect his burned hands, Haynes, wearing just the pants to his pajamas, made his way down a passageway that led to the wardroom. Only a few hours earlier it had been populated with ensigns, lieutenants and commanders drinking coffee and talking of rpm's, rating exams, and people they hoped to meet when the ship reached Leyte. He felt the ship drop off suddenly to starboard and steadied himself by pressing his left shoulder against a bulkhead. Upon reaching the wardroom he dropped heavily into a chair. The friendly social atmosphere was gone and he felt only fatigue and nausea. A red glow from nearby fire reflected on swirling, boiling smoke in the compartment. The feeling of illness gave way to one of complacency, and Lewis L. Haynes, MD, USN, drifted off into a sort of delightful somnolence. As a doctor he knew subconsciously that he was dying but it did not seem to make much difference. It was so easy to sit there in that comfortable wardroom chair and let nature take its course.

Suddenly, as in a dream, he heard a muffled voice that seemed to come from a long way off. "My God, I'm fainting!" Just at that moment a body fell across him and the shock caused him to rally slightly. He pushed himself unsteadily to his feet and struggled to bring his dazed mind back into focus. He could hear men talking in excited voices.

"Don't light a match!" Another voice shouted, "Open a port! Open a port!" Of course, that was the thing to do. Open a port and get some fresh air. Haynes wondered why he had not thought of doing that. He realized there were others in the wardroom with him, but how many he did not know and who they were he could not even guess. Just men stumbling about and speaking with voices that choked from the hellish smoke.

Lunging about, he found the bulkhead and felt along it with his burned hands until he contacted a port. It was shut, dogged down tight. If only he could locate a dog wrench maybe he could get it open. Walking crabwise along the bulkhead, he continued to explore with his hands until he came to another port. It was open! Who had opened it? Doctor Haynes would never know, nor would anyone know for sure, but perhaps it was Ensign Woolston. To be sure he had been in the wardroom a few minutes earlier and he had opened one for himself and one for the steward's mate with him. Doctor Haynes shoved his head outside. The air felt cold, almost painful, as it rushed down into his tortured lungs, but the effect was like magic. As he gulped breath after breath, his mind began clearing. Just then something brushed against his face. He reached one of his arms out and felt around. It was a line. Where it came from he did not know, but when he closed a burned hand around it and tugged, it seemed to be secure. Could he do it? Would the pain in a pair of scorched palms permit him to go hand over hand up a hard Manila line? There was only one way to find out. Pulling himself out of the porthole, he hung on to the line and inch by hard-earned inch made his way to the forecastle deck and the blessed luxury of clean cool air.

From the forecastle Doctor Haynes went aft to the ladder that led down to the quarterdeck and across to the port hangar. Even as he approached, he could hear the cry, "Doctor! Doctor!" The port hangar was rapidly becoming an emergency sick bay. As he came on the scene he saw Chief Pharmacist's Mate John Schmueck moving about, doing what he could for some thirty wounded men, which was not much because he had little better than nothing with which to work: a small box of bandages, all of which could have been used on one victim and still not been enough; a few tubs of burn ointment; and most welcome of all, a small box of morphine capsules. These tiny containers could for a time dull the pain of a man who had been horribly burned or had lost a limb. Doctor Haynes and his chief pharmacist's mate worked rapidly in the few remaining minutes, and then a seaman waddled into the hangar with far more kapok life jackets than any normal man should have been trying to carry.

"Hey, Doc," he called. "Here's some jackets. Better get them on the wounded. They say the ship's going to sink and the order is out to abandon ship."

Like the blind leading the blind, some of the wounded helped others, while some fought back. One man with the flesh on his burned arms hanging in rags resisted the attempt of a shipmate to slip a jacket on him. "Leave me alone. Don't touch me," he whimpered. He knew that without a jacket his agony would soon be over. But for all of his cruelty to those of his kind, man often leans over backward in an effort to save his fellowman in times of catastrophe.

Aviation Radio Technician Second Class Robert Funkhouser from Wauseon, Ohio, and his buddy Aviation Radio Technician Third Class John Ashford from Lubbock, Texas, were fairly new aboard the *Indianapolis*. They had spent Sunday evening helping to belt fifty-caliber ammunition for the OS2U scout planes carried aboard. The endless business of clipping the big shells in long metal belts had begun just after the evening meal of cold cuts and continued well into the night while others were watching the movies. When the job was finished, Funkhouser, Ashford and a few more made their way across darkened decks and sat around in the port hangar and entertained themselves with a little harmony singing. It was late when the last cigarette was snubbed out and the final song was sung. In all, it had been an evening of simple pleasure. One by one they settled themselves in crowded bunks and drifted off to sleep. Robert Funkhouser awoke as he felt the ship stagger under the impact of the torpedoes. His first thought was that she

was going to roll all the way over, but he relaxed as
she righted herself.

"Ashford," he shouted. "This is it!" Hurriedly he
pulled on his dungarees, shirt and shoes. He was worried about his friend, who had been trying to shake
off a morbid dread of sinking ever since the *Indianapolis* had put to sea on her final voyage. Now the bad
dream had come true. There were few if any men in
the port hangar who had any serious doubts that the
ship was bound for the bottom.

Funkhouser and Ashford tried to help launch a life
raft, but it was a job for ten men and only four were
present. When the vessel began falling over on her
starboard side, they clawed their way through the lifelines on the port side of the quarterdeck and walked
down the hull and into the water. Both were wearing
pneumatic tubes around their waists, but Funkhouser
lost his as he was going through the lifelines—a severe
loss that could not be helped. He started swimming,
or trying to swim, but the weight of his clothes and
shoes dragged him down in the oil-coated water, first
five and then ten feet. He kicked off his shoes and
bobbed back to the surface. Next he squirmed out of
his dungarees and then his shirt and finally he was
swimming free.

With every tick of the second hand the *Indianapolis*
was drawing closer and closer to her end. The torpedoes had torn great gaping holes in the starboard side.
Later there were those qualified to voice an opinion
who would say that the entire bow section had been
blown off, but because those who knew for sure will
never be heard from, it can only be surmised. Nevertheless, tons of seawater were pouring into the ship,
bringing her down by the head and causing the lighter
stern to rise slowly but inexorably out of the water.
The roll was to the starboard in animated slow motion
like a great lean whale beginning to sound.

Of course in the first few minutes there had been a
feeling of shock and dismay from bow to stern and
bridge to engine rooms, but the general belief was that

the trouble could be quickly corrected and the ship would survive. There were those with a sort of sixth sense or those with a more realistic view of the situation because they had a clearer picture of what had happened, who knew immediately that the *Indianapolis* was going to sink.

Aft on the first platform and far down under the fantail, Marine Private First Class Giles McCoy leafed through a magazine. It did not have much of interest, and the dull red light from the battle lamp did not make the effort of reading any more enticing. When the torpedoes struck, the noise and shock seemed far away but not far enough to prevent McCoy from being dashed to the deck. The stern of the ship seemed to thrash about like the cracker on the end of a bullwhip. Bunks were torn from the bulkhead and in a matter of seconds everything was in a shambles. Men were screaming and yelling. Some were injured; others were just scared. In the sullen red light from the battery-operated battle lamp McCoy picked himself up and stumbled back to the brig where his two prisoners were still locked behind bars. He remembered the regulations clearly: *In time of disaster at sea the prisoners are to be released from their cells and taken topside.* They had been written into the manual back in the days of wooden ships and iron men when those in the old-time brigs were generally murderers and mutineers. McCoy's prisoners were just a couple of young seamen who had made the mistake of drinking a little too much while on liberty or failing to get back to the ship on time. He was not concerned with rule books at the moment. Unlocking the cells, he released his prisoners and told them to help him clear a pathway to the ladders that led topside. The two young sailors went to work in a hurry along with their friendly jailer.

The first platform aft near the brig was already swarming with confused men. Some were struggling to help wounded shipmates and two were fighting to pull a pile of metal bunks away to extricate another who had been trapped by the explosion. Seamen, petty officers, marine guard and prisoners all worked together. Now there was no rate or status. The important thing was to get out of the close confines of the stern section and to the weather deck. An endless chain of frightened men scrambled up the steel rungs of the ladder that led topside. Suddenly, in a brief lull of the exodus, McCoy heard a chilling order shouted down from the second deck.

"Stand by to dog down the hatch!"

He had been in the Marine Corps long enough to know the rules—if a ship is in danger of sinking, certain compartments will have to be closed off to preserve watertight integrity even if it means sacrificing lives of personnel still below. Tonight McCoy was not prepared to commit himself and the others unnecessarily to such a fate.

"We've got a lot of wounded down here," he shouted back. "Give us time to get them out."

"No!" the voice came back. "Only a few more minutes and then we dog the hatch."

McCoy was not the only one who heard the fatal words. Almost instantly a solid human chain of sailors formed on the ladder leading topside, and the injured were quickly passed up like cordwood. McCoy led his two prisoners to the second deck and then up to the fantail, where he met Lieutenant Edward H. Stauffer.

"Here are my prisoners, sir," he announced.

Lieutenant Stauffer took charge of them and sent McCoy forward to his battle station on the boat deck. In the ways of the old Navy the prisoners should have been shackled and bound, but now hundreds of sailors were crowding the stern as the ship's bow settled lower and lower into the water. Stauffer and his prisoners were almost alone. It was not an easy job for a young Marine officer.

Nineteen-year-old Private First Class Paul R. Uffelman from Fort Wayne, Indiana, another member of the Marine Guard on board, had been in his first year of college in 1943 when he realized that many of his friends had already enlisted in the services. He abruptly left college, joined the Marines, and was eventually stationed aboard the *Indianapolis*. On the night of 29 July he had set his pad outside the laundry room and was fast asleep when he suddenly found himself being slammed first into one bulkhead and then another. When he could get to his feet, he wandered into the laundry. A sailor was there trying to shut off a valve, and the whole area was cloaked in a dense cloud of steam.

Quickly remembering that his battle station was up on one of the 40-mm guns, Uffelman left for topside in a rush. Once on station he saw that conditions were not normal. There was no communication with other parts of the ship and no electric power to swivel the gun mount. It was being cranked around by hand. He suddenly realized that he was at his general quarters station without a life jacket and he knew one was required. He remembered a great bag of them that had hung on the boat deck and hurried to the spot. What he found was a limp canvas sack. Poking his arm inside, he found only empty space. But wait— what was that way back in the corner? It was a single kapok jacket that had been overlooked. Paul Uffelman dragged it out and tied it around his chest. Now, at least, he was dressed properly for general quarters and if the ship might be going to sink he was ready to go over the side.

Watertender Second Class Harold J. Flaten picked himself up off the deck in the Oil King's shack and tried to make himself believe he was just having a bad dream, but his conscious mind would have none of it. This was real! His ship had been hit and hit hard. Instantly, he remembered the main valve in the after engine room that shunted the water from the evaporators to the feed tanks in the inner bottom. In time of emergency this valve had to be shut off, and it was Flaten's responsibility to see that it was closed. Grabbing the soundpower phone, he tried to call the after engine room, but the circuit was dead.

A good-natured sort of fellow, Flaten had been tagged with the nickname of "Happy" and this was quickly shortened to just "Hap." As he hurriedly pulled on his dungarees and shoes he felt anything but happy. His main concern was to close that valve. Ahead of him lay a long route, but he made it through mess halls and sleeping compartments and down steel ladders only to find when he reached the after engine room that someone had already closed off the valve.

On the way back toward topside he stopped to help two men carry a badly burned engineer who had found his way out of the forward fireroom. As the three struggled with their wounded shipmate, Coxswain Keyes ran up to them and shouted the order to get topside and prepare to abandon ship.

"Hap" Flaten became more acutely aware of the plight of his ship and the severe toll the torpedoes had caused to his shipmates as he made his way back through the mess hall. He came across more and more badly burned sailors, and one man was lying on the deck clutching his legs in agony. Both of his feet had been crushed by a falling object. An even more terrible scene awaited him just a minute away when he gained the weather deck.

Already the *Indianapolis* was beginning to lie over on her starboard side. "Hap" hurried through the port hangar and back toward the fantail. Just as he passed the butcher shop he saw a group of men struggling to get the twenty-six-foot whaleboat over the side. There was a metal cover over it and as the ship gave a sudden lunge the cover broke loose and hit one of the men like a broadsword, cutting him in half. Flaten pressed a splayed palm against his face to shut out the sight and struggled to repress a shudder.

Seaman First Class Grover Carver, who was close behind Flaten, saw the whaleboat suddenly break loose and crash into the after deckhouse, carrying half a dozen men with it and crushing them like a battering ram. A moment before, Firecontrolman Third Class Cleatus Lebow, who had earlier indulged in the lemonade binge in the armory, had been helping to launch that very same craft, but as the list became more acute he had given it up as a bad job and gone on to the boat deck.

That same murderous whaleboat almost cost Electrician's Mate Third Class David Thompson his life and did take away one of his friends. Thompson, who had unwittingly but fortunately picked up his life jacket before going off duty in number one fireroom, was making his way topside with his friend Electrician's Mate Second Class David L. McClure. McClure had fallen and injured his back and Thompson was trying to get him to the fantail. When they reached the group around the whaleboat, McClure stopped.

"I've got to sit down," he panted. "My back's killing me. You go on and do what you can."

Thompson hesitated but then decided that if the men were successful in launching the boat McClure would have a better chance of getting aboard if he were there at the time. Thompson tried not to look back when the boat broke loose because he knew he would never again see his friend.

As her final moment drew nearer, the *Indianapolis* seemed to hold steady suddenly. It was a hopeful, if brief, period for many of the men on board. In the three and a half years that World War II had been raging, the records were filled with accounts of ships that had been seriously damaged and come perilously close to sinking yet stubbornly refused to take the final plunge. It was this thin thread of hope that kept many of the officers and seasoned enlisted men struggling to the last to keep the ship afloat. These men lost their lives in this hopeless effort but they could not know at the moment, and it will never be known fully, the extent of the damage inflicted by the torpedoes. But had the enemy been permitted to bring his torpedoes aboard and make a careful study of the ship from bow to stern, he could hardly have placed them more strategically.

Radarman Third Class Tommy Reid was not usually

a heavy sleeper, but he gave a pretty fair example of one that night. He had strung his hammock just outside his battle station, which was the radar shack on the boat deck, and he was sleeping there when the torpedoes struck. He awakened slightly and grumbled that people should be more careful about bumping into a sleeping man's hammock. Seconds later he was back in dreamland. Again he was awakened by someone shaking his hammock violently. Now this was going too far. If the guys on duty did not have anything better to do than indulge in this horseplay of running around waking people . . . He leaned over the side of his hammock to speak his mind and stared into the face of Seaman Second Class William Ault.

"Hit the deck, Reid," Ault said in an excited voice. "We've struck a mine or something and I think we're getting ready to sink."

Reid did hit the deck and he hit it running. First he ducked into the radar room to see if general quarters had been sounded, but of course it had not. With all of the circuits dead no one knew anything. Hurrying back out on deck, he ran across to another compartment that housed part of the extensive radar equipment. He saw his friend Radarman Third Class William Arnold Heggie in the shack.

"Hey, Heggie," he called. "See those dungarees and shoes over there on the bench? Hand 'em out to me, will you? They're mine."

As the tidal wave continued to gush into the forward section, the *Indianapolis*'s bow dipped lower and lower, and because the weight of the water as on the starboard side, she naturally began to roll that way.

After issuing abandon ship orders, Captain McVay became increasingly disturbed that none of those he had sent to the radio shack with orders to send out the distress message had returned with word that it had been sent. He could sense that time was growing short and he decided to go down and investigate what was happening in Radio Central.

The *Indianapolis* rolled farther over on her starboard side, and McVay stared down into the darkness. Radio Central was underwater! If the fatal message had not already been dispatched, it would never leave now. Doggedly he reversed his direction and began to pull himself up the communication deck hand over hand along the lifeline. When he reached the hull he stepped out onto it and paused momentarily to look back down on the sinking remains of his once proud ship. Turning away, he started walking aft. The water deepened around him until gradually he found himself floating.

Suddenly the pressure-tortured bulkheads in the ship gave way in a rush. The *Indianapolis* flopped over flat on her starboard side and, with her stern lifting high out of the dark sea, began to go down by the head. A vast wave of 40-mm shells that had been stacked outside the radar shack broke loose, swept across the deck and crashed against the door, sealing it shut as surely and effectively as a mine cave-in would block off a tunnel. Horror-stricken, Tom Reid realized Heggie and the others were hopelessly trapped inside! There was nothing he could do to help them.

Amid the confusion of shell racks breaking loose, smoke and the dull red glow of fire from the forward part of the ship, Reid saw Chief Firecontrolman Clarence Benton. Just a few minutes before Benton had been suddenly turned out of his bunk in CPO quarters under the fantail by Coxswain Keyes running in and calling for everyone to abandon ship. Grabbing a flashlight, Benton had looked out onto a scene of destruction. His battle station was up on the boat deck, and he had let nothing stand in the way of his getting there.

When the *Indianapolis* made her second big roll to starboard Chief Benton drew on his years of naval experience. He had first boarded her in the spring of 1938 and he knew the old ship as well, if not better, than any man aboard. He had lived with her in many of the good times and through most of the battles, but now he knew she was going to sink and he wasted little time in telling the men around him to put on life jackets and get over the side in a hurry.

On the port side of the forecastle men climbed through lifelines and walked along the sinking hull until solid footing dropped away. For those on the starboard side there was no choice. They were simply dumped into the sea when the ship fell over on her side. Near the quarterdeck men slid, stumbled, and ran along the port side of the hull as they raced for the fringe of water that continued to draw nearer and nearer. On the fantail some five or six hundred men were clustered in a confused mob. A large percentage were young sailors, many of whom had been at sea for hardly a fortnight. Some did not know how to swim. Others had not found a life jacket, and there were a few who were so new to the Navy that they did not even know how to put one on properly. One man put his on backward and somehow managed to knot the ties up his back and others had their legs through the armholes. The problems of donning a life jacket or what to do once they were in the water were of small significance compared to the other frightening developments. Gear was breaking loose and crashing into men. Every moment or so someone would lose his grip and go sliding down the deck. As the stern lifted higher and higher out of the water, however, the challenge to jump became increasingly hard to accept.

Tom Reid found his friend, Gunner's Mate Second Class Carlos La Paglia, and together they started up the deck. Reid thought how much they resembled big four-legged spiders crawling up an almost vertical web. When they reached the port side of the hull the two men joined hands and walked off into the water.

Firecontrolman Third Class Cleatus Lebow did not really become alarmed until he pulled himself over the gun shield and started walking down the side of the ship. As he pushed off into the water he was shaking with fear and he uttered a short but earnest prayer: "Oh, Lord, help me." Out of the darkness he immedi-

ately heard Him answer in a clear, calm voice, "Fear
not, for I am with you." Lebow quickly looked
around, but there was no one near him and at once a
feeling of well-being enveloped him and his fears were
gone. From that moment on he knew that no matter
what happened, he would be delivered from the sea.

Young Ensign Harlan Twible looked at the milling
throng of sailors scrambling about and clinging onto
the lifelines. Instinctively he knew that the longer they
waited, the less would be their chances of survival,
and his eyes searched through the gloomy moonlight
for a superior officer to give the word to abandon
ship. With so little time at sea he knew he was not
really qualified to take charge and issue major orders,
but his years of training at Annapolis had left an indel-
ible mark. He was an officer and as such he must be
prepared to take command when necessary. Ignoring
the fact that a few of the sailors had been at sea longer
than he had been on earth, Twible mustered his
courage.

"All right men, let's go. We can't stay here any
longer. Jump off the low side and swim away as fast
as you can," he called.

He heard a confused murmur of dissent—the rules
said to go off the high side. Twible knew this was true
but the high side of the stern was already too far out
of the water. There was also the danger of falling into
the screws or crashing into the side of the hull. When
he saw that his orders were not going to be obeyed
without an example being set, he adopted the same
maneuver Boatswain's Mate Second Class Raymond
McClain had used minutes earlier up on the hangar
deck. Of course, Twible had not witnessed McClain's
success, so when he dropped into the sea and started
swimming he did not know if any of the men would
follow him. But it seemed to be the only thing to do.
It was with relief that he saw dozens of men immediately jump into the water behind him and begin to
swim away.

Quartermaster First Class Robert Gause and Yeoman Second Class Victor Buckett, along with a hundred or more other men, had left the ship on the port side near the quarterdeck.

A few minutes earlier Ensign John Woolston had come down from the gun deck over the hangars. When the ship rolled on her side he quickly climbed through the port lifelines. Suddenly, he saw a steward's mate lunging through the crowd toward him, his eyes wide with fear. Woolston noticed that he was not wearing a life jacket and reached out and grabbed his hand. For a moment he considered peeling off his own kapok and giving it to the mess attendant, but there was not time. All he could do was take the young sailor in tow and swim away from the ship to escape the suction she would create when she went down.

The *Indianapolis* finally tossed her stern straight up into the night sky, and fuel oil, black, sticky and stinking, spurted forth like blood from severed arteries. Some two hundred feet of the stern towered like a sinister spire above the cluster of men who had been the last to leave.

"She's going to fall on us," a young seaman cried.

"Don't look back—swim for all you've got!" Seaman Grover Carver answered.

The dread that the great black shape might suddenly topple over on them like a falling building was an unreasoned fear, of course, because already the entire forward section of the ship was filled with water. It was physically impossible for it to do anything but drop straight down like a shaft.

The crashing and banging of objects tearing loose blended in a hideous discordant symphony with the cries of men trapped inside or still hanging to the lifelines on her stern as the *Indianapolis* slipped more swiftly beneath the waves. Then came the shout: *There she goes!* Every man turned to watch in awe as faster and faster and deeper and deeper the *Indianapolis* dropped, accompanied by great belches of steam and smoke and strange hissing and sucking noises. Then there was nothing save a vanishing wisp of smoke and a few big bubbles.

FOUR

≋

"SOMEBODY HELP ME"

CAPTAIN Charles Butler McVay III watched his ship disappear and then he started swimming—toward what, he did not know, but it just seemed the logical thing to do. After a while he came upon a floating potato crate. Clinging onto this, he looked around and in the intermittent moonlight spotted two life rafts bobbing about on the swells. He climbed aboard and a few minutes later he heard voices. Calling out, he watched as Quartermaster Vincent J. Allard helped two seamen through the water. McVay assisted the three men aboard the raft.

By a strange quirk of circumstances the captain, the quartermaster and the two seamen were to go through the remainder of the night without hearing the sound of another voice. They could only believe that out of nearly two thousand men aboard they were the only four survivors.

No one but a sailor who has watched his ship disappear and leave him floating on the surface of a hostile sea can dare to imagine the awful loneliness that swept over the survivors of the *Indianapolis* that Sunday night of 30 July 1945 at 134 degrees 48 minutes East, 12 degrees 2 minutes North.

For most there was the brief moment of relief that came with the realization that they had actually managed to survive the sinking. Then came the sledge-hammer blow of disbelief. How was it possible for a ship so large and strong, a ship that had been through so many battles simply to turn her stern to the sky and vanish so swiftly? But how or why made little difference now. The important thing was that over eight hundred men were now afloat in the water, where the bottom was about two miles straight down, and the nearest islands were those of the Palau group some 250 miles to the south.

Countless thousands of gallons of diesel oil had spilled from the ruptured tanks that had been filled just before leaving Guam. To get strangled by a clean sunlit comber while frolicking about in the surf at a beach resort is not the most pleasant experience, but to be smothered by a breaking wave and swallow a mixture of dark seawater and fuel oil is enough to turn the stomach of the strongest. Within minutes after leaving the ship there were three predominant sounds that rose up from the small clusters of survivors. The voices of men calling to one another, trying to get together, trying to make some order out of the chaos or maybe just shouting because the sound of their own voices momentarily dispelled the terrible aura of aloneness that enveloped so many. Perhaps the most terrifying of all were the pitiful cries from the wounded and the dying. "Somebody help me . . . please, somebody help me. I can't stand the pain."

God only knows how this timeworn cry has seared itself into the very souls of every man who has been forced to hear it in time of battle and know there is nothing he can do to help.

Everywhere men were vomiting or trying to vomit, heaving and coughing, doing any and every thing they

could to rid themselves of the mixture of oil and salt
water they had swallowed. These were the sounds of
shipwreck. Pleading, lonely, dirty sounds that men
make when the heat of battle has suddenly cooled.
Radarman Third Class Tom Reid listened and shuddered. The magnitude of the hackneyed phrase *war is
hell* suddenly swelled up around him. With ten battle
stars on his service ribbons he had heard the sounds
before but never so terrible. These were the sounds
of hell. He made up his mind at that moment that he
did not want to go to hell.

Robert Funkhouser, who had lost his life belt as
he left the ship, shouted for his friend Ashford, who
miraculously found him in the darkness and swam up
to him. For a while the two clung together, depending
upon the limited buoyancy of Ashford's pneumatic
tube to keep them afloat. Funkhouser knew the life
belt could hold one man fairly safely on the surface
but not two, and he knew that if he continued holding
on to Ashford, both would sink. He did not want to
drown, but if he was going to, he was not dragging
his good friend down with him. Without a final word
he turned loose and swam away, ignoring Ashford's
demands that he come back.

An hour passed—or maybe it was only thirty minutes—and he was rapidly running out of strength. He
had always been a pretty good swimmer and he knew
all the tricks: Turn over on your back and float, make
slow easy strokes with your arms; above all, conserve
your energy. But this was different. The surface of the
sea was coated with a thick blanket of slick, stinking
fuel oil. If you opened your mouth a split second before your head was out and clear you gulped a mouth-
ful of the oil and the result was a spasm of
uncontrolled retching. Funkhouser was in the final
stages of a feeble dog paddle when he heard someone
calling his name. It was Ashford again and he was not
far away. "Come over here. I have a life jacket for
you—a life jacket!" he shouted.

Drawing on the last few ounces of strength that re-

Captain Charles Butler McVay III. (*Corbis*)

The USS *Indianapolis* being outfitted for its final mission at the Mare Island Navy Yard, 12 July 1945. Circles mark recent alterations.
(*Naval Historical Center*)

The *Indianapolis* prepares to leave Tinian after delivering parts for the first two atomic bombs, July 1945. She was lost a few days later en route to the Philippines.
(*Naval Historical Center*)

The *I-58* and *I-53* at Kure, October 1945, three months after the *I-58* sank the *Indianapolis*. (*Naval Historical Center*)

Torpedo room and three crew members of the *I-58*.
(*Naval Historical Center*)

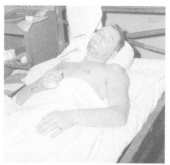

Lt. Cmdr. (Doctor) Lewis L. Haynes, USN. (*National Archives*)

Ens. John Woolston, USNR. (*National Archives*)

Willie Hatfield (seaman second class) and Cozell Lee Smith (coxswain) in recovery. Smith's left hand is still bandaged and healing from a shark attack. (*National Archives*)

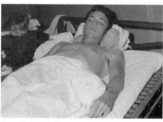

Lt. (jg) Melvin W. Modish, USNR. (*National Archives*)

Ens. Ross Rogers Jr., USN. (*National Archives*)

USS *Indianapolis* survivors being taken to the Navy Base Hospital at Peleliu following their rescue. (*National Archives*)

Transfer of survivors from a landing craft to the USS *Tranquility*. (*National Archives*)

Injured survivors aboard a landing craft. (*National Archives*)

Admiral Raymond A. Spruance awards a Purple Heart to Joseph J. Moran (radioman first class). Moran keyed out the distress signal.
(*National Archives*)

Lt. (jg) Wilbur G. Gwinn, USNR, pilot of the PV-1 Ventura patrol bomber that sighted the survivors of the *Indianapolis* floating in the Philippine Sea.
(*National Archives*)

Captain Charles McVay discussing the ordeal suffered by his officers and men with a group of war correspondents. (*National Archives*)

Commander Mochitsura Hashimoto (*left*), captain of the *I-58*, flown in by the Navy from Tokyo to testify at McVay's court-martial hearing. (*National Archives*)

USS *Indianapolis* survivors in formation at the decommissioning ceremony for the USS *Indianapolis* (SSN 697) submarine. Pearl Harbor, 8 February 1998. (*US Navy Photos*)

Survivors posing in front of the submarine *Indianapolis*. Left to right: Harold Schechterle, Eugene Morgan, Glenn Morgan, Richard Paroubek (back), Mike Kuryla, John Spinelli, Buck Gibson (face obscured), Robert McGuiggan, Cleatus Lebow, Paul Murphy, Lyle Umenhoffer. Top right corner: Captain William J. Toti, Mike Kuryla, and Paul Murphy. (*US Navy Photos*)

mained in his body, he swam toward the voice of his friend. It was true! Ashford was bobbing about on the surface holding a fresh kapok jacket in front of him. Funkhouser put it on and hung limp for a few minutes while he caught his breath. Together the two began swimming toward the sound of other voices. In the moonlight of early morning they only knew that there were many men from the *Indianapolis* still afloat, but it was a comforting feeling.

Seaman First Class Felton J. Outland from Sunbury, North Carolina, was one of those who knew what it was like to go down with his ship and live to tell about it. He and his buddy, Seaman First Class George S. Abbott, had been standing the midwatch on the 40-mm gun just aft of number two stack when the torpedoes struck. Outland was wearing the phones and he asked Abbott to find some life jackets while he stayed with the phone circuit. In a matter of minutes the stocky young seaman from Kentucky was back, but he had only one life jacket. He stuffed it in Outland's hands and raced out of the gun tub calling over his shoulder that he would get a jacket for himself on the way down. Outland had stayed until ammunition began spilling out of the racks around the port shield.

Pulling off the headphones, he realized that the ship had fallen over so far to starboard that walking was out of the question. From one stanchion to another he pulled himself along until he could stand upright on the port bulkhead. As he continued to make his way aft, the ship started her dive. He floated free and then something snagged his right foot. It felt like wire or a length of line or maybe a tangle of electrical cable. Whatever it was, it was attached to some part of the ship and was carrying the nineteen-year-old sailor down into the inky blackness with her. After seconds that seemed like ages had passed, he managed to break free of the entanglement. His ears were popping, and his air-starved lungs were demanding a fresh breath, but he could sense that the buoyancy of his new kapok jacket was bearing him swiftly to the sur-

face. He determined to hold his breath until either he
reached the surface or lost consciousness. Luck was
with him and in that final desperate moment the whole
upper portion of his body bounced up out of the water
beside not just one but four life rafts. They were still
lashed together just as they had been on the deck of
the ship. There was no way of knowing whether they
had been cut free by someone in the final minutes or
whether they had simply broken loose by accident.

Outland had just climbed on to the rafts when another sailor swam up and the two began to separate
the life rafts. As they worked they shouted out across
the dark rolling waves. Now and then they would receive an answering call. Slowly as the night wore on,
other survivors reached them.

According to specifications, each raft could accommodate twenty men—not luxury accommodations, to
be sure. Just a little rectangle of canvas-covered balsa
wood, but it was a place where a man could relax now
and then and catch a few winks of sleep without being
afraid of drowning before he awoke.

Seaman First Class Joseph Malski was another survivor who was sucked under with the ship and he, too,
came up to find a raft. The messenger from the 40-
mm gun mount on the starboard side near Radio Central had either overlooked him or simply could not
find him, so Malski had not awakened until about
three minutes before midnight. Becoming groggily
aware that he was already late in relieving the evening
watch on his gun, he jumped into his dungarees and
shoes and finished buttoning his shirt as he scurried
from the crew's berthing quarters aft, across the quarterdeck and up to the gun tub on the starboard side
forward. With this fast footwork he got there before
the witching hour, but he was annoyed because he had
not been awakened early enough to stop by the galley
for a cup of coffee. It had become almost a ritual with
him. Lots of times the cook on duty would have a
tray of sweet rolls or some other kind of goodies set

out for the men who had to spend four hours wide-awake on the weather decks behind a gun.

Malski thought about his friends in the galley. That cup of coffee and maybe a roll, if he was lucky, would have taken the edge off the boring job of staring out into the darkness during the better part of the sleeping hours. He had just adjusted himself in the seat when he was knocked flat by the first blast. As he began to stand up he saw a buddy, Seaman First Class Charles Marciulaitis, from his home town of Grand Rapids, Michigan, holding out a kapok life jacket to him. He was reaching for it when the second torpedo exploded almost under the gun mount.

Smoke and steam and a rapidly developing list had driven the gun crew out of the mount in a hurry. Malski headed for the port side, and as the *Indianapolis* rolled over, he started walking aft. He was still tying the strings on his jacket when the ship plunged. He tried to swim free, but the swirling water was coming up around him fast. He felt himself being drawn down. Time after time he managed to overcome the suction, and after he had gone under four times he found himself swimming free on the surface and as he looked around he could see no one. For an awful moment, Malski, like so many others, had to hang there in the black water and wonder if he might possibly be the only survivor. All around him there was nothing but big black waves crested with little fringes of yellowish-white curls of luminescent foam. Surely, he thought, there must be someone else around nearby. Of course there was. He heard a shout and then in the moonlight he saw a raft sliding down the back of a big wave. A sailor jumped over the side of the raft and swam toward him and helped him aboard. As he scrambled in, Malski looked down at his left leg. A great angry gash ran down the side. How had it happened and when had it happened? He did not know. All he knew was that now when he could see it, his injured leg began to hurt and he was worried about the quantity

of blood that was spilling out. He tried to stanch the
flow by clutching both hands tightly around the thigh.

There seemed to be a great throng of men around
the raft into which he had been pulled. Someone said
there was another raft close by, and he heard men
yelling to one another as they tried to unroll a floater
net that had drifted free from the sinking ship.

There were some six or seven different groups scattered out in a long irregular line that stretched for as
much as a mile or more across the sea. With only
twelve minutes from torpedoes to sinking, it is difficult
to understand how the survivors could have become
so widely separated. But the ship had been under
power until she went down, and men had left all the
way from the forecastle to the fantail at different times.
The waves were choppy with twelve-foot swells running, and now and then the ten-knot wind that was
pushing up from the southwest became gusty, blowing
the rafts and other high-floating objects off to the
northeast. Those who found rafts were naturally
higher out of the water and were blown along more
swiftly than men who floundered about in life jackets.
Also there were those who were struggling in a vast
pool of oil that had been vomited out by the sinking
ship. Almost every survivor ran afoul of the oil slicks
at one time or another shortly after the sinking, but
as is always the case, there must be an exception here
and there. One of the more notable of these was Fire-
man Second Class William Gooch from Martinsville,
Indiana. He left the ship at the last moment, and as
he hit the water a lifeline struck him across the back
and dragged him under. This would have been serious
for even a good swimmer with a life jacket to help
him along, but Bill Gooch could not swim a stroke,
plus he had lost his life jacket when he was fighting
his way out of number one turret on the bow. Neither
Gooch nor any of those around him will ever be able
to explain how he managed to be transported underwater for something better than a hundred yards from
the point where he jumped overboard to the spot

where he came up right beside a life raft. When willing hands helped him aboard, he sputtered and gagged for a few seconds and then looked about him. Every man aboard was painted black with fuel oil but he was as clean as if he had just stepped out of a shower.

"I don't know, Gooch," one sailor said as he tried to wipe the sticky ooze out of his own mouth and eyes. "Maybe you just fell into a clean spot and got washed under the oil until you bobbed up in another clean spot beside the raft."

In another location conditions were far more frightening. Lieutenant (j.g.) Melvin Modisher, the junior medical officer, had left the ship from the forecastle deck and as he had watched her sink, he realized there were many badly injured survivors who could not last through the night. A sensitive man and a qualified doctor of medicine, Modisher was heartbroken. At a field hospital or even back aboard in the limited confines of the sick bay, most of the men could have been helped. Here in the empty sea with every man, wounded and able-bodied alike, attempting to rid his stomach of oil and salt water, he knew there was nothing he could do as a doctor. But Melvin Modisher was not only a doctor—he was a religious man, as most of the crew knew. In happier days many had affectionately tagged him with the nickname "the Protestant chaplain" of the *Indianapolis*. Before the first night was done, scores of strong men swam up beside the junior medical officer and asked not that he give them medicinal assistance but rather that he intercede with divine Providence to deliver their souls.

Doctor Modisher was with by far the largest group of survivors, the one at the southwest end of the long line. In the early hours it was actually not one large group but mostly just small clusters of men ranging in number from as few as three or four up to a couple of dozen. Some were not more than a hundred yards apart. Others were scattered out a thousand yards or even more in all directions. Viewed from above, this main group of survivors would have resembled inkspots shaken out on a sheet of paper from an over-filled fountain pen. The largest of these units consisted of somewhere between one hundred and one hundred and fifty men. Most were wearing life jackets, and as a sort of focal point to rally around, there was a huge canvas bag bulging with spare life jackets. Had it not been for a fortuitous error on the part of the Bureau of Supplies and Accounts while the ship was in dry dock at Mare Island, the pitiful few who did manage to survive might have been far fewer. Shortly after going into dry dock, a requisition had gone out from the *Indianapolis* for new kapok life jackets for the crew. When the order had not been filled in a reason-able length of time, the supply officer sent a second requisition. Again there was a delay. Then, just before the *Indianapolis* put to sea on her last voyage, the life jackets began to arrive. Not just one order, which would have provided a nice fresh jacket for every man aboard, but twice that many in two separate ship-ments. Storekeepers and boatswain's mates wailed in anguish as they wrestled with the problem of stowage. But after jackets were issued to the crew, the sailmak-ers made large canvas bags for the extras and they were hung about the ship at various points. It was around one of these still unopened bags that had been cut down and had floated free that the largest single collection of survivors was gathered. There was an ad-mixture of officers and enlisted men, but all were cov-ered in the thick black fuel oil and the fair-haired, dark-complected, brunettes and redheads, officers, petty officers and seamen looked the same.

Doctors Haynes and Modisher were in this same general group, but they were not aware of one anoth-er's presence for many hours. Father Thomas Michael Conway was there and so was Captain Edward L. Parke, who had been in charge of the Marine detach-ment on board. Most severely injured of all the offi-cers among them was Commander Stanley Lipski, the ship's gunnery officer. That he had even managed to fight his way off the ship was a testimony to his undying courage as a man. His hands and arms were so badly burned that the bones were exposed through the hanging flesh and his eyes were fried crisp. The men took turns supporting him, doing their best to protect his face and arms from the sting of the salt water.

From all directions came the cry, "Doctor, Doctor." Commander Haynes and Lieutenant Modisher swam among the clusters of men examining limp forms lolling in life jackets. The average man, suspecting that his friend had died, knew only to shake him and shout to him, pleading for a word. Haynes and Modisher followed the more professional approach of gently lifting an eyelid and touching a finger to the eyeball. If there was no reflex, then there was no life, and the body was divested of the jacket and allowed to drop quickly into the deep. When close friends were so parted, the extra life jacket was passed on to another sailor who had been patiently paddling about or hanging on to the shoulder of a buddy for temporary support.

At nineteen minutes after midnight Signalman Third Class Kenley Lanter stopped swimming long enough to wipe the oily scum from the face of his watch and check the time. When he had first entered the water, there had been hundreds of men around him. Now he suddenly realized he was all alone. Like so many others, he had been swimming hard to get as far away from the ship as possible before she went under. Resting in his jacket, he began looking around in hopes of seeing someone. Then, suddenly, he caught sight of a large dark object riding high on the surface. In the hazy moonlight it looked to him like one of the OS2U float planes that had been carried aboard ship, and there seemed to be someone hanging on to it. Deciding it must have broken free as the ship went under, he began swimming for the plane, but just before he reached the object, it slipped quietly beneath the waves. Once again he stopped swimming and rested. The sea was not rough, but the endless swells were twelve feet from the bottom of a trough to the crest. In one of these watery valleys a man had to take hold of himself to overcome the feeling that he was being drawn down into the sea, but when a moment later he was floating high on the ridge he could relax and look out over the surface. It was while he was riding the crest of a swell that Lanter spotted another floating object. Not as large as the one he had seen earlier, but anything would be better than this awful rising and falling, rising and falling in the water over and over again, not knowing where he was or how many others might have survived the sinking. Once more he began to swim, and as he drew nearer he gradually made out the shape of a balsa raft. Not the most desirable place to spend the night at sea, but what a blessed relief to find something solid. As he reached the raft, he wanted to shout with joy, for he was no longer alone in the frightening darkness of the sea. Another man was approaching.

They hoisted themselves aboard and lay on the wet latticed platform that was the bottom of the raft. After a brief rest they quickly found they were far from strangers. The newcomer was Radioman First Class Joseph Moran from Johnstown, Pennsylvania. Radiomen and signalmen are frequently friends on a warship. For a while the two huddled together and stared into the black night while they talked over the explosions and the sinking of their ship.

"I wonder where everybody else is?" Lanter mused. "I know a lot of the guys got off when I did. You don't suppose they've all drowned, do you?"

"I don't think so," Moran said. "They must be out here somewhere."

"What about an SOS? Did we get one off?"

Moran did not know for sure. He remembered the terrible turmoil and fire he had seen when he left his bunk in the Flag coding room and rushed to Radio Central. He knew that no message had left Radio Central because he had tested the keys, but he knew, too, that Radio II was trying to get on the air. Whether they did or not he could only guess.

Examining their newfound raft they discovered only a bag of kapok life jackets, which had been lashed onto the floor. Feeling sure there must be other survivors, it seemed wrong to be sitting in the comparative safety of the raft while only a short way off there might be men struggling to stay afloat without a life jacket. Whether it would do any good there was no way of knowing, but they opened the bag and began tossing the jackets as far as they could over the dark heaving swells.

Hardly more than half a mile away, Ensign Ross Rogers found himself the only officer in charge of three other life rafts. Rogers had been on the fantail when the *Indianapolis* was standing on her beam's end. When she took her final plunge, he went down with her. How far down he had no way of knowing, but before he came up he felt that his lungs would explode in the next second unless he could have a breath of fresh air. Then he bobbed to the surface like a cork, and a few minutes later bumped against a raft. Climbing aboard, he saw that two men were already there, a rangy Kentucky mountain boy, Seaman Second Class Willie Hatfield, and Chief Machinist's Mate Albert E. Ferguson. The chief had just come off duty and had been taking a shower when the torpedoes struck. The blast had slammed him against some sharp protuberance and made a bad gash in his right leg just below the knee. Trying to ignore the pain, he had made his way topside stark naked. A seaman, seeing his plight, tossed him a pair of pants. Not exactly a sterile bandage, but better than nothing. Ferguson had tied the pants around his leg before going over the side.

Ensign Ross Rogers hated the sight of blood and he had known that he could never be a doctor, but when fate cast him on a raft with a badly injured man he remembered that he was an officer and as such was expected to take charge. He ripped off a section of the white pants the chief had been using as a bandage and formed a tourniquet above the knee to stanch the flow of blood.

As the night wore on, they spotted another survivor and helped him aboard. There was not much the four could do for the rest of the night except sit in the raft and talk and wonder what had happened to the rest of their shipmates. Every few minutes Rogers would release the tourniquet around Ferguson's leg in an effort to prevent gangrene.

In the confusion aboard the mortally wounded ship, Chief Engineering Officer Richard Banks Redmayne had been unable to find a life jacket before she began her final plunge. As the water swirled up around him, he had slipped off the side of number three turret and begun swimming hard to escape the suction. When the ship was gone and there was no longer the urgent need to swim, he had looked about for something to hold on to while he caught his breath. There it was. An empty five-inch ammunition can. Ignoring the pain in his burned palms, Redmayne clung to the can and looked around him. A small dark object was floating nearby. Paddling over to it, he was relieved to find that it was a kapok jacket. He wriggled into it and for the first time since the torpedoes had landed he allowed himself to relax fully.

Around him he could hear voices and when the excess fatigue had drained from his body he began swimming in their direction. As he drew nearer he could see several dozen men clinging onto the sides of a life raft. Some seemed to be in control of themselves and were trying to maintain a semblance of order among the frightened sailors, who were fighting to scramble aboard. Every few minutes the raft would become overloaded and begin sinking, and everybody would fight to get free. But once its cargo had been dumped, the raft would bob back to the surface, and the scene would be repeated.

"Listen to me, you stupid bunch of knuckleheads," a foghorn voice shouted. It was a voice that could have belonged only to a tough boatswain's mate. "This raft ain't big enough for us all to get in it. We've got to put the wounded in here and the rest of us just hang on to the sides. That way it'll hold us all up."

Lieutenant Redmayne approached the excited group with caution. He could well understand that another survivor was just about the last thing the men wanted around the already overcrowded raft but he knew, too, that the whole group would fare better in the long run if there were many instead of a few. He also realized that leadership would become increasingly important as the time in the water lengthened.

Among those clustered around the lone raft were Ensigns Harlan Twible and Donald Blum, Chief Firecontrolman Clarence Benton and Gunner Duward Horner. During the night they could hear other voices nearby and they knew they were not alone.

When the report had come that all tubes had been fired and the torpedoes were running true, Commander Mochitsura Hashimoto had brought his *I-58* around to a parallel heading and watched the results—two violent explosions, followed by a third of even greater magnitude! It had been most gratifying from his point of view. The enemy ship was mortally wounded!

With all forward tubes empty, Commander Hashimoto had decided to make a quick dive while they were being reloaded. Excitement ran high on the *I-58* for the next hour. Even the rats seemed to feel the desire to join in the celebrations. They harassed the cooks in the galley and boldly jumped up on mess tables. Although a modern ship and well appointed in every respect, she had acquired a colony of rats during her construction that had defied eradication. But the noisome rodents were ignored now. The supply officer called the cooks together and told them to prepare the best meal they could for the following day. "Spare nothing," he said. "This is a time for great celebration."

The meal would not be just a big bowl of rice, unintentionally flavored faintly with rat urine, or canned sweet potatoes that tasted like a mixture of sand and ashes. Nor would there be the equally monotonous serving of boiled onions. This would be different. Corned beef and canned eels would provide the meat course, and there would be a specially favored vegetable, a kind of canned parsley. And to be sure, there was a bountiful supply of *sake* for all hands.

When an hour had passed, Hashimoto brought the *I-58* back to the surface. Cautiously he upped his periscope, hoping to be rewarded with the sight of a great battleship burning furiously. Searching the horizon, he saw nothing. His hydrophone operators listened— there was no sound. Frustrated, Hashimoto gave the order to surface. He had been a submarine officer for many years and he knew when a ship was mortally wounded. He was glad that he had given the conning tower crew a chance to look through the periscope before they had made their dive. At least they could bear witness to the severity of the damage the torpedoes had inflicted. Hashimoto knew beyond a shadow of a doubt that the ship simply could not have made a quick recovery and sped away to safety under the cover of night.

As compressed air forced the water out of the ballast tanks, the *I-58* rose to the surface. With the decks still awash, the yeoman of signals undogged the conning tower hatch and stepped out onto the bridge followed quickly by Hashimoto and several other officers. As a student of naval history the captain of the Japanese submarine knew that torpedoed ships occasionally sink in record time. The *Lusitania,* which went down in a short eighteen minutes after being struck by German torpedoes off the Irish coast on 7 May 1915, was an outstanding record of fast sinking, but that was thirty years earlier and modern warships had watertight integrity systems that could keep them afloat for hours.

Certain that he would find an abundance of flotsam

on the surface, Hashimoto cruised slowly through the area, with every man on the weather decks keeping a sharp lookout for survivors or anything that might suggest that an empty warship had been sunk. But the sea was black and lonely. Big swells laced with luminescent foam curled across the submarine decks, and now and then the moon shone through scudding clouds. Could this possibly be the place where he had sunk a great ship? He stared out into the darkness and wondered. With each passing moment he became increasingly nervous. Logically he reasoned that a capital ship, such as the one he was sure he had sunk, would not be traveling without an escort. Any moment now a speedy destroyer would be boring in and laying a pattern of depth charges. Hashimoto decided to get away as quickly as possible. Reluctantly he ordered his crew below and once again dropped beneath the surface to beat a hasty retreat to the northeast.

After Marine Private First Class Giles McCoy had delivered his prisoners to Lieutenant Edward H. Stauffer, he had headed for his 40-mm gun mount, but before he could get there, the ship had fallen over on her starboard side. He had fought desperately to get up to the port rail, but a man cannot climb a vertical wall. Just as the young marine was about to lose hope, he saw a bunch of electrical wires hanging down from one of the five-inch gun turrets. Hand over hand he had pulled himself up to the port side, climbed out on the hull and then stopped to untie his shoes. Suddenly he slipped, caught himself in a sitting position and bounced along down the side on his back end like a kid on a rough sliding board.

McCoy had lost his shoes by the time he hit the water, but he was still wearing his pants and T-shirt, and the heavy .45 automatic was still slung around his waist on the web belt. With one arm through a life jacket he started swimming. He had not made much progress before he heard a frightening hissing and bubbling sound close behind. The stern of the *India-*

napolis was slipping beneath the waves, and then McCoy felt himself being pulled under. It was as though someone had grabbed him by his ankles and was dragging him down deeper and deeper into the cold black water. When he was sure the mounting pressure would pop his eyes out of their sockets, whatever was holding to his ankles suddenly let go, and he bobbed back to the surface. Nearby he heard the cries of many frightened men. He swam toward the sound of their voices and soon came up beside Boatswain's Mate Second Class Eugene Morgan. Neither man knew the other very well, but they had met several times on board ship and once or twice had made a liberty together. From the beginning McCoy had liked the big dark-haired bosun. Somehow they just seemed to talk the same language.

As he and Morgan paddled around together, the young marine found a five-inch powder can and climbed up on it long enough to put both arms through his life jacket and tie it on. All around them men were in small groups talking excitedly. Still straddling the can, McCoy heard someone shouting louder than the rest, and when he looked in the direction of the voice, he saw the dim shape of a life raft. It seemed a long way off and he could not tell how many men were aboard.

"Let's swim for that raft," he said.

Morgan shook his head. He felt that the raft was too far away and he was afraid they would not be able to swim through the blanket of oil that covered the water. "Besides," he argued, "we'll have a better chance of being spotted if we all stay together in a big group."

McCoy respected the big boatswain's judgment, but he had his own opinions too. "I'd rather be on that raft than bobbing about out here like a fishing cork on a millpond." Aware that his life jacket would slow him down, he took it off and shoved it toward Morgan. "You take this," he said. "I'm going to try to make it."

With no further ado McCoy started swimming toward the raft underwater to avoid the oily film that covered the entire sea around him. When he had to have a breath of air, he would rise to the surface and breathe deeply while he got his bearings. Time after time he repeated this maneuver, but instead of getting nearer, the raft seemed to be getting farther and farther away. Something was wrong. Then he realized there was a steady wind from the southwest blowing the raft on ahead of him.

Desperately he looked around and knew there was no turning back now because he was too far away from the others. Exerting as much strength in each stroke as he could muster, he kept on swimming, but just when the raft was within arm's reach, it seemed that someone had suddenly cut off all the current. His arms and legs became bars of lead and he felt himself sinking. In that final moment of total exhaustion strong fingers clutched his hair. He was pulled aboard and shoved across the latticed floor. With his head resting against the balsa ring he almost turned his stomach wrong-side-out in a spasm of heaving to rid it of the salt water and oil he had swallowed during his swim.

"I didn't think I was going to make it," he gasped, wiping an oily hand across his face.

"You almost didn't," a sailor answered.

But by determination, a lot of luck and a little help Marine Private First Class Giles McCoy was beating the odds. He had narrowly managed to escape the compartment just before it was dogged shut, he had delivered his prisoners safely topside, he had been sucked down with the ship and come back to the surface and now he had swapped a life jacket for a seat in a life raft.

For a long while he lay in a state of semiconsciousness. Finally he began to rally and after vomiting up more salt water and oil he looked around him. There were six other men on board. The only petty officer was Ship's Cook Third Class David P. Kemp. The other five were Seamen Edward Payne, Robert Brundige, Farrell Maxwell, Willis Gray and Felton Outland. By strange coincidence both McCoy and Outland had been drawn down by the suction of the sinking ship, managed to get back to the surface and now were aboard the same tiny raft. Two other rafts were floating nearby. There was not enough light to see how many survivors they carried but there were a number of voices to be heard.

Suddenly someone shouted, "There's a ship!"

Everybody immediately became alert. Those suffering from wounds, men who had been badly burned and even those who had not stopped heaving seemed to come alive.

McCoy looked off into the darkness and sure enough there was the silhouette of some kind of ship. The triangular shape was black against the night sky and a light was flashing.

"I'll bet it's a destroyer that picked up our SOS and they're searching for us," someone said.

This seemed a logical idea. The tin can probably was out on patrol, had caught the message and was coming in for the rescue.

The survivors began to shout, but their voices were swallowed by the slosh of waves slapping against the rafts.

"They're too far away to hear us," McCoy said. His hand subconsciously went to the big .45 automatic he still wore on the web belt around his waist. "Hey, no wonder I was having trouble catching up with you guys," he laughed. "I might as well have been swimming with an anchor tied around me. Look. I've still got my gun. Do you suppose if I shoot it they'll see the flash?"

Everyone agreed. Getting up on his knees, McCoy steadied himself with his left hand while he dug the gun out of the holster. Shucking it to put a fresh shell in the chamber, he pointed toward the dark silhouette and fired. The blast slammed against their ears like the report from a cannon, and a spurt of yellow light jumped out into the night. Again and again he pulled the trigger. Then, with his ears still ringing, he sank back on his heels and waited. Everyone in the cluster of three rafts waited and watched and hoped with everything that was in them that there would be some quick sign of recognition. Perhaps the winking on of a bright searchlight, or a couple of rocket flares from a Very pistol or even the shriek of the ship's whistle, but there was nothing. Just the same dark object with the little blinking light.

"They couldn't have seen those little flashes anyway," someone said. "And even if they did, it would just look like specks of phosphorescence on the water."

"What if it's the sub that sank us?" another asked. "Maybe they've come up to find us."

That it might be an enemy submarine was a sobering thought, and the men suddenly grew quiet.

"To hell with them!" came a strong voice from another raft. "There's plenty of us here and you've got a gun. If it's a damn Jap sub sitting up there on the water, let's go over and capture the bastard."

Excitement ran high as the would-be John Paul Joneses planned their naval encounter, until the courageous rafters discovered the hopelessness of propelling their avenging crafts through the water without paddles. Finally there was no longer a blinking light, and the dark shape disappeared. Nothing had been accomplished, but at least the men had been willing to give it a try.

In the years to come the survivors of the *Indianapolis* who saw these dark shapes that to some resembled a destroyer and to others a sinking plane would wonder if perhaps it had not been the conning tower of the Imperial Japanese Navy's *I-58*. Of course no one will ever know for sure.

Electrician's Mate Second Class Charles Zink had been relieved from the switchboard in the main generator by Electrician's Mate Third Class Bruce McLean at about ten minutes before midnight. Having been

awake for some twenty hours, Zink had hurried to his
bunk and dropped down in an exhausted heap. The
torpedoes slammed home before he had even begun
to relax, and it had seemed that some terrible force
was shaking the ship to pieces. When he could stand
up, he had fumbled around until he found his clothes
and then hurried topside. Someone tossed him a
kapok jacket as he made his way aft through the port
hangar, and when he reached the fantail he stood for
a short while listening to men debate the question of
whether they should abandon ship or wait for orders.

*If those guys don't know this ship is sinking, then
they can just stand here and fuss with one another until
their white hats float off their heads,* Zink thought.
Then aloud he said, "I'm getting off while there's still
time." Squirming through the lifelines, he skidded
down the side of the hull until he was close to the
water and then jumped as far as he could.

Not all of those who survived the sinking of the
Indianapolis had left the ship from the high side or
from the fantail. Many went off the starboard side
either because they could not make it to the port side
or because they simply decided there was nothing
wrong with that method of departure. Seaman Second
Class Curtis Reid was one of these. A farm boy from
Blount County, Alabama, Reid had been in the Navy
almost a year. He had boarded the *Indianapolis* in
December 1944 and been assigned to the Fourth Division. Just before the ship had begun to sink, he had
gone on duty on one of the five-inch antiaircraft guns
and before the midwatch had officially begun, someone noticed that the gun captain was not present.

"Hey, Reid," a petty officer had called. "Scout
around and see if you can locate Pait. He's probably
still sleeping somewhere on the boat deck."

Reid left in a hurry and it was not long before he
found the gun captain, Boatswain's Mate Second Class
Robert Pait. He awakened him, and both were back
at the gun just seconds before the torpedoes struck.
In the bedlam that followed, Reid was making his way

aft along the starboard side when the ship began to lie over in the water. He took one look up the slanting deck, the shell cases, potato crates and all manner of loose debris tumbling down, and decided he would be unwise to try to make his way up through all of that. He simply stepped off into the water and started swimming.

For every rule there must be a few exceptions and First Sergeant Jacob Greenwald and Chief Boatswain's Mate Harold Daniel unintentionally proved that a man can stay with a ship to the very last moment and then swim away with no more struggle than if they had stepped off a float down at the old swimming hole. Greenwald had stayed on his 40-mm gun station until the *Indianapolis* tossed her stern to the night sky. As she began to slip deeper and deeper, he began working his way aft. In the final moment he climbed down on the rudder and there he met Chief Daniel. As the water closed around them, both started paddling away, and Greenwald did not even get his hair wet.

The hours that stretched between the torpedo blasts and the gray light of dawn were to hold something special for almost every man. For those who had been severely wounded the first dark hours in the water meant the end of life or, perhaps more properly, the end of suffering. Other men who had been positive that they could not swim a stroke were surprised when they found themselves still on the surface looking for a life jacket. Some experienced the thrill of finding a buddy they had never hoped to see again and at the same time still others saw their closest friends die and slip beneath the waves.

FIVE

"THEY'LL FIND US TODAY"

THE moon was no longer visible when the first light of dawn began to swell up in the eastern sky. It was still too dark to see clearly, but gone was the inky blackness. In their raft, Signalman Kenley Lanter and Radioman Moran scanned the waves and spotted a lone swimmer. He was wearing a jacket and making a feeble attempt at pushing himself along with labored strokes. They shouted, and the man turned. He came slowly toward the raft, and the two men helped him aboard. He was not a pretty sight. He had been badly burned and blood oozed from a ragged wound in his hip.

With no first-aid equipment there was nothing they could do but give him a place to relax and listen sympathetically as he told them how he had gashed his hip when he struck a sharp object while trying to leave the ship.

As the light grew stronger in the morning sky, Lanter and Moran continued to search the sea. There was nothing to be seen save the endless heaving swells, but somewhere they could hear human sounds. They shouted across the water, and soon two more life-jacketed sailors bobbed into view. Moran and Lanter reached out and helped them aboard.

When there are no clouds, full daylight comes swiftly at sea. There is a brief gray haze, and then the sun lifts above the horizon and suddenly the waves are sparkling bright. Monday morning 30 July 1945 at approximately 134 degrees 48 minutes East, 12 degrees 2 minutes North the sun rose, but not in a blaze of glory.

Lanter and Moran and the three men they had collected during the early-morning hours looked out over the bright water. They saw three more rafts and it was like a shot in the arm to each man aboard. If there were other survivors so near there must be many more not far away. The sea was not running as high as it had been earlier, and the four rafts got together.

The warming rays of the morning sun brought a great flood of hope to more than seven hundred men scattered out in that long line that stretched from the northeast to the southwest. Men who had been cold and frightened during the night began to come alive and shout words of encouragement to their shipmates. The wind that had blown all night subsided with the rising sun, and the waves flattened and changed into gently heaving swells. Every man knew that the sinking of the *Indianapolis* was a terrible tragedy and there was not one afloat who was unaware of the fearsome loss of life the ship's company had suffered in the preceding five hours, but war has always meant loss of life and it has also meant survivors. The dead have given their all and those that live must get ready to fight again.

Lieutenant Redmayne, Ensign Twible and the others who were clustered about their lone raft were astounded at the men they could see in the water around them. The number had seemed large during the dark hours of the night, but now it was swelled tenfold when they saw just how many were actually still afloat. There were two more rafts in the immedi-

ate area with ten or fifteen people on and around
these and at least one hundred and fifty swimmers.
While most of them had either kapok life jackets or
pneumatic tubes around their waists, others had none
and were either swimming or sharing a jacket or tube
with a buddy. During the night these swimmers had
stayed near a large bulky object, which the daylight
revealed to be an unrolled floater net. It was quickly
opened and spread out on the water. This net was a
big square of strong manila line knotted together with
canvas-covered chunks of balsa tied on at regular intervals to give it buoyancy. While not an ideal place
to settle down for a rest, the spread of rope and floats
gave the men at least a soggy island to cling to, and
those who were wearing jackets could even lie on their
backs upon it and doze for short periods.

This group, in which Lieutenant Redmayne was the
senior officer, was the second largest collection of survivors from the *Indianapolis*. But during the early-
daylight hours of Monday morning the number began
to dwindle. The badly wounded, who had somehow
managed to hold on to life during the dark hours,
weakened quickly with the coming of the heat of day
and one by one gave up the struggle.

It was not just the wounded, however, who began
to die quickly. Logic would suggest that the big, husky
specimens who had only months earlier been letter-
men on the high school football squad or track team
would be the ones who could withstand the stress and
deprivation. Conversely, it would be assumed that
middle-aged men who had allowed themselves to grow
soft with reduced physical activities would be the first
to go. While nothing new to those who have studied
man's survival under stress, the sinking of the *Indianapolis* proved once again that in disaster survival is
not based on age, rank or social standing. Commanders, seamen, the older as well as the young died at
about the same rate. The senior officers who had not
been killed in the first few minutes and the leading
petty officers who had wives and families ashore wait-

ing for them seemed to have the greatest tenacity to life. Still, there was no hard-and-fast pattern. A skinny little nineteen-year-old seaman would find an untapped reservoir of strength and suddenly become a pillar for other seemingly stronger and more resourceful men to hang on to.

Every man was black with the fuel oil that had been vomited up by the *Indianapolis* when she sank, and it took a sharp eye for even close friends to recognize one another. Officers, seamen and petty officers all looked the same. Time after time men would drift alongside one another and begin talking. "What division you in, Mac?" a seaman would ask of his new-found companion. "I'm Lieutenant Commander Henry," or Stout, or some other officer, would be the reply, and the two black-faced men would look at each other and chuckle.

The chief topic of interest and conversation was whether or not a distress message had been sent. When a young sailor would recognize an officer or leading petty officer and earnestly ask this important question, the answer was likely to be much the same. "Sure we got off an SOS. Those guys in the radio shack knew we were going to sink the instant the first torpedo struck us. If they didn't have power up in Radio Central, they had a couple of other places on the ship they could send a message from."

Some of the more realistic who could not place such divine faith in the dependability of modern communications replied with a more guarded answer, sincerely wishing they could believe their own words. "What the hell difference does it make? They know we're on our way to Leyte and when we don't show up in the next few hours they'll come looking for us."

"Sure they will. Hey, Joe, they'll be searching for us soon now," the word would be passed on to the wounded. "Just hang on for a little while longer, huh? They'll be here."

The *wonderful house of they*. How efficient *they* seemed. How certain the men were that port authori-

ties in Leyte were at this moment practically standing
out on the dock looking for the first sight of CA-35
as she steamed in from the eastern Pacific. When they
failed to sight her on the horizon at the appointed
hour, the wheels of a massive sea rescue would be put
in effect.

First would come the search planes. They would
circle overhead, radio transmitters would hum as exact
latitude and longitude locations were transmitted back
to shore bases, and then there would be the rescue
planes—large fat amphibious planes that could land
on the open ocean, pick up survivors and carry them
back to safety. Behind them would come the fast PC's
and destroyers to search the area for stragglers. Yes,
rescue would be in full effect sometime today!

The men gathered in small groups and talked about
what they would do after they were rescued. Most
agreed they were going to take the world's biggest
shower to get all of that stinking fuel oil off their
bodies and then they were going ashore and really live
it up. Such talk was good fun for nearly an hour after
sunrise, and then the enthusiasm began to fade as the
big hot yellow ball of fire climbed higher and higher
into the eastern sky. Having suffered through some
five cold hours of darkness, most of the men tried to
pretend they were reveling in the reflected heat.

From all directions came the shout, "A plane! A
plane! See him? There he comes!" All eyes looked to
the sky. Sure enough, there was a plane. It was big
and fast and it was speeding northward at an altitude
of about 1500 feet. This was the first search plane!
They began to kick their feet and wave their arms and
shout at the top of their voices. The plane came in
steady, passed over them and continued on.

"Well," a sailor rationalized, "he was just not looking. The next one will see us for sure."

Near almost all of the groups the surface of the
water was littered with a variety of flotsam that had
spilled off the ship as she was sinking—boxes, pieces
of wooden furniture, boards, chunks of paper and shell

cases. Gunner's Mate First Class Johnny Fitting saw a big fat Bermuda onion bobbing about on the water nearby. He reached out and picked it up. It did not look inviting as a breakfast but then again it might come in handy, so he stuffed it inside his shirt.

As the sun reached its zenith even the most cheerful were beginning to grumble. The brilliance of the reflected light on the layer of fuel oil was bringing about photophobia so intense in some cases that the victims were totally blind. Even with their lids shut tight the pain was intense, almost as if their eyeballs had been seared with fire.

For those who were not seriously bothered by photophobia there were things to see that would almost have made blindness a blessing rather than a curse. The intense breathless heat of noonday was rapidly sapping the strength of every man, but for the wounded who had managed to survive the first few hours it was agony. A burned sailor whose tortured body could no longer endure the pain would suddenly untie his life jacket and disappear beneath the waves. Again, one who had been injured and was steadily losing blood would topple over and lie facedown in the water until someone swam up beside him to help. Sometimes he would rally for a short while, but usually there was nothing anyone could do but untie the jacket and let the lifeless body drift down.

Immediately after the sinking there had been many sailors swimming about without a jacket. By Monday afternoon, however, life jackets were becoming fairly plentiful. Some men were even wearing two, and here and there an empty could be seen floating on the surface.

Another menace was beginning to make itself felt in the groups—a menace that did not restrict itself to preying only on those who were injured. Sharks! They were few at first, but as the day wore on the tall triangular fins that cleaved the surface like the conning towers of submarines became more numerous. Timid at first, the rapacious scavengers patrolled the perimeters of the little groups of survivors. Now and then, as if on reconnaissance, a lone shark would make a swift trip right through the very middle of a group and then vanish like a shadow.

When a man died and was released from his life jacket, those who watched the body drift downward shuddered at the sight of three or four and sometimes as many as a dozen sharks converging on the corpse and tearing it to pieces with all of the savagery of a pack of jackals.

Quickly the word spread, and whenever the shout of *shark* was nearby, the men gathered into little knots and screamed and flailed the water with their arms and legs. There were no hard-and-fast rules in the *Bluejackets Manual* saying what to do when a shark was attacking, so the men just did what came naturally. In almost every case where fifteen or twenty were gathered together the kicking and screaming maneuver had the desired effect and the menacing sharks were driven off for a while. It was those who drifted away from the larger groups who were the most susceptible to attack. The lone swimmer would be seen thrashing about on the surface; then there would be a startled cry of pain that was stifled suddenly as his body was dragged under by hungry jaws.

The man-eating sharks were a real threat and the men were afraid. "Besides the sharks," a sailor asked, "what else is there out here that is liable to get us?" And a secondary fear was born, bastard seeds of half-truth, half-fancy planted by men with little scientific knowledge and great imagination, germinated in darkness and fertilized with the abundant fear of the unknown that is so much a part of every human.

"You got to watch out for moray eels and poisonous sea snakes," came one answer.

"They call the barracuda the *tiger of the sea*," another added. "Their jaws work like the blades of a mowing machine and they can cut your leg off like a bandsaw."

"They say there's a jellyfish out here with a sting

so violent that it can kill a man just as sure as if he had grabbed hold of a high-tension electric wire."

Every man listened, and many tossed in their own little bit of partly accurate information. "There's a small fish out here no bigger than your hand called the lion fish, and his fin is so poisonous that he can strike a man dead in five seconds."

"The giant squid is the most dangerous," one petty officer with several years at sea offered. "They come up from the bottom to feed after the sun goes down. They've got arms a hundred feet or more in length and they've been known to swallow whole ships."

Not exactly bedtime stories, these tales of the terrible creatures that lurked just beneath the surface, and they had a demoralizing effect on many as the nightfall grew darker. Suddenly there was a high-pitched scream of terror, and a man began fighting the water and everything about him.

"It's got me! Help! Somebody help! Don't let it kill me!"

Several of the men swam up to the sailor and forcefully subdued him. When he could be made to listen to reason, he was able to laugh feebly at the "thing" that had been clutching at his neck—a drifting length of Manila line.

But of such stock nightmares are born. Sunday night—with the excitement of the torpedoes, the sinking ship and the wholesale confusion—had been bad, but Monday night was worse. All day every man had seen death around him. He had seen the sharks and heard wild stories, and what was more, no plane or ship had come to rescue them. The darkness was filled with screams and frightened sobs and the voices of men praying.

Shortly after midnight on 31 July every man from the great pod floating to the southwest to Captain McVay and his rafters at the northeast end saw the running lights of a plane flying east toward Guam. Those in the water could only look up at the tiny lights and listen to the rumble of engines, but almost every raft had a Very pistol and a handful of shells and as the approaching plane drew near they fairly set the sky ablaze with signal flares.

The plane was a rugged old C-54 on its way from Manila to Guam, piloted by Captain Richard G. Le-Francis of the Army Air Force. Captain LeFrancis saw the pyrotechnics out of his starboard window as he pressed on along an eastward track. To him it looked like a small naval battle. Two ships shelling another vessel, he thought. Not the sort of engagement that his tired C-54 could take part in. He watched the bright balls of fire jut up from the sea and made a note of the location in his log book.

When Captain LeFrancis touched down at Guam he made a full report of the "naval battle" he had witnessed, but those in authority told him to forget it. What the Navy was involved in was no concern of the Army Air Force. Captain LeFrancis nodded and bowed out. He had made his report, and it had been tossed aside.

The pathetic tragedy is that LeFrancis had not vec-tored in on the display of tiny rocket shells and found the destitute band of survivors. Had he done so, many hundreds of lives would have been saved.

The sun came up on Tuesday morning as it had done on the preceding day. In each group of swimmers and rafters many had vanished. Some had died of wounds, others had been taken by sharks and still oth-ers had simply given up what to them was a hopeless struggle for survival.

Ensign Ross Rogers looked at the sea around him and at the survivors in the raft with him. By now he had ten men aboard. Chief Ferguson showed no signs of improvement, but neither did he seem to be getting any worse. Rogers tried hard to remember their posi-tion when the ship went down. He had been on the bridge Sunday afternoon and he had also listened to some of the other officers talking in the wardroom that evening. Either through conversation or by look-ing at the charts, he had somehow gotten the impression that there was a group of islands less than thirty miles to the south.

Fully aware that they could hope only to make a few miles each day if they began to paddle in a southerly direction, Ensign Rogers pondered the thought for several hours. Except for Ferguson and two other men who had been sounded, the sailors on his raft were growing restless. Paddling to those vague islands to the south seemed the best idea, so Rogers gave the orders and the men set about the task. At least they had a goal, and it did not seem unattainable. If even one man aboard had known that the Palau Island group nearly 250 miles away was the nearest land, the paddles would have been promptly tossed over the side. Another fact they were unaware of was that the slow southern drift of ocean currents was more than matched by the prevailing wind that pushed up to the northeast, and their labored strokes did little more than keep the raft in one position. But Ensign Rogers and his men had a job to do. They were on their way to salvation and they knew that if they kept trying they would reach a sun-drenched beach and there would be natives in canoes to greet them, coconut palms and plenty of freshwater to drink.

By and large almost every man who still remained afloat on Tuesday morning was in fairly good spirits. It had been common knowledge aboard ship that the *Indianapolis* was to be met that day by tractor planes towing sleeves for the antiaircraft gun crews to practice on as they neared Leyte. Even the most informed and pessimistic officer was counting on this being the trigger that would set off an immediate search. The planes would be on station at the appointed hour and when no heavy cruiser hove into view they would begin to make contact with home base, and the big wheels would start to turn in a hurry.

And rightly they should have. No one knows for sure just where things went wrong. It is a matter of record that the sleeve-towing planes were on station and they gave up and returned to base when the ap-

pointed hour of rendezvous was passed. No one paid
much attention to the abortive contact. For those who
were later to be taken to task and exposed to public
scorn and Navy discipline, there was one saving fac-
tor—the time-honored regulation that combatant ships
of cruiser and battleship class were not required to
operate on a hard-and-fast timetable.

But men and officers who had scrambled off the
Indianapolis in the twelve minutes she remained afloat
after being struck by the torpedoes from Commander
Hashimoto's *I-58* did not believe they would not be
missed on Tuesday morning. Today would be the day
for sure, the day when they would be rescued. Who
can say how many would have given up the struggle
had they known the apathy that existed at their appointed port of call?

Tuesday's hot sun intensified the men's suffering.
For the most part each knew that he was not to drink
salt water under any circumstances. Such basic fundamentals had been drilled into every sailor and officer
from the first moment they had joined the service.
Those who had also read magazine articles or books
and newspapers had gained an instinctive awareness
that a sailor's quickest route to self-destruction upon
being cast into the sea is to yield to the temptation of
swallowing salt water.

Marvin Kirkland, the freshwater king who had tried
to find a fire hose for his division officer, Lieutenant
Commander K. C. Moore, in the ship's final moments,
bobbed about on the surface near a raft. His head
throbbed with excruciating pain from the teeth that
had been driven up into his face. He had a frantic
craving for water, but he remembered an article he
had read only a few nights before in a dog-eared copy
of the *Reader's Digest* someone had left on his watch
station down near the freshwater tanks on the second
platform. The article had told of the sinking of the
Juneau with the loss of 676 men, including the five
Sullivan brothers. The inherent hazards of drinking
salt water had been explained in great detail. Kirkland

reread the article a thousand times in his mind's eye and whenever the desire for water became almost overpowering, he ducked his face into the sea, filled his mouth and while his system begged him to swallow he would spew the deadly liquid back out through his torn lips.

No one was hungry on Tuesday morning, but there was a growing need for water. The sea which enveloped them seemed cool and clear. Soon some were unable to rationalize. There could certainly be nothing wrong with taking one swift gulp. Like a drink of soda pop it ran down their gullets cool and tingly, but once it hit their stomachs, it became pure poison. The saline content brought about acute diarrhea. The passage of body fluid caused dehydration, and the body's demand for more fluid to replace that which was lost quickly brought on strange behavior. Victims of this temptation began to babble like fools, they became violent and thrashed the sea around them until brown foam bubbled from their mouths and they collapsed in lifeless heaps. Some began to believe that those around them were trying to harm them and they fought with even their closest friends, unable to listen to reason. They gulped more and more salt water in a wild frenzy to quench the fire in their stomachs. In this final deadly attempt they would drink twice, even three times as much water as they could possibly have swallowed had the water been cool and fresh and had they been in the peak of physical condition. Whatever form it took, death was inevitably the victor over those who yielded to those first few gulps.

Radiomen Joe Moran and Elwyn Sturtevant, along with Signalman Kenley Lanter and seventeen other men who shared four rafts far away by themselves, had managed to cheer each other and maintain fairly good order from the time they had assembled early Monday morning. Next to their increasing desire for water their greatest concern was for Lieutenant (j.g.) Howard Freeze, who had been badly burned while attempting to escape from the compartment he had shared with Lieutenant Charles McKissick on the starboard side of the *Indianapolis*. Freeze, however, stubbornly refused to complain and just lay quietly on the bottom of one of the rafts.

In the early part of the evening a strange episode began for the men, similar to that which had occurred late Sunday night to Marine Private First Class Giles McCoy and his group when they saw what they believed to be the running lights of a nearby ship.

Signalman Lanter was looking out across the dark sea when he suddenly began to see a blinker light winking. Nudging Moran, he pointed to the signal and quickly those in the other three rafts were alerted. A small battery-operated signal light had been found in one of the rafts and it was hurriedly handed to Lanter.

Quick with the visual dots and dashes, Lanter rapidly spelled out a plain-language message: "Four rafts, wounded men aboard, need help."

There was a brief delay and then the blinking light started flashing again. They were dots and dashes, all right, but they did not make sense.

"I'll send him an IMI," Lanter said. The two dots, two dashes and two more dots in the International Morse Code means *question mark—I did not understand your last transmission*. Right away the blinking light on the dark horizon answered, but again it was nothing but a scrambled series of dots and dashes.

While Lanter and Moran fumed over the shortcomings of the inept operator at the other end, someone suggested that the signals might be coming from an enemy ship. As the idea took hold, Lanter put his lamp aside, and every man lay still. While rescue was their greatest desire, no one in the group wanted to be taken prisoner by a Japanese submarine. Also there was the eminent threat of being machine-gunned.

When an hour had passed and there were no other signals from the horizon, the men began once again to talk in normal voices. Lanter remembered the burned officer and called over to ask how he was doing.

"I'm fine, except for the pain," Lieutenant Freeze

answered. Before the night was over he very quietly died, but because of the sharks around the raft the men decided to wait until morning to put him in the water.

A short way to the north, Captain McVay and his eighteen fellow survivors were a bit more organized, but they were not faring much better. There was no drinking water, and except for the usual can of Spam and bottles of malted milk tablets that were in some of the rafts there was nothing to eat. There was a fishing kit aboard, however, and they caught a few fish but because no one knew if they were edible they were tossed overboard. Captain McVay looked at his little fleet of rafts and wondered if the eighteen men who shared his watery domain were the only survivors from the *Indianapolis*. As with Doctor Haynes, Lieutenant Redmayne, Ensign Rogers and Signalman Lanter, there was no way that he could know. Now they were all little islands unto themselves populated with suffering men.

Sunday night, all day Monday, Monday night and for the better part of Tuesday the survivors in the water had fought to stay alive because they were certain rescue was imminent. Man can endure great physical suffering when there is hope. When, however, they commenced to believe there was no hope that rescue would ever come, the will to continue the struggle began to evaporate for many.

Machinist's Mate Third Class Gabriel George had suffered the loss of his father in a train accident when he was very young. It was during those early and often bleak years, when there was only his mother to make a living for a cluster of brothers and sisters who bore the name of George, that Gabriel discovered he had a good voice. In his early school days he was in demand whenever there was entertainment in store, and from the day he joined the Navy in January of 1944 his singing became popular with those around him. He led his platoon in songs while he was in training at the Great Lakes Naval Training Station and when he reported aboard the *Indianapolis* he redoubled his efforts and was "on stage" at every smoker. Everybody, officers and enlisted men alike, knew and liked "Gabe." When he had left the sinking ship he had narrowly missed falling into the port screw, and although he could not swim, he had found his way somehow to one of the rafts.

All day Monday he had tried to keep up the morale of the men around him by occasionally bursting forth into song. On Tuesday, however, most of the music of life drained from him. One of the boys who was part of the Flag was badly injured and unconscious, and Gabe held his head in his lap. With no first-aid supplies there was nothing Pharmacist's Mate Third Class Harold Anthony could do but watch the boy die. When he had pronounced him dead, the men said prayers and then because of the sharks around the raft they tied their shoes to his body to help sink it in the water.

By Tuesday many of the men in the raft were beginning to act strangely, trying to go below deck for milk or seeing beautiful Hollywood girls and wanting to swim to them. Gabe George, Marine First Sergeant Jacob Greenwald and Pharmacist's Mate Anthony struggled with the men, trying to bring them back to their senses.

Most of the survivors on the rafts, however, were still in good spirits. They were far better off than those in the water because, although suffering the pangs of hunger and thirst, an exhausted man could relax without the pressing fear that if he dared let go for one moment his head would drop over into the water and before somebody roused him he would drown.

When darkness came on Tuesday night, conditions began to deteriorate rapidly among them all. This was especially so in the largest group of survivors at the southwest end of the line. Life jackets were becoming more and more waterlogged. As the men continued to sink lower into the water some would suddenly lose control and begin screaming or trying or climb up on the shoulders of a fellow survivor. Again another would jerk off his jacket and swim about until he contacted someone and then try to take this man's jacket from him by force. Fights broke out and some of the men had knives, which added to the terror.

Father Thomas Michael Conway swam from group to group, never stopping to rest, praying with the men, encouraging those who were frightened, trying to reason with the maddened. His faith and his prayers gave solace to many.

Tuesday night also brought a real-life nightmare for the nearly one hundred and fifty men around the net to the northeast and those in and around the three life rafts nearby. Two factors, one real and one imagined, contributed to their plight. The real and terrifying threat was the man-eating sharks that had found the survivors late Tuesday afternoon. Joseph Dronet, seaman second class, had watched in horror as first one sailor and then another were attacked and dragged under by sharks. The seventeen-year-old sailor from New Iberia, Louisiana, was the youngest in a family of eight children, and four of his brothers were already serving in various branches of the armed forces around the world. Sunday night he had been sleeping on the forecastle on the starboard side and the explosion had all but tossed him overboard. He had gone over the side with a friend from Eufaula, Oklahoma, Coxswain Cozell Smith.

Now the two watched the sharks as they attacked in waves, drew back, waited for a while and then rushed in again, almost like Indians harassing a wagon train. Dronet remembered a class he had attended while in boot training at San Diego. It had been concerned with things to do and not to do in order to survive in the water after a shipwreck. "If you are attacked by sharks," the instructor had said, "don't thrash the water. You have a much better chance of escaping if you just turn over on your back and lie still. The shark is like a cowardly hyena. He would much rather attack something he thinks has already been wounded. He may mistake your thrashing as a feeble attempt to escape."

Young Dronet did not know much about shark psychology, but the Navy would not have hired the man to teach the course unless he knew what he was talking about, he reasoned. Each time the shark alert was sounded, he rolled over on his back and tried to remain as immobile as a floating plank. Several times he felt the swirl of water directly beneath his body, but he was never touched. He and many of the others watched three of the men in the group around the net caught in rapid succession by the rapacious jaws and dragged screaming beneath the surface.

The shark attack was bad enough, but as night came an even more frightening specter began to spread among the group—the wildly fantastic belief that Japanese sailors had infiltrated their ranks and were slowly killing the men with knives.

"Get away from me!" a man suddenly screamed. "You're a Jap! You're a dirty Jap bastard and you were trying to drown me."

Forty-some hours of drifting about in the water with nothing to eat or drink was playing tricks on the men's minds. Before the long night was over, countless friends had fought and now and then when one was stronger and sufficiently frightened he would get a half nelson on his adversary and hold his head underwater until he stopped struggling. In an equally hideous manner a man would whip out a sheath knife and stab to death the companion next to him in the firm conviction that he was an enemy trying to kill him.

In the large group at the southwest end of the line Ensign John Woolston, Ensign David Park, one of the OS2U pilots and several other officers and enlisted men were in better control of their faculties and still hoped for rescue. They realized that if order was not maintained, men were going to die unnecessarily. They went to work late Tuesday night breaking up the fights when they began and swimming out to round up the strays who drifted away from the group. Cowboy

Duty was what they called it. Neither rank nor age nor experience seemed to play much of a part in determining whether a man was willing and able to help those around him. Now and then one of these self-appointed guardians would be a seaman with only a few months' sea duty behind him. Some of these men gave too much of their own strength. Many watched with admiration as Ensign David Park swam tirelessly from one trouble spot to another, reasoning with a frightened man, helping another find a life jacket and always giving the impression that he did not feel the situation was quite so bad as it looked. Another was a young seaman, Garland Rich, from the west Texas town of McCamey. Seaman Rich, Ensign Park and many other unknown heroes worked too hard to keep their fellow men alive and because of this the life in their own weakened bodies burned out.

Ensign John Woolston was a good swimmer. As a youngster he had spent his summers in the San Juan Islands in Puget Sound, where his grandparents owned a lime business. At the age of nine he learned to swim and then just to prove to himself that he had learned well he crossed by boat to the opposite side of a three-quarter-mile-wide bay and promptly dived in and swam all the way back.

This early training was proving invaluable now as time after time he would strike out across the moonlit water toward the sound of a frightened voice, find the man and talk to him for a few minutes, then lead him back to the main group. On many occasions he hurried over to a spot on the dark waves where men were fighting over the possession of a jacket. It was tricky business and doubly so in the watery blackness. First it was necessary to decide which of the fighting men was temporarily deranged. When this was determined, he would swim in and pin the man's arms to his sides until he had been talked back to normality. When the crisis had passed, the man was helped to find a floating jacket and then guided over to a small group of survivors who were fairly well under control.

Even as the sun began to light the eastern sky on
Wednesday morning, conditions did not improve. A
new threat had been born in the minds of some men
who had taken almost as much as they could. It was
the call for mass suicide. Ashore, under normal conditions, exponents of such a drive would either have
been completely ignored or shouted down, but now
after better than fifty hours of hanging in the water
their delirious doctrine almost seemed to make sense.

"Listen to me, you sailors," a voice called out.
"They haven't even missed us at Leyte. We're not
going to be rescued. What's the sense of hanging here
in these damned jackets until the flesh rots off our
bones and the sharks pull us to pieces? We've all got
to die today or tomorrow, so let's get it over with in
a hurry."

"I go along with that," a sailor said.

"You're right!" another answered.

"Come on, men," the voice called. "Pull off your
jackets. Let's go."

"You go on and feed yourselves to the sharks if
you want to," a voice called back, "but me—I gotta
get home. They're gonna come find us sooner or later
and when they get here, if there's just two of us left,
I'm gonna be the other one."

For most who heard this thick-lipped and tongue-
swollen conversation the final statement with its sar-
donic touch of levity seemed to break the frightening
spell, and a few began to laugh. Here and there men
called back, "I'm right there with you, Mac!"

But for many the call for suicide had implanted the
idea as a panacea for their suffering. Fingers that had
grown soft with hours of immersion fumbled with tie
strings on kapok jackets and the buckles of inflated
life belts, and soon there were numerous pieces of
flotation gear awaiting those whose own life jackets
were beginning to grow waterlogged.

Father Conway, like Ensign Park, Seaman Rich and
many others, burned himself out keeping up a constant patrol among the men, ministering to the dying,

talking reason into others who had become momentarily deranged and calming the frightened with prayers until all at once he reached the limit of his endurance, and his life drained away. A sobbing seaman clutched the lifeless body to him, refusing to remove the jacket and commit his padre to the depths.

"He's dead because of us. He used up his life helping us. He prayed for everybody—not for himself but for me and you and you," he sobbed. "I don't know how to, but I can't let him go until he's been prayed for." The sailor clutched the body tighter, his eyes pleading with the blackened faces around him.

A sailor swam up to them. "He doesn't need our prayers," he said. "God knows what he has done. But I know the Lord's Prayer. Come on, you guys, gather around." The small group hung in the water, their heads bowed, and joined quietly with the man who led them. When the prayer was finished, the young sailor slowly and gently removed the jacket and committed Father Conway's body to the depths.

Wednesday morning was just like the two preceding days—hot in a still sea. The frenzy of Tuesday night was stilled to some extent, primarily because most of those who survived were too exhausted to continue fighting. Now all the men wanted was a drink of water.

Doctor Lewis Haynes and his junior medical officer, Doctor Melvin Modisher, were themselves undergoing the pangs of thirst, but both managed to hold on to some semblance of reality. Every few minutes a man would paddle up and say his gut was hurting or his eyesight was failing, and the two doctors were expected to offer advice and worthwhile council just as they would have back on board the *Indianapolis*.

Radioman Elwyn Sturtevant looked around him and saw that most of those on the raft were still asleep. He searched the water and saw no signs of sharks and knew that it was time to bury Lieutenant Howard Freeze. Motioning to the few who were awake, they quietly committed the body to the deep with a silent prayer on their lips.

The men were weaker now. They had been so long without water that they were ready to grab at any straw.

"Hey, Doc," a thirst-crazed sailor exclaimed, swimming up beside Haynes. "I bet that if I hold a double handful of water up to the sun for a few minutes it will become as fresh as spring water. Don't you think I'm right?"

Lieutenant Commander Lewis Haynes quickly shook his head. In carefully selected words he explained why the water would not be good and begged the man not to drink it.

Assistant Master-at-Arms G. S. Crane was helping to hold Commander Stanley Lipski's burn-tortured body out of the water. Although blind and in intense pain he had been coherent and talkative since their first night in the water and seemed aware of everything going on around him. In the early hours of the morning, however, life quietly left his body, and death mercifully ended his suffering. A sailor watching nearby pressed a hand across his eyes and muttered, "Thank You, God, for taking him at last." Because of the sharks that were beginning to circle them again, many of those who had helped support Lipski in his final hours were reluctant to let his body down into the water. But as they gathered sadly around the limp form and said the Lord's Prayer, Crane relaxed his grip and the commander's body dropped swiftly down into the deep.

Tuesday night Lieutenant (j.g.) Charles McKissick and Quartermaster First Class Robert Gause had helped round up strays and quell fights and now many men were gathered around them asking them for advice and discussing their chances of rescue. Suddenly, one of the men lifted his arm and pointed toward the eastern sky.

"Look at that bank of clouds!" he shouted.

"That's a rain squall," Gause said, "and it's coming this way."

"Rain! Oh, God, please let it rain on us," the sailors prayed reverently.

Next to immediate rescue, water was most important to every one of the over four hundred men who were still fighting death. One prolonged downpour would be all that was needed to put new life into men who were rapidly dehydrating.

"How are we gonna get any of that water when it gets here?" one man asked. "We haven't got anything to catch it in."

"Take off your shirt or T-shirt, even your skivvies," Gause said. "When the rain starts, hold the cloth up and let it get good and wet, then wring it out. That will get rid of most of the salt. Then hold it up and let it get soaked by the rain again and squeeze that water into your mouth. It will be good and clean."

The great dark cloud with the long columns of falling water had been seen by other groups, and excitement was running high. It had now been nearly sixty hours since most of the survivors had tasted freshwater. What a blessed relief it would be to swallow even a few drops.

Closer and closer came the black rain cell. They could see the falling water now—less than a quarter of a mile away—volumes of it pouring in wasteful abandon on the surface of the sea. The men made ready. The dusky shelf of cloud that preceded the rain reached out over the survivors, and each man held up his undershirt or shorts or any other piece of cloth that he could find. In just a minute or two now the rain would reach them.

But fate had no supply of water in store for the survivors of the *Indianapolis*. When the storm was only a few hundred yards away, a fresh breeze sprang up, the sullen swells were laced with foam, and slowly the vast cloud spilling its countless gallons of life-saving liquid turned. Gradually the leading edge withdrew, the breeze vanished as the rain squall swept off to the south, and once more the sun set the sea to sparkling. Unable to accept the reality that they had been cheated by such a narrow margin, many of the men hung there in their jackets for a long while holding their pitiful rags up toward the sky in hopeless supplication.

"We don't have to worry about trying to catch rainwater," one of the men suddenly yelled. "Come with me. I've just found a stream of freshwater about twenty feet below. It must be a river boiling up from the bottom. I just went down and had a drink and I'm going back after another. There's plenty for everybody, so come on!"

For many of the men the invitation was too enticing to be ignored. One after another they untied their jackets and swam down for that coveted drink of water. Big silver bubbles wabbled to the surface and some of the men came back declaring there *was* freshwater a short way down. But within the hour they were going into convulsions. The luckier ones did not have the strength to fight their way back to the surface, and sometimes those who still waited in their jackets could look down and see the lifeless bodies being torn to pieces by the sharks.

Aside from the physical torture that grew steadily worse with each passing hour, there was the torment of the endless parade of airplanes that crossed over the area day and night. Sometimes as many as five planes would be sighted in a single day. Each time the far-off drone of engines began to pulsate against eardrums, the men looked up toward the sky. Was this the search plane that would finally spot them? After many false alarms the miserable survivors only turned their eyes away from the sky and clapped their hands over their ears to shut out the sight and sound of the salvation that came so near to torture them by reminding them that there was still a real world of people and machines, while blandly failing to notice them as if they did not exist anymore. But hope does spring eternal in the human breast and try as they would to ignore the sound of the approaching plane, the men could not conquer the temptation of becoming increasingly alert. As an aircraft would crawl up over the horizon and draw nearer, they would again call out, wave their arms and thrash the water.

"Why can't they see us?" they would demand as the planes roared overhead and finally faded into the haze on the horizon.

"They don't see us because all pilots are stupid blind," one sailor sobbed. "All the fools can do is just sit there watching little dials."

Ironically, the sailor was not far from right. After a man has logged a hundred or so hours flying over an empty ocean he loses interest in looking down. There is nothing to see save the endless expanse of waves, sometimes slick and greasy like a great pool of oil or again a purplish blue flecked with little feathers of white foam—no more interesting than looking down at the rug on the floor. Added to this, in the closing days of World War II radar provided an electronic eye that searched the surface of the sea. If there was a ship below, she would show up as a little yellow pip on the dial, but men alone were beyond its vision. When the radar "found" something, then was the time to begin looking.

Had any of the crews who passed over the area been informed that there was even the slightest chance of finding survivors they would have kept a constant watch, but no one knew a ship was missing. Months earlier the business of searching for downed pilots in that section of the Pacific had come to a close. Naval battles were a thing of the past here too. The Army pilot, Captain LeFrancis, who had seen the rockets and flares Monday night had not been able to stir up any interest when he turned in his report. Certainly it was not thoughtlessness on the part of any individual or branch of the service. It was simply that no one knew the *Indianapolis* was missing and no one was searching for her survivors.

Such hindsight, even could it have been known at the time, would have been little consolation to the men in the water who looked up hopefully at the approaching planes, then dropped off into a stupor of despair as the "blind aviators" went on their merry way.

Wednesday afternoon the hallucinations worsened. About three o'clock a man bobbed to the surface without his life jacket and shouted to all of those around him that he had just been down to the ship and had a full meal and a long drink of cool water.

"They said we were sailing over real deep water," the crazed sailor shouted. "Don't believe it! *Indy* is just a few feet down and the cooks are hard at work in the galley. There's plenty of food and freshwater and the skipper is down there getting ready to bring the ship back to the surface."

"Can I go down and get some water without having to wait for them to get the ship back to the surface?" a sailor asked.

"Sure you can," the man replied as he dog-paddled slowly about. "But you better let me show you the way. They got most of the hatches dogged good and tight, and you have to know the way if you want to get in."

"Hey! How about it?" a third half-crazed man asked. "Can I go with you guys?"

Then all at once a dozen men were clamoring around the sailor. "Now everybody stop yelling and listen to me," he commanded. "The exec is trying to keep the decks cleared so the repair parties will have room to work. He don't mind if a few of us come down at a time, but he'll start raising hell if the whole crew tries to get aboard. Now I'll take four of you down there and you can get a drink and then I'll come back and get four or five others. He won't mind if we take turns."

They held their little caucus as if working out a fair plan of who would go on liberty and who would stay aboard. As they were trying to decide who would stay first and who would wait for the second turn, a sailor paddled over to the group.

"You crazy jerks are just going to drown yourselves

if you keep listening to this man," he pleaded. "There isn't any ship down there, and if you try to dive for it you won't come back."

"Listen to him," a man grumbled. "He's probably already been down and drunk all the water he wants and he don't want us to get any."

No amount of reasoning could stop them. Four thirsty sailors pulled off their jackets and on signal arched over and followed the first one down. When nearly a minute had passed, one suddenly bobbed back to the surface gasping for air and fighting to find the life jacket he had so lightheartedly abandoned.

"There ain't no ship down there!" he sputtered. "That guy was crazy."

Water Tender Second Class Harold "Hap" Flaten was trying hard to hold on to the belief that they would be rescued soon, but he had not closed his eyes since Sunday night and the struggle to stay awake was becoming increasingly difficult. In the water around him close to the big floater net were men like Seaman Second Class Joseph Dronet and Seaman Second Class Marvin Kirkland and close by in a raft was the senior officer, Lieutenant Richard Redmayne. Ensign Harlan Twible was hanging on to the side of another raft. These men Flaten recognized, but there were many others around him whose sunken faces and fear-crazed eyes defied identification. He and another ship-mate talked about their desire for sleep and decided to pair off from the rest of the survivors. They were aware that this would increase their chances of attack by sharks, but at the same time they knew that right now both were rational and they would not have to fear that one would suddenly turn on the other and try to kill him.

"You take a nap," Flaten said. "I'll stand watch and be sure your head doesn't drop over into the water. When you are rested, you can watch after me."

Using this method, "Hap" Flaten and his buddy managed to each get a few minutes of badly needed sleep. But then as they grew closer to the point of complete exhaustion, even they could not trust each other.

All around them men were giving up or would take off their life belts or jackets and start to swim for an island they were sure had lots of fresh water to drink and plenty of fresh food. No one had the strength to stop them. One could only watch until they disappeared from sight, never to be seen again. One of the men started away but appeared again swimming hard toward the group.

"I've got to have some help," he said, approaching a sailor whom he knew was married and had a family. "There's a woman out there having a baby. I don't know what to do for her, but I told her you would know and that I'd come get you."

Flaten and several others tried to keep the father from going. "You know there couldn't be a woman out there," they argued. But nothing they said could stop him, and the two sailors swam away out of sight.

By now it had ceased to make much difference whether a man was sitting in a raft, hanging on to a floater net or simply bobbing up and down in a life jacket that barely kept his head out of the water. In fact, many of the sailors who had earlier considered themselves fortunate because they had found a raft were beginning to question their luck. While the men around the floater net were plagued with outbreaks of hysteria and frequent attacks by sharks, they were at least not being sunburned since only their faces and ears were exposed. Any uncovered parts of the body of those on the rafts began to blister after the first few hours. The ones with fair complexions were suffering the most.

Chief Machinist's Mate Albert Ferguson in the raft with Ensign Ross Rogers was completely naked. Rogers had looked at the sunburned injured chief on Tuesday and taken pity on him. Pulling off his own trousers he had helped Ferguson wriggle into them. Seaman First Class George Kurlick from Akron, Ohio, another who had been taking a shower when the torpedoes struck, was now in the group with Captain McVay. Since there were plenty of kapok jackets aboard the raft, however, he kept the sun from his exposed body by covering himself with jackets. And there was Electrician's Mate Third Class Richard Houck, who had run out of the showers with only a towel wrapped around his middle and a pair of shoes on his feet. He had lost both when he hit the water, and now his only article of clothing was a kapok jacket.

No group was without the hallucinations that were becoming increasingly numerous by late Wednesday afternoon. A big sailor who still retained the strength of a bull thrashed up to Radarman Third Class Tommy Reid and stared glassy-eyed into his face. Reid nodded his head in a sign of recognition, expecting the sailor to pass along some trivial comment. Instead, the man suddenly lifted a long sheath knife out of the water and stuck the point of the blade to Reid's throat!

"O.K., you bastard," he snarled. "I want to know where you hid my milk!"

Reid glanced down at the glint of cold steel beneath his chin and looked back into the eyes of a man who only a day before had simply been a scared sailor cast adrift from his ship. A week earlier the two had been talking to one another on the quarterdeck and cutting in on the chow line together.

"You know where we put your milk," he said quickly, fishing for words as he went along. He was almost too exhausted really to care whether he lived or died, but he was still horrified at the thought of having his throat cut. He was confident the menacing sailor was nearing the end of his rope. "Don't you remember?" he urged. "We put the milk down in the water so it would keep cool."

The ruse seemed to work. The excited sailor withdrew his knife and began nodding his head in agreement. Meticulously he replaced the knife in its sheath and swam away.

Wednesday afternoon Firecontrolman Operator Third Class Rudolph Gemza counted the men in the water with him. The one hundred and fifty who had been around the big floater net Monday morning had now dwindled to less than a third of that number! He had seen men killed by sharks, men killing others and men killing themselves. As with many of the other groups there were those who were positive that there was freshwater just below the surface and he watched in pity as one man after another went down for a drink.

Close beside him a sailor fished a white handkerchief out of a pocket and held it up over his face. "Say, if one of you will scoop up some water and pour it on this handkerchief what comes through will be pure and I can drink it."

"Knock it off," Gemza said. "You can't strain the salt out of seawater like it might be grains of sand. If you drink that water it'll kill you."

"I know what I'm doing," the sailor said. "You tend to your business, and I'll tend to mine."

Gemza turned away, helpless to prevent the man from drinking the water. Thirty minutes later he could hear him screaming, and before the hour had passed he was dead.

Radarman Allan Altschuler saw the group growing smaller, and fearing he would soon be alone, he decided to strike out in search of a larger group someone had said was not far away. He had been a student at UCLA and was a member of the water polo team. To say the least, he was a better-than-average swimmer. After he had been swimming for some time, he came to Doctor Haynes's and Doctor Modisher's group and found several friends from his own division. Except that there were more men here he soon realized they were no better off than the group he had left. He saw sailors resting on three and four jackets while others shared one. Around him men were praying for forgiveness for past mistakes, others were asking for matches for cigarettes that were soaked and disintegrating in their hands and he could still hear the cries for help.

In the late afternoon a boatswain's mate who had drifted far away from the group during the day came swimming back across the darkening water.

"Good news!" he shouted as he approached a small cluster of men. "The ship broke in half just after she sunk and the whole stern section is back on the surface. I've just been there and had a drink and ate a peanut butter sandwich."

"Take us over there," the sailors clamored.

Glancing up at the sky, the boatswain stroked the stubble on his chin. "I'm too tired to swim back right now," he said. "Besides, it's getting dark, and we might miss her. You guys stick with me, though, and just as soon as the sun comes up we'll go. I promise I'll take you there."

Crazy? Well perhaps, but perhaps too the boatswain's mate realized he could not go another hour without sleep. Now, however, he could relax because he knew at least ten dedicated disciples would watch over him during the night and not let him drown while he slept.

Perhaps because they were fewer in number or because they had good leadership and more opportunity to rest, the survivors on the captain's rafts were not subjected to the relentless torture. True, an occasional shark did circle around them, but the men had the sanctuary of the four rafts. When the sharks were not there they put out lines and now and then caught a few fish. They were strange-looking little fish, bright blue in color, and because everyone had heard of the deadly poisonous fish in the Pacific, the skipper insisted that they be tossed back over the side. The ones they caught were probably perfectly safe to eat since the poisonous fish are reef dwellers found near shallow water around islands, but it was probably providential that the men were not sure. It is true that the flesh of saltwater fish is composed largely of pure freshwater, but when ingested by the human stomach

there must be an extra supply of liquid to offset the
normal loss of body fluid passed in the simple body
chemistry of digesting the protein contained in the fish
flesh. With plenty of drinking water to go along with
it, raw fish is of high nutritional value. Eaten alone, it
can lead to serious dehydration.

Over eight hundred men had managed to abandon
ship as the *Indianapolis* went down, but by Thursday
morning the number still alive had dwindled to less
than four hundred, and these were nearly dead. They
had watched the sun come up four times. They had seen
a score of planes pass overhead. It did not seem to
matter now. You joined the Navy, served aboard a ship
for a time, and then you were sunk. Who was there to
care? Who was there to look for you? Total disintegra-
tion of the survivors was rapidly approaching. Officers
and enlisted men who had fought desperately to hold
their waning groups together had endured all of the suffering their bodies could absorb.

SIX

THE LONG WAIT IS OVER

THURSDAY, 2 August 1945, dawned hot and clear over the naval air station at Peleliu, where VPB 152 was based. Lieutenant (j.g.) Wilbur C. Gwinn finished an early breakfast and ambled across to the runway where his PV-1 Ventura was waiting for takeoff. His copilot, Lieutenant (j.g.) Warren Colwell, was already there. Gwinn had the morning patrol and except that as one of the squadron's engineering officers he was to test a new type of trailing wire antenna, this flight promised nothing new.

Here in the summer of 1945 the Palau Islands were well behind the hotter spots of the Forward Area, and the planes that took off on their endless patrols did not expect much excitement. Their main job was to watch for enemy supply ships that might try to bring aid to the bypassed Japanese in the Palaus.

At 0800 Lieutenant Gwinn shoved the throttles ahead and the twin-engine Ventura rumbled down the runway. Reaching takeoff speed he pulled back on the

yoke and the plane lifted. A moment later there was
a snapping sound.

Chief Aviation Radioman Bill Hartman pressed the
button on his intercom mike. "That was the antenna
weight, sir," he said. "It snapped off just as I started
reeling out."

"O.K.," Gwinn said. "We'll just go back and get
another one." He began a slow turn and a few minutes
later they were back on the ground. Radioman Hartman assisted by the other two enlisted crew members
hurriedly scrambled outside and attached a new
weight that would carry out the trailing wire antenna.

Once more the Ventura pounded down the runway
and this time Hartman was not in so much of a hurry
to test the new antenna. He and Machinist's Mate
J. K. Johnson and Ordnanceman Hickman pulled the
plug out of a large Thermos jug, and everybody indulged in a cup of hot coffee.

VPB 152, commanded by Lieutenant Commander
George C. Atteberry, consisted of eighteen active
crews. While they could have done with twice the
number of men and planes, they were a congenial
group. There were no odd-balls in the squadron and
in general the day-by-day routine under the command
of Lieutenant Commander Atteberry worked as
smoothly as an efficient little airline.

While Lieutenant Wilbur Gwinn flew his Ventura
along at 1800 feet for the first hundred miles on his
northeast leg, he fell into a reflective mood. He had
been born on 1 September 1920 on an orchard and
cattle ranch outside of Gilroy, California, about
twenty miles inland from Monterey Bay. After graduating from high school in 1939, he had gone to Los
Angeles to continue his schooling, and while there he
took a job with Douglas Aircraft at Santa Monica.

As he worked at his trade as an apprentice metal-
smith, Gwinn could not help but notice the increasing
number of youngsters who were dropping out of
school and quitting their jobs to join the armed forces.
Many of his close friends had their sights set on the

Army Air Force. "What's wrong with naval aviation?" twenty-year-old Wilbur Gwinn had asked during a coffee-break bull session.

"Nuts to the Navy," one of the smiths in his crew replied. "You've got to be a *brain* to pass the entrance exams."

To Gwinn this became a challenge. He did not consider himself of superior intelligence, but he wanted to find out if he could make the grade. He took the entrance exams and passed. Before he could hardly realize what was happening, he was in the first stage of the early training that was to make a Navy pilot of him. On 2 February 1944 he received his gold wings at Corpus Christi, Texas.

His first assigned duty was in the Aleutians but he failed to get any further north than Seattle, Washington. There he received a change of orders that sent him back to Clinton, Oklahoma, for special duty with a newly formed squadron. There was secret talk about the squadron being trained for something as important as the Doolittle Raid over Tokyo, but then suddenly one day all of the excitement evaporated and VPB 152 simply moved out into the Pacific and wound up based at Peleliu.

Like all young naval aviators, Gwinn had privately hoped to emblazon his name in the hall of fame along with the great aces of World War II: Butch O'Hare, Bong, Boyington and Foss. With the war in the Pacific rapidly drawing to a close, he now knew this could never be. Little did he suspect that this humble patrol flight was destined to cause his name to live longer in the minds of 317 men than had he single-handedly defeated an entire squadron of Zeros.

About one hundred and fifty miles out at sea on a northeast course, Lieutenant Gwinn pulled his Ventura around to a true north heading and climbed to 4000 feet. The morning sun had turned the ocean's surface into a blinding polished mirror, and now he and copilot Colwell depended on the unblinking eye of radar to spot an enemy ship. Gwinn instructed

Radioman Hartman to make another try with the new trailing wire antenna.

After a brief silence Hartman came back on the intercom. "Skipper, it's about seventy feet out but the weight broke off again and it's fouled up."

Annoyed, Gwinn nudged Colwell and motioned with his thumb for the younger man to take control while he went aft to see what new problem had developed. Back in the tail section he and Machinist's Mate J. K. Johnson examined the antenna. Without the weight that held the copper wire in place the antenna was jumping around in the air behind the plane like a buggy whip gone wild. Together the pilot and machinist's mate got the wire free to reel in. When the crisis was over, Gwinn was about to leave the job to Johnson, when he sighted an oil slick on the water four thousand feet below.

A submarine had just made a crash dive! A whole war had almost slipped away from him and he had yet to fire a shot in anger. Now he was sitting squarely on top of an enemy submarine and he did not intend to let it get away. He hurried forward to take over the controls. Excitement began running high throughout the plane. Gwinn briefed Colwell in clipped sentences. Orders were passed, bomb bay doors unfolded, and bombs were armed as Gwinn arched the Ventura over in a 180-degree diving turn. In a matter of seconds they would be on target!

With the sun out of their eyes, pilot and copilot could see the surface clearly as they raced in for the kill. But what were those little black balls bobbing about in the middle of the oil slick? And there seemed to be things splashing on the water.

"Secure from bomb run," Lieutenant Gwinn ordered quickly as he pulled back on the throttles. "Let's get a better look at what we've found."

Dropping lower and slowing the speed, the twin-engine plane coasted over the oil slick, circled and came back for a second look. This was not just oil belched out by a quick diving sub. There were men down there. Maybe as many as twenty or thirty.

"Bust in on all traffic and tell the base we've found about thirty survivors," Gwinn told Radioman Hartman as he climbed back to a higher altitude. Hartman adjusted the headset over his ears and switched on the transmitter. Part of the gyrating antenna was still flipping about in the air behind the tail section, but maybe it would work anyway. Putting his fingers on the key, he began tapping out the message: "Sighted thirty men in water. Position 11 degrees 30 minutes North, 133 degrees 30 minutes East."

The message was received but in the jargon of the Navy it was *sat on*. One high-ranking admiral was made cognizant of its contents, but he simply wagged his head slowly and muttered under his breath about aviators who were allowed to fly on morning patrol while still suffering from a hangover.

Lieutenant Gwinn and his crew of four were cold sober and while he did not know where the men had come from or even whether they were from Allied forces, he was convinced they had found survivors from some kind of shipwreck. After a second trip around the area Gwinn ordered another message to be transmitted.

"Seventy-five men floating in open sea. Request immediate rescue. Am circling area."

Still no reply. Gwinn was becoming worried. He knew his antenna was damaged and maybe home base was not hearing his cry. He made an even larger sweep of the area and sent back a third message. This time he informed his base that he was wheeling over at least one hundred and fifty floating men. Still he did not know his estimate was less than half of what he had actually found. Ordnanceman Hickman bent over and shouted into Gwinn's ear.

"Those men down there need help. How about letting me bail out."

It took a brave man to volunteer for such an assignment, Gwinn knew. No man wants to leave his plane by parachute unless it is in the last extremity. He looked at Hickman and then down at the sea.

"No soap!" he said. "We don't even know they are our own men. Even if they are, they may have been down there a long time. If they have, they could be crazy and kill you."

It was 1115 hours when those survivors in the larger group to the southwest saw Gwinn's Ventura headed toward them. Doctor Haynes and three other men around him lifted their heads and watched the approaching plane through eyes that had grown weak from oil and exposure. Was this just another false hope in a long line of disappointments? Would this plane, like all the rest, sweep proudly over them and vanish on the distant horizon? Haynes and his companions offered up a humble prayer that this time they would not go unnoticed.

The Ventura drew nearer and nearer, but there was no change in the speed of the engines, no waggle of wings, nothing even to suggest they had been sighted. Some of the men, still clinging to a rapidly weakening thread of reality, lifted feeble arms into the air and waved. As the plane swept relentlessly on, the arms fell back into the sea and eyes were again shut to keep out the searing brilliance of a noonday sun.

"Look!" someone croaked. "He's seen us! He's turning around! He's coming back!"

Many refused to believe it. They would not open their eyes even when a buddy shook them and tried to get them to show some interest.

"Leave me alone," a man said. "I've got to get some sleep."

"Don't go to sleep now. This is what we've been waiting for. They've finally come for us. Look, they're dropping things out of the plane."

Chief Radioman Bill Hartman was hard at work on his newly established rescue circuit. At last the earlier messages had been acknowledged and he knew there was big excitement back at Peleliu. He began sending a string of MO's at regular intervals. MO's in the language of the Morse Code are two long dashes, a brief space, then three more long dashes. Their purpose is to enable anyone within range to tune in with a radio direction finder and get an accurate fix on the exact location of the transmitting station, which in this case was Gwinn's PV-1 Ventura.

Glancing off to the east, Lieutenant Gwinn saw a PBM with Army markings headed toward him. He needed help and he was delighted to see the plane. Maybe it would be able to land on the water and pick up some of the survivors. But the PBM pilot must not have been in the mood for rescue that day. He did not contact Gwinn but made a few quick turns around the area, dropped three rafts and continued on his westward course across the Pacific.

Back at Peleliu things were beginning to hum at the naval air station. Lieutenant Adrian Marks from the little town of Ladoga, Indiana, was on standby in the Quonset hut headquarters of VPB 23, consisting of a squadron of PBY's, the large clumsy airplanes more popularly known as Catalinas. What the PBY's lacked in speed and grace was more than made up for in moral fortitude. Since long before World War II they had been lumbering about over the oceans of the world and from Pearl Harbor until now they had been used for just about every job an aircraft could be expected to perform. They had sunk submarines by dropping depth charges affixed to the underside of their wings; they had dropped five-hundred-pound bombs on enemy ships; they had engaged in air-to-air combat with fighters; and more than once they had ignored a hail of antiaircraft fire to bore in and sink enemy ships with wing-borne torpedoes. Out of the fragments of several squadrons based on Oahu on 7 December 1941 the famed Black Cat Squadron was born. In the battle of Guadalcanal these black PBY's roamed the seas by night rescuing survivors of ship and air disaster, spotting enemy fleets and even hauling cargo when necessary.

On Thursday morning Marks had the third flight

and if things went according to schedule he would not get in the air that day. But this was not to be a normal day in more ways than one. The first flight was sent off to Ulithi to pick up some repair parts, and a short while later the second flight was called out to assist a Marine Corps landing craft in capturing some by-passed Japanese soldiers up on Babalthuap who had come out on a reef and started waving a white flag. This left Marks and his crew on the line ready for take-off when Lieutenant Wilbur Gwinn's first message finally filtered back down to VPB 23.

The general feeling was that the message had been badly garbled through encoding, transmitting, receiving and decoding. Probably when they reached the scene they would find a carrier pilot who had ditched his plane and was on a raft awaiting rescue or maybe a bomber crew. Whatever the case, at least one man's life was at stake—perhaps even several—and Marks hurried his crew into action. Survival gear, droppable rafts and other lifesaving equipment were already aboard for just such an emergency, but the PBY pilot delayed his departure for just a few minutes while he topped off his wing tanks to maximum capacity of 1250 gallons of gasoline. This would give him enough fuel to fly to the rescue location and remain there for at least twelve hours, which would give a rescue vessel ample time to arrive, and still have enough to return to home base.

If there was one thing PBY's were not noted for it was speed. Under normal cruising conditions they plodded along through the clouds at little better than a hundred knots. In a real emergency they could be urged up to something like one hundred and fifty knots, but like an old plow horse they responded best when allowed to set their own pace. Unhurried, they were dependability personified. Once in the air, Marks talked with the crew chief, Aviation Machinist's Mate Second Class Donald M. Hall, and asked for a report on the engines. Hall answered, saying that everything was normal. It reminded Marks of a famous quip handed back by a crew chief in another PBY earlier in the war when the pilot had asked for a routine report on the engines.

"Port engine running perfect. Starboard engine running perfect," the mechanic had replied. "Shut 'em both off, and she'll fly on reputation."

Such was the confidence pilot and crew alike placed in the PBY's.

Departing Peleliu at 1242, Marks headed in a northerly direction of 11 degrees 30 minutes North latitude by 133 degrees 30 minutes East longitude. When he had been in the air only a few minutes, a PV-1 Ventura passed him and the radio opened up. He recognized Lieutenant Commander George C. Atteberry's voice. Using the voice call of Gambler Leader, Atteberry asked Marks to pardon him for playing through but there was important business up ahead. He was hightailing it out across the ocean to relieve Gwinn, who was beginning to run short of fuel. Leaving Marks in his slipstream, he streaked out of sight. Marks steadied down on course and forgot about the speedy Ventura.

As soon as Lieutenant Commander Atteberry reached the scene, Lieutenant Gwinn took him on a quick survey of the area. When he was ordered to take a bow and head for home, Gwinn did not need to be told good-bye but once. He had been doing a little figuring on his fuel supply and was beginning to worry. Climbing higher into the sky, he throttled back to the most economical cruising speed and crossed his fingers. And his fears were not ungrounded. The Ventura made it back to Peleliu with only fifteen minutes of fuel left in the tanks when they touched down on the runway!

Lieutenant Marks's PBY was lumbering across the sky on course when suddenly he began to hear a loud and clear transmission coming through the earphones from Gambler Leader. Aviation Radiomen Roland A. Sheperd and Robert G. France copied the message

and after it had been decoded they handed it to
Marks.

"One hundred fifty survivors Latitude 11 degrees 54
minutes North, Longitude 133 degrees 47 minutes
East."

Something was a bit screwy, Marks thought. He was
out to aid in the rescue of a single pilot or at most a
bomber crew. Now they were giving him a different
location and were talking in numbers that sounded
more like the crew of a destroyer. Altering his heading
accordingly, he continued on and within the hour he
was able to "home in" on the Ventura that had passed
him shortly after takeoff.

On her way south toward her station at Kossol
Roads on the northern end of Babelthuap in the Palau
group, the destroyer escort *Cecil J. Doyle,* under the
command of Lieutenant Commander W. Graham
Claytor, spotted Marks's PBY and called him on voice
radio just to pass the time of day. Marks explained
that he was vectoring in on a Ventura that had spotted
an unusually large number of survivors some two hundred miles to the north.

Commander Claytor contemplated the newly acquired information and decided he would be receiving
orders eventually to proceed to the scene of rescue,
so why not turn around now and save time? For once
he outguessed the high command. An hour after
Doyle had reversed her course the radio circuits
started popping and Commander Claytor was ordered
to make all possible speed to assist in the rescue. The
trim new DDE 368 had not seen much action in the
war except for occasional shelling of Japanese concen-
trations hiding in the hills of the Palau Islands. Now
this was real grist for the mill and Commander Claytor
intended to make the most of it. He took the con and
his trim little ship raced ahead like a deerhound on a
hot scent, a long white wake fading away astern as
Doyle reached a speed of twenty-four knots. Another
insignificant brick in the strange wall of coincidences
that had dogged the *Indianapolis* since she put to sea,

but it just so happened that Captain McVay's wife was also Commander Claytor's cousin.

Radios from all areas were open now. No one knew what had happened, but it had to be something big for one hundred and fifty men to be in the water. Two cans from Ulithi—the *Madison,* commanded by Commander D. W. Todd, and the *Ralph Talbot,* under Commander W. S. Brown—were ordered to the area. The Philippine Sea Frontier command ordered the attack transport *Bassett,* the DDE *Dufilho* and the *Ringness* to the rescue scene.

In midafternoon at approximately 1550 hours Lieutenant Marks made visual and voice contact with Gambler Leader. Lieutenant Commander Atteberry was justifiably excited at what he had found when he flew into the area and relieved Gwinn. It seemed that men were everywhere, some hanging on to rafts, others lolling on floater nets and still more, many more, in life jackets.

"Hold off dropping any rafts until you have seen the big picture," Gambler Leader suggested. "Stay on my tail and I'll show you what we've found."

Down on the water Seaman Second Class Loel Dene Cox from Sydney, Texas, watched in horror as a large shark swept in and grabbed a sailor next to him. There was a scream of terror as they thrashed about for a brief moment on the surface, and then the shark was gone. The injured man was badly torn, the blood quickly drained from his body, and he was dead.

Hallucinations were running rampant among the survivors by the time the planes began wheeling over them. Two men swam up beside Seaman Loel Dene Cox and told him they were officers and had heard there was an officers' island only a short distance away. In hushed voices they explained to the young sailor that no enlisted man would be allowed ashore but that if he would guide them to the island they would put in a good word and they were sure the authorities would let him ashore.

Cox thought about this with a brain that was becoming more and more clouded. Where was this island and why did the officers think he could lead them to it? He did not know, but he wanted to get to land again so he allowed himself to be talked into the scheme. Together the three began paddling away from the group. When they had separated themselves from the others by approximately five hundred yards, Cox suddenly stopped swimming and told the two men he simply did not believe there was an island nearby, and if it existed, he did not know how to guide them to it.

"O.K." one of the men said. "If you want to, you can go back, but we're going on."

Cox spent a while trying to talk the other two out of going off in search of the island, but when it was obvious they were adamant in their decision, he left them and swam back to the main group. As luck would have it he joined up with several other men who were in the throes of a different hallucination. This time the leader thought he had a very small radio that only he could operate and he claimed he had just made contact with a submarine a short way off. They were coming to take the survivors aboard.

"But there's one thing the sub commander wants me to ask you guys," the man with the *radio* said. "Do any of you wet the bed at night?"

"I guess I do now and then," a young seaman confessed.

"Well, that lets you out," the leader replied in a compassionless voice. "You'll just have to stay here."

Any man who was supported only by a kapok jacket was in bad shape. The life jackets had offered a wonderful sense of security for the first twenty-four hours, but they were designed to keep one afloat for a maximum of forty-eight hours, and now with the time almost doubled, they afforded hardly enough buoyancy to keep a man's chin out of the water.

Little Ernest McKenzie, with all of his five feet four inches, was still holding on to life fairly well. From the first night he and his buddy, Tommy Lockwood, had formed a team. They tied themselves together at night and took turns sleeping while the other stayed on watch. The system had faltered badly on Wednesday night, however, and McKenzie drifted off by himself. He thought he had been picked up by an English ship and taken to port. One of the British sailors told him that he was free to go on liberty but explained that he would have to wear the pneumatic tube all of the time he was ashore.

Never one to take orders seriously, McKenzie agreed to the stipulation but as soon as he was ashore he slipped around behind a building and removed the life belt that had already begun to rub his chest raw. Suddenly the dream was over and McKenzie, who had survived the sinking of the *Bismarck Sea,* snapped back to reality. He was off by himself and in his delirium he had removed his belt and was managing to stay afloat only by swimming. Somewhere, it seemed a long way off, he could hear men talking and he began swimming in that direction. When he reached the group, he fortunately found an empty kapok jacket and in a little while he located his buddy, Tommy Lockwood.

"What the hell did you leave me for?" Lockwood demanded. "I had over a hundred cases of cold beer."

"Beer?" McKenzie said. "Where the hell did you get any beer?"

"Never mind where I got it," Lockwood said. "If you hadn't gone running off, you could have handed it out while I collected the money. But damn you, the guys rushed me and took it away from me and I didn't get a damn dime."

In another group a man began swimming among the men explaining that they had drifted over a submerged island where his mother ran a large resort hotel. He had been down to see her, and she had told him that there was only one vacant room but the men were welcome to come down one at a time, take a shower, and get some water, food and rest for a while. As the news spread, men began to form a long line.

Doctor Haynes asked what they were queuing up for, and the men replied in hushed tones.

"We're waiting for sack time, Doc. You have to get in line and wait your turn like the rest of us, though."

As more and more planes appeared in the sky and dropped survival gear, Cleatus Lebow watched in awe. Somebody said something about a B-29, and he let his tortured mind have full rein. That was it! The planes had spotted them, but because they were dropping crates of parts for a B-29. All they had to do was to collect the crates, open them and assemble an airplane. When it was done, all could be loaded aboard and they would fly off to the nearest land.

Lieutenant Charles McKissick watched the same objects dropping from the planes. Some came down by parachute, and others simply spilled out on the sea in big fat bundles that landed with a tremendous splash. He asked another survivor what the planes were dropping, and the man said that it was an experimental maneuver to hurry up the delivery of U.S. mail. Lieutenant McKissick swam up to one of the big inflatable rafts that bobbed about on the surface in a folded condition. All he needed to do was pull the plunger on one of the CO_2 bottles and the raft would be quickly inflated. Subconsciously he knew this, but as he fumbled about the big yellow package he heard a man shouting to him.

"You better keep your hands off of that! If you don't watch out, you'll be charged with tampering with government mail."

McKissick thought about this and reasoned that he had been given good advice. He turned and swam away from the floating bundle.

Doctor Haynes and several men near him watched the bulky objects spill out of the circling planes and swam over. In a momentary flash of clear thinking an experienced sailor grabbed the toggle attached to the CO_2 bottle and gave it a tug. Because of his weakened condition, however, nothing happened. He called for help, and with Doctor Haynes and several others working with him the seal was finally punctured and the raft blossomed on the water. Haynes crawled inside and began looking at the objects of survival. One which attracted his attention was labeled FRESH-WATER KIT.

There were now two rafts inflated and bumping together on the surface. One after another, sailors climbed aboard. Some who were more dead than alive flopped over into them and lay there like the near skeletons they were. Doctor Haynes's befuddled mind struggled with the simple and explicit instructions printed on the container for making sea water potable with chemicals, but try as he would, he could not understand them. They were just words with no meaning. While he was staring, almost unseeingly, at the printed label a sailor broke open a package and suddenly let out a yell.

"Look here, Doc, we got water!"

It was true. The raft not only supplied a desalting kit but there were cans of freshwater. Haynes opened one and tested its contents. The water was fresh. He passed it to the next man and opened another. Thirsty as the men were, they showed remarkable courage in restricting themselves to only a small sip and then passing the container on to the next outstretched hand that trembled with the excitement of that coveted swallow.

Seaman Marvin Kirkland watched as more and more planes began to fill the air above them. He was hanging on to the side of a raft in which Lieutenant Redmayne lay in an exhausted heap. Now and then he saw a parachute and wondered if men were jumping out to assist in the rescue. Then, wonder of wonders, a B-17 came slowly toward his group and all at once there was a parachute swinging about in the sky and at the bottom of the shrouds was a boat, a real boat and it was going to land nearby! Kirkland started to swim and even as he turned loose the raft, he wondered where he had found the sudden reservoir of energy. His broken teeth and swollen face had ceased to hurt except for brief periods, but as he thrashed along across the water toward the trim little boat that landed with a splash and bobbed about pertly on the water he felt the pain returning. No time to bother about a little pain now, however. The important thing was to get to that boat and climb aboard.

Reaching the side he took hold of the gunwale and hung there trying to gather enough strength to hoist himself up. When he regained his breath, Grover Carver came up beside him, but Kirkland was the first man in the boat. He and the oil-blackened Carver began examining the various containers. They were sure that among them there would be water and they desperately wanted a drink. The first thing Kirkland found, however, was a can marked hard candy. He clutched the prize in hands grown soft from the constant immersion in water. Candy, real old-fashioned Christmas candy! He stared down at it and held it close to his chest like a miser fondling a purse of coins. The candy was going to be his and his alone. It was his own personal reward for living through four horrible days and nights in the water. With a furtive glance over his shoulder, he quickly slipped the prize inside his soggy jacket.

Kirkland and Carver watched another man swimming toward the little lifeboat and shouted words of encouragement. Still wearing the life jacket he had gone all the way back down to the evaporators to retrieve after the *Indianapolis* had been torpedoed, George Horvath struggled toward the boat. When only one hundred yards away, he felt his strength failing. He stopped swimming and hung in the water breathing hard. It was then that he looked down and saw a dark object beneath him. It was coming closer and he suddenly realized it was a shark, larger than any he had previously seen. The creature rolled over on its side and the failing light of afternoon reflected back from the cotton white belly.

"Oh, God, not now!" Horvath prayed. After such a long, long time in the water and seeing so many of

his shipmates taken by sharks, was he going to suffer the same fate when he was only one hundred yards away from the protection of a boat? The big shark continued to move toward him, swimming leisurely and rolling from side to side. The creature was obviously in no hurry. He had singled out his victim and he would take his time.

"I'll bet I can outswim you," Horvath said aloud and with that he began stroking for the boat. Carver and Kirkland saw him coming and hurriedly helped him aboard. A dozen yards behind, the shark rose close to the surface, his tall dorsal fin sliced through the side of a swell and then he was gone.

There were cans of freshwater in the boat, but as more and more men came aboard it was soon exhausted.

"Look," someone called out. "Here's a kit that will turn seawater into drinking water." Like Doctor Haynes some five miles to the southwest, the men in the lifeboat tried to understand the directions, but they could not force the words to make sense.

"To hell with it!" one man suddenly babbled. "If these chemicals will take the salt out of water in this can, then it can do the same in my belly." Grabbing a handful of the crystals from one of the packets and stuffing it into his mouth, he began scooping up handfuls of seawater to wash it down. A short while later he was rolling about in the bottom of the boat heaving in agony.

Total rescue was now only hours away, but some of the men could wait no longer. Aroused from their lethargy by the sounds of low-flying planes and the shouts of their shipmates, they used up their last few ounces of strength and collapsed. Nor had the patrolling sharks let up their relentless attacks. On more than one occasion men would be in the process of pulling a survivor into a newly found lifeboat only to have him snatched from their grasp by the jaws of a shark that had suddenly closed in.

Many of the men had gone insane. A sailor watched

the excitement around him and thought the Japanese had found them and were taking them prisoner. "You dirty Japs ain't gonna take me back to your stinking island and feed me fried rats and make me walk forever like you did them guys on Bataan."

"Snap out of it, buddy," a sailor said, holding out a helping hand. "We're your friends. It's all over now. The Navy has come for us."

"Git away!" the life-jacketed sailor snarled. Suddenly he was brandishing a sheath knife. The sailor in the raft jerked back and looked at the dark red blood that welled up from the palm of his hand.

"Forget him!" another said. "There's plenty of men that *want* to come aboard."

Eight men climbed up on a newly dropped raft and for a moment sat in exhausted little heaps. Then someone discovered a small wooden keg that was full of freshwater. He twisted out the bung and took a drink.

"Water!" he said, handing the small keg to the man beside him. "Everybody have a good drink. I'm buying this afternoon."

Men who had long ago forgotten how to laugh began to chuckle. The keg passed from one pair of hands to another. Suddenly, one sailor who had not laughed snatched it from the hands of a frail seaman beside him.

"Goddamn you little son of a bitch!" The half-emptied keg fell to the bottom of the boat and a precious stream of water bubbled out. One man made a dive for it while the others watched in horror as the stronger man grabbed the youngster by the neck and forced his head over the side and down into the sea. "I'll teach you to drink more'n your share," the demented sailor raved. There was not much of a struggle. It did not take much strength to drown a man who by all rights should have been dead two days earlier.

"Let him alone!" a sailor screamed, stumbling across the raft. But by now it was to late. The emaciated body was pulled back into the raft, but he no longer needed their protection. The little crew sat in stunned silence. Death had been their companion for days and they had grown accustomed to it, but to witness murder in the hour of rescue was too much to bear.

Lieutenant Adrian Marks in his PBY and Lieutenant Commander Atteberry in his Ventura circled the survivors who were scattered out over an area that stretched nearly ten miles north and south and five miles east and west. Marks, disregarding security, sent a CW plain-language message with an "Urgent" prefix.

"Between one hundred and two hundred survivors at position reported. Need all survival equipment available while daylight holds. Many survivors without rafts. We will transmit MO's for five minutes after each half hour on emergency frequency."

More and more planes arrived on the scene and began crossing and crisscrossing the area, dropping survival equipment. If conditions had been nearly perfect there would have been enough supplies on the water by late afternoon to fill the immediate needs of most of the men. Conditions, however, were far from perfect. Some of the gear, including water containers, was ruptured or badly damaged on impact. Again, a raft or boat would fall too far away from those who needed it most. Coupled with this was the physical and mental condition of those on the surface. In a delirious moment one man explained to those around him that they were being bombed because there were so many dead men floating on the sea. The Navy thought that was the best way to clean up the litter. Fearfully they watched the objects falling from the sky and when one landed nearby they would use their waning strength trying to swim away from it.

Lieutenant Marks had no way of knowing about this, but as he made endless trips around the egg-shaped scattering of survivors one single observation became increasingly clear to him. Many of the men toward the south were swimming alone and others were so low in the water that their heads appeared as

floating coconuts. He was sure these could not last
through the night or for that matter even a few more
hours. If a ship were down there right now many could
be rescued that otherwise would be lost.

In the early days of the war the sturdy PBY had
made some rather outstanding rescues by landing in
open sea. In the overall picture, however, there had
been far too many tragic losses as brave PBY crews
threw caution to the wind and were killed in a flaming
crash or at best had to join the survivors they sought
to rescue. True, the PBY could take a rough beating
on the sea and sometimes manage to fly another day,
but its primary role was best played in open-sea rescue
by dropping survival gear and then hovering over the
spot until surface vessels could "home in" on them.

Marks mulled over the fleet order concerning the
open-sea landing of a PBY. *It shall not be attempted
except in the last extremity.* Right now he felt that he
was faced with a last extremity. Still in voice contact
with Lieutenant Commander Atteberry in the second
Ventura, Marks pressed the button on his mike and
told the superior officer he was going to attempt a
landing. He did not request permission or ask for advice. He simply stated his plan. Atteberry's reply is
not on record but those who knew the commander
feel that he secretly wished he too was in a flying boat
instead of a land-based aircraft.

The sea was not rough, but twelve-foot swells were
running and under these conditions an aircraft could
take a severe beating if the pilot misjudged his landing
altitude by as much as two or three feet. Marks was
not particularly worried. He had been sitting on the
port side of PBY cockpits for many hours since pin-
ning on his gold wings and he had a good idea of what
the old Catalinas could take in the way of rough
landings.

Informing his crew of his intentions, Marks made a
pass over an empty spot at the south end that was
free of survivors and studied the wind drift and the
fetch of the swells. Shoving the throttles ahead, he

climbed and circled. Every member of the crew took his ditching station, just in case, as once again Marks headed for the surface.

With his nose into the wind, which was out of the north at about eight knots, Marks dropped his wing-tip floats and settled down. When the sea was just beneath him, he yanked back on the yoke, putting the PBY in a power stall. A split second later the boat-like hull made violent contact with a rising swell and the plane was enveloped in a shower of foam. Once again she was off and flying. A hundred yards more there was the crest of another swell and a blast of spray. When the PBY hit the third swell the speed was killed, and the men inside were beginning to relax. The ordeal was over but there were certain things that had to be looked after right away. Here and there seams were split and water was spurting through the holes left by a few popped rivets.

When they were steady on the water, Marks turned the controls over to his copilot and stepped back into the radio compartment to have a look at the damage. It was not severe, and his crew was already at work plugging up the leaks with wads of paper while one man was busily jabbing pencils into the rivet holes.

Back at Peleliu, Marks's squadron commander had received word that an open-sea landing was being attempted, and the "old man" took off like a scalded cat. When and if that pilot returned he would be court-martialed!

Marks did not care. He had taken the bit in his mouth, effected a reasonably safe landing, and with Atteberry in the air to "see" for him, the two began functioning like a pitcher and catcher on a winning ball team.

Atteberry directed Marks to a couple of survivors swimming off by themselves and he revved up the starboard engine and taxied ahead for a few seconds. There they were—two men, both wearing jackets that were almost waterlogged. Even at this distance it was impossible to tell whether they were Americans or

Japanese. To Marks and his crew it did not matter. They were humans who needed their help. As the PBY closed in on the swimmers, airmen leaned out of the port blister and tossed them a line. The first two survivors were hauled aboard, and Marks and his crew were stunned to learn they were from the heavy cruiser USS *Indianapolis*. Marks considered passing the information to the *Doyle* but refrained for reasons of security.

Ensign Morgan F. Hensley from Arlington, Virginia, an amateur wrestler, assumed the role of pickup man on the PBY. When a survivor was in reach, he grabbed him under the armpits and lifted him over into the plane. Not a slight feat of strength, considering that Hensley was standing in a blister some two feet above the surface.

Men were quickly pulled aboard as Marks, directed by Lieutenant Atteberry, moved from first one spot to another. There was a single life ring aboard and one of the crew made a line fast to it so it could be thrown to a survivor. By dusk a plane that normally carried a crew of seven had picked up fifty-six survivors. The pickups had been stationed at safe places about the inside of the hull and on the wings.

When his fuel supply was dangerously low, Atteberry wished Marks and his crew good luck and returned to Peleliu. Among the aircraft circling and dropping equipment was another PBY manned by an army crew and flown by Lieutenant Richard C. Alcorn. As darkness began to close in, the various planes left to return to base, all, that is, except Lieutenant Alcorn. He could see Marks's plane rising and falling with the swells and taxiing about picking up the men. Except for insignia, there was no difference in an Army PBY and those that flew for the Navy. The danger of open-sea landing was just as great, and Lieutenant Alcorn hated to take the risk, but as Marks had done, he, too, felt it was his duty. With only a few minutes of light left in the sky, he went down and by luck made better contact than Marks with the swells. When he had drifted to a standstill, he found his plane was in good shape. Relieved at this piece of good luck, he quickly taxied toward a nearby survivor, and his crew picked the man up and placed him on a bunk.

Now that he was down, Alcorn found himself faced with a problem. Darkness had closed in and while he had made a mental picture of how the survivors were scattered out across the water, he knew there were numerous stragglers littering the path he would have to follow. There was the danger of running over these men if he revved up his engines and started to taxi. Deciding the risk was too great, he shut off the engines and stationed his crew in the blisters and up on the wing in hopes that they could hear someone calling.

As the night grew blacker he switched on his lights. That way, if there were any survivors nearby, they would be guided to the plane. But the plan had to be quickly abandoned as an approaching aircraft, spotting the lights and assuming it to be some kind of marker, began to spill out its cargo of survival equipment. There were no direct hits, but some very near misses convinced Alcorn it would be far safer to remain blacked out.

Lieutenant Commander W. Graham Claytor, on the bridge of the *Doyle,* had eavesdropped on the messages being transmitted between pilots Marks and Atteberry and the other rescue planes. He heard Army Lieutenant Alcorn as he vectored in on the area and made plans for an open-sea landing. As he listened, Claytor slowly became aware of the magnitude of the rescue operation he was racing toward. With the coming of darkness he tried to think of himself as a survivor out there on the water for no telling how many hours. What would he want most? he asked himself. He knew his answer would be *hope*. He called the signal bridge and told the petty officer of the watch to fire up the big twenty-four-inch carbon arc lamp and direct the beam skyward. On hearing the order

several men on the navigation bridge and down on
the signal bridge made a few murmuring protests.
Everyone knew there were Japanese submarines in
the area and the shaft of white light would be an open
invitation for a torpedo shot. But it was a calculated
risk Lieutenant Claytor felt he must take.

Lieutenant Marks and Lieutenant Alcorn saw the
white beam of light stab up into the sky and bounce
off the clouds and so did the survivors of the *Indianapolis*. Could they hold out a few more hours until that
shaft of light became a ship with solid decks and water
and medical aid? All about the sea little clusters of
men banded together, the strongest lifting the heads
of their weaker comrades and saying over and over
again, "Don't give up now. Look. See that light? It's
a ship and it will be here in a little while." Men who
were moments from death responded, and a flicker of
hope returned to minds that had grown dull with pri-
vation and despair.

"If it's a Limey ship," one spunky little seaman said,
"they'll have beer aboard and I'll tell you what I'm
gonna do. I'm gonna buy all you guys a nice cold
brew."

Someone managed a feeble chuckle, pointing out
that the generous sailor would have a hard time pay-
ing for the offered beer since he had lost all of his
clothes.

Lieutenant Marks and his crew aboard the PBY
made good psychological use of the *Doyle's* searchlight beam. Once out of the water the men had begun
to realize the pain with which they had almost learned
to live. Emaciated bodies long ago grown soft with
constant immersion felt the pressure of bones, and
saltwater ulcers stung anew in the chill of night air.
The crew of the PBY were all experienced airmen,
but they had made shambles of their plane as they
attempted to station the survivors on the wings. Everywhere feet had accidentally stepped through the fabric
and down below water was having to be pumped out
of the bilge from leaking seams that had been sprung

during landing. Early in the evening Lieutenant Marks had decided that his plane was already so badly damaged that it would never fly again, and when he saw the survivors shivering from the cold he told his crew to pop the parachute packs and use the abundance of cloth to cover the men.

As the PBY crew doled out their meager sixteen-gallon supply of freshwater and tried to make their fifty-six guests comfortable, they would frequently point to the steadily approaching *Doyle*'s searchlight and say, "Look over there, Mac. See that light? It's a ship and it will be here in a short time and then they will take you aboard and you can lie down in a real bunk. Just keep watching that light."

Ten miles off to the northeast other men saw the steady shaft of white light and to most it was the signal that their period of torture was rapidly drawing to a close. Some, like Marvin Kirkland, had climbed into a lifeboat and were able to relax for the first time in nearly eighty hours.

Scattered about the area were numerous rafts. Manning them were scores of sun-blackened men who had weathered the ordeal a little better than those who had spent the time suspended in life jackets. But they were nonetheless thirsty and equally close to delirium.

All afternoon Captain McVay and his crew of nineteen on the four rafts had watched the rescue operations. The planes were concentrated over the survivors to the south, and now McVay and his companions could only wonder if they had been overlooked. The captain decided they should make some kind of signal. Dumping a few fragments of life jackets, torn rubber life belts and other bits of scrap into a powder can, he set it burning with a ball of fire from a Very pistol. The men clung to the hope that the smile would attract the rescuers. They watched dejectedly, however, as it drifted out flat across the sea.

On Thursday afternoon Signalman Kenley Lanter, Radioman Joe Moran and the other men on the rafts with them realized they had floated far away from

their group. Time after time they caught sight of
planes wheeling and diving and they were sure the
main body of the survivors had been located, but now
they began to worry for fear they would be overlooked. Lashing two paddles together to form a jury
mast, the men hoisted a sheet of canvas and attempted
to sail back to the main group, but as night came on
they lost their sense of direction. Lanter and Moran
were kept busy watching after a sailor who had gone
out of his head and rolled off the raft time after time.

"Don't drown me," he would plead as he drifted
away. "Just throw me a jacket, and I'll take care of
myself."

Exhausted as they were, Lanter and Moran would
slip over the side and corral their charge.

"Nobody wants to drown you," Lanter explained.
"If we did, why would we keep coming back to get
you? Now sit down and be still."

After several bouts the sailor stared at Lanter for a
long moment and then relaxed. The spell was broken,
and he seemed to realize they were trying to help him.
For the first time in hours he closed his eyes and
caught a few winks of badly needed sleep.

Near midnight, with her twenty-four-inch carbon arc
lamp still reaching a long white finger of hope into
the sky, the *Doyle* arrived on the scene. The steady
MO's from the transmitter on Marks's PBY had led
Lieutenant Commander Claytor straight toward the
spot. In short order the captain and pilot were in voice
contact. Fearful that he might run down some of the
men, Claytor stopped his destroyer and let her stand
dead in the water while whaleboats went over the side.
The first intention had been to send the boats straight
to the PBY and pick up the survivors that Marks and
his crew had collected, but the first whaleboat had
hardly cleared the davits before it was coming back
with men. What were they on top of? Commander
Claytor wondered, as boats continued to deliver gaunt
men with eyes staring half seeing from sunken sockets.

What ship were these men from, and why were they in such a deplorable physical condition?

A whaleboat pulled up alongside a raft and helping hands reached down. Doctor Haynes started to talk to the rescuers, but a naked sailor beside him began shouting in a loud voice, demanding to know whether the rescue vessel had any water.

"Plenty of water," came the reply. "Come on, let me help you aboard and we'll take you to it."

The naked sailor looked at Doctor Haynes and shook his head slowly. He had been fooled before. At first everyone had said the *Indianapolis* was not going to sink, but when she did they said rescue would come on the following day and then they said it would come the next day. Now here was a man leaning over the side of a boat claiming there was plenty of drinking water aboard. Repeated disappointments burn into a man's soul. Better to have no hope at all than to be disillusioned time after time. Doctor Haynes turned away from his rescuers and talked with the emaciated sailor until he had convinced him these men were telling the truth. Slowly the sailor lifted himself to a kneeling position and joined hands with those who sought to hoist him into the safety of the whaleboat.

On board the *Doyle,* Doctor Haynes slumped to the deck, but after a few minutes he rose unsteadily to his feet and walked toward an officer. In faltering words he introduced himself, and for the first time Commander Claytor learned that the survivors whom the *Doyle* was rescuing were from the heavy cruiser *Indianapolis,* torpedoed and sunk just about ninety-six hours earlier.

It was raining now—not a deluge but a slow, steady rain that made rescue operations a little more difficult. How the men would have welcomed that rain yesterday or the day before. Marks and his PBY crew watched as a whaleboat came near. A fresh breeze had sprung up, and the boat crew exercised good seamanship in maneuvering alongside the lee blister, but try as they would they could not help accidentally ramming the PBY and holes were gouged and additional seams were split. Lieutenant Adrian Marks did not worry because he knew his plane would never fly again anyway. Men from the overcrowded hull were transferred first, and when another boat came the crew carried survivors down from the wings. After the last of the fifty-six men had been transferred into the whaleboat, Marks told one of the coxswains to come back for the PBY crew in an hour. During that time they set about the job of salvaging all usable equipment from the plane.

Whaleboats from the *Doyle* continued to work through the dark morning hours. There were no rules to govern the method used in rescuing men who had been floating in the sea this long. Coxswains and boat crews made up their own—run slowly to avoid hitting a man who might be too weak to call or get out of the way, cut the engine every three minutes and try to listen above the whistle of wind and the slap of waves. Before the night was over the boat crews had picked up thirty-six men and these, along with the fifty-six from Marks's PBY and the one on Alcorn's plane, made a total of ninety-three survivors. Most of the men were more nearly dead than alive. The *Doyle*'s crew became Florence Nightingales in white hats. They handled the survivors with all of the tenderness they would have shown newborn babies. They gave them little sips of water and carried them into the shower rooms where they cut off their few rags of clothes and washed their ulcer-covered bodies gently in an effort to remove the fuel oil. Sailors dug into their seabags and produced clean skivvies and T-shirts and then carried the men to their own bunks.

Ensign John Woolston, exhausted by the long hours trying to keep the survivors in his group from disintegrating into a savage mob, knew that he had gone beyond the limit of his endurance. Even as willing hands helped remove his clothes, he felt sure there was something wrong with him, but he had no idea that he was suffering from a case of pneumonia and that his life would hang in the balance for days to come.

Now and then a man would be lifted aboard and the crew would listen as he muttered a few incoherent words, then watch helplessly as the feeble light of life that had doggedly continued to flicker throughout the long ordeal winked out. For some reason this was harder to take than to pull a corpse out of the sea. One young sailor who had never before seen a man die broke down in grief and knelt beside the emaciated body of one who had lived only long enough to be plucked from the sea.

"We're sorry, Mac," he sobbed. "If we had've known you were out here like this we would've come sooner."

A first class gunner's mate who had seen the war from its beginning at Pearl Harbor put his right hand on the young sailor's shoulder and pulled him to his feet. But he turned his head away so the seaman would not see the moisture that welled up in his own pale blue eyes. "Don't worry no more about that one, son," he said in a husky voice. "Get below and see what you can do to help some of those men who ain't had a drink of water in days."

Ships were moving in from several directions now. The destroyers *Madison* and *Ralph Talbot* were coming across from Ulithi to the east. The destroyer transports *Ringness* and *Bassett* were speeding from the Philippine Sea Frontier, as was the destroyer escort *Dufilho*. While these vessels were converging from east and west at about the same time, the *Bassett,* under the command of Lieutenant Commander Theriault, was the first of them to begin rescue operations.

Having run blacked out for the better part of the night while approaching the scene, the *Bassett* saw the sky beam from Claytor's *Doyle,* and also lighted ship. Theriault was under orders from Commodore N. C. "Shorty" Gillette to tell him which vessel had been sunk as soon as rescue operations were begun.

The first boat over the side was commanded by En-

sign Jack Broser. Having no idea what he was coming
up against, Broser cautiously drew his .45 automatic
and slipped off the safety as the nearest raft was approached. When the men called across and told him
they were from the *Indianapolis,* the young ensign
feared a Jap trick. Scuttlebutt had it that many Japs
could talk good English and would lure their rescuers
in with soft talk and then blow the whole works to
kingdom come with a hidden grenade or bomb. Ensign
Broser was not going to be taken in so easily. He
squinted his eyes and looked at the survivors on the
raft. The beam of a flashlight revealed half a dozen
frail men. They were blackened with fuel oil and sunburned, but they did not look like Japs.

"We don't know who you are or where you've come
from," a voice called back, "but we want to get out
of this water."

Ensign Broser quickly holstered his gun. These were
no Japanese sailors. In the next five minutes the *Bassett* made her first rescue. Lieutenant Commander
Theriault briefly interrogated a few of the men and
then ordered his communication officer to send a message to Commodore Gillette, telling him that the *Bassett* was picking up survivors from the *Indianapolis.*

As the *Bassett*'s landing craft scurried about in the
water, some of the men could only lie in crumpled
heaps on rafts or hang motionless in life jackets and
wait. Others pulled off their jackets and swam toward
the small boats.

Cleatus Lebow had spent the late hours of Thursday
afternoon wondering how they were going to assemble
the B-29 from the parts being dropped by the planes.
After dark he puzzled over the lights from the *Doyle,*
unable to understand that they were coming from a
rescue vessel. Suddenly out of the darkness strong
hands were lifting him into a landing craft. When he
opened his eyes he found himself in a large, well-
lighted room with four men bending over him. Instantly a mixed-up dream began forming in his mind.
He was a bank robber and he had just stolen four

thousand dollars from the Bank of America in San Francisco. These men were trying to force him to tell them where he had hidden it. Well, that was something they could never make him do. The money was his, and it was going to stay hidden until he could go get it. He struggled, and the men began torturing him with all kinds of strange devices. Then as dreams will do, his bank-robbing nightmare evaporated, and he found himself staring up at an inverted bottle suspended by a hook over his head and connected to his arm by a long rubber tube.

"It's glucose," a hospital corpsman said in answer to his unspoken question. "You sure gave us a hard time when we were trying to start you on it. Took four of us to hold you in the sack."

The meaning of the words slowly sank in, and Lebow told the corpsman about his dream and the stolen money.

"Well, no wonder you were fighting so hard," the corpsman chuckled, and a few minutes later Lebow heard his story being related to the other three men as he drifted off into a peaceful sleep.

Loel Dene Cox was brought aboard at the same time and he, too, sank back in the luxury of sleep as sailors stretched him out on a mattress. He did not know where he was and he could not have cared less. He just knew that he was no longer in the water and it felt good to lie there and rest. Sleep came quickly, but when he awoke and attempted to turn over, his hands seemed bound to the mattress. Lifting his head he looked down. The days in the salt water had so softened his skin that it had fused to the canvas. As he struggled to free himself the flesh was torn away, and he was left with two bleeding hands.

Joseph Dronet was lifted up on deck and the first thing he asked for was a drink of water. A sailor led him to a scuttlebutt and told him to drink all he wanted. Dronet thought, *Now these guys are going to see a man do some real water drinking.* But something was wrong. He could only manage a few swallows. He tried again and again, but the liquid would not go down his throat. The sailor gently turned him away, helped him belowdecks, and eased him down into a bunk. A short while later someone brought him a half of an orange, and Dronet began squeezing the juice into his mouth. He decided it was the best food he had ever tasted.

By early morning the *Bassett* had picked up nearly all of the survivors she could handle. Lieutenant Commander Theriault ordered a count made and when it was discovered that he had one hundred and fifty aboard, he notified Leyte that he was returning.

David Thompson and several other men had climbed aboard a rubber raft that had been dropped late Thursday afternoon, and it had been a wonderful place to be during the long night. They knew rescue was coming at any minute and they allowed themselves to relax. When dawn did come, however, Thompson and the others awoke to the frightening realization that during the night their raft had been blown a long way from the rescue zone. Far off to the south they could see numerous planes gliding about like little specks in the sky and here and there could be seen puffs of smoke as ships blew their tubes.

"I think this raft has fouled us up," one of the men said. "All of those planes and ships are working way over there, and we're just going to keep on blowing across the water until we're too far away to be seen."

"They'll find us all right," Thompson said, trying hard to believe his own words.

The longer they thought about it, however, the more frightening the prospects of being overlooked became. There was a sheet of rubberized canvas in the bottom of the raft. Someone suggested that perhaps they could hold it up as a sail and get back to the main group. To those who knew even the basic fundamentals of the art of sailing it was immediately obvious that this would not work. With no mast and no means of tacking they were accomplishing nothing more than speeding up their drift when they held the canvas up to catch the morning breeze.

Resignedly they began to fold the canvas and as they were shaking out the wrinkles a lookout on the destroyer *Ralph Talbot,* under the command of Commander Winston S. Brown, caught a yellow flash in his 7×50 binoculars. Adjusting the focus of his glasses, the seaman studied the area more closely. Just a false alarm. There was nothing yellow out there—but wait, there was a dark spot that could be a survivor. He pointed it out to one of the bridge officers, and minutes later the old destroyer that had been in the thick of the Pacific war since Pearl Harbor and had been daggered by a kamikaze in the latter part of the previous April was off and running. After he was safely aboard, David Thompson wanted to find the man who had spotted them through the binoculars and thank him, but he discovered he was too exhausted to stand.

Lieutenant Commander William C. Meyer in command of the destroyer transport *Ringness* moved in close behind the *Bassett* and began picking up survivors. By midmorning on Friday the lookouts on the *Ringness* spotted rafts far off to the port. Lieutenant Commander Meyer watched the specks on the sea as his ship drew nearer and when they were alongside he counted nineteen men. All seemed in fairly good shape considering that they had spent almost five days adrift without water and with precious little food. Meyer was on the bridge when a badly sunburned and obviously weakened man walked up to him, saluted and announced that he was Captain Charles Butler McVay III, commanding officer of the CA-35.

Captain McVay gave Meyer a thumbnail sketch of the sinking and abandonment of the *Indianapolis* and then went below for water and some much-needed rest.

Late Thursday evening Giles McCoy had stood up in his raft and watched a rain squall sweeping across the sea toward him.

"Water! We're going to get some water!" he called to the others.

Some of those on the raft with him were nearly too far gone to care, but McCoy had worked swiftly. He dug out a pocket knife and split his inflatable tube. As the shower moved in and big drops began spattering down over the area Willis Gray and Felton Outland helped him hold the opened tube so that it formed a flexible trough. The rain thundered down, stinging their sunburned bodies and puddling in the improvised cistern. The men watched hungrily as the first few ounces swelled to a pint and then to a couple of quarts.

The rain was gone as quickly as it had come, but they had managed to catch some of it—real drinking water, pure and fresh out of the clouds. McCoy placed the end of the rubber tube between his parched lips while the others lifted it until a little trickle ran into his mouth. All at once he jerked his head away gagging and spitting. The inside of his mouth felt like he had eaten a green persimmon.

"We can't drink it," he sputtered.

In their haste to prepare a vessel to catch the rainwater the men had failed to notice the thin dust of white powder that coated the inside of the tube. It had been put there during the manufacture to preserve the rubber and prevent it from sticking together when the tube was not inflated. It was this that had ruined the rainwater. Reluctant to accept the fact that their precious supply was unfit to drink, two others sampled it and, like McCoy, gagged and wished they had never drawn the evil concoction into their mouths. The men slumped down in the raft and cried and soon they began passing out from exposure and dehydration.

McCoy and Felton Outland huddled together and discussed the possibilities of survival. As they looked at the unconscious sailors around them they knew their time was drawing near. Although they did not realize it, there were moments when they were both mentally deranged now. They decided that if they were going to die they should at least be clean and began trying to bathe the baked oil from their bodies. In his mind each lived over his early life and thought how he would like to go home and relive some of it and go on to a future that he knew was now coming to a close.

They kneeled in the rocking raft and prayed as darkness once again enveloped them. They were certain they would not be alive when morning came. When they raised their bowed heads they suddenly saw a brilliant light pointing skyward and bouncing off the clouds in the overcast sky. Excitedly they tried to arouse the others in the raft with them. They were going to be saved!

"That *has* to be one of our ships," McCoy insisted. "They're looking for us. They know we're here!"

As the night wore on the men eagerly watched the beacon flash. The excitement induced chills and fever, but the vision of being rescued by morning was like a shot of adrenaline and their weakened bodies found a reserve to fight back.

When Friday dawned they could see ships on the horizon and there seemed to be an abundance of aircraft in the distant sky. As the day progressed and no ship came near them, they began trying to attract the attention of the planes, but the airmen were too far away to see their signals.

"What are they doing? Why don't they come get us?" an emaciated sailor asked, his head lying on the gunwale and his sunken eyes staring at the faint outline of the ships.

No one could answer. They could only sit in a lethargic stupor and pray and search the water with dimming eyes. The suffocating heat from the sun brought on unconsciousness again for the weaker ones, but Giles McCoy and Felton Outland continued their watch, every so often standing up in the raft and waving a shirt and shouting. The rescuers had to find them soon; they had to. And then the survivors stared in disbelief at a suddenly empty sea. The ships had vanished over the horizon!

"They've gone!" Outland said. "They didn't see us."

Night was coming on, and the men knew they would not be alive in the morning even if the ships came back to search some more. To have come so close and yet been passed over—Giles McCoy and Felton Outland dropped their heads into their hands and cried. Then they heard a motor droning closer and closer. They looked up, hardly daring to believe their ears. They searched the darkening sky but could see nothing. Then low over the water came a PBY and as it passed overhead they could see men in the blisters waving their hands at them. They had been found! The plane banked, came back around, and dropped a metallic dye bomb near the raft. Then it waggled its wings, the men in the blisters waved, and the craft flew on out of sight. Joyously Felton Outland and Giles McCoy crouched in their raft with nearly a dozen other men who were barely alive and watched a ship appear on the horizon and head their way. As the vessel grew nearer they saw that it was the *Ringness,* and McCoy and Outland felt a surge of reserve strength course through their bodies.

The destroyer transport came alongside, and a deck hand heaved a monkey fist over to the raft. McCoy caught the line attached to the weighted pellet and made it fast. This was the proper thing to do, but the *Ringness* was still under way and as the line suddenly grew taut the raft began to plow under. McCoy and Outland fought to hold the bodies of seemingly lifeless survivors aboard and shouted to their rescuers to slow down. A boatswain's mate on the *Ringness* quickly appraised the situation, slipped the towline and let the raft right itself. A seaman from the ship plunged over the side, climbed aboard the raft, and quickly snugged it alongside.

McCoy, suddenly feeling his importance as a marine, decided he would not let the honor of the corps down by being assisted aboard. He waited until all of the helpless had been taken off the raft and then he made his way up the landing net to the deck. As he stepped over the life lines, he gathered himself to full height and announced in his best training station voice that he had never thought the day would come when he would want to kiss the deck of a Navy ship, but now he did. As he leaned over he suddenly became as limp as a wet sock and fell flat on his face. It felt very good to have strong young sailors pick him up and carry him down to a clean dry bunk and give him cups of water. Far back in his mouth was still the taste of the foul liquid from the pneumatic tube. Now, however, everything seemed far away.

Half a dozen fast destroyers, destroyer escorts and attack transports were closing in on the rescue area. For the most part living survivors were being picked up, but here and there the ships were finding men who had not been able to wait for them. There was one young seaman lying dead in the middle of a raft still clutching a water-stained Testament in his lifeless hand. Frequently a landing craft would come up alongside a floating jacket and find only the upper part of a man's body still afloat. Sharks had cut off the lower half.

Shortly after dawn on Friday morning Lieutenant Adrian Marks made a final inspection of his PBY and informed Lieutenant Claytor of the *Doyle* that the plane was unsalvageable. It was decided to destroy it by gunfire.

Quartermaster Robert Gause had just dropped off to sleep when the *Doyle*'s guns were opened up on the PBY and the ship began shaking and rattling. Opening his eyes he looked up at the bunk above him. *It just can't be true,* he thought. Here he had hardly been aboard long enough to dry off, and now the ship was engaged in a naval battle.

"Go on back to sleep, Mac," a hospital corpsman said. "They're just sinking the plane that picked you up yesterday afternoon."

Gause lay there for a few minutes wondering why in the world they would want to sink such a wonderful plane. Deciding the skipper must have a good reason, he sighed and went back to sleep.

By noon on Friday Lieutenant Richard C. Alcorn had transferred his survivors to the *Doyle* and made a successful takeoff and returned to base. The *Bassett,* with her one hundred fifty survivors, was on the way back to Leyte, but there were still five ships in the area with seriously wounded men aboard. Of these the *Doyle* led the list with ninety-three; the *Ringness* was next with thirty-nine; the *Ralph Talbot* had twenty-four; the *Register* had picked up an even dozen; and the *Dufilho* trailed with a single survivor. Commander D. W. Todd on the *Madison* made a quick check of the situation and during the early afternoon he sent the *Doyle* on her way to Peleliu. The *Ralph Talbot* transferred her casualties to the *Register* and the *Dufilho's* single man was put aboard the *Ringness.* The two ships carrying the remainder of the survivors continued working until well after dark and then they too turned south and followed the *Doyle's* wake.

The *Ralph Talbot* and the rapidly approaching destroyers *Helm* and *Aylwin* stayed on the job for days to come. After discharging her wounded, the *Doyle* refueled quickly and returned to the scene in the company of the destroyer escort *French.* Search patterns were laid down, and surface craft in the company of dozens of aircraft combed the area, locating and examining even the most insignificant piece of flotsam. The urgent excitement which had existed on Thursday afternoon, all that night and well into Friday was gone now. This was simply a mopping-up operation. There were no more survivors. The few who had been missed on Friday were now corpses, but for miles around there were pieces of broken life rafts, floating powder cans and an endless number of life jackets. All had to be either picked up or sunk. When the dead were found, an effort was made to identify them, and then they were buried at sea in keeping with naval tradition.

The *Bassett* reached Samar and duly discharged her one hundred fifty survivors while the other 169 were hospitalized at Peleliu late Saturday night—almost exactly six days and nights after the *Indianapolis* went down. Some were too far gone even to know they had been picked up from the sea.

Ensign John Woolston had come close to death during his last hours in the sea. When he was finally carried ashore, he was placed on the critical list, and the chart at the foot of his bed showed that he was suffering from pneumonia. For two days he lay in a state of semiconsciousness. A friend came in with a shot glass and a bottle of bourbon, but he could not arouse any interest in the young officer. When the corpsman turned the friend away, Woolston rallied briefly and asked for water, but he could only take a small swallow at a time and the medical force at Peleliu had already decided he would not be listed among the survivors. On the third day after rescue, however, he rallied. The congestion in his lungs began to clear up and shortly thereafter the junior damage control officer of the *Indianapolis* was on his way to recovery.

Assistant Master-at-Arms Granville S. Crane stayed close beside the bunk occupied by Gunner's Mate Third Class Robert Lee Shipman. They had been buddies for years, and Crane broke down and wept when a doctor stopped by and pronounced the gunner dead. To have seen his friend come so close to survival and then pass away was doubly hard on Crane. For a long while he sat beside Shipman's bed and tried to understand why help had not come a day or even a few hours earlier.

Ensign Harlan Twible managed to walk unaided into the hospital ward at Samar and as he was making his way toward a bunk he saw a familiar face.

"Captain Thompson!" he said, extending a hand that had grown thin during the past week. "Remember Midshipman Twible from Annapolis?"

Captain Thompson recognized the young ensign all right. Doctor Thompson had been in charge of "Misery Hall," the affectionate name for the dispensary at Annapolis. He asked Twible what he thought his men would best like to have, and a tub of cold beer was suggested. The order was filled on the double but those who brightened up momentarily at the sight found to their dismay that the best they could do was quaff a few ounces of the brew, put the can aside and drop off to sleep.

Ernest McKenzie had been picked up by the *Doyle* and spent a few hours in a bunk at Peleliu, but early Saturday morning he arose, pulled on a pair of pants and a shirt and walked outside to survey his new surroundings. The air was warm but not oppressively so. McKenzie looked about and saw a bicycle leaning against a Quonset hut. He straddled it and began to pedal about the island. There was a basket in front of the handlebars and with so many coconuts lying around McKenzie began to make a collection. Several times during the day he stopped by various billets and swallowed a few gulps of water and then around lunchtime he ate an egg salad sandwich. That night he finished off a plate of chow in the mess hall and took a seat at the movie. One of the doctors watched and shook his head in wonder—at death's door one day and spry as a cricket the next.

Glen Milbrodt lay in his bunk at the Navy hospital at Peleliu and reflected on his time in the service. His first day at sea had begun on 16 July. Two weeks later on 30 July he had been dumped into the sea—three weeks out of port and a third of the time spent hanging in a life jacket.

For most of the 317 men who had survived the sinking and the long ordeal in the water their fight was about over. But for some—Captain Charles Butler McVay III in particular—a new battlefront was suddenly opened and it was one that would not be secured in a week, a month or forever, for that matter.

SEVEN

≋

CONCLUSION

AT exactly fifteen and a half minutes after nine a.m. on 6 August 1945 a B-29 bearing the name *Enola Gay* piloted by Army Colonel Paul W. Tibbets flew over the Japanese industrial town of Hiroshima at a height of 31,600 feet. A switch was flipped, and one single bomb dropped from the plane's belly and exploded with a blast equivalent to 20,000 tons of TNT. The city all but evaporated, over 60,000 people were killed, 20,000 more were seriously injured and 171,000 left homeless. The *Indianapolis,* now lying at the bottom of the Pacific Ocean, with 879 of her 1196 men dead, had brought the component parts of this bomb to Tinian. Three days later a similar bomb was dropped over Nagasaki, and Japan admitted defeat.

The *Indianapolis* survivors at Samar and Peleliu heard the news and were pleased to know that their tragic voyage had played such an important part in bringing the war to an abrupt termination. Now the invasions of the Japanese home islands would not have to be carried out, and millions of American men could start thinking about doing such things as carving a turkey and decorating a Christmas tree instead of wading ashore on another hostile beach.

In keeping with Navy regulations, Admiral Chester W. Nimitz promptly ordered a Court of Inquiry to convene at Guam as soon as the survivors were well enough to be moved from their first hospital beds. This action on the Admiral's part was in no way a reflection on Captain Charles Butler McVay III. A naval tragedy had occurred, and it was necessary to get the true story on record as quickly as possible for two reasons: The understanding of the full facts might prevent the same mistakes being made in the future, and then there was the press. Throughout the war rigid censorship had allowed unpleasant stories to be securely bottled until all loose ends were tied up and the armed forces were ready to let the public be informed. Now, with Japan's surrender obviously only days off, the sheltering arm of censorship would suddenly fall away.

On the morning of 13 August the inquiry began on Guam with Vice Admiral Charles A. Lockwood, Jr., Commander Submarines Pacific, as president of the court. The court stayed in session until 20 August, during which time dozens of witnesses from Guam, Leyte and the *Indianapolis* were heard. It would be something of an understatement to say that the hearing was confused from the outset. At that stage no one knew with positive assurance exactly how the *Indianapolis* had been sunk. The general consensus was that she had been hit by Japanese torpedoes, but there was still the possibility she had struck floating mines. At the moment the biggest question was not how the cruiser had been sunk but rather why she had not been missed and reported overdue.

Just before the survivors were to leave Peleliu aboard the hospital ship *Tranquility* a touching scene transpired when Commander George C. Atteberry took Lieutenant Wilbur C. Gwinn aboard and called for attention. He made no speech. Instead, he told the survivors that he thought they might like to say hello to the man who had spotted them.

Did they! Gwinn had been somewhat reluctant to invade the privacy of the wards in the hospital ship, but the reception he received from nearly two hundred men was something he will never forget. Those in the best physical condition bounced off of their bunks and ran toward him like fans rushing a movie idol. They shook his hands and pounded him on the back and forced him to promise he would visit them when everyone was back in civilian life. Others just rolled over in their bunks and their thin bodies shook with sobs that had been long overdue. The flood of emotion was almost more than the young Navy pilot was prepared to cope with.

Another group of survivors, those being flown from Samar to Guam, were treated to quite a different experience by the pilots. They had heard the men complaining about not having been sighted sooner by the many planes that passed overhead, and on the flight that lasted nearly five hours, they invited the sailors to the cockpit in groups of twos and threes to see why they had been missed so often. It was a morning flight, and the plane was headed east.

"Look down there, lads," the pilots said. "For all we know there may be another group of survivors from another ship waiting for rescue."

The men looked through the cockpit windows. The morning sun was in their faces and below them was the polished silver mirror of the sea. For the first time they could understand why the "blind aviators" had passed them by, but even more they were made to realize the miracle of their rescue.

Another scene which will never be forgotten took place after the survivors had rendezvoused at Guam. The band was playing, and those able to walk were assembled and each man was presented with a Purple Heart medal. Then Admiral Raymond A. Spruance went to the hospital to complete the presentation. He stopped at each bedside and personally pinned the medals to pajama tops, often pausing long enough to talk with an emaciated sailor who most likely looked on an admiral as just a few steps lower than God himself. Material for poignant memories for an admiral and the men who had sailed his flagship.

The war was over, and official surrender papers were signed on the deck of the *Missouri* on 2 September 1945. Survivors of the *Indianapolis* were still on Guam, but now they had been transferred to the submarine rest camp, where the men were treated like so many kings. If a bowl of onion soup was desired for lunch, all one had to do was ask for it. If it was a two-inch T-bone it was there, waiting for dinner and cooked to exact specifications. The same was true if there was an urge for a peanut butter sandwich at midnight or a glass of cold milk at bedtime. There was a library and a recreation room with all types of games, and authorities failed to take notice of some fast and furious poker sessions. For a few who still had not lost their urge to paddle about in the salt water there was a glorious stretch of sandy beach shaded by coconut palms with sunlit waves forever curling shoreward.

Too bad the story could not have ended here. But the war was over now, and the lid of censorship had been blown away weeks ago. Newspapers carried the story, and there were people who would not accept the news of this seemingly needless tragedy without striking back. Just hating the Japanese was not enough. Someone had to be punished! Newspapers, sparked by influential people, refused to let the story die. The Navy Department and President Truman continued to receive letters. There were those who felt that it must surely have been the captain's fault. If not, why had he survived the ordeal sitting on a raft while hundreds more fought for their lives in the water, some without even a life jacket? Nothing could have been more unfair. Captain McVay had left the ship in the same way as every other man aboard, and only through the strange workings of fate did he chance upon a raft shortly after entering the water. Nor did he have any control over the happenstance that he and the other three rafts with him drifted off by themselves. Still, he *was* the captain and he had come through the ordeal alive and in better physical shape than hundreds of others. To several thousand people touched by the tragedy and those who did not know the sea and could never know the details of the sinking it just did not seem right. Such is and always will be the penalty of command.

When it was obvious the public at large would not give up, the Navy Department announced in November that Captain McVay would be court-martialed. Already, Commodore Norman C. "Shorty" Gillette, acting Commander Philippine Sea Frontier, had received a letter of reprimand as had his port director and operations officer at Tacloban in Leyte. The basic theme of these letters was that the men in charge of ship movement had used bad judgment in failing to report the nonarrival of the *Indianapolis* at Leyte on Tuesday.

Letters of reprimand and admonishment are serious in the lives of career naval men because they play an important part when promotions in rank are being considered, but such letters seldom make newspaper headlines. The public, however, quickly pricks its ears when it learns that the captain of a warship will be court-martialed. In McVay's case interest was doubled because the story of the sinking had been so much in the news. The Navy announced it would bring the enemy submarine commander who had actually sunk the ship to Washington to testify, and this unprecedented action actually tripled the interest, and the court-martial was on the front page of most newspapers. Seldom, if ever, has a Navy captain who lost his ship in time of battle been subjected to such harsh treatment. The noted naval historian, Rear Admiral Samuel Eliot Morison, likened the court-martial to the famous trial and execution of Admiral John Byng (RN) in 1757 when Byng failed to defeat the French off Minorca—a court-martial that provoked Voltaire's barbed observation: "It is found good, from time to time (in England), to kill one admiral to encourage the others."

Captain Charles Butler McVay III accepted his trial without protest, and it was a credit to his quality as a naval

officer that he did not fight back through the medium of
the press, something he could surely have done. Many
persons in responsible positions were convinced he was
being used as a whipping boy. Somebody had to be
blamed and the captain was the most convenient
scapegoat.

The trial, which began in early December of 1945,
confronted McVay with two charges: (1) hazarding his
ship's safety through failure to zigzag, and (2) failing
to issue timely orders to abandon ship. Scores of people were called to testify, many from the slim ranks
of the survivors.

Commander Mochitsura Hashimoto took the stand
and gave testimony that became a two-edged sword.
By claiming the moonlight conditions were sufficient
for him to keep the westbound cruiser in his periscope
sights for nearly six miles, he offered strong proof that
the *Indianapolis* had not been following fleet orders
to zigzag in times when the enemy might be watching.
In the same testimony, however, he discounted the
value of this practice by saying he could have sunk
the ship with the same ease had she been zigzagging.
His latter observation, however, was discounted to a
large extent, since the fleet order was still in full effect
at the time of the sinking.

McVay was quickly cleared of the charge of failing to
issue timely orders to abandon ship. Many men came
forth to testify that with the total loss of communications
there was no way for the order to be passed except by
word of mouth, and it was obvious that every effort had
been made in this direction. Coxswain Edward Keyes
told how, following bridge orders, he had run through
the ship—those parts he could reach—calling all hands
topside. There were others, too, who had heard the
order, and each gave his own personal account.

When the trial came to a close Captain McVay had
nothing to do but await the verdict. In February 1946
the court decided that he would lose one hundred
numbers in grade. Unlike Admiral Byng in eighteenth-
century England he would not be taken out and exe-

cuted, but he might as well have been so far as his professional career was concerned.

During the seemingly endless testimony one question was forever unanswered: How much faith could be placed in Mochitsura Hashimoto's assertions? He claimed he had the cruiser in view for nearly half an hour, yet throughout this time he failed to distinguish the fact that the ship was a heavy cruiser instead of a battleship. There are certain other questions concerning Hashimoto's reliability as a witness that must forever go unanswered. For example, why did the submarine crew fail to see any sign of the approximately eight hundred men who had managed to escape the sinking ship or the litter of crates, furniture, powder cans and the normal assortment of flotsam including many tons of fuel oil belched up from the ruptured ship? It may be the *I-58* never returned to the surface. To discount this, however, is the Japanese submarine commander's own admission that he did surface about an hour after the sinking. Also it is logical that had he been sure of a successful torpedo attack he would have wanted to return to the scene and have a look at the destruction.

It could be argued that Hashimoto did return to the surface as he claimed, but in the wrong spot, perhaps several miles away. This could hardly be the case, however, since he was an experienced naval officer with many years of training behind him. What was more, he had a fully competent navigator aboard.

In all probability Hashimoto's *I-58* did resurface, judging from the eyewitness accounts that some kind of ship was noticed shortly after the sinking. Perhaps the submarine lookouts did see the survivors but, fearing escort vessels were approaching the area, decided to get away from the scene. Hashimoto admitted that he departed for fear of reprisals from ships or aircraft that he thought were in company with his late enemy.

Of all questions left unanswered the most mysterious is whether the type of torpedoes used were mechanically operated or controlled by man. It is known that *I-58* carried a complement of six Kaiten pilots when she left Kure on 16 July 1945. After nearly a fortnight of patrol without contact, *I-58* met the enemy on the afternoon of the 28th at about 1400 hours. Running at periscope depth in the early afternoon, Hashimoto caught sight of a large American tanker traveling in company with a destroyer. Two Kaitens were launched, their fanatical pilots shouting the traditional "three cheers for the emperor" before departing.

To Hashimoto's disappointment the tanker disappeared over the horizon, and the destroyer was lost in a rain squall. The best he could claim were the sounds of two explosions nearly an hour later. In true Japanese fashion, the crew of *I-58* prayed for the happiness of the late Kaiten pilots in a future existence.

There were four Kaiten pilots and four suicide submarines still left aboard *I-58* when the *Indianapolis* was first sighted. Hashimoto stated he did not launch any of them on the night of 29–30 July and perhaps he told the truth. But what happened to the four remaining Kaiten pilots is a question that still exists.

After leaving the scene of the *Indianapolis* sinking, *I-58* continued on her northeast course. Two nights later she was running on the surface when a dark blot was spotted on the horizon. Hashimoto studied the approaching ship and decided it was a fat merchantman on a westbound course. He tried to close in for an attack, but the vessel outdistanced him. On 10 August, he reported that he sank two destroyers with two of his Kaitens and a large ship which he described as a "fifteen-thousand-ton seaplane carrier" with the remaining Kaitens two days later. Naval records show no such losses in the final days of the war, and there are those who wonder if perhaps Hashimoto did not use the Kaitens to sink the *Indianapolis*. It is generally accepted that only two torpedoes struck the ship. But many of the survivors have a vivid recollection of a third explosion. While there are no facts to back up the conjecture, one cannot help wondering if this third blast was not perhaps one of the Kaitens who made contact with the hull as she was slipping beneath the waves. It is known that *I-58* returned to Kure as one of the defeated enemy on 18 August 1945 with no Kaitens aboard. For Commander Mochitsura Hashimoto it was the inglorious end of an old way of life.

He had been involved in the war with the United States from the first to the last day. When he was the torpedo officer on the Japanese submarine *I-24*, one of the twenty-eight fleet-type subs accompanying the task force that attacked Pearl Harbor on 7 December, it had been his duty to see to the launching of one of the five midget submarines in the predawn hours of that fateful day. It was an experiment in naval warfare that proved a miserable failure. None of the tiny two-man subs made the slightest contribution to the surprise attack, and the one launched by Hashimoto had all but brought disgrace to the entire Japanese submarine fleet. Ensign Kazuo Sakamaki had been the officer in charge of the midget, and his crewman had been Kyoji Inagaki. Doubtless the two men had done their best, but a faulty gyrocompass had caused them to go astray while trying to find their way into the entrance to Pearl Harbor. Unable to do so they wandered around like a blind whale, bumping against one reef after another until they finally stranded on a bar near the Naval Base at Kaneohe Bay on the windward side of the island. When he realized their mission was a failure, Seaman Inagaki followed the time-honored tradition of Japanese warriors and took his own life, but Ensign Sakamaki swam ashore and was captured. Ten fanatical young men had manned the five midget subs, and nine had died gloriously for the emperor. Only Sakamaki from Hashimoto's *I-24* survived to become the first Japanese prisoner of war. After the attack, Hashimoto devoted the following three and a half years to war, and much of it had been spent under the surface as a submarine officer. He had assisted in the opening battle between Japan and the United States and wound up his career by sinking the last major warship to go down in World War II.

When Captain McVay's court-martial was finished, Commander Hashimoto was returned to Japan. In the months that followed, a few top-ranking admirals and

many newspapers were not content with the treatment
Captain McVay had received and they did not hesitate
to say so. On 23 February 1946 Secretary of the Navy
James Forrestal signed a statement to the effect that the
sentence of Captain Charles Butler McVay III had been
remitted in its entirety and he would be restored to duty.

In April of 1946 McVay was ordered to duty as
Chief of Staff and Aide to the Commandant, Eighth
Naval District in New Orleans, Louisiana. He remained at this station until his retirement on 30 June
1949 and stepped into civilian life with the expected
graveyard promotion to Rear Admiral.

The death of the USS *Arizona* with her loss of 1104
lives will perhaps forever stand as the monument to
the greatest number of lives lost on a single United
States warship. But the *Arizona* was securely anchored
at Pearl Harbor at the time of her sinking, while the
Indianapolis was at sea and in a condition of full battle readiness.

Second only to the *Indianapolis* for loss of life at
sea was the carrier *Franklin*—the ship that refused to
die. Struck by two Japanese bombs on 19 March 1945,
she suffered the staggering loss of 724 lives and 265
wounded. Refusing to give up his ship, Captain Leslie
H. Gehres and what remained of his crew fought monstrous ammunition and gasoline fires until the following morning and then sailed the torn ship back to New
York with only one stop, at Pearl Harbor.

Close to the *Franklin*'s record is that of the light
cruiser *Juneau,* sunk on 13 November 1942 in Iron
Bottom Sound off Guadalcanal. When she went down,
she carried 676 men, including the five Sullivan brothers. Only eleven survivors were rescued.

The escort carrier *Liscome Bay,* sunk by a Japanese
submarine just a year later a few miles north of Tarawa, went down with 644 dead and 272 survivors.

But standing apart from all of these because of the
number of lives lost and the long tragic wait of the
survivors for rescue, the sinking of the *Indianapolis* is
listed as the greatest open-sea disaster in the history
of the United States Navy.

AFTERWORD

by Captain William J. Toti, USN

I intend to use this afterword to update this story based on the events occurring after the 1963 publication of *Ordeal by Sea*. I must first point out that the Navy is not a single, homogeneous entity—it is a collection of individuals, each with different opinions. Some within the Navy will agree with what I write here; some will not. I have not cleared this with anyone, and I absolutely do not speak for the Navy on this matter. The opinions I am about to present are mine alone, nothing more.

One issue that isn't controversial, however, relates to a dichotomy with respect to the number of crew members rescued. Many reports list the number rescued as 316, while others say 317. Although it should not be difficult to count the number of people you pull out of the water, the discrepancy was caused by how you define who was actually rescued. One of the

first accounts was a narrative prepared by Captain
McVay as his official report to the Navy, which was
recorded on 27 September 1945, as an input to the
Court of Inquiry. Amazingly, Captain McVay freely
offered this twenty-page testimonial two days *after*
Admiral King recommended that the Secretary of the
Navy convene a court-martial. Clearly, this was a man
who felt he had nothing to hide and nothing to fear
from the court-martial.

In this report, McVay states that 316 crew members
survived. He based that number on the fact that 320
officers and enlisted men were picked up alive, where-
upon two died in Samar and two died in Palau. What
McVay didn't know at the time was that a passenger
on the ship, Captain Edwin Crouch—a classmate and
friend of McVay's who was aboard only because
McVay offered to ferry him to his next duty station—
had been counted against the number of crew members killed when in fact he was not part of the crew.
Hence, the actual number of surviving crew members
is 317, but the error in the original report has been
carried forward over the years in books and articles
too numerous to count.

Regardless of how you categorize the survivors, it
is safe to say that when the *Indy* controversy erupted
in August 1945, just after the atomic bombs had been
dropped, the American public was clearly outraged at
the loss of more than eight hundred lives in the waning days of the war. It was perfectly proper for the
Navy to convene a Court of Inquiry to investigate the
tragedy, something Admiral Chester Nimitz did on 9
August 1945, soon after Captain McVay's rescue and
return to Guam. McVay was designated an "interested
party" and afforded counsel and the opportunity to
examine witnesses and present evidence. The Court of
Inquiry placed "serious blame" on Captain McVay for
his failure to zigzag and recommended trial by general
court-martial.

As indicated by my old Academy professor, Edwin B.
Potter, Admiral Nimitz disagreed with the recommen-

dation of the court and instead issued the captain a letter of reprimand—an act that would not have received much publicity, but one that would have been nearly career ending in and of itself.

For reasons that can only be speculated, Chief of Naval Operations, Admiral Ernest King, overturned Nimitz's decision, as was his right to do, and convened a court-martial in the Washington Navy Yard in late 1945. Admiral Nimitz's letter of reprimand to Captain McVay was then withdrawn. As is routine in such matters, the Navy's Inspector General, Admiral Charles P. Snyder, also initiated an investigation that would normally have been expected to provide the foundation for any court proceedings.

In a move that had at least the appearance of impropriety, King then interceded directly with Secretary of the Navy James Forrestal to proceed with the court-martial *parallel to* the Inspector General's investigation, saying that any findings of fact could come out in court.

As the survivors like to point out, a court-martial is a criminal proceeding, not an investigatory tool. If King's concern was simply a lack of information, why didn't he allow the Inspector General to issue his report before ordering the court-martial? Whatever his true motivation, it is understandable why some survivors believe that King may not have been confident that the Inspector General's conclusions would support his predetermination to initiate the court-martial, so he ordered the court proceeding to begin with all due haste.

In anticipation of the trial, the Navy Judge Advocate General, Rear Admiral Oswald S. Colclough, was also asked to review the referral. As part of his review, he addressed other accusations and charges that had been recommended, including failure to maintain watertight integrity.

Although Colclough concluded that no other charges were supported by the evidence, his response contained the curious statement that the charges included in the initial referral were "the only ones that can be supported," as if he had been asked to explore the possibility of charging McVay with even more violations. From the survivors' point of view, this was yet another indication that the deck was stacked against them. On 29 November 1945, as Thomas Helm points out, the Secretary of the Navy referred the two charges to a general court-martial: Captain McVay suffered his vessel to be hazarded by failing to zigzag and failed to give the order to abandon ship in a timely manner. McVay's counsel, Captain John Cady, reportedly handpicked by King to defend McVay at the Court of Inquiry, was asked by McVay to represent him at the court-martial. Cady had never argued a case in court before.

The most appalling issue in the trial had to be the Navy's audacity in bringing in the commander of the submarine that sank the *Indy,* Mochitsura Hashimoto, to testify against McVay. In a matter of historic irony, much of Hashimoto's extended family had been killed by the Hiroshima bomb that *Indianapolis* delivered to Tinian, so Hashimoto had reason to believe that, when armed Americans came to his door to take him away, he wouldn't be coming back. Most of the American public saw Hashimoto not as a tragic figure caught up in events beyond his control, but as a man who was still the enemy—a prisoner of war, in fact, who was responsible for a great number of dead Americans and who should not have been brought into the country to contribute to the downfall of a brave American captain.

Although Hashimoto was brought in by the prosecution to help convict McVay, much of what he said actually helped to lessen the case against McVay since he said that zigzagging might have complicated the attack, but would not have changed the outcome. Hashimoto expressed his concern with the way the court-martial progressed in a 1999 interview, where he said:

I understand English a little bit even then, so I could see at the time I testified that the translator did not tell fully what I said. I mean it was not because of the capacity of the translator. I would say the Navy side did not accept some testimony that were inconvenient to them. . . . I was then an officer of the beaten country, you know, and alone. How could I complain strong enough? . . . At the time of the court-martial I had a feeling that it was contrived from the beginning. . . .

In the end, the court found Captain McVay guilty of the charge "Through Negligence Suffering a Vessel of the Navy to Be Hazarded."

In that Charles B. McVay, 3rd, captain, U.S. Navy, while so serving in command of USS *Indianapolis,* making passage singly, without escort, from Guam, Marianas Islands, to Leyte, Philippine Islands, through an area in which enemy submarines might be encountered, did, during good visibility after moonrise on 29 July 1945, at or about 10:30 P.M., minus nine and one-half zone time, neglect and fail to exercise proper care and attention to the safety of said vessel in that he neglected and failed, then and thereafter, to cause a zigzag course to be steered, and he, the said McVay, through said negligence, did suffer the said USS *Indianapolis* to be hazarded; the United States then being in a state of war.

The court claimed that McVay was not being convicted for any deficiency that led to the sinking of his ship. They made a strong case that the "*Indianapolis* was hazarded before she was ever detected by *I-58,* and would have been hazarded if she had never been detected by *I-58.*" In essence, McVay could have been found guilty in a court-martial even if his ship had not been sunk. This is a meaningless legal distinction, since absent the sinking there would have been no prima facie case that the vessel had been hazarded.

Put all these facts together, and it is understandable

why most of the survivors believe that Admiral King was doing all he could to tilt the scales of justice against McVay. Even Admiral Nimitz would later say to one survivor that the entire affair involving the court-martial was a mistake and should never have happened. The depth of Admiral Nimitz's disagreement was such that later, after he became CNO himself, he took the rather unusual step of publicly announcing the fact that he disagreed with the way the McVay affair had been resolved, saying that "the [Navy] department in Washington saw fit to disregard my recommendation." The great naval historian Samuel Eliot Morison, when asked about the incident, quoted Voltaire with an appropriate air of cynicism: "It is found good, from time to time, to kill one admiral to encourage the others."

When contemporary figures like Nimitz disagreed so strongly with the formal Navy position, the survivors are apt to wonder how it can be that fifty-six years later, the Navy position remains so unwavering.

In more recent times, of course, the story of the *Indianapolis* has approached legendary status. Unfortunately, the legend has in some cases overwhelmed the truth.

For example, some of McVay's proponents opine that the Navy is still involved in some sort of cover-up to hide the corporate Navy's culpability in the events that led up to McVay's court-martial. Any such notion is patently ludicrous. No one on active duty today has any stake in a court-martial decision made in 1945. None of today's decision makers has any personal capital invested in a sequence of events that occurred fifty-six years ago. It would reflect poorly on none of them if someone were to declare that Captain McVay should not have been court-martialed at the end of World War II. It is reasonable to conclude, therefore, that any contemporary declaration on the case is likely to be unbiased.

Which leads to the issue of recent reviews of this incident by the Navy. Since 1946, there have been numerous inquiries into the sinking of the USS *Indianapolis,* the resulting loss of life, and the court-martial of Captain McVay. This case was reviewed in 1975 by Senators Hartke and Eagleton, in 1992 by independent attorneys commissioned by Senator Lugar, and in 1996 by the Navy internally. Each review found that no further action could be taken to ameliorate McVay's condition. But the survivors refuse to back down.

Why? It's because the questions answered by the Navy aren't always the ones that are asked. Most reviews have looked into the legality of the conviction itself and have rightly concluded that the conviction was perfectly legal. But the survivors are less interested in whether the conviction was legal than they are with whether it was just.

The most recent review of the case was completed by a Navy lawyer, Commander (later Captain) R. D. Scott, in 1996. The study is thoroughly researched, logically sound, and I will assume, legally correct. Nevertheless, some statements in the report show a lack of professional knowledge of the naval art, weaken the overall presentation, and unfortunately lend credence to those who contend that the Navy still is engaged in shaping the argument against Captain McVay.

For example, in one of his footnotes, Commander Scott says, "The Navy has never challenged Captain McVay's uncorroborated account that he did not go down with his ship because he was swept over the side by a wave." The implication here is that it was McVay's duty to go down with his ship—a notion that is steeped in folklore but has no foundation in regulation or naval tradition.

Worse, Scott implies here that Captain McVay—a man who was awarded the Silver Star for gallantry under fire, a man who spoke freely and honestly about the fact that he had not been zigzagging at the time when he was torpedoed—was lying about something as trivial as how he found himself removed from his sinking ship. This is an implication that most of the survivors consider personally offensive, as do I. I

deeply regret that the official Navy representative in
this matter found it necessary to include that statement in his official report.

Scott also writes that existing naval-warfare publica-
tions directed commanding officers to zigzag anywhere
a threat of submarine attack existed. But by July 1945
the Imperial Navy barely existed, and the Philippine
Sea where the *Indianapolis* was sunk was thought of
as a backwater with an imperceptibly small probability
of encountering the enemy.

Much is made of the fact that McVay was given
routine warning of three submarine-contact reports in
the area within two hundred miles of his planned track
and that these reports should have caused McVay to
continue zigzagging even after visibility became obscured. But submarine sightings are a daily occurrence
in war. Inexperienced crews frequently characterized
glints on the water, flashes on the horizon, and indis-
tinct flotsam as periscopes.

In this regard, naval operations haven't really im-
proved over the past fifty-plus years. On my last deployment in 1997, while I was in command of the
submarine *Indianapolis,* we were attached for a time
to a United Kingdom battle group during the hand-
over of Hong Kong. Our flagship, HMS *Illustrious,*
frequently tasked me with conducting simulated attacks on battle-group vessels. After a few days of this,
sightings were so prevalent that my submarine was
given the call sign "Lion" in reference to the popular
movie of the moment, *The Ghost and the Darkness,*
which portrayed a turn-of-the-century African bridge
construction project that was ravaged by a single pair
of lions that seemed to be everywhere at once. My
Indianapolis was similarly sighted by sailors of that
battle group in widely dispersed locations simultaneously, a notion which they knew to be impossible but
found difficult to sort out.

It's even worse in real war. In the Falklands campaign of 1982, Britain expended over two hundred
antisubmarine weapons against a single unlocated Ar-

gentine submarine, one that remained in close proximity to Royal Navy forces for over a month without ever really being detected. Throughout history, continuing to today, the best submarine-detection sensor has been the eyeball.

In World War II, Pacific forces were working against dozens of Imperial Japanese submarines, as well as hundreds of nonexistent phantom submarines, so the ratio of false sightings was extremely high. If every ship captain reacted to every reported sighting, the fleet would have been so busy defending itself that nothing would have ever been done. That's why so much is left up to the discretion of the captain. His role is to measure benefit versus risk in a process called operational risk management, to get the most effective warrior performance from his ship at a reasonable level of risk.

It was McVay's best judgment that the risk of submarine attack was low enough that he could cruise to Leyte at a more efficient speed. It was well within his authority to make that decision. The *Indianapolis*'s routing order, which even Admiral Nimitz admitted took precedence over the other publication, gave McVay authority to zigzag "at his discretion." McVay had been zigzagging throughout the daylight hours and ordered a straight-line course only late in the evening, when the sky was obscured and visibility was poor. These facts weakened this line of reasoning so acutely that the prosecution never pursued a strategy of convicting McVay for failing to follow a lawful order.

Also in the official 1996 Navy report, Commander Scott performed a naive assessment of the *I-58*'s attack, concluding that, if the *Indy* had zigged at the time the submarine launched her torpedoes, the weapons would have missed. Notwithstanding the laws of probability that argue against this kind of fortuitous timing, combat is not a kid's game where everybody goes home after experiencing initial frustration.

Even if the *I-58* had missed with the first salvo, she

had other options at hand. She could have employed
her Kaiten suicide minisubmarines, or she could have
surfaced, repositioned, and pressed on the attack.
Many of the U.S. Navy's most successful submarine
commanders of World War II missed their initial attack but still achieved success. These men sank more
than 4,000 ships, most of which were zigzagging. Scott
exaggerates the difficulty that zigzagging would have
presented to the commander of the *I-58,* and to pro-
pose that the *Indy* would have been spared had she
zigged at time of fire weakens his overall argument.

In addition, Scott's assertion that zigzagging would
have helped save the *Indianapolis* weakens his later
statement that "whether zigzagging would have defeated submarine *I-58*'s targeting of *Indianapolis* was
not the issue at Captain McVay's court-martial." If
the efficacy of zigzagging was not the issue, then how
could failure to zigzag be considered hazarding your
vessel? And why did the Navy's advocate in this matter spend so much effort trying to show that zigzagging
would have been effective? Because he had to overcome the weight of evidence, most of which was provided during McVay's court-martial by Hashimoto
himself, as well as an experienced U.S. submarine
commander, both of whom agreed that the *Indy* would
probably have been sunk regardless of McVay's
maneuvers.

While *Indy* was provided with routine, relatively
trivial reports of submarine sightings, McVay was not
told of a more significant event: the sinking of the
USS *Underhill* by a submarine on 24 July 1945, within
two hundred miles of the *Indy*'s path. This is staff
officer malfeasance of the worst sort—certainly worse
than the decision McVay made regarding his ship's
suspension of zigzagging. Yet none of those staff officers who failed to provide this critical information
were punished.

There's another matter. It turns out that prior to
taking command of the *Indianapolis,* McVay was
chairman of the intelligence committee of the Com-

bined Chiefs of Staff—a precursor to the Joint Chiefs of Staff. That position would probably have given McVay knowledge of the fact that the U.S. Navy was breaking ULTRA codes of the Imperial Japanese Navy and routinely knew where Japanese naval vessels were operating.

If he was aware that we had this great capability, then that knowledge would undoubtedly have affected his decisions, even if he had no direct access to that information prior to his ship's final voyage. If he knew that this intelligence existed and was in the hands of the routers who sent him on his way, men who told him that they didn't expect any submarine activity—the reason they gave for denying him an escort—then in his mind this would be tantamount to them telling him: "We know where the bad guys are and you don't have to worry."

As every captain knows, you have to make decisions based on what others are *not* telling you, as well as what they are. This may have been part of the unwitting trap set for Captain McVay and his crew.

Despite the Navy's claims to the contrary, all evidence available to the survivors points to the notion that McVay was convicted for having his ship sunk. In the end, Commander Scott's assessment only served to heighten the survivors' concern that their skipper continues to receive unjust treatment at the hands of the Navy.

I opened my foreword by saying that I was reluctant to answer the survivors' call to provide my assessment. The truth is that, while Commander Scott got much of his analysis wrong, his conclusions are essentially correct, if only because he missed the real point.

There is no question that the Navy's policy for reporting ship movement in effect at the time was flawed. There is also no question that the failure to notice *Indianapolis*'s nonarrival in Leyte was directly responsible for the delay in rescuing the crew. That is why letters of reprimand punished the officers responsible for those failures. The Navy understood its culpa-

bility in this regard and changed its policy affecting
the way ship movements were reported upon comple-
tion of the investigation that followed the *Indianapolis* disaster.

When dealing with this tragedy, it is important to
separate the events that led up to the sinking from
the events that led up to the delay in rescue. These
are two separate occurrences, both tragic, but the result
of two separate strings of events that must be evalu-
ated individually.

With respect to the sinking, the question that should
be asked is, if a ship with no antisubmarine capability
is sunk by a submarine in a war zone, is the commanding officer always free from culpability?

The short answer is no. Regardless of legal wran-
gling, a commanding officer's responsibility and his accountability are absolute in matters that affect the
safety of his ship. This tenet is founded in Section
5947 of Title 10, United States Code, which states:

> All commanding officers . . . in the naval service
> are required . . . to take all necessary and proper
> measures, under the laws, regulations, and cus-
> toms of the naval service, to promote and
> safeguard . . . the physical well-being, and the
> general welfare of the officers and enlisted per-
> sons under their command or charge.

Or as Captain Larry Seaquist, USN (Ret), wrote in
"Iron Principle of Accountability Was Lost in *Iowa*
Probe," *Navy Times*, December 9, 1991:

> In the American Navy, the principle of account-
> ability for the safety of one's crew derives directly
> from our long-standing tradition of the citizen-
> soldier. The Founding Fathers explicitly rejected
> the European tradition of a professional officer
> caste that puts its own stature and survival above
> that of troops forcibly drawn from the peasantry.
> Instead in our democracy, the military leader's

authority over his troops was linked to a parallel responsibility to them as fellow citizens.

Accountability is a severe standard: the commander is responsible for everything that occurs under his command. Traditionally, the only escape clause was an act of God, an incident that no prudent commander could reasonably have foreseen. The penalties of accountable failure can be drastic: command and career cut short, sometimes by court-martial.

These factors favor the argument that a commander can and should be court-martialed for a failing that results in members of his crew being hurt or killed. Any deficiency in the ship is the captain's responsibility, even if he had no direct, causal relationship with the deficiency. This is because it is the commanding officer's responsibility—more than that, his duty—to ferret out and correct problems before they manifest in failure. If he fails at that task, there is no one to back him up.

Captain McVay was the son of an admiral, a second-generation Naval Academy graduate, and he knew this well. He even acknowledged his accountability on two separate occasions. First, after his rescue, he told *The New York Times,* "I was in command of the ship and I am responsible for its fate." Later, in his court-martial, he testified, "I know I cannot shirk the responsibility of command."

I was reminded of this linkage every time I stepped aboard my submarine, for Navy custom required my watch to pipe me aboard every day with the words "*Indianapolis,* arriving." They don't say, "Captain of the *Indianapolis* arriving." They say, "*Indianapolis,* arriving," because in naval tradition, the captain isn't merely a member of the ship's crew—he *is* the ship.

Captain McVay's ship was lost. He failed to take "all necessary measures" to protect his ship. In our system of responsibility of command, it does not matter whether that action would have been effective—

he should have tried. That is why he was found guilty. The members of the court-martial—the *jury* in civilian parlance—had no choice but to find him guilty.

So it seems that Captain McVay's conviction was legally correct. But was it just?

Remember that out of several hundred ships sunk during World War II, Captain McVay was the only commanding officer ever to be court-martialed for having his ship sunk out from under him. Was every one of those other commanding officers faultless? Did every one of them take "all necessary measures" to protect his crew? Of course not. If those sinkings were subjected to the same level of scrutiny as the sinking of the *Indy,* we probably would find some kind of failure in each event.

Why doesn't the Navy routinely court-martial commanding officers when their ships are sunk? Consider how polite society responds to the death of a child. The parents sometimes have some degree of responsibility. Perhaps he left the child home alone. She let the child play too close to the street. Or they left matches in an accessible location. The parents could have prevented the tragedy—they might even be criminally negligent—but a humane society considers the impact of the tragedy on the accused and understands that, absent the grossest kind of malfeasance, the parent has suffered enough and should not be prosecuted. This is the concept of prosecutorial discretion. So it is with the sinking of a ship. The captain almost always can be found technically guilty of some form of negligence.

Indeed, a captain's responsibility is so vast that on almost any day, on almost any ship, any one of us could walk on board and find something for which the captain could be held legally culpable. Except for the worst kind of deliberate misconduct, captains are not routinely prosecuted, because pursuing this tenet too aggressively would result in an effusion of action tailored to prevent failure, rather than to pursue success.

Captain McVay was a man who, because of the

unique and absolute nature of the responsibility of command, was culpable for the misfortune that befell his ship. There was nothing he could have done to prevent that misfortune, and he never should have been prosecuted in the first place. The lesson here is that a decision can be legally correct and still be unjust.

It is worth pointing out that McVay's jury understood this paradox, and as a result, his sentence was light. As Thomas Helm points out, McVay did not get demoted as is commonly thought, but was merely set back in line for promotion. In addition, the members of the court-martial were unanimous in recommending that the reviewing authority exercise clemency. Why? Because they knew that, but for the grace of God, any one of them might have found himself in the same position as Captain McVay.

In fact, following the court-martial, Secretary Forrestal set aside even this token punishment. Nevertheless, McVay's career was sufficiently tarnished by this front-page event that it was effectively over, so he retired in 1949 with a promotion to rear admiral, consistent with the practice of the day.

From 1945 on, McVay received hate mail every Christmas from a few persistent relatives of sailors killed on the *Indianapolis*. The support he received from fellow survivors did little to assuage his feelings of inadequacy and guilt, made worse by the fact that his conviction rendered him not only legally culpable for the death of his shipmates, but a felon as well.

After retiring from the Navy, Captain McVay took a job with an insurance firm and then a consulting firm in New Orleans. In 1961, his beloved wife, Louise—the woman who stood by his side throughout the court-martial and the vitriol that followed—died of cancer, leaving him a lonely, defeated man. Although he did remarry a year later and move to Litchfield, Connecticut, he was never again the same. On 6 November 1968, he dressed in his Navy uniform, picked up a toy figure of a sailor, walked onto his front porch,

put a handgun into his mouth, and pulled the trigger—
yet another victim of a battle that claimed too many.

Because Captain's McVay's punishment has been
set aside, the only historical vestige of the *Indianapolis*
incident is that his service record continues to reflect
the conviction. This causes him to be viewed as a
felon, and it continues to rankle the survivors, who
insist their captain should not be considered a criminal
because of an event over which he had no control.
Hence, they continue to work to get even this black
mark removed from his legacy.

Unfortunately, there is no legal authority to overturn or reverse a final court-martial conviction. Even
if the President agrees that remedial action is war-
ranted, no such action is legally available. For example,
a presidential pardon does not overturn a conviction,
but merely sets aside or mitigates the punishment im-
posed. In this case, since the Secretary of the Navy
remitted the sentence in its entirety, a pardon would
affect nothing. Finally, statutory secretarial authority
to correct records does not extend to final convictions
of courts-martial.

So the survivors, in desperation, have taken their
battle to the court of public opinion and into the halls
of Congress. As part of the fiscal 2001 defense authori-
zation bill, Congress included a nonbinding resolution,
which includes the following language:

**(B) Sense of Congress Concerning Charles Butler
McVay III**—With respect to the sinking of the
USS *Indianapolis* (CA-35) on July 30, 1945, and
the subsequent court-martial conviction of the
ship's commanding officer, Captain Charles Butler McVay III, arising from that sinking, it is the
sense of Congress—

(1) in light of the remission by the Secretary
of [the] Navy of the sentence of the court-martial
and the restoration of Captain McVay to active
duty by the Chief of Naval Operations, Fleet Admiral Chester Nimitz, that the American people

should now recognize Captain McVay's lack of culpability for the tragic loss of the USS *Indianapolis* and the lives of the men who died as a result of the sinking of that vessel; and

(2) in light of the fact that certain exculpatory information was not available to the court-martial board and that Captain McVay's conviction resulted therefrom, that Captain McVay's military record should now reflect that he is exonerated for the loss of the USS *Indianapolis* and so many of her crew.

(C) Unit Citation for Final Crew of the USS *Indianapolis*—Congress strongly encourages the Secretary of the Navy to award a Navy Unit Commendation to the USS *Indianapolis* (CA-35) and her final crew.

Although this action by Congress was significant, the survivors still haven't achieved satisfaction because our Constitution does not allow matters such as court convictions to be overturned by Congress—that's left to the judicial branch. Nor does it allow Congress to modify a serviceman's record of service—that's the responsibility of the Executive Branch. In the end, since none of the other two branches of government followed Congress's advice on this matter, the resolution didn't change anything. The survivors still work toward their goal, and they work with an intensity that reveals the fact that they know their time is limited.

I fulfill my obligation to the survivors by reporting that, in my opinion, since the failure to zigzag had no direct effect on the outcome of this horrendous event, Captain McVay should never have been prosecuted for hazarding his vessel. Nevertheless, once the decision was made to prosecute, the jury had no choice but to find McVay guilty of the suffering his vessel to be hazarded since he failed to take "all necessary measures" to protect his ship.

For those who would have preferred a black-and-white response, I apologize, but sometimes life is not conducive to black-and-white answers.

For those who feel let down by the fact that I have not found evidence to cleanly exonerate Captain McVay, I again apologize if this failure is due to any weakness on my part. I hasten to point out that none of this lessens in any way the heroic nature of the survivors' sacrifice.

It is also clear to me that the years of pressure they've put on the Navy has paid off in ways they might never have imagined. The recent USS *Cole* tragedy is evidence of this. There are many who said the captain of the *Cole* also failed to take "all necessary measures" to protect his crew, in that he did not do some of the things that were required of him, like manning fire hoses to fend off small boats. Rather than admonishing that captain publicly and quickly, our present Chief of Naval Operations has looked at the case and said, sure, the captain might not have done everything right. But even if he did, would that have changed the outcome of the disaster? Our top admiral has decided it wouldn't, and as a result, the *Cole*'s captain will not suffer the same fate as Captain McVay.

So the Navy does get it.

I believe that all the *Indy* survivors are asking for at this point is someone to tell them that it wasn't their fault their ship was sunk and they spent five days in the water, losing over eight hundred of their shipmates in the interim. That's all they've been asking for the past fifty-six years. By punishing Captain McVay and nobody else, even bringing the enemy captain in to testify against him, the Navy took a stand that said only McVay was to blame for his sinking.

That's a position they refuse to tolerate. It was not the crew's fault their ship was sunk. They will not go gently into that good night.

Every two years, the survivors hold a reunion in the city of Indianapolis during the month of August, usually on the anniversary of their rescue. Since their last reunion in 1999 thirteen survivors have died, leaving just 124 alive as of this writing. Most of those say they will attend the 2001 reunion, but at this point we're losing about two to three a month, so who knows how many will really attend? A few say they will refuse to die until their cause is won, and I darn near believe them. Charitable organizations have begun "sponsor a survivor" initiatives, which help the survivors defray the cost of traveling to these reunions.

The saddest thing of all is that as the publicity of this incident has risen in recent times, so has the presence of those who would take advantage of these men for their own personal gain. Sharks fed on them in the water, and since their rescue, a different kind of shark has continued to victimize them, with various entities profiting at their expense, both politically and financially. Unfortunately, and largely as a result of these profiteers, divisions have developed among this once united crew over who can best tell their story. Even the original tragedy had not generated fissures like these. This has been a development that heaps travesty on top of tragedy.

In the end, what we are still left with is the wonderment of their rescue. The fact that these men were found at all—even after five days of waiting—remains absolutely incredible. No one has expressed this amazement better than Adrian Marks, the brave pilot who landed his PBY on the open sea in order to save lives.

After the war, Mr. Marks left the Navy to become a small-town lawyer. When asked, he would travel to VFW halls and other gatherings of men to describe the wonderment of it all. On more than one occasion, he spoke to gatherings of survivors, men who owed him everything. And although he died a few years ago, his words still resonate in the minds of those who had the delight of hearing his rich description of one night in the South Pacific.

I have recorded some of Mr. Marks's words here so they might be remembered:

I have known you through a balmy tropic night of fear.

I suppose that through the years, which have so swiftly run, I have recalled some portion of the day when our fates crossed nearly ten thousand times. But the memories that would surface in my retrospection are not of horror, not of blackness, not of fear. I think of little things, of things as small as courage, honor, and a simple honesty. Things so small and yet so great that they form the cornerstone of our society.

When I think of these little things, I am humbled by the thought that I have seen true greatness in my time. Some of my reflections have been so startling, as to make me think of miracles. Sometimes I believe we are living in a world of miracles. Things that would have been thought of as unimaginable by our forefathers are now everyday experiences. We sit in our living rooms and watch events transpire half a world away. We bounce our messages off artificial moons in the sky. The computer that sits alongside my desk is a never-ending source of astounding revelations to me. These miracles I have come to accept, even understand. But there is one miracle that is beyond all of my powers of understanding. It is the miracle that you are here today and not with your shipmates at the bottom of the sea.

What were the chances that you would be found? They were so minute as to be unbelievable. I flew many air-sea rescue missions where I searched for men who would be deliberately placed in the water to test various survival techniques. It was axiomatic that you could never find a lone man floating in the ocean. He could only be seen if he had some sort of survival aid. . . .

But you had none of these aids. You were simply out there, unknown and unseen. Floating in a dull gray life jacket which blended into the color of the water.

A man's head is about six inches wide by about nine inches tall. If a pilot is flying a search mission such as Wilbur Gwinn was flying, at about ten thousand feet looking down at an angle of thirty degrees, what will he see? He will be looking down at an angle, at the water about four miles ahead. The span of his vision will be about five miles. He will see twenty square miles at a glance. How apparent will be the head of a man floating? It will look as big as the diameter of a cross section of human hair seen endwise across the room. It will be lost in the countless waves and whitecaps of the ocean. He simply won't be seen.

Even if the pilot knew that somewhere out there a man was swimming, how could he search? I turn to my computer. There are 6,080 feet in a nautical mile. There are 36,966,400 square feet in one square mile. Three-quarters of a billion square feet in one twenty-square-mile glance. And a floating man will occupy less than one square foot of that space.

A search mission went out over six hundred miles. The aircrew was supposed to make a visual search of ten miles on each side of this track. A radar search such as Wilbur Gwinn was making would be much wider.

I type these figures into my computer. Six hundred miles by twenty miles, twelve thousand square miles on each pass, and it would take five passes to visually search a hundred-mile strip. Multiply these figures, the computer overloads and goes into scientific notation. It can only write the figure in terms of exponents, and the very first exponent goes to the twelfth power.

Even the national debt starts to look small.

A pilot and his aircrew normally look out at an angle at the water. They search the water for ships and the sky for aircraft. And the pilot won't see a man in the water unless he looks right straight down on him. The only way a pilot can

look straight down is to conduct a very steep turn
or execute a dive-bombing maneuver. What pilot
would do a silly thing like that in the forlorn
stretch of ocean where you were swimming?

What were the chances of that? What were the
chances that Wilbur Gwinn would fly a course
that would take him directly over you? What
were the chances that his radio antenna would
break while he was out on this mission? What
were the chances that he would open his bomb
bay door and look down momentarily? And what
were the chances that he would look straight
down at one of you? You didn't have a chance
in a million.

I know that most of you prayed a lot, and I
know that some of you feel that it made a difference. Wilbur Gwinn is a wonderful man and a
fine pilot. He never said that he heard a voice
speak to him. But was there an unseen hand upon
his shoulder? Did he find you by pure chance?
The odds against it were one in a million—more
than that—one in a billion! Somehow he was chosen as the instrument to overcome these astro-
nomical odds. Wilbur Gwinn looked down at the
split second that would become one of the great
moments of history. . . .

I have seen greatness. And I have been compelled by the evidence of my own eyes to believe
in miracles.

It is already too late for Captain McVay to know
that the battle being fought on his behalf may one day
be won. The survivors endured one of the most terrible ordeals in human history. We were at war, and in
war the nation calls upon its finest to perform greatly,
and sometimes to suffer greatly, in defense of free-
dom. Now they wonder if any one of them will be
around to see how the final chapter of this tale will
be written.

What should we do about the *Indianapolis*?

We should celebrate the ship—she served us nobly, keeping her crew well and safe in dangerous times for nearly the entire war. My submarine crew tried to do this. We took pride in the knowledge that our ship carried the name of such a glorious vessel. That is why during our last deployment we were proud to travel the same seas steamed during the cruiser's final days— Okinawa, Tinian, Guam, and the Philippine Sea, where we conducted a ceremony and laid a wreath in her honor.

I'll never forget standing on the deck of my boat at the site of the sinking. When you're standing on the deck of a submarine, you are only a few feet above the surface of the sea. On that day, waves were washing over the deck and filling our shoes in a scene that reminded me of the closing shot of *In Harm's Way*. Looking out on the ocean, I was able to get some sense of how it must have felt for them with nothing in sight.

At that moment a single thought gripped me.

In a few moments, my *Indianapolis* would, like her predecessor, also slip silently beneath the surface, but would do so by design and for an altogether different purpose. When it did, we would again be on patrol, just as the cruiser whose name our sub bore is still on patrol. As we took our station beneath the sea, we would recall in silent tribute the faithful service of those *Indianapolis* sailors who went before us. May we never forget their sacrifice.

It saddens me to realize that today the colors of the United States no longer fly over a ship named *Indianapolis*. Perhaps one day that will be rectified.

For today, let us be inspired by the presence of the remaining survivors. We should rejoice in service well rendered, and in peace well maintained, and that ships like mine can be put to rest with solace rather than with violence. Our achievements were built on the shoulders of their sacrifice.

And to my friends, the survivors of that proud ship, USS *Indianapolis* (CA-35), I say finally, I am honored by your service. I am forever in your debt. I am eternally grateful for all the inspiration you have given me all these years.

In the end, the image that lingers with me is the vision of Mochitsura Hashimoto, the captain of the *I-58*, returning home from testifying at the court-martial of an American hero, Captain Charles Butler McVay III. Hashimoto returned home laden with armloads of gifts provided by the American government. Upon Hashimoto's departure, the Navy released to the press a statement (dated 12 December 1945) that described Hashimoto as having had a "pleasant visit." He left the Navy shortly thereafter, first becoming a merchant harbor pilot and then later a Shinto priest. He lived to a ripe old age of ninety-one and died a peaceful death on 25 October 2000. Before he died, he wrote a letter to Senator John Warner that said, "I do not understand why Captain McVay was court-martialed. I do not understand why he was convicted . . . because I would have been able to launch a successful torpedo attack against his ship whether it had been zigzagging or not. . . . Our peoples have forgiven each other for that terrible war and its consequences. Perhaps it is time your peoples forgave Captain McVay for the humiliation of his unjust conviction."

Captain McVay, in contrast—a man who earned a Silver Star for valor and a Purple Heart for wounds received in battle—died on a lonely, sullen, gray day, a death suffered at his own hand, feeling unloved and unforgiven by the country that he gave so much.

It seems that we sometimes treat our enemies better than we do ourselves.

APPENDIX

USS *INDIANAPOLIS* (CA-35) FINAL SAILING LIST

30 JULY 1945

Abbott, George Stanley, S1c — Dead
Acosta, Charles Mack, MM3c — Dead
Adams, Leo Harry, S2c — Wounded
Adams, Pat L., S2c — Dead
Adorante, Dante W., S2c — Dead
Akines, William Roy, S2c — Wounded
Albright, Charles Erskine, Jr., Cox (T) — Dead
Allard, Vincent Jerome, QM3c (T) — Wounded
Allen, Paul Franklin, S1c — Dead
Allmaras, Harold Dean, F2c — Dead
Altschuler, Allan Harvey, S2c (RdM) — Wounded
Alvey, Edward Suites, Jr., AerM2c — Dead
Amick, Homer Irvin, S2c — Dead
Andersen, Lawrence Joseph, SKD2c — Dead
Anderson, Vincent U., BM1c — Dead
Anderson, Erick T., S2c — Wounded

Anderson, Leonard Ole, MM3c (T)	Dead
Anderson, Richard Lew, F2c	Dead
Anderson, Sam G., S2c	Dead
Andrews, William Robert, S2c	Wounded
Annis, James Bernard, Jr., CEM	Dead
Anthony, Harold Robert, PhM3c	Dead
Antonie, Charels J., F2c	Dead
Anunti, John Melvin, M2c (T)	Wounded
Armenta, Lorenzo, SC2c (T)	Dead
Armistead, John H., S2c	Wounded
Arnold, Carl Lloyd, S1c	Dead
Ashford, Chester Windell, WT2c	Dead
Ashford, John "T," Jr., ART3c	Wounded
Atkinson, "J" "P", Cox	Dead
Aull, Joseph Harry, S2c	Dead
Ault, William Frazier, S2c (RdM)	Wounded
Ayotte, Lester James, S2c	Dead
Backus, Thomas Hawkins, Lieut. (jg)	Dead
Baker, Daniel Albert, S2c	Dead
Baker, Frederick Harold, S2c (RdM)	Dead
Baker, William Marvin, Jr., EM2c (T)	Dead
Baldridge, Clovis Roger, EM1c	Wounded
Ball, Emmet Edwin, S2c	Dead
Ballard, Courtney Jackson, SSMB3c	Dead
Barenthin, Leonard William, S1c (FC)	Dead
Barker, Robert Craig, Jr., RT1c, USNR	Dead
Barksdale, Thomas Leon, FCO3c	Dead
Barnes, Paul Clayton, F2c	Dead
Barnes, Willard Merlin, MM1c	Dead
Barra, Raymond James, CGM (AA) (T)	Dead
Barrett, James, B., S2c	Dead
Barry, Charles, Lieut. (jg)	Dead
Barto, Lloyd Peter, S1c	Wounded
Barton, George Stewart, Y3c (T)	Dead
Bateman, Bernard Byron, F2c (WT)	Wounded
Batenhorst, Wilfred John, MM3c	Dead
Batson, Eugene Clifford, S2c (RdM)	Dead
Batten, Robert Edmon, S1c (GM)	Dead
Batts, Edward Daniel, StM1c	Dead
Beane, James Albert, F2c	Wounded

Beaty, Donald Lee, S1c	Wounded
Becker, Myron Melvin, WT2c (T)	Dead
Beddington, Charles Earnest, S1c	Dead
Bedsted, Leo A. K., F1c (MoMM)	Dead
Beister, Richard James, WT3c (T)	Dead
Belcher, James R., S1c (RM)	Wounded
Bell, Maurice Glenn, S1c	Wounded
Bennett, Dean Randall, HA1c	Dead
Bennett, Ernest Franklin, B3c (T)	Dead
Bennett, Toney Wade, St3c (T)	Dead
Benning, Harry, S1c	Dead
Benton, Clarence Upton, CFC (AA)	Wounded
Bernacil, Concepcion Peralta, FC3c	Wounded
Berry, Joseph, Jr., StM1c	Dead
Berry, William Henry, St3c (T)	Dead
Beukema, Kenneth Jay, S2c	Dead
Beuschlein, Joseph Carl, S2c	Dead
Biddison, Charles Lawrence, S1c	Dead
Billings, Robert Burton, Ensign	Dead
Billingsley, Robert Frederick, GM3c (T)	Dead
Bilz, Robert Eugene, S2c	Dead
Bishop, Arthur, Jr., S2c	Dead
Bitonti, Louis Peter, S1c	Wounded
Blackwell, Fermon Malichi, SSML3c (T)	Dead
Blanthorn, Bryan, S1c (GM)	Wounded
Blum, Donald Joseph, Ensign	Wounded
Boege, Raynard Richard, S2c	Dead
Bogan, Jack Roberts, RM1c	Dead
Bollinger, Richard Howard, S1c	Dead
Booth, Sherman Chester, S1c	Wounded
Borton, Herbert Elton, SCB2c (T)	Dead
Boss, Herbert George, S2c	Dead
Bott, Wilbur Melvin, S2c	Dead
Bowles, Eldridge Wayne, S1c	Dead
Bowman, Charles Edward, TC1c	Dead
Boyd, Troy Howard, GM3c	Dead
Bradley, William Hearn, S2c	Dead
Brake, John, Jr., S2c	Dead
Brandt, Russell Lee, F2c	Wounded
Braun, Neal Frederick, S2c	Dead

Bray, Harold John, Jr., S2c	Wounded
Brice, "R" "V", S2c	Dead
Bridge, Wayne Aron, S2c	Dead
Bright, Chester Lee, S2c	Dead
Briley, Harold Vinton, MaM3c (T)	Dead
Brinker, David A., Pfc *(Marine)*	Dead
Brooks, Ulysess Ray, CWT (AA) (T)	Dead
Brophy, Thomas D'Arcy, Jr., Ensign	Dead
Brown, Edward Augustus, WT3c	Dead
Brown, Edward Joseph, S1c	Wounded
Brown, Orlo N., Pfc *(Marine)*	Dead
Bruce, Russell William, S2c	Dead
Brule, Maurice Joseph, S2c	Dead
Brundige, Robert Henry, S1c (GM)	Wounded
Bruneau, Charles Albino, GM3c	Dead
Buckett, Victor Robert, Y2c (T)	Wounded
Budish, David, S2c	Dead
Bullard, John Kennith, S1c (SF)	Wounded
Bunai, Robert Peter, SM1c (T)	Wounded
Bunn, Horace G., S2c	Dead
Burdorf, Wilbert John, Cox	Wounded
Burkhartsmeier, Anton Tony, S1c	Dead
Burkholtz, Frank, Jr., EM3c (T)	Dead
Burleson, Martin LaFayette, S1c	Dead
Burrs, John William, S1c	Dead
Burt, William George Allan, QM3c (T)	Dead
Burton, Curtis Henry, S2c	Wounded
Bush, John Richard, Pvt. *(Marine)*	Dead
Bushong, John Richard, GM3c (T)	Dead
Cadwallader, John Julian, RT3c	Dead
Cain, Alfred Brown, RT3c	Dead
Cairo, William George, BUG1c	Dead
Call, James Edward, RM3c (T)	Dead
Cameron, John Watson, GM2c (T)	Dead
Camp, Garrison, StM2c	Dead
Campana, Paul, RdM3c	Dead
Campbell, Hamer Edward, Jr., GM3c (T)	Wounded
Campbell, Louis Dean, S1c	Wounded
Campbell, Wayland Dee, SF3c	Dead
Candalino, Paul Louis, Lieut. (jg)	Dead

Cantrell, Billy George, F2c	Dead
Carnell, Lois Wayne, S2c	Dead
Carpenter, Willard Adolphus, SM3c	Dead
Carr, Harry Leroy, S2c	Dead
Carroll, Gregory Krichbaum, S1c (FC)	Dead
Carroll, Rachel Walker, Cox (T)	Dead
Carson, Clifford, F1c (WT)	Dead
Carstensen, Richard, S2c	Dead
Carter, Grover Clifford, S2c	Wounded
Carter, Lindsey Linvill, S2c	Wounded
Carter, Loyd George, Cox (T)	Wounded
Carver, Grover Cleveland, S1c	Wounded
Cassidy, John Curron, S1c (RM)	Wounded
Castaldo, Patrick Peter, GM2c	Dead
Castiaux, Ray Vernon, S2c	Dead
Casto, William Harrison, S1c	Dead
Cavil, Robert Ralph, MM2c	Dead
Cavitt, Clinton Columbus, WT3c (T)	Dead
Celaya, Adolfo Valdo, F2c	Wounded
Centazzo, Frank Joseph, SM3c	Wounded
Chamness, John Desel, S2c	Wounded
Chandler, Lloyd Nyle, S2c	Dead
Chart, Joseph, EM3c (T)	Dead
Christian, Lewis Enock, Jr., Elec. (Warrant Officer)	Dead
Clark, Eugene, CK3c (T)	Dead
Clark, Orsen, S2c	Wounded
Clements, Harold Preston, S2c	Dead
Clinton, George William, S1c	Wounded
Clinton, Leland Jack, Lieut. (jg)	Dead
Cobb, William Lester, MoMM3c	Dead
Cole, Walter Henry, CRM (AA)	Dead
Coleman, Cedric Foster, Lt. Comdr. (CD) USNR	Dead
Coleman, Robert Edward, F2c	Wounded
Collier, Charles Rives, RM2c	Wounded
Collins, James, StM1c	Dead
Colvin, Frankie Lee, SSMT2c (T)	Dead
Condon, Berna Theodore, RdM1c	Dead
Connelly, David Fallon, Ensign	Dead

Conrad, James Patrick, EM3c (T)	Dead
Conser, Donald Lynn, SC2c	Dead
Consiglio, Joseph William, FC2c	Dead
Conway, Thomas Michael, Lieut.	Dead
Cook, Floyd Edward, SF3c	Dead
Cooper, Dale, Jr., F2c	Dead
Copeland, Willard James, S2c	Dead
Costner, Homer Jackson, Cox	Wounded
Countryman, Robert Earl, S2c	Dead
Cowen, Donald Rodney, FC3c	Wounded
Cox, Alford Edward, GM3c	Dead
Cox, Loel Dene, S2c	Wounded
Crabb, Donald Calvin, RM2c	Dead
Crane, Granville Shaw, Jr., MM3c	Wounded
Crews, Hugh Coachman, Lieut. (jg)	Dead
Crites, Orval "D", WR1c (T)	Dead
Cromling, Charles J. Jr., Sgt. *(Marine)*	Dead
Crouch, Edwin Mason, Capt. *(Passenger)*	Dead
Crum, Charles Junior, S2c	Dead
Cruz, Jose Santos, CCK (AA) (T)	Dead
Curtis, Edwin Eugene, CTC (T)	Dead
Dagenhart, Charles Romeo, Jr., PhM2c	Dead
Dale, Elwood Richard, F1c (B)	Dead
Daniel, Harold William, CBM (AA) (T)	Wounded
Daniello, Anthony Gene, S1c (SM)	Dead
Davis, James Clark, RM3c (T)	Dead
Davis, Kenneth Graham, F1c	Dead
Davis, Stanley Gilbert, Lieut. (jg)	Dead
Davis, Thomas Edward, SM2c	Dead
Davis, William H., Pfc *(Marine)*	Dead
Day, Richard Raymond, Jr., S2c	Dead
Dean, John Thomas, Jr., S2c (RdM)	Dead
DeBernardi, Louie, BM1c (T)	Wounded
DeFoor, Walton, RdM3c (T)	Dead
DeMars, Edgar Joseph, CBM (AA) (T)	Dead
DeMent, Dayle Pershing, S1c	Dead
Denney, Lloyd, Jr., S2c	Dead
Dewing, Ralph Otto, S1c (FG)	Wounded
Dezelske, William Bruce, MM2c	Wounded
Dimond, John Nelson, S2c	Dead

Dollins, Paul, RM2c	Dead
Donald, Lyle Herbert, EM1c	Dead
Doney, William Junior, F2c	Dead
Donnor, Clarence W., RT2c	Wounded
Dorman, William Burns, S1c	Dead
Dornetto, Frank Paul, WT1c (T)	Dead
Doss, James Monroe, S2c	Dead
Doucette, Roland Ordean, S2c	Dead
Douglas, Gene Dale, F2c	Wounded
Dove, Bessil Raymond, SKD2c	Dead
Dowdy, Lowell Steven, ChCarp.	Dead
Drane, James Anthony, GM3c	Dead
Drayton, William Harry, EM2c (T)	Wounded
Driscoll, David Lowell, Lieut. (jg)	Dead
Dronet, Joseph "E" "J", S2c	Wounded
Drummond, James Joseph, F2c	Dead
Drury, Richard Eugene, S2c	Dead
Dryden, William Howard, MM1c (T)	Wounded
Dufraine, Delbert Elmer, F1c (MM)	Dead
Dunbar, Jess Lee, F2c	Dead
Dupeck, Albert, Jr., Pfc *(Marine)*	Dead
Durand, Ralph Joseph, Jr., S2c	Dead
Dycus, Donald, S2c	Dead
Eakins, Morris Bradford, F2c (WT)	Dead
Eames, Paul Harford, Jr., Ensign	Dead
Eastman, Chester Steve, S2c	Dead
Eck, Harold Adam, S2c	Wounded
Eddinger, John William, S1c	Dead
Eddy, Richard LeRoy, RM3c (T)	Dead
Edwards, Alwyn Curtis, F2c	Dead
Edwards, Roland James, BM1c (T)	Dead
E'Golf, Harold Wesley, S2c (RdM)	Dead
Elliott, Harry William, S2c	Dead
Elliott, Kenneth Albert, S1c	Dead
Emery, William F., S1c	Dead
Emsley, William Joseph, S1c	Dead
Engelsman, Ralph, S2c	Dead
Epperson, Ewell, S1c	Dead
Epperson, George Lensey, S1c	Dead
Erickson, Theodore Mentzer, S2c	Wounded

Ernst, Robert Carl, F2c	Dead
Erwin, Louis Harold, Cox	Wounded
Ethier, Eugene Edwin, EM3c	Wounded
Eubanks, James Harold, S1c (I)	Dead
Evans, Arthur Jerome, PhM2c	Dead
Evans, Claudus, GM3c	Wounded
Everett, Charles Norman EM2c (T)	Dead
Evers, Lawrence Lee, CMM (AA) (T)	Dead
Eyet, Donald Archie, S1c	Dead
Fantasia, Frank Alfred, F2c (WT)	Dead
Farber, Sheldon Lee, S2c (RdM)	Dead
Farley, James William, S1c	Dead
Farmer, Archie Calvin, Cox	Wounded
Farris, Eugene Francis, S1c (RM)	Wounded
Fasthorse, Vincent, S2c	Dead
Feakes, Fred Atkinson, AOM1c	Wounded
Fedorski, Nicholas Walter, S1c	Wounded
Feeney, Paul Ross, S2c (RM)	Dead
Felts, Donald "J", BM1c	Wounded
Ferguson, Albert Edward, CMM (AA) (T)	Wounded
Ferguson, Russell Myers, RT3c (T)	Dead
Figgins, Harley Dean, WT2c (T)	Dead
Firestone, Kenneth Francis, FC2c (T)	Dead
Firmin, John Alden Homer, S2c	Dead
Fitting, Johnny Wayne, GM1c (T)	Wounded
Flaten, Harold James, WT2c (T)	Wounded
Fleischauer, Donald William, S1c	Dead
Fleshman, Vernon Leslie, S2c	Dead
Flynn, James Madison, Jr., S1c (FCO)	Dead
Flynn, Joseph Ambrose, Comdr.	Dead
Foell, Cecil Duane, Ensign	Dead
Fortin, Verlin Leverre, WT3c	Wounded
Foster, Verne Elmer, F2c	Wounded
Fox, William Henry, Jr., F2c	Wounded
François, Norbert Edward, F1c (MM)	Wounded
Frank, Rudolph Anthony, S2c	Dead
Franklin, Jack Ray, RdM3c	Dead
Freeze, Howard Bruce, Lieut. (jg)	Dead
French, Douglas Orrin, FG3c	Dead
French, Jimmy Junior, QM3c	Dead

Fritz, Leonard Albert, MM3c (T)	Dead
Frontino, Vincent Fred, MoMM3c	Dead
Frorath, Donald Henry, S2c	Dead
Fuchs, Herman Ferdinand, Mach.	Dead
Fuller, Arnold Ambrose, F2c	Dead
Fulton, William Clarence, CRM (AA) (T)	Dead
Funkhouser, Robert Morris, ART2c	Wounded
Gabrillo, Juan, S2c	Wounded
Gaither, Forest Maylon, FC2c (T)	Dead
Galante, Angelo, S2c	Wounded
Galbraith, Norman Scott, MM2c	Wounded
Gardner, Roscoe Wallace, F2c	Wounded
Gardner, Russell Thomas, F2c	Dead
Garner, Glenn Richard, MM2c	Dead
Gause, Robert Pritchard, QM1c	Wounded
Gause, Rubin Conley, Jr., Ensign	Dead
Gemza, Rudolph Arnold, FCO3c (T)	Wounded
George, Gabriel Vincent, MM3c	Wounded
Gerncross, Frederick Joseph, Jr., Ensign	Dead
Gettleman, Robert Alfred, S2c (RdM)	Wounded
Gibson, Buck Warren, S1c	Wounded
Gibson, Curtis Woodrow, S2c	Dead
Gibson, Genola Francis, LM3c (T)	Dead
Gilbert, Warren, Jr., S1c (I)	Dead
Gilcrease, James, S2c	Wounded
Gill, Paul Edward, WT2c (T)	Dead
Gilmore, Wilbur Albert, S2c (I)	Dead
Gismondi, Michael Vincent, S1c	Dead
Gladd, Millard, Jr., MM2c	Wounded
Glaub, Francis Anthony, GM2c	Dead
Glenn, Jay Rollin, AMM3c	Wounded
Glovka, Erwin Samuel, S2c	Dead
Godfrey, Marle Roy, RM3c (T)	Dead
Goeckel, Ernest Stanley, Lieut. (jg)	Dead
Goff, Thomas Guy, S1c	Wounded
Golden, Curry, StM1c	Dead
Golden, James LaVonne, S1c (I)	Dead
Gonzales, Ray Adam, S2c	Dead
Gooch, William LeRoy, F2c	Wounded
Good, Robert Kenneth, MM3c (T)	Dead

Goodwin, Oliver Albert, CRT (AA) (T)	Dead
Gore, Leonard Franklin, S2c	Dead
Gorecki, Joseph Walter, SK3c	Dead
Gottmann, Paul James, S2c	Dead
Gove, Carroll Lansing, S2c	Dead
Gray, Willis Leroy, S1c	Wounded
Greathouse, Bud "R", S1c	Dead
Green, Robert Urban, S2c	Dead
Green, Tolbert, Jr., S1c	Wounded
Greene, Samuel Gile, S1c	Dead
Greenlee, Charles Ians, S2c	Wounded
Greenwald, Jacob, First Sgt. *(Marine)*	Wounded
Greer, Bob Eugene, S2c	Dead
Gregory, Garland Glen, F1c	Dead
Greif, Matthias Daniel, WT3c (T)	Dead
Gries, Richard Charles, F2c	Dead
Griest, Frank David, GM3c (T)	Dead
Griffin, Jackie Dale, S1c	Dead
Griffith, Robert Lee, S2c	Wounded
Griffiths, Leonard Sylvester, S2c	Dead
Griggs, Donald Ray, F1c	Dead
Grimes, David Elimer, S2c	Dead
Grimes, James Francis, S2c	Dead
Grimm, Loren E., Pfc *(Marine)*	Dead
Groce, Floyd Vernon, RdM2c	Dead
Groch, John Thomas, MM3c (T)	Dead
Guenther, Morgan Edward, EM3c	Dead
Guerrero, John Gomez, S1c	Dead
Guillot, Murphy Umbroise, F1c (EM)	Dead
Guye, Ralph Lee, Jr., QM3c (T)	Dead
Guyon, Harold Louis, F1c (WT)	Dead
Haberman, Bernard, S2c	Dead
Haduch, John Martin, S1c	Dead
Hale, Robert Baldwin, Lieut.	Dead
Hale, William Franklin, S2c	Dead
Hall, Pressie, F1c	Dead
Halloran, Edward George, MM3c	Dead
Ham, Saul Anthony, Cox (T)	Dead
Hambo, William Perrin, PhM3c	Dead
Hammen, Robert, PhoM3c	Dead

Hamrick, James Junior, S2c	Dead
Hancock, Thomas A., Pfc *(Marine)*	Dead
Hancock, William Allen, GM3c	Dead
Hankinson, Clarence Winfield, F2c	Dead
Hansen, Henry, S2c	Dead
Hanson, Harley Clarence, Mach.	Wounded
Harland, George Alfred, S2c	Dead
Harp, Charlie Hardin, S1c	Dead
Harper, Vasco, StM1c	Dead
Harrell, Edgar A., Corp. *(Marine)*	Wounded
Harris, James Davis, F2c	Dead
Harris, Willard Eugene, F2c	Dead
Harrison, Cecil Manly, ChGun.	Wounded
Harrison, Frederick Elliott, S2c (QM)	Dead
Harrison, James McLaurin, S1c	Dead
Hart, Fred Junior, RT2c	Wounded
Hartrick, Willie Boomer, MM1c	Dead
Hatfield, Willie, S2c	Wounded
Haubrich, Cloud David, S2c	Dead
Hauser, Jack Isaac, Sk2c	Dead
Havener, Harlan Carl, F2c	Wounded
Havins, Otha Alton, Y3c	Wounded
Hayes, Charles David, Lt. Comdr.	Dead
Hayles, Felix, Ck3c (T)	Dead
Haynes, Lewis Leavitt, Lt. Comdr.	Wounded
Haynes, Robert Albert, Lieut.	Dead
Haynes, William Alexander, S1c (GM)	Dead
Heerdt, Raymond Edward, F2c	Dead
Heggie, William Arnold, RdM3c (T)	Dead
Heinz, Richard Anthony, HA1c	Dead
Heller, John, S2c	Wounded
Heller, Robert Jacob, Jr., S2c	Dead
Helscher, Ralph John, S1c	Dead
Helt, Jack Edward, F2c	Dead
Henderson, Ralph Lewis, S1c	Dead
Hendron, James Raymond, Jr., F2c	Dead
Henry, Earl O'Dell, Lt. Comdr.	Dead
Hensch, Erwin Frederick, Lieut.	Wounded
Hensley, Clifford, SSMB2c	Dead
Herbert, Jack Erwin, BM1c	Dead

Herndon, Duane, S2c	Dead
Hershberger, Clarence Lamar, S1c (FC)	Wounded
Herstine, James Franklin, Ensign	Dead
Hickey, Harry Todd, RM3c (T)	Dead
Hicks, Clarence, S1c (SC)	Dead
Hiebert, Lloyd Henry, CM1c	Dead
Hill, Clarence Max, CWT (T)	Dead
Hill, Joe Walker, StM1c	Dead
Hill, Nelson Page, Jr., Lieut.	Dead
Hill, Richard Norman, Ensign	Dead
Hind, Lyle Lewis, S2c	Wounded
Hines, Lionel Gordon, WT1c	Dead
Hinken, John Richard, Jr., F2c	Wounded
Hobbs, Melvin Dow, S1c	Dead
Hodge, Howard Henry, RM2c	Wounded
Hodgins, Lester Byron, S2c	Dead
Hodshire, John William, S2c	Dead
Hoerres, George Joseph, S2c	Dead
Holden, Punciano Aledia, St1c	Dead
Holland, John F., Jr., Pfc *(Marine)*	Dead
Hollingsworth, Jimmie Lee, StM2c	Dead
Holloway, Andrew Jackson, S2c	Dead
Holloway, Ralph Harris, Cox (T)	Dead
Hoogerwerf, John, Jr., F1c (MoMM)	Dead
Hoopes, Gordon Herbert, S2c	Wounded
Hopper, Prentice William, S1c	Dead
Hopper, Roy Lee, AM1c	Dead
Horner, Duward Richard, Gunner	Wounded
Horr, Wesley Alan, F2c	Dead
Horrigan, John Gerard, F1c	Dead
Horvath, George John, F1c (MoMM)	Wounded
Hoskins, William Orson, Y3c	Wounded
Houck, Richard Eugene, EM3c (T)	Wounded
Houston, Robert Garvis, F1c	Dead
Houston, William Howard, PhM2c	Dead
Hov, Donald Anthony, S1c (RM)	Dead
Howison, John Donald, Ensign	Wounded
Hubbard, Gordon R., Pfc *(Marine)*	Dead
Hubbard, Leland R., Pfc *(Marine)*	Dead
Hubeli, Joseph Francis, S2c	Wounded

Huebner, Harry Helmut, S1c (CM)   Dead
Hughes, Lawrence Edwin, F2c (WT)   Dead
Hughes, Max M., Pfc *(Marine)*   Wounded
Hughes, Robert Alexander, FC3c   Dead
Hughes, William Edward, SSML2c (T)   Dead
Humphrey, Maynard Lee, S2c   Dead
Hunter, Arthur Riles, Jr., QM1c   Dead
Huntley, Virgil Clair, CshClk.   Dead
Hupka, Clarence Elmer, Bkr1c (T)   Wounded
Hurley, Woodrow, GM2c   Wounded
Hurst, Robert Huntley, Lieut.   Dead
Hurt, James Edward, S2c   Dead
Hutchison, Merle Byron, S2c   Dead
Igou, Floyd, Jr., RM2c   Dead
Izor, Walter Eugene, F1c   Dead
Jackson, Henry, StM1c   Dead
Jacob, Melvin C., Pfc *(Marine)*   Wounded
Jacquemot, Joseph Alexander, S2c   Wounded
Jadloski, George Kenneth, S2c   Dead
Jakubisin, Joseph Sylvester, S2c   Dead
James, Woodie Eugene, Cox (T)   Wounded
Janney, Johns Hopkins, Comdr.   Dead
Jarvis, James Kenneth, AM3c   Wounded
Jeffers, Wallace Mansfield, Cox (T)   Dead
Jenney, Charles Irvin, Lieut.   Dead
Jensen, Chris Alstrum, S2c   Dead
Jensen, Eugene Wenzel, S2c   Wounded
Jewell, Floyd Raymond, SKV1c   Dead
Johnson, Bernard John, S2c   Dead
Johnson, Elwood Wilbur, S2c   Dead
Johnson, George Glen, S2c   Dead
Johnson, Harold Bernard, S1c   Dead
Johnson, Sidney Bryant, S1c (FC)   Dead
Johnson, Walter Marion, Jr., S1c   Dead
Johnson, William Albert, S1c   Wounded
Johnston, Earl Rankin, BM2c (T)   Dead
Johnston, Lewis Eugene, S1c (RM)   Dead
Johnston, Ray Frances, MM1c   Dead
Johnston, Scott Albert, F2c   Dead
Jones, Clinton LeRoy, Cox   Wounded

Jones, George Edward, S2c	Dead
Jones, Jim, S2c	Dead
Jones, Kenneth Malcolm, F1c (MoMM)	Dead
Jones, Sidney, S1c	Wounded
Jones, Stanley Fairwick, S2c	Dead
Jordan, Henry, StM2c	Dead
Jordon, Thomas Hardin, S2c	Dead
Josey, Clifford Odell, S2c	Dead
Jump, David Allen, Ensign	Dead
Jurgensmeyer, Alfred Joseph, S2c	Dead
Jurkiewicz, Raymond Stanley, S1c	Wounded
Justice, Robert Eugene, S2c	Wounded
Karpal, Daniel Larence, BM1c	Dead
Karter, Leo Clement, Jr., S2c	Dead
Kasten, Stanley Otto, HA1c	Dead
Katsikas, Gust Constantine, S1c	Wounded
Kawa, Raymond Philip, SK3c	Dead
Kazmierski, Walter, S1c	Wounded
Keeney, Robert Allan, Ensign	Dead
Kees, Shelous Eugene, FM2c	Wounded
Keith, Everett Edward, S1c	Dead
Kelly, Albert Raymond, S2c	Dead
Kemp, David Poole, Jr., SC3c (T)	Wounded
Kenly, Oliver Wesley, RdM3c	Wounded
Kennedy, Andrew Jackson, Jr., S2c	Dead
Kennedy, Robert Arthur, S1c (Y)	Dead
Kenny, Francis Joseph Patrick, S2c	Dead
Kenworthy, Glenn W., Corp. *(Marine)*	Dead
Kephart, Paul, S1c	Dead
Kerby, Deo Earl, S1c	Wounded
Kern, Harry Gilbert, S1c	Dead
Key, S. T., FM2c	Dead
Keyes, Edward Hiram, Cox	Wounded
Kight, Audy Carl, S1c	Dead
Kilgore, Archie Clinton, F2c	Dead
Killman, Robert Eugene, GM3c	Dead
Kinard, Nolan Dave, S1c	Dead
Kincaid, Joseph Ercel, FC2c (T)	Dead
King. A. C., S1c (Y)	Wounded
King, Clarence, Jr., StM2c	Dead

King, James Thomas, S1c   Dead
King, Richard Eugene, S2c   Dead
King, Robert Harold, S2c   Dead
Kinnaman, Robert Leroy, S2c   Dead
Kinzle, Raymond Arthur, Bkr2c (T)   Wounded
Kirby, Harry, S1c   Dead
Kirchner, John H., Pvt. *(Marine)*   Dead
Kirk, James Roy, SC3c   Dead
Kirkland, Marvin Foulk, S2c   Wounded
Kirkman, Walter William, SF1c   Dead
Kiselica, Joseph Frederick, AMM2c   Wounded
Kittoe, James William, F2c   Wounded
Klappa, Ralph Donald, S2c   Wounded
Klaus, Joseph Frank, S1c   Wounded
Klein, Raymond James, S1c   Dead
Klein, Thiel Joseph, SK3c   Dead
Knernschield, Andrew Nick, S1c   Dead
Knoll, Paul Edward, Cox (T)   Dead
Knot, Elbern Louis, S1c (FC)   Dead
Knudtson, Raymond Arthur, S1c   Dead
Knupke, Richard Roland, MM3c (T)   Dead
Koch, Edward Chris, F1c (EM)   Wounded
Koegler, Albert, S1c   Dead
Koegler, William, SC3c   Dead
Kolakowski, Ceslaus, SM3c (T)   Dead
Kollinger, Robert Eugene, S1c   Dead
Konesny, John Mathew, S1c   Dead
Koopman, Walter Frederick, F2c   Dead
Koppang, Raymond Irwin, Lieut. (jg)   Dead
Kouski, Fred, GM3c   Dead
Kovalick, George Richard, S2c   Dead
Koziara, George, S2c   Wounded
Kozik, Raymond, S1c   Dead
Krawitz, Harry Joseph, MM3c   Dead
Kreis, Clifford Eddie, S1c   Wounded
Kron, Herman Edward, Jr., GM3c   Dead
Kronenberger, William Maurice, GM3c   Dead
Krueger, Dale Frank, F2c   Wounded
Krueger, Norman Frederick, S2c   Wounded
Kruse, Darwin Glen, S2c   Dead

Krzyzewski, John Michael, S2c   Dead
Kuhn, Clair Joseph, S1c   Dead
Kulovitz, Raymond Joseph, S2c   Dead
Kurlick, George Robert, S1c   Wounded
Kuryla, Michael Nicholas, Jr., Cox   Wounded
Kusiak, Alfred Meciuston, S2c   Dead
Kwiatkowski, Marion Joseph, S2c   Dead
Labuda, Arthur Al, QM3c (T)   Dead
La Fontaine, Paul Sylvester, S1c   Dead
Lakatos, Emil Joseph, MM3c (T)   Dead
Lake, Murl Christy, S1c   Dead
Lamb, Robert Clyde, FM3c (T)   Dead
Lambert, Leonard Francis, S1c   Dead
Landon, William Wallace, Jr., FCO2c   Dead
Lane, Ralph, CMM (AA) (T)   Wounded
Lanter, Kenley Mackendree, S1c (SM)   Wounded
La Paglia, Carlos, GM2c (T)   Wounded
La Parl, Lawrence Edward, Jr., S2c   Dead
Lapczynski, Edward William, S1c   Dead
Larsen, Harlan D., Pfc *(Marine)*   Dead
Larsen, Melvin Robert, S2c   Dead
Latigue, Jackson, StM1c   Dead
Latimer, Billy Franklin, S1c (RM)   Dead
Latzer, Solomon, S2c (I)   Dead
Laughlin, Fain Heskett, SK3c (T)   Dead
Laws, George Edward, S1c   Wounded
Leathers, William Ben, MM3c   Dead
Lebaron, Robert Walter, S2c   Dead
Lebow, Cleatus Archie, FCO3c   Wounded
Leenerman, Arthur Louis, RdM3c (T)   Wounded
Lees, Henry W., Pfc *(Marine)*   Dead
Leluika, Paul Peter, S2c   Dead
Lestina, Francis Joseph, S1c   Dead
Letizia, Vizencio, S2c   Dead
Letz, Wilbert Joseph, SK1c   Dead
Levalley, William Delbert, EM2c   Dead
Leventon, Mervin Charles, MM2c   Dead
Le Vieux, John Joseph, F2c   Dead
Lewellen, Thomas Edgar, S2c   Dead
Lewis, James Robert, F2c   Dead

Lewis, John Robert, GM3c (T)   Dead
Linden, Charles Gerald, WT2c (T)   Dead
Lindsay, Norman Lee, SF3c (T)   Dead
Link, George Charles, S1c   Dead
Linn, Roy, S1c   Dead
Linville, Cecil Harrison, SF2c   Dead
Linville, Harry Junior, S1c   Dead
Lippert, Robert George, S1c   Dead
Lipski, Stanley Walter, Comdr.   Dead
Little, Frank Edward, MM2c   Dead
Livermore, Raymond Irving, S2c   Dead
Lloyd, John Francis, WT2c   Dead
Loch, Edwin Peter, S1c   Dead
Lockwood, Thomas Homer, S2c   Wounded
Loeffler, Paul Eugene, Jr., S2c   Dead
Loftis, James Bryant, Jr., S1c   Wounded
Loftus, Ralph Dennis, F2c   Dead
Lohr, Leo William, S1c   Dead
Lombardi, Ralph, S1c   Dead
Long, Joseph William, S1c   Dead
Longwell, Donald Jack, S1c   Dead
Lopetz, Sam, S1c   Wounded
Lopez, Daniel Balterzar, F2c   Wounded
Lorenc, Edward Richard, S2c   Dead
Lucas, Robert Andrew, S2c   Wounded
Lucca, Frank John, F2c   Wounded
Luhman, Emerson David, MM3c (T)   Dead
Lundgren, Albert Davis, S1c (FCO)   Dead
Luttrull, Claud Ancil, Cox (T)   Dead
Lutz, Charles Herbert, S1c   Dead
Maas, Melvin Adolph, S1c (SF)   Wounded
Mabee, Kenneth Charles, F2c   Dead
Mace, Harold A., S2c   Wounded
MacFarland, Keith Irving, Lieut. (jg) Dead
Machado, Clarence James, WT2c (T)   Dead
Mack, Donald Flemming, Bug1c   Wounded
Maday, Anthony Francis, AMM1c   Wounded
Madigan, Harry Francis, BM2c   Dead
Magdics, Steve, Jr., F2c   Dead
Magray, Duwain Frederick, S2c   Dead

Makaroff, Chester John, S1c	Wounded
Makoeski, Robert Thomas, CWT (AA)	Dead
Maldonado, Salvador, Bkr3c	Wounded
Malena, Joseph John, Jr., GM2c (T)	Wounded
Malone, Cecil Edward, S2c	Dead
Malone, Elvin C., S1c	Dead
Malone, Michael Leo, Jr., Lieut. (jg)	Dead
Malski, Joseph John, S1c	Wounded
Maness, Charles Franklin, F2c	Dead
Mankin, Howard James, GM3c (T)	Dead
Mann, Clifford Eugene, S1c	Dead
Mansker, LaVoice, S2c	Dead
Mantz, Keith Hubert, S1c	Dead
Marciulaitis, Charles, S1c	Dead
Marple, Paul Thomas, Ensign	Dead
Marrmann, Frederick Henry, WT1c	Dead
Marshall, John Lucas, WT2c	Dead
Marshall, Robert Wallace, S2c	Dead
Martin, Albert, S2c	Dead
Martin, Everett Gilliland, S1c	Dead
Marttila, Howard W., Pvt. *(Marine)*	Dead
Massier, George Arcade, S1c	Dead
Mastrecola, Michael Martin, S2c	Dead
Matheson, Richard Robert, PhM3c (T)	Dead
Mathulla, John, S1c (FCO)	Wounded
Mauntel, Paul John, S2c	Dead
Maxwell, Farrell Jacob, S1c	Wounded
McBride, Ronald Gene, S1c	Dead
McBryde, Frank Eugene, S2c	Dead
McCall, Donald Clifton, S2c	Wounded
McClain, Raymond Bryant, BM2c (T)	Wounded
McClary, Lester Earl, S2c	Dead
McClure, David LeRoy, EM2c (T)	Dead
McComb, Everett Albert, F1c	Dead
McCord, Edward Franklin, Jr., EM3c (T)	Dead
McCorkle, Ray Ralph, S1c	Dead
McCormick, Earl William, MoMM2c (T)	Dead
McCoskey, Paul Franklin, S1c (RdM)	Dead
McCoy, Giles G., Pfc *(Marine)*	Wounded
McCoy, John Seybold, Jr., M2c (T)	Dead

McCrory, Millard Virgil, Jr., F1c   Wounded
McDaniel, Johnny Alfred, S1c   Dead
McDonald, Franklin Gilreath, Jr., F2c   Dead
McDonner, David Pious, Jr., F1c (EM)   Dead
McDowell, Robert Earl, S1c (SM)   Dead
McElroy, Clarence Ernest, S1c (GM)   Wounded
McFall, Walter Eugene, S2c   Wounded
McFee, Carl Snyder, SC1c (T)   Dead
McGinnis, Paul Wendle, SM3c (T)   Wounded
McGinty, John Matthew, S1c   Dead
McGuiggan, Robert Melvin, S1c   Wounded
McGuire, Denis, S2c   Dead
McGuirk, Philip Arthur, Lieut. (jg)   Dead
McHenry, Loren Charles, Jr., S1c (RM)   Wounded
McHone, Ollie, F1c   Dead
McKee, George Edward, Jr., S1c   Dead
McKenna, Michael Joseph, S1c   Dead
McKenzie, Ernest Eugene, S1c   Wounded
McKinson, Francis Moore, Y3c   Dead
McKissick, Charles Brite, Lieut. (jg)   Wounded
McKlin, Henry Theodore, S1c   Wounded
McLain, Patrick Joseph, S2c   Wounded
McLean, Douglas Bruce, EM3c (T)   Dead
McNabb, Thomas, Jr., F2c   Dead
McNickle, Arthur Samuel, F1c   Dead
McQuitty, Roy Edward, Cox (T)   Dead
McVay, Charles Butler, III, Capt.   Wounded
McVay, Richard Calvin, S2c   Wounded
Meade, Sidney Howard, S1c   Dead
Mehlbaum, Raymond Aloysius, S1c (SC)   Dead
Meier, Harold Edward, S2c   Dead
Melichar, Charles Harry, EM3c (T)   Dead
Melvin, Carl Lavern, F1c (FM)   Dead
Mencheff, Manual Angel, S2c   Dead
Meredith, Charles Everett, S1c   Wounded
Mergler, Charles Marlen, RdM2c (T)   Dead
Messenger, Leonard J., Pfc *(Marine)*   Dead
Mestas, Nestor A., WT3c   Wounded
Metcalf, David William, GM3c (T)   Dead
Meyer, Charles Thomas, S2c   Wounded

Michael, Bertrand Franklin, Bkr3c (T)	Dead
Michael, Elmer Orion, S1c	Dead
Michno, Arthur Richard, S2c	Dead
Mikeska, Willie Wodrew, S2c	Dead
Mikolayek, Joseph, Cox (T)	Wounded
Milbrodt, Glen LaVerne, S2c	Wounded
Miles, Theodore Kerr, Lieut.	Dead
Miller, Artie Ronald, GM2c (T)	Dead
Miller, George Edwin, F1c (MM)	Dead
Miller, Glenn Evert, S2c	Dead
Miller, Samuel George, Jr., FC3c (T)	Dead
Miller, Walter Raymond, S2c	Dead
Miller, Walter William, B1c (T)	Dead
Miller, Wilbur Harold, CMM (T)	Dead
Mills, William Harry, EM3c (T)	Dead
Miner, Herbert Jay, RT2c	Wounded
Minor, Richard Leon, S1c	Dead
Minor, Robert Warren, S2c	Dead
Mirich, Wally Mayo, S1c	Dead
Mirrs, Carl Emerson, S2c	Dead
Miskowiec, Theodore Francis, S1c	Dead
Mitchell, James Edward, S2c	Wounded
Mitchell, James Hamilton, Jr., Sk1c	Dead
Mitchell, Kenneth Earl, S1c	Wounded
Mitchell, Norval Jerry, Jr., S2c	Wounded
Mitchell, Paul Boone, FC3c (T)	Dead
Mitchell, Winston Cooper, S1c (FC)	Dead
Mittler, Peter John, Jr., GM3c	Dead
Mixon, Malcom Lois, GM2c (T)	Dead
Mlady, Clarence Charles, S1c	Wounded
Modesitt, Carl Elsworth, S2c	Wounded
Modisher, Melvin Wayne, Lieut. (jg)	Wounded
Moncrief, Mack Daniel, S2c	Dead
Monks, Robert Bruce, GM3c (T)	Dead
Montoya, Frank Edward, S1c	Dead
Moore, Donald George, S2c	Dead
Moore, Elbert, S2c	Dead
Moore, Harley Edward, S1c	Dead
Moore, Kyle Campbell, Lt. Comdr.	Dead
Moore, Wyatt Patton, Bkr1c	Dead

Moran, Joseph John, RM1c (T)   Wounded
Morgan, Eugene Stanley, BM2c   Wounded
Morgan, Glenn Grover, Bgmstr3c (T)   Wounded
Morgan, Lewis E., S2c   Dead
Morgan, Telford Frank, Ensign   Dead
Morris, Albert Oliver, S1c   Wounded
Morse, Kendall Harold, Lieut. (jg)   Dead
Morton, Charles Wesley, S2c   Dead
Morton, Marion Ellis, SK2c (T)   Dead
Moseley, Morgan Millard, Sc1c (T)   Wounded
Moulton, Charles Calvin, S2c   Dead
Mowrey, Ted Eugene, S1c   Wounded
Moynelo, Harold Clifton, Jr., Ensign   Dead
Mroszak, Francis Alfred, S2c   Dead
Muldon, John James, MM1c   Wounded
Mulvey, William Robert, BM1c (T)   Wounded
Munson, Bryan C., Pfc *(Marine)*   Dead
Murillo, Sammy, S2c   Dead
Murphy, Allen, S2c   Dead
Murphy, Charles T., Pfc *(Marine)*   Dead
Murphy, Paul James, FC3c   Wounded
Musarra, Joe, S1c   Dead
Myers, Charles Lee, Jr., S2c   Dead
Myers, Glen Alan, MM2c   Dead
Myers, H. B., F2c   Wounded
Nabers, Neal Adrian, S2c   Dead
Naspini, Joseph Anthony, F2c (WT)   Wounded
Neal, Charles Keith, S2c   Dead
Neal, George M., S2c   Dead
Neal, William F., Pfc *(Marine)*   Dead
Neale, Harlan Benjamin, S2c   Dead
Nelsen, Edward John, GM1c   Wounded
Nelson, Frank Howard, S2c   Wounded
Neu, Hugh Herbert, S2c   Dead
Neubauer, Richard, S2c   Dead
Neuman, Jerome Clifford, F1c   Dead
Neville, Bobby Gene, S2c   Dead
Newcomer, Lewis Willard, MM3c   Dead
Newell, James Thomas, EM1c   Dead
Newhall, James Franklin, S1c (GM)   Wounded

Nichols, James Clearence, S2c	Wounded
Nichols, Joseph Lawrence, BM2c (T)	Dead
Nichols, Paul Virgil, MM3c	Dead
Nielsen, Carl Aage Chor, Jr., F1c	Dead
Nieto, Baltazar Portales, GM3c	Dead
Nightingale, William Oliver, MM1c	Wounded
Miskanen, John Hubert, F2c	Dead
Nixon, Daniel Merrill, S2c	Wounded
Norberg, James Arthur, CBM	Wounded
Norman, Theodore Raymond, GM2c	Dead
Nowak, George Joseph, F2c	Dead
Nugent, William Gerald, S2c	Dead
Nunley, James Preston, F1c	Dead
Nunley, Troy Audie, S2c	Wounded
Nutt, Raymond Albert, S2c	Dead
Nuttall, Alexander Carlyle, S1c	Wounded
Obledo, Mike Guerra, S2c	Wounded
O'Brien, Arthur Joseph, S2c	Dead
O'Callaghan, Del Roger, WT2c	Dead
Ochoa, Ernest, FC3c (T)	Dead
O'Donnell, James Edward, WT3c (T)	Wounded
Olderen, Bernhard Gunnar, S1c	Dead
Olijar, John, S1c	Wounded
O'Neil, Eugene Elbert, S1c	Dead
Orr, Homer Lee, HA1c	Dead
Orr, John Irwin, Jr., Lieut	Dead
Orsburn, Frank Harold, SSML2c (T)	Wounded
Ortiz, Orlando Robert, Y3c	Dead
Osburn, Charles William, S2c	Dead
Ott, Theodore Gene, Y1c (T)	Dead
Outland, Felton James, S1c	Wounded
Overman, Thurman David, S2c	Wounded
Owen, Keith Nichols, S2c	Wounded
Owens, Robert Seldon, Jr., QM3c (T)	Dead
Owensby, Clifford Cecil, F2c	Dead
Pace, Curtis, S2c	Wounded
Pacheco, Jose Cruz, S2c	Wounded
Pagitt, Eldon Ernest, F2c	Dead
Pait, Robert Edward, BM2c (T)	Dead
Palmiter, Adelore Aurthor, S2c	Wounded

Pane, Francis William, S2c	Dead
Parham, Fred, St2c	Dead
Park, David Ernest, Ensign	Dead
Parke, Edward L., Capt. *(Marine)*	Dead
Paroubek, Richard Anthony, Y1c	Wounded
Pasket, Lyle Matthew, S2c	Wounded
Patterson, Alfred T., S2c	Dead
Patterson, Kenneth George, S1c	Dead
Patzer, Herman Lantz, MM1c	Dead
Paulk, Luther Doyle, S2c	Wounded
Payne, Edward Glenjoy, S2c (I)	Wounded
Payne, George David, S2c	Dead
Pena, Santos Alday, S2c	Wounded
Pender, Welburn Morton, F2c	Dead
Perez, Basilio, S2c	Wounded
Perkins, Edward Carlos, F2c	Wounded
Perry, Robert J., S2c	Dead
Pessolano, Michael Richard, Lieut.	Dead
Peters, Earl Jack, S2c	Dead
Peterson, Avery Clarence, S2c (FC)	Wounded
Peterson, Darrel Erskine, S1c (FC)	Dead
Peterson, Frederick Alexander, MM3c	Dead
Peterson, Glenn Harley, S1c (RM)	Dead
Peterson, Ralph R., S2c	Dead
Petrincic, John Nicholas, Jr., FC3c	Dead
Peyton, Robert Carter, StM1c	Dead
Phillips, Aulton Newell, Sr., F2c	Dead
Phillips, Huie Harold, S2c	Wounded
Pierce, Clyde Alton, CWT	Dead
Pierce, Robert William, S2c	Dead
Piperata, Alfred Joseph, MM1c	Dead
Pitman, Robert Fred, S2c	Dead
Pittman, Almire, Jr., St3c (T)	Dead
Pleiss, Roger David, F2c	Dead
Podish, Paul, S2c	Wounded
Podschun, Clifford Albert, S2c	Wounded
Pogue, Herman Crawford, S2c	Wounded
Pohl, Theodore, F2c (MOMM)	Dead
Pokryfka, Donald Martin, S2c	Dead
Poor, Gerald Melbour, S2c	Wounded

Poore, Albert Franklin, S2c	Dead
Potrykus, Frank Paul, F2c	Dead
Potts, Dale Floyd, S2c	Wounded
Powell, Howard Wayne, F1c	Dead
Powers, R. C. Ottis, S2c	Dead
Poynter, Raymond Lee, S2c	Dead
Praay, William Theo, S2c	Dead
Prather, Clarence Jefferson, CMM (AA) (T)	Dead
Pratt, George Roy, F1c (EM)	Dead
Price, James Denny, S1c	Wounded
Priestle, Ralph Arthur, S2c	Dead
Prior, Walter Mathew, S2c	Dead
Puckett, William Charles, S2c	Dead
Pupuis, John Andrew, S1c (Bkr)	Dead
Purcel, Franklin Walter, S2c	Dead
Pursel, Forest Virgil, WT3c (T)	Dead
Pyron, Freddie Harold, S1c	Dead
Quealy, William Charles, Jr., Pr3c	Wounded
Rabb, John Robert, SC1c	Dead
Ragsdale, Jean Obert, S1c	Dead
Rahn, Alvin Wilder, SK3c (T)	Dead
Raines, Clifford Junior, S2c	Dead
Rains, Rufus Brady, S1c	Dead
Ramirez, Ricardo, S1c	Wounded
Ramseyer, Raymond Clifford, RT3c	Dead
Randolph, Cleo, StM1c	Dead
Rathbone, Wilson, S2c	Wounded
Rathman, Frank Junior, S1c (FC)	Dead
Rawdon, John Herbert, EM3c (T)	Wounded
Realing, Lyle Olan, FC2c	Dead
Redd, Robert F., Pvt *(Marine)*	Dead
Redmayne, Richard Banks, Lieut.	Wounded
Reed, Thomas William, EM3c (T)	Dead
Reemts, Alvin Thomas, S1c	Dead
Reese, Jesse Edmund, S2c	Dead
Reeves, Chester O. B., S1c	Wounded
Reeves, Robert Arnold, F2c	Dead
Regalado, Robert Henry, S1c	Dead
Rehner, Herbert Adrian, S1c (SM)	Wounded
Reid, Curtis Franklin, S2c	Wounded

Reid, James Edgar, BM2c	Wounded
Reid, John, Lieut.	Wounded
Reid, Tommy Lee, RdM3c (T)	Wounded
Reilly, James Francis, Y1c	Dead
Reinert, LeRoy, F1c	Dead
Reinold, George H., Pfc *(Marine)*	Dead
Remondet, Edward Joseph, Jr., S2c	Dead
Reynolds, Alford, GM2c (T)	Wounded
Reynolds, Andrew Eli, S1c	Dead
Reynolds, Carleton Clarke, F1c	Dead
Rhea, Clifford, F2c	Dead
Rhodes, Vernon Lee, F1c (WT)	Dead
Rhoten, Roy Edward, F2c	Dead
Rice, Albert, StM1c	Dead
Rich, Garland Lloyd, S1c	Dead
Rich, Raymond A., Pfc *(Marine)*	Wounded
Richardson, John Richard, S2c	Dead
Richardson, Joseph Gustave, S2c	Dead
Rider, Francis Allan, RdM3c	Dead
Riggins, Earl, Pvt. *(Marine)*	Wounded
Riley, Junior Thomas, BM2c (T)	Dead
Rineay, Francis Henry, Jr., S2c	Wounded
Roberts, Benjamin Ellsworth, WT1c	Dead
Roberts, Charles, S1c	Dead
Roberts, Norman Harold, MM1c	Wounded
Robison, Gerald Edward, BT3c	Dead
Robison, John Davis, Cox (T)	Wounded
Robison, Marzie Joe, S2c	Dead
Roche, Joseph Martin, Lieut.	Dead
Rockenbach, Earl Arthur, SC2c (T)	Dead
Roesberry, Jack Roger, S1c	Dead
Rogell, Henry Tony, F1c	Dead
Rogers, Ralph Guy, RdM3c	Wounded
Rogers, Ross, Jr., Ensign	Wounded
Roland, Jack Anderson, PhM1c	Dead
Rollins, Willard Eugene, RM3c (T)	Dead
Romani, F. J., HA1c	Dead
Roof, Charles Walter, S2c	Dead
Rose, Berson Horace, GM2c (T)	Dead
Rose, Francis Edmund, Pfc *(Marine)*	Dead

Ross, Glen Eugene, F2c   Dead
Rothman, Aaron, RdM3c   Dead
Rowden, Joseph Geren, F1c   Dead
Rozzano, John, Jr., S2c   Dead
Rudomanski, Eugene William, RT2c   Dead
Rue, William Goff, MM1c   Dead
Russell, Robert Avery, S2c   Dead
Russell, Virgil Miller, Cox   Wounded
Rust, Edwin Leroy, S1c   Dead
Rutherford, Robert Arnold, RM2c   Dead
Rydzeski, Frank Walter, F1c (EM)   Dead
Saathoff, Don William, S2c   Wounded
Saenz, Jose Antonio, SC3c   Dead
Sain, Albert Franklin, S1c   Dead
Salinas, Alfredo Antonio, S1c   Dead
Samano, Nuraldo, S2c   Dead
Sampson, Joseph Raymond, S2c   Dead
Sams, Robert Carrol, StM2c   Dead
Sanchez, Alejandro Vallez, S2c   Dead
Sanchez, Fernando Sanchec, SC3c   Wounded
Sand, Cyrus Harvey, BM1c   Dead
Sanders, Everett Raymond, MoMM1c   Dead
Sassman, Gordon Wallace, Cox   Dead
Scanlan, Oscela Carlisle, S2c   Wounded
Scarbrough, Fred Richard, Cox   Dead
Schaap, Marion John, QM1c (T)   Dead
Schaefer, Harry Winfield, S2c   Dead
Schaffer, Edward James, S1c (GM)   Dead
Scharton, Elmer Daniel, S1c   Dead
Schechterle, Harold Joseph, RdM3c   Wounded
Scheib, Albert Eddie, F2c   Dead
Schewe, Alfred Paul, S1c   Dead
Schlatter, Robert Leroy, AOM3c   Dead
Schlotter, James Robert, RdM3c   Dead
Schmueck, John Alton, CPhM   Wounded
Schnappauf, Harold John, SK3c (T)   Dead
Schooley, Dillard Alfred, Cox (T)   Dead
Schumacher, Arthur Joseph, Jr., CEM   Dead
  (AA) (T)
Scoggins, Millard, SM2c (T)   Dead

Scott, Burl Down, StM2c	Dead
Scott, Curtis Marvin, S1c	Dead
Scott, Hilliard, StM1c	Dead
Seabert, Clarke Wilson, S2c	Wounded
Sebastian, Clifford Harry, RM2c (T)	Dead
Sedivi, Alfred Joseph, PhoM2c (T)	Dead
Selbach, Walter Herman, WT3c	Dead
Sell, Ernest Frederick, EM2c (T)	Dead
Sellers, Leonard Edson, SF3c	Dead
Selman, Amos, S2c	Dead
Setchfield, Arthur Lawrence, Cox	Wounded
Sewell, Loris Eldon, S2c	Dead
Shaffer, Robert Patrick, S1c	Wounded
Shand, Kenneth Wallace, WT2c	Dead
Sharp, William Hafford, S2c	Wounded
Shaw, Calvin Patrick, GM2c (T)	Dead
Shearer, Harold James, S2c	Wounded
Shelton, William Enloe, Jr., SM2c	Dead
Shields, Cecil Norris, SM2c (T)	Dead
Shipman, Robert Lee, GM3c (T)	Dead
Shown, Donald Herbert, CFC	Wounded
Shows, Audie Boyd, Cox	Wounded
Sikes, Theodore Allan, Ensign	Dead
Silcox, Burnice Rufus, S1c	Dead
Silva, Phillip Gomes, S1c	Dead
Simcox, Gordon William, EM3c (T)	Dead
Simcox, John Allen, F1c	Dead
Simpson, William Edward, Cox (T)	Wounded
Sims, Clarence, Ck2c	Dead
Sinclair, James Ray, S2c	Wounded
Singerman, David, SM3c	Dead
Sipes, John Leland, S1c	Dead
Sitek, Henry Joseph, S2c	Wounded
Sitzlar, William Clifton, F1c	Dead
Sladek, Wayne Lyn, BM2c (T)	Wounded
Slankard, Jack Crocker, S1c	Wounded
Smalley, Howard Earl, S1c	Dead
Smeltzer, Charles H., S2c	Wounded
Smeraglia, Michael, RM3c (T)	Dead
Smith, Carl Murphy, SM2c (T)	Dead

Smith, Charles Andy, S1c	Dead
Smith, Cozell Lee, Jr., Cox	Wounded
Smith, Edwin Lee, S2c	Dead
Smith, Eugene Gordon, BM2c (T)	Dead
Smith, Frederick Calvin, F2c	Wounded
Smith, George Robert, S1c	Dead
Smith, Guy Nephi, FCO2c (T)	Dead
Smith, Henry August, F1c	Dead
Smith, Homer Leroy, F2c	Dead
Smith, James Wesley, S2c	Wounded
Smith, Kenneth Dean, S2c	Dead
Smith, Olen Ellis, CM3c (T)	Dead
Snyder, John Nicholes, SF3c	Dead
Snyder, Richard Redhaffer, S1c (SM)	Dead
Solomon, William, Jr., S2c	Dead
Sordia, Ralph, S2c	Dead
Sospizio, Andre, F1c	Wounded
Sparks, Charles Byrd, Cox	Dead
Speer, Lowell Elvis, RT3c	Dead
Spencer, Daniel Frederick, S1c	Wounded
Spencer, James Douglas, Lieut.	Dead
Spencer, Roger, S1c	Wounded
Spencer, Sidney Ancil, Bos'n	Dead
Spindle, Orval Audry, S1c	Dead
Spinelli, John Anthony, SC2c (T)	Wounded
Spino, Frank J., Pfc (Marine)	Dead
Spomer, Elmer John, SF2c (T)	Dead
Spooner, Miles Lewis, Pvt. (Marine)	Wounded
Stadler, Robert Herman, WT3c (T)	Dead
Stamm, Florian Marian, S2c	Wounded
Stanforth, David Earl, F2c	Dead
Stankowski, Archie Joseph, S2c	Dead
Stanturf, Frederick Robert, MM2c (T)	Dead
Stauffer, Edward H., 1st Lt. (Marine)	Dead
Steigerwald, Fred, GM2c	Dead
Stephens, Richard Park, S2c	Wounded
Stevens, George Golden, WT2c (T)	Wounded
Stevens, Wayne Allen, MM2c	Dead
Stewart, Glenn Willard, CFC	Wounded
Stewart, Thomas Andrew, S2c	Dead

Stickley, Charles Benjamin, GM3c	Dead
Stier, William George, S1c (FC)	Dead
Stimson, David, Ensign	Dead
Stone, Dale Eugene, S2c	Dead
Stone, Homer Benton, Y1c	Dead
Stout, Kenneth Irwin, Lt. Comdr.	Dead
St. Pierre, Leslie Robert, MM2c	Dead
Strain, Joseph Mason, S2c (RDM)	Dead
Straughn, Howard V., Jr., Corp. *(Marine)*	Dead
Streich, Allen Charles, RM2c (T)	Dead
Strickland, George Thomas, S2c	Dead
Stricter, Robert Carl, S2c	Dead
Stripe, William Stanley, S2c	Dead
Strom, Donald Arthur, S2c	Dead
Stromko, Joseph Anthony, F2c (WT)	Dead
Stryffeler, Virgil Lee, F2c	Dead
Stueckle, Robert Louis, S2c	Dead
Sturtevant, Elwyn Lee, RM3c	Wounded
Sudano, Angelo Anthony, SSML3c (T)	Dead
Suhr, Jerome Richard, S2c	Dead
Sullivan, James Patrick, S2c	Dead
Sullivan, William Daniel, Ptr2c	Dead
Suter, Frank Edward, S1c	Wounded
Swanson, Robert Herman, MM2c	Dead
Swart, Robert Leslie, Lieut. (jg)	Dead
Swindell, Jerome Henderson, F2c	Dead
Taggart, Thomas Harris, S1c (RdM)	Dead
Talley, Dewell Emanuel, RM3c	Dead
Tawater, Charles Hoyt, F1c	Wounded
Teerlink, David Sander, ChPayClk	Dead
Telford, Arno John, RT3c, USN-SV	Dead
Terry, Robert Wayne, S2c	Dead
Thelen, Richard Peter, S2c	Wounded
Thielscher, Robert T., CRT	Dead
Thomas, Ivan Mervin, S2c	Wounded
Thompson, David Alvin, EM3c (T)	Wounded
Thomsen, Arthur A., Pfc *(Marine)*	Dead
Thorpe, Everett Nathan, WT3c (T)	Dead
Thurkettle, William C., S2c	Wounded
Tidwell, James Freddie, S2c	Dead

Tisthammer, Bernard Edward, CGM (AA) (T)   Dead
Tock, Nicolo, S2c   Dead
Todd, Harold Orton, CM3c   Dead
Torretta, John Mario, F2c   Wounded
Tosh, Bill Hugh, RdM3c   Dead
Tracy, Richard I., Jr., Sgt. *(Marine)*   Dead
Triemer, Ernst August, Ensign   Dead
Trotter, Arthur Cecil, RM2c (T)   Dead
Trudeau, Edmond Arthur, Lieut.   Dead
True, Roger Glenn, S2c   Dead
Truitt, Robert Edward, RM2c (T)   Dead
Tryon, Frederick Braum, Bug2c   Dead
Tull, James Albert, S1c (GM)   Dead
Turner, Charles Morris, S2c   Wounded
Turner, William Clifford, MM2c   Dead
Turner, William Henry, Jr., ACMM (AA) (T)   Dead
Twible, Harlan Malcolm, Ensign   Wounded
Uffelman, Paul, R., Pfc *(Marine)*   Wounded
Ulibarri, Antonio De Jesus, S2c   Dead
Ullmann, Paul Elliott, Lieut. (jg)   Dead
Umenhoffer, Lyle Edgar, S1c   Wounded
Underwood, Carey Lee, S1c   Dead
Underwood, Ralph Ellis, S1c (RdM)   Wounded
Van Meter, Joseph William, WT3c (T)   Wounded
Wakefield, James Newell, S1c (QM)   Dead
Walker, A. W., StM1c   Dead
Walker, Jack Edwin, RM2c   Dead
Walker, V. B., F2c   Wounded
Wallace, Earl John, RdM3c (T)   Dead
Wallace, John, RdM3c (T)   Dead
Walters, Donald Henry, F1c (EM)   Dead
Warren, William Robertson, RT3c   Dead
Waters, Jack Lee, CY   Dead
Watson, Winston Harl, F2c   Dead
Wells, Charles Orville, S1c (RdM)   Wounded
Wells, Gerald Lloyd, FM3c (T)   Dead
Wenzel, Ray Gunther, RT3c, USNR   Dead
Wernerholm, Wayne Leslie, Cox (T)   Dead

Whalen, Stuart Denton, GM2c	Dead
Whallon, Louis Fletcher, Jr., Lieut. (jg)	Dead
White, Earl Clarence, TG1c	Dead
White, Howard McKean, CWT (PA)	Dead
Whiting, George Albert, F2c	Wounded
Whitman, Robert Taft, Lieut.	Dead
Wilcox, Lindsey Zeb, WT2c	Wounded
Wileman, Roy Weldon, PhM3c	Dead
Willard, Merriman Daniel, PhM2c	Dead
Williams, Billie Joe, MM2c	Dead
Williams, Magellan, StM1c	Dead
Williams, Robert Louis, Mach.	Dead
Wilson, Frank, F2c	Dead
Wilson, Thomas Beverly, S1c	Dead
Wisniewski, Stanley, F2c	Wounded
Wittmer, Milton Robert, EM2c (T)	Dead
Witzig, Robert Marian, FC3c	Wounded
Wojiechowski, Maryian Joseph, SM1c	Dead
Wolfe, Floyd Ralph, GM3c	Dead
Woods, Leonard Thomas, CRdoE.	Dead
Woolston, John, Ensign	Wounded
Wych, Robert A., Pfc *(Marine)*	Dead
Yeaple, Jack Thomas, Y3c	Dead
Zink, Charles William, EM2c	Wounded
Zobal, Francis John, S2c	Dead

Index

Born in St. Augustine, Florida, THOMAS HELM grew up in Richmond, Virginia, and attended Birmingham Southern College in Birmingham, Alabama. He worked as a radio newscaster, newspaper reporter and forest ranger.

In the Navy during World War II he served aboard the USS *Indianapolis* and was wounded at Pearl Harbor where he was officially credited with shooting down a Japanese Zero with a Springfield rifle, for which he received a citation from Admiral Nimitz.

He contributed frequent articles to such magazines as *Field and Stream, Sports Afield, Outdoor Life* and *Argosy.* His previous books include *Treasure Hunting Around the World, Shark!: Unpredictable Killer of the Sea,* and *Monsters of the Deep.*

CAPTAIN WILLIAM J. TOTI was the tenth and final commanding officer of the submarine USS *Indianapolis* (SSN 697). He lives in Springfield, Virginia, with his wife, Karen, and his two children, Sara and Billy. When not at work in the Pentagon, he can usually be found cruising about the Potomac in his old boat, *Little Indy.*

More informantion about USS *Indianapolis* can be found at the survivors' Website:

http://www.ussindianpolis.org